Just in time for t
Nelson is giving
two more bo

MEN (

These hot Soutnern heroes have spent years
taking on anything the military could throw at
them and they always came out on top. So why
do they get knocked off course by the first
sexy woman who crosses their path?

There's nothing like a man in uniform...
or out of it!

Dear Reader,

To tell you the truth, I haven't given a lot of thought about where I'll spend my older years, but I sincerely hope that it's somewhere like the fictional Twilight Acres featured in this book. The residents are all young at heart, with enough money in the bank for the expensive things they couldn't afford in their youth. (And not all of it is strictly good for them!) They're an interesting bunch with lots of life experience, history and a whole lot of sass…which is more often than not directed at the hero and heroine.

When several residents of Twilight Acres realize that they've all had expensive pieces of jewelry stolen, one of the families calls in Ranger Security's Jeb Anderson to get to the bottom of the thefts. Having been given a brooch by one of the ladies, massage therapist Sophie O'Brien inadvertently winds up at the top of Jeb's suspect list.

Jeb is autocratic, irritating and unbelievably mysterious, and Sophie wants nothing more than to crack that cool reserve and tap into the heat she feels bubbling just below the surface. And once she does…*mercy*.

I love to hear from my readers, so please be sure to check out my website, www.readrhondanelson.com, like me on Facebook or follow me on Twitter @RhondaRNelson.

Enjoy!

Rhonda Nelson

THE PROFESSIONAL

BY
RHONDA NELSON

MILLS & BOON

First published in Great Britain 2013
by Mills & Boon, an imprint of Harlequin (UK) Limited,
Eton House, 18-24 Paradise Road, Richmond, Surrey TW9 1SR

© Rhonda Nelson 2012

ISBN: 978 0 263 90291 4
ebook ISBN: 978 1 408 99650 8

14-0113

Harlequin (UK) policy is to use papers that are natural, renewable and recyclable products and made from wood grown in sustainable forests. The logging and manufacturing processes conform to the legal environmental regulations of the country of origin.

Printed and bound in Spain
by Blackprint CPI, Barcelona

A Waldenbooks bestselling author, two-time RITA® Award nominee, *RT Book Reviews* Reviewers' Choice nominee and National Readers' Choice Award winner **Rhonda Nelson** writes hot romantic comedy for the Mills & Boon® Blaze® line and other Mills & Boon® imprints. With more than thirty-five published books to her credit, she's thrilled with her career and enjoys dreaming up her characters and manipulating the worlds they live in. She and her family make their chaotic but happy home in a small town in northern Alabama. She loves to hear from her readers, so be sure to check her out at www.readrhondanelson.com, follow her on Twitter @RhondaRNelson and like her on Facebook.

For quintessential Southern lady Jean Hovey,
who makes me cornflake cookies and provides
emergency plotting advice. Hugs, my sweet friend.
Love you!

Prologue

"YOU'RE CERTAIN THEY'RE twins?" the nurse asked as she peered skeptically into the bassinet.

Olga Montrose, the RN who'd assisted with the delivery, nodded, a smile on her lined face. "They most certainly are," she confirmed. "The blond one came first, then the dark-haired one less than two minutes after his brother. That's fast, particularly for a natural birth."

The nurse harrumphed under her breath. "They don't look like any set of twins I've ever seen," she said. "Even fraternal twins typically bear some sort of resemblance. These boys…don't."

Olga couldn't argue there, so she didn't try. She'd been working the maternity ward for over thirty years and had seen all manner of babies come into this world. Perfect and imperfect, big and small, identical twins and those of the fraternal variety.

But even she had to admit she'd never seen anything quite like the Anderson boys.

Weighing in at exactly seven pounds each—ordinarily one was smaller than the other—and both twenty-three inches long, they couldn't be any more different in appearance. The oldest boy, Jeb, was fair-haired, with startling especially blue eyes, even for a newborn, and had a visible dimple in his right cheek. The younger twin, Judd, had inky black hair and eyes that were so dark blue they already appeared brown and the same dimple as his brother, only on his left cheek. Exact opposites, but mirror images.

How inconceivably bizarre.

Both boys had thrashed around in their bassinets and wailed until, at a loss, Olga had put them in one together and the caterwauling had instantly stopped, as though a switch had been thrown. Presently the two lay facing one another and, though it was impossible, she got the distinct sense that they were somehow communicating. Ridiculous, she knew. Still…

She'd never seen a pair of twins more different or more distinctly bonded and knew a fleeting pang of sympathy for their parents.

For whatever reason, Olga suspected the two of them were going to be more than a handful to raise. Anyone charged with the dubious task of their upbringing would need lots of patience, fortitude and divine intervention.

With one last look at the pair and a shake of her head, she muttered a heartfelt, "Thank God it isn't me," then went on about the rest of her duties.

1

THIRTY-TWO years later...

Former Ranger Jeb Anderson was more accustomed to dodging bullets and IED's than a geriatric retiree with a Dale Earnhardt complex, on a tricked-out scooter, but luckily it took the same skill set.

"Move it, sonny!" an old man bellowed at him, narrowly avoiding Jeb's ankle with his back tire.

Interestingly enough, he wasn't certain what had been more dangerous—the potential bombs or these vision-impaired senior citizens on the only form of transportation they were legally allowed to drive without a proper license.

Sheesh.

Another older gentleman roared up next to him, his scooter candy-apple red with custom orange flames shooting down the sides, racing flags winging along behind him on the back. A cloud of Old Spice suddenly enveloped Jeb, making his nose burn and his eyes water.

"Psst," the older player stage-whispered, darting a covert look around them. He leaned closer. "You want to score some V?"

Jeb blinked. He wasn't altogether certain what V was, but he was relatively sure that he didn't need to score it.

"V," the man repeated impatiently, evidently in response to Jeb's blank look. "The Tent-Maker, the Rocket Launcher, Vitamin V, the Miracle of Manhood," he added with a suggestive waggle of his bushy brows.

Ah. That *V.*

"I get my next script in a few days and I can spare a couple of pills. Two for fifty. What do you say?"

Fifty dollars for two pills? Seriously? He'd say that was highway robbery. Of course, he wasn't familiar with the street value of Viagra, so for all he knew this was actually a bargain price. Fortunately—*blessedly*—he wasn't in the market for any sexual performance enhancement drugs, so he merely shook his head and the gentleman moved on.

Because Lex Sanborn—a fellow friend and former soldier—had warned him in advance that some of the jobs that came Ranger Security's way were a bit unorthodox, Jeb hadn't batted a lash when the three founding members—Jamie Flanagan, Brian Payne and Guy McCann—had told him that his first assignment with the firm would be to try and locate a jewel thief at an exclusive retirement home for those clients who needed specialized care.

Jeb considered working with the three legendary Rangers a real privilege. Known as The Specialist, Brian Payne's unmatched attention to detail, cool, unflappable confidence and keen observation skills had set the gold standard for every Ranger serving in Uncle Sam's army. With a supposed genius IQ and more brawn than even the traditional soldier, Jamie Flanagan was a force to be reckoned with, one who had married Colonel Carl Garrett's grand-daughter. He grinned. That sure as hell took nerve. And Guy McCann's almost providential ability to skate the fine line between sheer genius and stu-pidity and always come out on top was still locker room lore.

He couldn't be working with finer men—men who *got* him, who knew precisely why he'd gone into the military and why he'd ultimately elected to come out.

After Mosul...

Jeb released a tense sigh and battled the images back, the horror of his friends' broken bodies. *His* team, the one *he* was supposed to protect, and yet he was the only one to survive. He swallowed.

He'd be lying if he said there were moments when he sincerely wished he hadn't.

And then the inevitable guilt of that followed, imagining the pain his death would have caused his parents, his family, but most particularly his twin brother, Judd, who'd joined him in Ranger School and was currently still serving, but at present on a much-needed leave. Time hadn't permitted Judd a state-side visit, but he'd been able to manage a trip to Crete. It was odd being so far away from his brother, Jeb thought, as though he was missing an imaginary appendage.

Because they looked so different—Heaven and Hell more than one person had joked over the years—they'd never struggled with having their own identity, but the twin thing, the bond between them, had always been substantial. Had they not been so close, sharing that connection might have been a curse, but Jeb could honestly say he'd never resented the tie. Anything that Judd might have picked up from him was something he would have shared anyway.

They'd been more than brothers—they'd been best friends from the womb.

And this was the first time in either of their lives that their feet hadn't been on the same path. Or even the same continent, for that matter.

No doubt that was going to require more adjustment than anything else. Selfishly he'd hoped that Judd would make the switch with him, but that was hardly fair. Though his younger (by two minutes) brother had gone into the military initially to follow Jeb, Judd had thrived in the Ranger School and had developed a passion for serving that had defined his life just as much as it had Jeb's. Like himself, he knew Judd would stay there until he could no longer do the work to the best of his ability. He just hoped it didn't involve a tragedy, especially one that came with a heavy burden of guilt.

He wouldn't wish this hell on anybody.

Rather than linger on what he couldn't change, he sighed and tried to focus once more on the job at hand.

Twilight Acres looked more like a trendy resort than a glorified nursing home. The grounds were meticulously kept, featuring live oaks, sugar maples and weeping willow trees, lots of perfectly cut grass and flower beds bursting with blossoms. In honor of the Thanksgiving holiday there were potted mums, bales of hay, dried corn stalks and bunches of Indian corn artfully displayed around the grounds. Wrought iron lamp posts were positioned closely along the especially wide sidewalks and the heart of the community had been fashioned to look like an old town square. There was a beauty salon, a barber shop, several diners, a drug store and movie theater, a florist, a dentist and a doctor's office, a small grocery and what looked like a '50s era soda fountain.

A large gazebo with assorted benches, chairs and tables enabled residents to sit and play a game of chess or checkers or simply relax with a drink and talk. Uniformed staffers periodically refilled drinks and offered snacks.

For those residents who still liked to cook, there was a community center with a kitchen adjacent to the pool area and even a small, steepled white clapboard church at the end of the street. A community garden and greenhouse enabled residents to grow some of their own food and flowers, and the houses themselves were quaint and picturesque, all of them equipped with front porches and connected with a maze of sidewalks that encouraged access to neighbors. Meals were always available and the community provided cleaning and laundry services. Specialized vans carried the seniors to local attractions and made sure any off-site doctor's appointments were never missed.

All in all, the developers of the community appeared to have thought of everything and wanted their residents to genuinely enjoy their golden years. Jeb had been told the waiting list was a minimum of two years long and no amount of money, so-called donation or other motivation would move a person into a better position.

Given the seeming impartiality and incorruptibility, it seemed odd that they'd have a thief in their midst, but the facts didn't lie. Over the past three years more than a quarter of a million dollars in jewelry had been taken, more often than not from those residents who suffered with bouts of dementia. He grimaced, feeling his anger spike.

It took a particularly heinous sort of person to do that, in Jeb's opinion, and he looked forward to helping do his part to bring the perpetrator to justice.

Hired on by the most recent victim's family—

Rose Marie Wilton, who lost a diamond and emerald brooch which had been designed by the infamous Tiffany Company for Rose Marie's own grandmother—Jeb was coming in undercover and would be posing as the grandson of Foy Wilcox, whose central location and popularity would make it easy for Jeb to blend in and investigate. Foy had one of the few houses with a guest bedroom and had been considered ideal for Jeb's purposes.

Consulting the house numbers, Jeb located Mr. Wilcox's residence and noted the red scooter with the orange flames parked by the front door with a dawning sense of dread. His lips twisted. *Damn*.

Naturally, the Viagra pusher would be his host.

Jeb mounted the steps and with a resigned sigh, knocked on the door.

"Is that you, Mary?" Foy called, a happy note of expectation in his voice.

Jeb opened his mouth to reply, but was cut off.

"Come on in and make yourself at home, my dear," he said. "I'm changing and will be ready to go in just a minute."

Because he didn't see an alternative, Jeb opened the door and let himself into the spacious living room. A cursory glance revealed quite a bit about his pretend "grandpa." Foy was a fan of original art, high-end electronics, leather furniture and remote controls given the half dozen that lay on the stand next to his recliner. Jeb was strongly reminded of the so-called boardroom at Ranger Security, which had the same sort of man-cave feel.

The scent of fine cigars and some sort of disinfectant spray hung in the air and various photographs—some in color, some in black and white—lined the mantelpiece, presumably family, at least one a bride.

"I'm ready, Mary," Foy announced as he returned to the living room. His flirty, hopeful smile capsized when he saw Jeb and he blinked. "You're not Mary."

Jeb could state the obvious, too—Foy wasn't dressed.

At least, not in the traditional sense, and there was nothing conventional about the turquoise and black zebra-striped Speedo the older man was wearing. Even more disconcerting, evidence suggested that Foy was a man-scaper, because other than the slicked back hair on his head he was as bald all over as a newborn. A silk robe and a towel had been tossed over one arm and he wore a pair of rubber flip-flops. Jeb gave himself a mental shake and forcibly directed his gaze to Foy's face.

"I'm afraid not, Mr. Wilcox. I'm Jeb Anderson, the agent from Ranger Security looking into the jewelry thefts that have been taking place over the past few years. Rose Marie Wilton's family hired me. You were consulted by my boss, Major Brian Payne," he prompted.

Foy's eyebrows united in a dark scowl. "I know who you are and I know why you're here. I'm not a child, so don't talk to me like I'm one. I'm old, not ignorant."

Shit. He hadn't meant to cause offense. They certainly hadn't gotten off to a good start. "That's not what I—"

"Yeah, yeah," Foy said, ignoring him completely as he picked up his smart phone and loaded the calendar. He glanced up at him. "You're early," Foy announced. "You weren't supposed to arrive until four o'clock. It's three-thirty. Who looks like the dumbass now?"

Jeb felt himself blush. Foy was right. He'd incorrectly assumed that the older man would be waiting for him and, once he'd packed a bag, had decided not to delay his departure.

Clearly Foy, the resident Romeo, had other plans.

A knock at the door made them both turn and Foy's expression instantly transformed into a smile so smooth Jeb was hard-pressed not to admire the guy.

"Mary," Foy said warmly, striding forward. "Looking lovely as always. Is that a new cover up?"

Mary grinned, clearly pleased that Foy had noticed something different about her. She was an elegant lady, with carefully arranged blond hair, just enough make-up to hint at a more youthful beauty and finishing-school posture that made her appear taller than her true height. "It is," she said, nodding primly. Her gaze shifted to Jeb and she smiled expectantly.

"Mary, this is my grandson, Jeb. He's recently out of the military and is going to be visiting me for a few days. I'm working on my memoirs and he's kindly offered to take notes for me."

That was certainly news to Jeb. Memoirs? What sort of memoirs? Though Jeb would like to discount the remark as a good lie—and he suspected Foy Wilcox could spin a yarn with the best of them—there was a disturbing ring of truth to the announcement that made him distinctly uncomfortable.

"How nice," Mary enthused. A slight frown puckered her brow. "Oh. I hate to take you away from—"

"No, no," Foy was quick to tell her, shooting Jeb a black see-what-you've-done look over his shoulder. "He's going to settle in and take a nap. He's exhausted, poor lad. Had a nightmare layover in New York."

Jeb barely smothered a snort. Excellent liar indeed.

"Well, if you're certain," she said, still looking unsure.

"I am," Foy told her, herding her back out onto the porch, his fingers in the small of her back. "I'll be back after while, son," Foy told him. "Make yourself at home. There's food in the pantry and drinks in the fridge, but stay out of the liquor cabinet. I've got scotch in there that's older than you are." He settled Mary onto his lap, instructing her to wrap her arms around his neck in the process, then fired up his scooter and took off.

Jeb watched the pair hurtle down the sidewalk toward the pool area and knew a momentary flash of unhappy insight. He imagined his "grandfather" was getting laid with more enthusiasm and much more frequency than he was.

Rather than linger over that little nugget of disappointing information, Jeb decided he'd better call in. Charlie Martin, resident hacker for Ranger Security and new mother, had promised to have some information for him this afternoon.

Considering he was basically working blind, he'd take anything he could get.

BRIAN PAYNE REVIEWED the information in front of him and wished he could give his newest agent more to go on. "Sorry, Jeb. There's just not a lot here. Whoever is doing this has been at it for at least three years, chooses their items and victims wisely and, oftentimes, it's months before anyone even notices that their jewelry is missing. The only reason that Rose Marie noticed that the brooch was gone was because she'd been trying to make her will more equitable." No doubt a fact her heirs greatly appreciated, Payne thought.

Jeb laughed. "Maybe she should have a talk with some of my family," he said. "I'm anticipating all sorts of conditions to my inheritance when the time finally comes."

No doubt, Payne thought. Jeb's family had lots of old railroad money they'd parlayed into an even more lucrative real estate business. The fact that he and his twin had opted for a military career as opposed to the family business hadn't really bothered their parents, who'd only wanted their kids' happiness, but had angered their grandmother to no end. Twila Anderson's temper was legendary and her memory long. If she proved to be as spiteful, Jeb and his brother could find themselves cut out more thoroughly than they might imagine.

Not that either one of them would care. Payne was familiar enough with wealth to recognize greed and Jeb Anderson didn't have the look of it.

At the moment he merely looked haunted, but given the circumstances—those eerily close to his own—he completely understood the expression.

"Once my cover is completely in place with Foy, I plan on going over and talking to Rose Marie," Jeb continued. "As well as the others, of course. I need to know who has had any sort of access to their things. I also want to review who has lived and worked in the community for that length of time. See if I can find any sort of correlation there."

"That should be something Charlie can help you with," Payne told him. He studied Charlie's notes again and hummed under his breath. "Actually, she tagged a potential suspect based on a complaint she found in an online review of the community. Apparently, a Sophie O'Brien, who supplies one of the shops there on site with handmade soaps and lotions, was accused of taking a piece of jewelry from a resident. The family complained to the director, but nothing was ever done to their satisfaction."

"That sounds like as good a starting place as any," Jeb said. "I'll definitely check her out."

"Can you think of anything else I can get for you?"

"Some bleach for my eyes would be nice," Jeb drawled, chuckling. "Foy was wearing a Speedo when I arrived and the image is clinging determinedly to my retinas."

Payne laughed. "I guess modesty goes by the wayside at his age."

"He also tried to sell me some Viagra. I don't think modesty has anything to do with it. I think it's more like advertising."

Payne smiled. "Is it working?"

"He just left with a woman on his lap," Jeb told him, sounding equally bemused and impressed. "So, as incredible as it sounds, yes, I suspect it is."

"I don't know whether to be encouraged or appalled," Payne remarked, taking a pull from the drink on his desk.

"Me either and I've seen him."

Still chuckling, Payne told him to keep him posted and to let him know if he needed anything, then ended the call. A few more leaves lost their hold on the Bradford pear tree outside his window and drifted to the ground, revealing just a little more of the downtown Atlanta landscape. He spied a couple of utility workers fastening Christmas decorations onto the street poles and grunted in disgust. It was barely a week into November. Couldn't they enjoy Thanksgiving before giving way to the sadly over-commercialized Christmas season? Geez, he was beginning to sound just like his wife. He'd certainly never given a damn about one holiday or the other before he'd married Emma and started a family. He resisted the urge to do a ball-check, just to make sure he still had them, and then laughed.

Jamie and Guy had strolled into his office and both wore a questioning expression. "What's so funny?" Jamie asked.

"Nothing," Payne lied. Judging from his happy expression, Jamie must have won the most recent game of pool in the boardroom.

"Any trouble?" Guy said.

"Not trouble, really," Payne remarked, passing a hand over his face. "Just precious little to go on. I don't think this is going to be as simple as we'd originally thought."

"That seems to be a running theme of late," Jamie remarked with a grimace. He dropped into a chair and crossed an ankle over his leg.

"Not much we can do about that," Guy said. "How do you think he's going to do?"

Payne knew the question Guy was asking had nothing to do with Jeb's abilities—those were top-notch and without doubt. He was a Ranger, after all, and there wasn't a soldier alive who reached that level of expertise without possessing a keen mind, top physical form and a will of iron. It took more than being smart and in prime physical condition. It took mental endurance as well, which was often what broke before anything else did.

"I think that he'll make the transition simply because he knows that's what expected of him," Payne said. And with any luck, like him, he'd come to like it.

"He reminds me of you," Guy remarked thoughtfully.

Payne didn't betray a blink of surprise, but felt it all the same. That's exactly what Emma had said when she'd met Jeb Anderson earlier in the week. She said he was "intense" and "brooding" and she'd be willing to bet "autocratic," as well. She redeemed herself by adding the "but not quite so handsome as my husband" bit, but it was interesting all the same.

Because he'd noticed it as well.

Jeb Anderson had asked the same questions Payne would have asked had he been tasked with this particular case. And his reasons for coming out of the military were so very much like his own, only instead of losing one man on a mission he'd coordinated, Jeb had lost three.

After speaking with Colonel Carl Garrett, who'd been more disappointed to see him go than any other recruit he'd sent their way thus far, Payne had known that they were getting a Class A agent. Not to say that they all weren't, because they were. But even Payne had recognized the difference in Jeb, a do-it-or-die-trying mentality that marked him as a natural born leader with a determined, unshakable sort of resolve. It commanded respect, trust and loyalty.

Payne also knew the Colonel was sad to see Jeb leave because he fully anticipated losing his twin brother, Judd, as well, who was also purported to be an excellent soldier. He inwardly grinned.

No doubt Uncle Sam's loss would be Ranger Security's gain.

And as assets went, it was damned hard to beat the Anderson twins.

2

"OH, SOPHIE," Clayton Plank groaned loudly as she kneaded his bony shoulders. "Sophie, Sophie, Sophie. You have *no* idea how good that feels."

Sophie O'Brien's lips twisted with humor. Oh, she believed she had some idea. Clayton certainly wasn't her most grateful client, but he was definitely the loudest. And to anyone who wasn't familiar with his noisy moans, groans, sighs and exaltations, those people would have undoubtedly imagined that Sophie was giving the eighty-seven-year-old man more than the traditional, strictly platonic massage.

Clayton, however, liked to put on quite a show and, because he had a standing appointment, local residents often dropped by Twilight Acres' General Store—where she sold her handmade lotions and soaps and kept a massage room—so that they could listen to him carry on.

Clayton, ever mindful of his audience, never failed to make it sound like he was receiving a variety of mind-blowing, imaginative sexual favors and never left her little room without looking hot, sweaty and pleasantly worn out.

She looked the same way, for that matter. But it was only because ninety-percent of her clientele were on blood thinners and required more heat than was ever comfortable, particularly during the summer months. She grimaced.

Georgia's zip code in August could easily be mistaken for Hell's.

"Same time next week, Clayton?" she asked, wiping the excess lotion from her hands and the sweat from her brow.

"It's a date," he said, his response predictable.

With a shake of her head, Sophie left the room so that he could redress and wasn't the least surprised to see several pairs of eyes dart in her direction. Most of the gazes were amused and familiar, though there were always a few more baffled ones that she didn't recognize. No doubt they thought she was a hooker, turning her tricks at the old folks' home as opposed to a seedy street corner. She mentally snorted.

As if the hookers didn't go directly to their houses.

She'd been around Twilight Acres long enough to know that the only difference between this place and a college campus was that everyone here was older and could better finance their vices. Pot, she'd learned, never went out of style, sexual enhancement drugs had replaced speed, and thirty year old scotch and fine wine had picked up where two-buck chuck and George Dickel had left off.

And considering that none of the residents had to cook, clean, work or hell, even drive for that matter, what was left to do there but get high or laid?

Golden years, indeed, Sophie thought, her lips sliding into a smile. She fervently hoped she'd be able to retire here as well.

"Oh, I'm so glad I caught you before you left," Cora Henderson said, hurrying forward. The older woman was practically quivering with excitement. Her long snowy white hair was loosely braided, the plait dangling just below her collar bone. A fan of jewel tones and bold jewelry, today she was wearing a white tunic shirt, a large turquoise necklace and matching earrings, multiple rings upon her long, elegant fingers and a skirt the shade of the Caribbean Sea.

Cora had been her grandmother's neighbor and dearest friend here at Twilight Acres. Since her grandmother's death two years ago, Cora had all but adopted her as another grandchild. She never forgot her birthday and insisted that Sophie spend the holidays with her and her family. She wasn't certain how Cora's relatives felt about that—especially after Cora had given her a cameo pendant her late husband had gotten for her while they'd honeymooned in Rome—but they were all too afraid of jeopardizing their inheritance to be anything less than polite.

Because she had no other family to speak of—or would speak *to*, for that matter—Sophie sincerely appreciated it.

Cora grasped her arm and leaned in excitedly. "Have you seen him yet?"

Sophie blinked. "Seen who?"

The older woman heaved a why-am-I-not-surprised sigh. "Of course, you haven't," she said. "You stay hidden away on that farm or in that massage room. Goats and old goats," she went on, a familiar refrain. "How do you expect to meet anyone if you're never out and about?"

If Sophie wanted to meet someone, then she'd go out and about. Since she wasn't so inclined, she was perfectly satisfied with the status quo. When and if she changed her mind, then she'd change her habits, but considering her last foray into the love department had netted her a two-week crying jag and a broken heart, she wasn't keen on revisiting Romance Land at the moment.

Sophie considered herself a relatively intelligent person, but to her eternal chagrin, she was nothing short of just plain stupid when it came to men. She'd been jilted just prior to the alter once and a string of broken relationships since had left her more than marginally gun shy. She never seemed to make the right choice, so she'd concluded that not choosing at all was her best bet. No more second-guessing herself, no more pining away for Prince Charming. Life was too short and she'd rather live it alone and happy than alone and miserable.

The "alone" part was the constant, but from here on out, she was in charge of the variables.

As for her goats, they provided the milk that she used to make her lotions and soaps—which she sold via the internet, here, and at several boutiques around Atlanta—and it was in her best interests to take care of them. Not that she wouldn't have anyway. Thanks to her grandmother, Sophie had always had a bit of a "Heidi" streak and loved animals. Growing up on a farm—the one she'd inherited when Gran passed away—would do that to a girl. In addition to her goats, she had chickens, geese, ducks, swans and peacocks. Then there was Antonio, the rogue raccoon who was forever getting into her garbage. He wasn't precisely a pet, but was around enough to feel like one.

The "old goat" comment didn't signify—she gave just as many massages to the women here as she did the men, possibly more. What had started as merely applying lotion to areas her grandmother and her friends couldn't reach had turned into an unexpected career path that had kept her here at the retirement village long after her grandmother had passed away.

Though she had a Business degree from the University of Georgia and had used her education to parlay her hobby soap-making—a craft she'd learned from Gran—into a lucrative career, she'd nevertheless gone back to school to get her massage therapy certification. Knowledge was power and she was a firm believer in doing things right. She grinned.

Another lesson learned from grandmother. Dozie O'Brien had been a force to be reckoned with. A war bride, she'd moved to the US with her grandfather at the tender age of seventeen. She'd left her family and country—Scotland—but, thwarting custom, had refused to give up her name, one that Sophie had ultimately taken. She hadn't appreciated what an honor her grandmother had bestowed upon her with that gift until she was in her teens and they'd visited Gran's family in St. Andrews. She'd always joked that she was a few pounds shy of an heiress— gesturing to her plump middle—but Sophie hadn't realized how close to the truth that was, joke or not, until they'd driven up to the gates of the family estate. It had been quite intimidating.

Sadly, she had few memories of her grandfather—he'd been thrown from a horse the year before Sophie had moved in with her grandmother, but through old photographs and the stories her grandmother would share, she'd always felt like she'd known him.

That her father could have been born of two such wonderful, kind people…

She grimaced and shook the thought away.

Naturally, Sophie hadn't been in favor of her

grandmother's move to Twilight Acres—selfishly she'd wanted her grandmother to stay at the farm they'd shared since she was six years old—but had to admit that, in the end, it had been the right decision. Her grandmother had flourished in the social setting, had made good friends and had the occasional romance. Sophie had been basically grafted in to the Twilight Acres family and the love and support she'd gotten from the community since the death of her grandmother had been unfailingly kind.

She cared about each and every one of the residents here—she had her favorites, of course, like Cora and Foy—but had come to know them all quite well and had developed an attachment to each and every one of them.

And to think that someone was stealing from them…

It made her blood boil.

Initially, Sophie had chalked up the misplaced necklaces, earrings, bracelets and brooches to nothing more than memory loss—this was a retirement village, after all, and many of the residents had a hard time keeping up with their teeth, much less other valuables. They were forever forgetting doctor's appointments, whether or not they'd taken their medication, things like that. But it wasn't until Rose Marie Wilton lost her vintage Tiffany brooch that Sophie had realized something much more sinister was going on.

In the first place, Rose Marie Wilton's memory

was tighter than a steel drum. She didn't misplace anything, let alone lose it or forget it. Secondly, when the odd pair of reading glasses was lost, then that was to be expected. But having several pieces of *especially* valuable jewelry go missing—at least a couple a year since she'd been on-site—then there was something more going on.

Sophie was determined to get to the bottom of it.

Evidently realizing that Sophie was treating the "out and about" question as a rhetorical one, Cora heaved a long-suffering sigh. "I have it on good authority that Foy's grandson is going to be here for several days. And Sophie, he's not just hot but *hawt*," Cora confided, using more of her newfound internet slang. "He's at the Four Square Diner in a booth against the window. If you walk by there right now, you can see him."

And if she had any interest in seeing him, she would do just that. As it was, she didn't and she had animals to feed. Furthermore, Foy didn't have any children. How could he have a grandchild, *hawt* or otherwise? Her friend had to be mistaken.

"Cora, I need to get—"

Cora tugged on her arm. "Just humor me, please. You can get a piece of pie to take home for dessert," she told her, shamelessly taking full advantage of Sophie's insatiable sweet tooth. Cora shoved open the door and propelled her into the chilly fall air. "Ethel made Japanese Fruit pie this morning. That's one of your favorites, right?"

Actually, yes. The raisin, pecan and coconut concoction was just about as perfect as a pie could be. Barring good old fashioned chocolate, of course, which would forever hold the top spot in her heart.

"Evidently he's a former Army Ranger," Cora pressed on. "I'm certain that he has at least one tattoo, but I haven't seen it yet. Don't all soldiers get ink?" she asked, more to herself than to Sophie. Cora typically liked to stroll, but Sophie felt more this was a power march. "I'm usually a tall, dark and handsome sort of girl," Cora went on. "But he's different. He's blond."

"Well, that's a deal-breaker then," Sophie told her with a matter of fact sigh. "I'm off blond guys at the moment. Luke was blond and you know what happened there."

Cora grunted indelicately. "Luke was an ass," she said. "Fake smile, fake tan and slicker than goose-shit. I warned you about him, remember? I told you he was a player, but would you listen to me? No. You were determined to see the good in him—determined to see the good in everybody and, while that's an admirable quality on the whole, it's not helpful when looking for a mate."

That was true enough, so Sophie could hardly argue there. Cora hadn't liked Luke from the onset. She'd said he reminded her too much of a bad used car salesman. Honestly, Sophie had just assumed that Cora hadn't warmed to Luke because he'd reacted poorly when her beloved parakeet, Jose, had landed on his shoulder and he'd smacked the bird away, when a simple shrug of his shoulder would have accomplished the same thing. He'd never particularly liked any of her animals either and the sentiment had definitely been mutual. She grinned. Her billy goat, Rufus, had never failed to nail him from behind when given the opportunity.

That definitely should have been a clue. After all, animals were generally a better judge of character than people were, weren't they? Perhaps that's what she needed to do? Introduce all potential dates to Rufus and see how he reacted. Anyone who got the head-butt didn't get a second date. The thought made her smile.

At any rate, Cora hadn't been the least bit surprised or unhappy when Sophie had told her that she and Luke had parted ways. In fact, she'd promptly lined Jose's cage with pictures of Luke she'd found online.

"Besides, Luke wasn't blond. His hair was brown with highlights. This guy, as you will soon see," she said, guiding her determinedly to the door, "is *blond*."

Indeed he was, Sophie thought, inexplicably stopping short at the sight of him. She hadn't walked into the door, but felt like she had all the same. An odd little thrill whipped through her middle and a tingling started behind her ears, making the hair on the back of her neck rise. Her belly clenched, no doubt to keep the bottom from dropping out of her stomach and her pulse suddenly hammered through her veins. Though she'd swear she'd never clapped eyes on him before in her life, an undeniable sense of recognition teased her, leaving her with the oddest sense of familiarity.

It was unnerving.

From the corner of her eye, she saw Cora's triumphant expression. "See. I told you. Man candy." She gave her a gentle nudge. "Move along, dear, and don't gawk. It's unseemly."

She'd just used the phrase "man candy" and had nerve to accuse her of being unseemly? Sophie thought dimly, shaken and out of sorts.

Though the restaurant was filled with its usual geriatric crowd—those early eaters who needed to take their medication with their meal—Foy's "grandson" would have stood out no matter where he was.

Blond, as far as a description went, was accurate. He *was* blond.

He was also forbiddingly large, gloriously muscled, impeccably dressed and unbelievably, *mouthwateringly* handsome.

His profile revealed cheekbones sharp enough to cut glass, an angled, well-defined jaw, a high forehead, a perfectly proportioned nose and a mouth that was so full it was almost sulky, for lack of a better description. His eyes were deep-set and heavy-lidded and, though she couldn't discern a proper color from this distance, intuition told her they'd be light, most likely blue. Though it was a cliché comparison, he put her in mind of a Greek God and she could easily see him holding court on Mount Olympus.

He was certainly holding court here, she thought, watching the hive of activity swirling around him. It was excessive, even for a newcomer and, though he hadn't so much as glanced in their direction, she got the distinct impression that he knew that she and Cora had entered the restaurant, that he was completely aware of everything that went on around him.

"Afternoon, ladies," Ethel said, beaming at them from behind the counter. She nodded at Sophie. "I expect you'd like some pie. For here or to go, dear?"

"For here," Cora interjected before she could respond. "I'll have a slice as well. Spiced tea for both of us."

Sophie leaned closer to her ear. "Cora, I told you—"

"Those animals aren't going to starve to death if you're a few minutes late with their feed," she interjected, heading toward an open table nearest the action. "Humor me. I've got a good feeling about this guy."

Sophie had gotten some feelings too, but whether they turned out to be good or not remained to be seen.

"Did you see those hands?" Cora asked under her breath. "They're huge and accustomed to hard work. That's rare these days."

Sophie determinedly avoided looking at the guy's hands, which took a galling amount of effort, then dropped into a chair. "For all we know he could have been hammering out license plates."

"Hogwash," she said, leaning forward. "I told you, he's former military. A Ranger," she added significantly. "Special Forces. That's impressive."

Yes, it was, she had to admit, particularly considering he'd served during a time of war. That took courage and a level of conviction and loyalty to a greater good that was becoming increasingly scarce. Both of her grandfathers had served in the military and even her father, possibly the most selfish man who'd ever walked the planet, had been in the reserves.

She considered it his one and only redeeming quality.

Thankfully, she hadn't heard from him—or her mother and brother, for that matter—in a couple of months. They'd always periodically terrorized her, even after she'd moved in with her grandmother. And since her grandmother's visitation service, when they'd cornered the family attorney and discovered she'd left them just enough to prevent contesting her will, and the rest of her estate to Sophie, things had only worsened.

Naturally the terms of the inheritance had gone over like a lead balloon and had resulted in a restraining order Sophie had faithfully updated every six months. The fear came from never knowing when they were going to strike. She'd been used to the occasional horrible letter, the unexplained vandalism of her car, the crank calls. Seeing them from a distance in a crowd.

But since Gran had died, they'd upped the viciousness with heart-breaking results.

When the restraining order had prevented them from coming near her or the house—they had just enough self-preservation to avoid jail—they'd lobbed poison over the fence and killed some of her animals. Did she have any proof? No. But she'd known it was them all the same. As a result, she'd had to build a fence within a fence to keep everything inside it safe. And while the three-hundred yards they were required to keep between them was enough to avoid physical injury, it wasn't enough to prevent her from hearing them. *"We're coming for you, Sophie, you little bitch."*

A bad seed, her grandmother had once confided, the heartbreak evident in her voice. Her father was living proof for the "nature" argument, that was for sure. He'd been nurtured by two loving, caring parents and had still turned out bad. The expulsions from school had started in the first grade, when he'd stabbed another child in the hand with a pencil just to see if he could pin it to the desk beneath. Having been permanently expelled from every public and private school in the area in his teens, he'd been sent to a "reform" school similar to a military boot camp. That's where he'd met her mother—who was even more…unstable—and the rest, as they say, was history.

They were bitter, twisted people, capable of horrible, horrible things, and she'd learned at an early age to steer clear of them. She absently rubbed the scar on the inside of her arm and shook off a sudden chill.

It was then that she caught him looking at her, a bold considering gaze that caught and held hers so thoroughly she couldn't have looked away if she'd wanted to. It left her feeling pinned and paralyzed, breathless and exposed, as though he were privy to each thought that tripped through her suddenly muddled head. Ridiculous, she knew, but the sensation held fast and quickly inspired…others. Impossibly, a spool of heat unraveled low in her belly and an answering warmth responded in her nipples, making them pucker behind her bra. She couldn't have been any more shocked if they'd caught fire. She'd never merely *looked* at a man and had that sort of reaction, much less in the form of the stranger-across-the-crowded-room scenario.

Thankfully, Ethel arrived with their pie, momentarily blocking his line of sight, and the brief interruption was enough to sever the bizarre connection.

Good Lord…

Right, Sophie thought, feeling a bit like a martini—shaken and stirred. Time to go, because this was as close to Foy's impossible grandson as she ever intended to be. He was off-limits. Out of bounds. Trouble in a pair of worn blue jeans. Sex on feet. And most definitely out of her league.

She waited until Cora put a bite of pie in her mouth, then abruptly stood and pressed a kiss onto the older lady's startled cheek. "I've got to get home. See you tomorrow."

Impulsively, she snatched her dessert—no point in letting it go to waste—and fled.

THANKS TO THE twin connection, Jeb was accustomed to a heightened sense of intuition. Though he and Judd weren't identical, the link was still there and unusually strong. As a boy he could remember having a sudden craving for strawberry ice cream, only to find his brother at the kitchen table, the carton in front of him, spoon in his mouth.

While in his teens, he'd been out on a first date with a girl when Judd had gotten a speeding ticket and the onset of panic and anxiety had ruined his evening. Even now, as early as last night, he'd felt a familiar spike of elation—much to their shared discomfort, an orgasm would do it every time—followed by a keen sense of loneliness. A text had arrived a minute later from Judd, a simple "I'm fine." No doubt the girl in the bed next to him prohibited a phone call.

At any rate, Jeb had learned to listen to his instincts and, after Mosul, would *never* ignore them again, regardless of "orders." Had he pulled back at the first prickling of his scalp instead of pushing forward as commanded, he would have avoided the ambush that had killed the rest of his team.

He'd been first, dammit. It should have been *him* coming home in a flag-draped coffin.

How he'd avoided the spray of bullets that had cut down everyone else was a mystery he didn't think he'd ever be able to explain. In fact, only the small camera attached to his helmet which had transmitted a live feed back to base—and had unequivocally proved his position—had kept him from an official inquiry.

Regret and remorse, his constant companions, pulled at him, but he beat back the sensation and focused on the unusual—even for him—intuitive cue currently yanking a knot behind his navel.

It had started the instant *she'd* walked into the diner.

She was a relatively unremarkable female, mid-twenties. Dark hair, dark eyes, average height and weight. Despite the chilly weather, her face bore the fading shade of a decent tan, suggesting she was fit and healthy. She wore a sensible jacket over a pair of orange scrubs, probably a nod to the Thanksgiving season, but put him in mind of a convict. His lips twitched. Undoubtedly, that wasn't the look she was going for. She was with an older woman with decidedly more style and a quick check of their body language revealed a certain reluctance in the younger woman and a sense of excitement from the other.

Odd.

The knot and jerking sensation intensified, then his fingers began to tingle and a ripple of awareness skidded down his spine. With effort, he resisted the urge to stare at her, though admittedly he didn't understand the impulse. Frankly, he could discern more from the corner of his eye than most men with the benefit of full-on vision and he didn't see anything remotely notable about her. She was neither beautiful nor ugly. She wasn't especially tall or short, thin or fat. Her hair was brown, not too dark or too light, but that basic common shade in between. It was shiny, he noticed, but the messy bun on the top of her head prevented him from recognizing the length. Based on everything else about her, he imagined it was shoulder-length. Again, not too…anything. She was rather plain, if he were honest.

And yet…

He shifted, determined to focus instead on the older couple who'd stopped to welcome him to Twilight Acres. He was of the opinion that the person he was talking to deserved the full benefit of his gaze. Looking elsewhere was rude.

"Yes, that's right. Foy's grandson," Jeb said for what felt like the millionth time in the last hour. He'd been greeted more out of curiosity than friendliness, but the more time he spent talking to people, the more information he was likely to be able to gather. As this was his first assignment for Ranger

Security, he wasn't too keen on the idea of blowing it.

The alternative had been working for his father—which really meant he'd be working for his grandmother—and that wasn't an option. The autocratic old biddy was about as warm as an ice cube, as sweet as a persimmon and better at giving orders than some of his former commanding officers.

And he was done taking orders.

"Carl," as he'd introduced himself, chuckled. "Foy's quite a pip."

His companion nodded. "And our reigning Scrabble champion." A hint of color bloomed in her lined cheeks and she patted her hair. "He's certainly got a way with words."

Hmm, Jeb thought, suppressing a smile. Clearly this lady had been for a ride on Foy's scooter as well.

Carl scowled, his wiry brows knitting. "Come along, Martha. We should let the boy finish his dinner."

At thirty-two, he was hardly a boy, but Jeb didn't take exception. The pair shuffled off, only to be replaced by another group. He smiled and nodded and repeated himself, and all the while his awareness of his mystery woman intensified, the compulsion to look at her causing a muscle ache in his neck from holding it in check.

Sheesh, Jeb thought, determinedly taking a sip of his iced tea. What the hell was wrong with him? When he looked up, another person had stopped at his table. The woman was in her mid-fifty's. Business casual dress, minimal jewelry and make-up. Short, no-nonsense hair.

"Let me guess," she said with an arch of a brow. "Foy's notorious grandson?"

Jeb chuckled. "Hardly notorious, but yes." He'd guessed her identity as well. "Marjorie Whitehall?"

She smiled. "That would be me. I'm the managing director, more affectionately known as the Drill Sergeant around here, but someone has to keep them in line."

He feigned a wince. "I don't envy you that." And based on what he'd seen so far, he really meant it.

"Your grandfather certainly doesn't make it easy, I can tell you that." She paused. "To tell you the truth, it would be especially helpful if he'd stop selling his Viagra pills. Everyone here is on some form of medication and the potential for a harmful combination is very real."

Jeb blinked, not altogether certain what sort of response was required. "I—"

"If you could have a word with him about it, I'd appreciate it."

Ah. He nodded. "Of course." Like hell.

She nodded her goodbye, then moved away and it was in that split second of unguarded disbelief at the turn this case had already taken—since when was he responsible for his faux grandpa's sexual enhancement drug racket?—that his gaze inexplicably moved to her.

The tug behind his navel jerked so hard it pulled the breath out of his lungs and, like a zoom lens, she loomed so clearly into focus that the rest of the room blurred. His mouth went bone dry and his pulse thundered in his ears as though he'd taken a shot of adrenaline directly into the heart. The forgotten fork in his hand clattered against the plate, revealing a slight tremor in his fingers.

Bloody hell...

He didn't get it, could not understand what it was about her that elicited this singularly insane reaction. She looked exactly the same as she had minutes before—perfectly ordinary—and yet something about her kindled a fire in his loins faster than he'd ever experienced. Heat slithered along his dick, making it stir, and his groin tightened.

She looked up then and caught him staring. The impact of her gaze when it met his made the hair on the back of his neck tingle, the soles of his feet vibrate and even more strangely, an odd sense of relief suddenly overwhelmed him, as though he'd found something presumed lost forever.

Predictably, his cell vibrated at his waist, but he didn't reach for it. No doubt Judd was picking up on his heightened emotional frequency. He couldn't begin to imagine what his twin was making of these feelings, because he sure as hell couldn't figure them out.

She continued to look at him, seemingly as trapped as he was. Her gaze was wide and startled and he'd been wrong, Jeb discovered. While the rest of her might be rather ordinary, her eyes most definitely were not. They were almond-shaped and large, the outer edges tilted just so to complement her cheekbones. And they weren't just dark, but a warm, melting brown, the color of good Swiss chocolate. He mentally frowned. How had he missed that before?

Before he could contemplate it any further a waitress arrived at their table, blocking his view. By the time she'd moved away, the object of his obsession was hastily kissing her friend goodbye on the cheek. He'd rattled her that much, had he? At the last second she snatched up the dessert, taking the plate and cutlery with her. For whatever reason, that made him smile.

The same waitress who'd serviced their table stopped by his. "Can I get you anything else, hon? A piece of cake? A slice of pie?"

He nodded at the woman making a beeline for the door. "I'll have what she's having."

The waitress followed his gaze and smiled indulgently, her grin fond. "Aw, that's our Sophie." She tsked. "Every tooth in that girl's head is sweet." She topped off his tea. "I'll be right back with your dessert. You might want to take a slice to Foy as well," she suggested. "It's his favorite."

Sophie? As in Sophie O'Brien? His one and only suspect?

That was…inconvenient.

3

"THANK YOU FOR the home visit," Lila Stokes said, looking pleasantly relaxed after her massage. Wrapped in a fluffy robe, a pair of satin slippers on her feet, she handed Sophie a cup of tea and a slice of orange cake.

"You're most welcome." She gestured to the plate and smiled. "I had an ulterior motive." Not really a lie, per se. She did have an ulterior motive, but it had nothing to do with this delicious cake.

After another restless night preoccupied with especially carnal thoughts of a certain blond former Ranger with big hands and beautiful lips—honestly, the man's mouth was hauntingly erotic, full and firm and just so damned sexy it made her long for it against her skin—Sophie had decided the best way to get him out of her mind was to occupy it with something else. While finding the thief had been a top priority for her, now it seemed almost essential.

Lila was one of the first residents who'd "lost" a

piece of jewelry and, though Sophie'd heard about it at the time, she hadn't really paid attention to the particulars. If she was going to get to the bottom of this, she'd need those facts along with a description of the item. Since gossip traveled faster than anything around here, discretion was key. The last thing she wanted to do was to tip off the thief and, considering all three burglaries had happened in the resident's home, then it was fair to assume the he or she lived on-site. Only someone with regular access could have pulled this off.

The idea made her a little sick at her stomach.

Lila settled into a wingback chair. "It was my mother's recipe," she said, smiling. "She made it every year for my birthday, even after I was grown. Said no matter how old I was, I was always going to be her baby."

"How lovely," Sophie said, flattening a moist crumb against her fork. It always made her uncomfortable when people talked about their mothers because she couldn't relate to any of their stories. Her mother had only ever had eyes for her father and her brother—the boys, as it were. She'd hated other women, other girls and always had to be the center of attention. She'd never had any use for Sophie and had made sure that the rest of them hadn't either. That was the thing about bullies, she thought. A lone bully was bad enough, but when a group of them lived together, they brought out the absolute worst in each other, a pack mentality.

Being their prime target had been sheer hell.

Sophie released a slow breath, pushing the memories back. The very best thing her father had ever done for her was dumping her at the end of her grandmother's driveway. She'd been six at the time. Bruised from head to toe, with a cut down the inside of her arm that had ultimately required twenty-four stitches to close.

"Get out," he'd said, glancing dispassionately at the bloody shirt wrapped around her arm. "I don't like you, but I don't want her to kill you either."

Terrified, but strangely relieved, she'd scrambled from the car, then had stood barefoot in the freezing December night and watched him drive away, back to Kentucky. After that night, her grandmother had completely cut him off, which had painted the ultimate target on her back.

Because, in their twisted minds, everything had become Sophie's fault.

"Can I get you a second slice, dear?" Lila asked.

Sophie blinked. "I'd better not," she said. "I've got to take some hand cream by Evelyn Hunter's when I leave here and she's sure to have a little something for me to try." Her stomach twinged. God help her.

Lila's eyes twinkled. "I'm sure she will. Just last week Evie made some sweet potato cookies for us to snack on during our bridge game."

Sophie hesitated. "That sounds relatively harmless." Lila was known for her rather unorthodox experimentation with flavor combinations. Sophie had recently bitten into a brownie the older woman had made, only to find a hidden layer of anchovies in the center. She squelched a gag, remembering.

"Oh, it would have been," Lila said, "had she not iced them with a salmon-flavored cream cheese frosting."

Sophie grinned and shook her head, then glanced at Lila. "She's really been on a fish kick lately, hasn't she?"

"Yes. I'd be wary of anything the size of a cake or pie if I was you." She hid her smile behind her teacup. "She could hide a catfish in one of those."

Chuckling, Sophie set her plate on the coffee table. "I'll be vigilant, I assure you." She paused. Time to get down to business. "Lila, did you ever find that necklace of yours that went missing awhile back?" she asked lightly.

The older lady blinked behind her glasses, evidently surprised at the subject change. She frowned, her face falling a bit with regret. "No, I didn't."

"Rose-Marie's brooch made me think of it," Sophie told her, which was true, of course, but not precisely why she was asking about the missing necklace.

Lila was thoughtful for a moment, her long elegant hands wrapped around her tea cup. She'd been a concert pianist in her younger days, traveling the world with various orchestras. Arthritis made playing difficult for her now, but she still sat down at her piano every morning, like clockwork, at seven. She'd once told Sophie that the music still itched in her fingers, desperate for the outlet.

Lila's gaze found hers and she released a small sigh. "To tell you the truth, I think my daughter might have taken it. Oh, she'd never admit to it, of course. But I have my suspicions. She was forever hounding me about putting it away in the safety deposit box with all my other jewelry, but that piece was so special I couldn't bear to part with it." A sad smile turned her lips. "It was a gift from my father, you see. My mother, too, to be fair, but my dad is the one who picked it out for me. It was a present for my coming-out party." She gestured toward the fireplace. "There's a picture of us over there."

Sophie stood and made her way across the room. Several photographs—some old, some new—lined the mantle, but the one Lila referred to was easy enough to spot. It was the one closest to her wedding photo. Black and white, and in a silver filigree frame, a sixteen-year-old Lila clung happily to the arm of her father. He'd been a handsome man, her father, and the proud smile on his face made an inexplicable lump form in Sophie's throat.

Standing at the foot of a grand double staircase, Lila was dressed in a white organza dress and white satin gloves extended to her elbows. She'd had dark hair then, black as a raven's wing, and it had been upswept into a sleek bun. She was radiant with happiness, her smile the epitome of youthful joy. The necklace circled her throat, a stunning sapphire and diamond choker. A pair of matching earrings glittered from her lobes.

Sophie turned and arched a brow. "Where are the earrings?"

"In the safety deposit box now," she said.

A jolt of surprise caught her. "They were with the necklace then?"

"Yes, I've always kept the set in the original box. Odd, isn't it?" she asked, looking baffled. "That the necklace went missing, but the earrings didn't."

Sophie felt a frown move across her face, then turned back to look at the picture once more. The necklace was memorable and she felt certain she'd recognize it if she ever saw it again. And, yes, it was most definitely odd that the thief hadn't taken the set, particularly when the earrings would have been worth a small fortune as well. Perhaps a set would have been more easily traced? Or was there another reason? Regardless, it was a terrible thing to do to someone. Lila had clearly treasured the jewelry.

"Monica was livid," Lila went on, referring to her daughter, "but she was only concerned about the reduction in her inheritance, which was foolish because the necklace was insured. She didn't lose anything, ultimately." Lila met her gaze, the older woman's suddenly sad. "But I did. An heirloom tied to a memory," she sighed. "To me, it was priceless."

Sophie swallowed. "I'm so sorry, Lila."

"Whatever for, dear? It's not your fault." She purposely brightened. "Aw, well. It's all water under the bridge now. I've accepted that I'll probably never know what happened to it."

Not if she had anything to do with it, Sophie thought, firming her resolve. "If you don't mind my asking, what makes you think that Monica is the one who took it?"

"Because, other than Marjorie, she was the only person who knew the combination to my safe. Marjorie's a tyrant, I'll grant you," she said with a dark chuckle. "But I don't think she's a thief."

Truthfully, Sophie didn't either. Marjorie ate, lived and breathed Twilight Acres and was a strict rule-follower. She was notorious for sending out her "Please don't" letters—please don't drive your power chairs on the lawn, please don't allow your dogs off a leash, please don't sunbathe naked by the pool. (Sophie had most heartily approved of *that* particular edict.) Overall Marjorie made sure that everything was strictly up to code and kept a close supervisory watch on everyone associated with the village. Though many of the residents complained about her rigid disposition and had even at one point considered taking up a collection to have the proverbial stick up her ass surgically removed, ultimately they knew Marjorie genuinely cared for their well-being.

As for the safes, much like those featured in hotels, they'd been part of the standard installation when the complex was built. Sophie was relatively certain every unit featured one. A thought struck.

"Did you set your combination or was it already coded?"

"It was coded, though I was assured when I moved in that the old code had been zeroed out and my new one set in its place."

Sophie supposed it was possible that someone could have broken into Marjorie's office and obtained the combinations to the safes, but if that was the case, why hadn't everyone been a victim? She knew for a fact that Arnold Hammerfield had an extremely valuable coin collection—he never failed to tell her about while he was on her table—and that several of the other residents liked to keep sizable amounts of cash on hand for emergencies. One resident was notorious for burying her stash in Mason jars around her lawn. The baffled groundskeeper had suspected a mole problem until the truth was revealed. Why not steal from them? Why was jewelry the only item taken?

"I suppose you've seen Foy's grandson," Lila remarked with a smile, seemingly ready for a subject change.

Sophie swallowed a sigh. "I have, at Cora's insistence," she added with a droll grin.

Truthfully, Foy's grandson was a topic she was getting mightily tired of—she hadn't talked to a single person over the past two days who didn't have something to say about the former Ranger. It was infuriating. And to make matters worse, like a bad penny, he kept showing up everywhere she went. Granted the village was relatively small, but it seemed like no matter where she was, he managed to be close by.

She'd avoided going to the diner for lunch yesterday because she'd been certain he'd be there again, laughing and smiling and looking all brooding and mysterious and sexy. She'd packed a lunch from home and, despite the chilly weather, had opted to dine al fresco on a park bench by the lake. She'd just spooned a bite of potato soup into her mouth when she'd looked across the water and spotted him. Evidently, he'd made the same choice and, smiling, had lifted his thermos in a salute to her.

Peevishly—hell, it wasn't his fault that she found herself wildly, inexplicably, horribly attracted to him—she pulled a book from her bag, stuck it in front of her face and pretended to read. While hiding in plain sight, she'd inadvertently dropped a glob of soup on her right breast and accidentally let her cake slide off her plate. She was so annoyed she'd abandoned the rest of her meal, gathered up her things and left in a foul mood.

And realizing that she'd let him put her in a foul mood had only angered her further. Where was this newfound control she was supposed to be exercising? What the hell had happened to it?

Just because he had the unique ability to make her body mutiny and melt like a popsicle on the

Fourth of July, and she'd caught him staring at her several times with that microscopic gaze as though she were an exotic specimen in a Petri dish didn't mean that she was destined to fail at celibacy.

It simply meant she needed to try harder.

Honestly, for a man who was supposedly here to visit his grandfather and make notes for his memoir—that little tidbit had made its way to her this morning—he certainly didn't spend a lot of time with Foy. If he wasn't in the diner, then he was in the general store. If he wasn't in the store, then he was at the pharmacy. If he wasn't at the pharmacy, then he was at the barber shop. Or the fitness center, or the recreation room, or simply visiting someone else. She frowned. It was odd and, combined with it being physically impossible for him to be Foy's grandson, she suspected he wasn't being completely honest with everyone about his purpose here.

Granted she didn't know every branch of Foy's family tree and if Foy said he was his grandson—which he did—then who was she to question it? Furthermore, Foy was shrewd and, of the residents here, he was the least likely to be taken advantage of.

Ultimately, though, it didn't matter. She just knew she needed to stay the hell away from him.

"Speak of the devil," Lila said, a smile in her voice.

Sophie blinked. "Pardon?"

A knock suddenly sounded at the front door and with a sense of impending doom, she turned and followed Lila's gaze. The devil, indeed, Sophie thought, her mouth parching at the sight of him. He wore a black cable-knit sweater which accentuated every impressive muscle from the waist up, and a pair of faded jeans which did the same thing from the waist down. Black boots and black sunglasses completed the look. A silver watch encircled his wrist and though she couldn't isolate a brand name on any particular item, everything he wore looked well-made and of quality.

In a word, expensive.

In her discount scrubs and worn tennis shoes, she suddenly felt like a slob. It wasn't that she couldn't afford nice clothes—she could—she just preferred to spend her money on other things. Like food for her animals, farm equipment and new furnishings for her house. She'd be willing to bet her tractor cost more than his, Sophie thought with an inward smile.

At any rate, his arrival combined with the sudden racing of her heart and the absurd impulse to lick him from one end to the other was her exit cue.

Thankfully, she'd already packed up her massage table and bag, and was ready to go. Trying not to look like she was in a hurry, she casually crossed the room and hefted the bag onto her shoulder. "I'd better get going, Lila," she said.

Rather than wait for an invitation into the house, to her chagrin Foy's grandson—Jeb, she'd heard—opened the door, came in and stood in front of it. Purposely, she was sure. Panic and irritation surged through her, impossibly heightening her awareness of him.

"I hope I'm not interrupting anything," he said, his voice a warm baritone with a cool, raspy finish. A shiver hit her middle, sending goosebumps over the tops of her thighs. He fastened his gaze on hers once more and, while it had been unnerving at a distance, this close it was practically debilitating. His eyes were so very blue, Sophie thought dimly. Vivid and clear. Mesmerizing. Deep. A girl could drown in them. *She* was drowning in them.

"Not at all," Lila trilled, obviously happy to be included on his visitation circuit. "Sophie humored me with a home visit this morning."

"Lucky you," he murmured so low Sophie was certain she was the only one who heard it. Latent humor glinted in his gaze and his sulky, sexy mouth lifted in a faint grin.

She swallowed, stunned. He was flirting? With her? "I did," Sophie said with a nod. Did that squeaky voice really belong to her? She cleared her throat. "And now I've got to get going. Mustn't get behind schedule," she continued with a brittle laugh and started toward the door.

Rather than move out of the way like anyone else would have done, he stood firm and extended his hand. "Jeb Anderson," he said. "I'm F—"

"Foy's grandson," she finished, unable to keep the skepticism out of her voice. "I've heard." She shook his hand for all of half a second, then snatched it back, ignoring the fire that streaked down her arm and the instant weakening of her knees at the contact.

Though she was certain he picked up on her tone, his expression didn't change. He smiled, revealing a deep dimple in his right cheek. A dimpled badass? Really? She smothered a whimper. How unfair was that?

"I imagine word travels fast through here."

"It does," she agreed.

"Can I get you a cup of tea, Jeb? A slice of orange cake?" Lila asked, seemingly unaware of the tense undercurrent humming between them.

"I'd love that, thanks." He arched a brow. "It's Sophie, right?"

"Yes." She didn't elaborate because she desperately wanted to leave. He smelled *really* good, too. Like a loamy forest and musk. It was a rich smell, very masculine and it suited him perfectly. She could feel her reflexes slowing, becoming sluggish, which was odd considering she felt like her insides were about to vibrate out of her body.

"You're the resident masseuse?"

She shifted her bag as though it were too heavy, hoping he'd get the hint. "Among other things, but yes, that's right."

"Excellent," he said with a nod. "I should set up an appointment while I'm here. I could use a good working over."

Whether the innuendo in that comment was real

or imagined—probably imagined, Sophie told herself—it had a devastating effect all the same. Visions of his large, magnificent, naked body sprawled out on her table, his skin slickened with oil and glistening in the low light while she rubbed his shoulders tripped rapid-fire through her mind, eliciting an odd little noise from the back of her throat.

She suspected it was a moan.

His suddenly humorous gaze confirmed it.

If only a hole would open up beneath her feet, Sophie thought, mortified. With effort, she attempted to salvage the moment by attempting to be a professional. She cleared her throat. "You're welcome to call and set up an appointment."

"She works wonders," Lila interjected. "She might be little, but she can get in there and work a knot out in nothing flat."

His lips twitched and his gaze drifted over her from head to toe, as though confirming Lila's description of her size. Her nipples beaded behind her bra and a flush of heat skidded over her belly. "I've got a few knots she could work out."

Sophie nearly swallowed her tongue. Oh, yes. He was definitely flirting with her. As impossible as it seemed, the suggestion in his tone wasn't open to misinterpretation. And the temptation to flirt back was almost impossible to resist. She got the impression that he was purposely trying to rattle her, that he enjoyed watching her wiggle like a worm on a hook.

Fine. She'd play along.

"Oh, I'm sure it's nothing a little time on my table couldn't fix," she said. "You'd be amazed how much good a little oil and a deep tissue massage can do."

Gratifyingly, a little of the satisfaction clinging to his smile dimmed.

"I like to heat the oil up," she went on. "Get it really hot so that it slides more easily across the skin."

He swallowed, the muscles working along his neck, and his jaw went a little slack.

"Peppermint is my favorite," Lila interjected, returning to the living room, her arms laden with more tea and cake. "It smells good and it tingles."

Sophie chewed the inside of her cheek to keep her smile from widening any further.

Jeb's eyes twinkled and he hummed under his breath. "Indeed. I'm tingling now just thinking about it."

She was, too. In inappropriate places. Right here in Lila's living room. When she was supposed to be avoiding him and catching a thief. All-righty then.

Time to go.

Jeb watched her go and felt his shoulders shake with a chuckle. Sophie O'Brien had been doing her dead level best to avoid him since the first time she'd clapped eyes on him. From her hasty retreat from the diner night before last, to the book she'd pretended to read to keep from looking at him yesterday at lunch—her performance might have been more convincing if she'd remembered to turn the page, he thought drolly—to, as early as this morning, seeing him on the street and purposely changing directions.

Though irritating—as his prime suspect, it was imperative that he talk to her—it had been endlessly entertaining. She had the most expressive, animated face he'd ever seen. Take this morning, for instance. When she'd looked up and noticed him coming in her direction, both her eyes and her mouth had rounded—though he knew it was impossible, he could have sworn he heard her swear—then she'd stopped short and wheeled in the other direction. And it wasn't even a good short stop, like a "Darn, I must have forgotten something and I need to go back and get it." It was more like a dreaded, "Oh, hell, there he is again."

Initially, her reaction had baffled him. Women, on the whole, didn't purposely avoid him. Quite honestly, it was ordinarily the other way around. Though Jeb liked getting laid as much as any man— probably more so than some—he'd never let his appetite for sex get in the way of being selective. When he chose a woman to bed, several key factors came into play. In addition to him finding her attractive, she had to be smart, self-sufficient, healthy—he didn't want any diseases, thank you very much, and a condom wasn't foolproof—and, equally important, she'd have no expectations of a permanent relationship.

If and when he ever decided to settle down, he was just old-fashioned enough to want to do things the same way his parents had. His father had always said that he'd known by the end of his first date with his mother that he was going to marry her. Jeb didn't necessarily expect that kind of fanciful certainty, but he liked to think he knew his own mind well enough to know when he'd found the right girl.

Presently, he wasn't looking for a girl—right or otherwise, though admittedly, Sophie O'Brien was proving to be much more intriguing than was strictly professional—he was looking for a thief. Barging uninvited into Lila's this morning was the closest he'd managed to get to her and that was only by happy coincidence. He'd seen her bicycle outside, an aqua blue retro number with a wicker basket attached to the front and his anticipation had spiked with victory.

She'd bolted from her chair as though she'd been hit with a cattle prod upon seeing him, then had started immediately gathering her things, preparing to escape once again. It had been horribly rude to block the door, but as a momentary trap it had worked beautifully.

Right up until he'd started flirting with her—he couldn't have been any more shocked if he'd started speaking Swahili—and then, in another turn of unpredictable events, she'd started flirting *back*. After avoiding him like the plague.

It boggled the mind.

And spoke directly to his groin.

Nothing a little time on her table couldn't cure, indeed. Her soft hands, hot oil… He'd gotten the sudden mental image of her naked body riding him on that table, both of them slick with *tingling* oil and he'd gone rock hard.

And that wasn't even the most significant reaction.

That bizarre yank behind his naval had given another significant pull, the balls of his feet had vibrated and a powerful bolt of heat struck his already tortured groin. Coupled with the irrational sexual attraction, he'd been hit with an even more illogical urge to protect her. From what? Who the hell knew? But the inclination to stand between her and harm's way was undeniable. There was something distinctly vulnerable lurking in that warm, chocolate gaze, a hidden hurt she couldn't fully conceal. He had no idea what had triggered the notion, but it was there all the same and, since he'd decided to never again disregard his gut instincts, clearly more intel on her was needed.

He made a mental note to ask Charlie to dig a little deeper into her background. The preliminary report he'd received on her revealed that she was financially secure, having inherited a farm from her grandmother and running her own successful business. He'd spotted her soaps and lotions in the General Store—Wisteria Grove Farms—and had been impressed with the simple packaging and product.

According to her website, her soaps were all organic and handmade and any scents were derived from essential oils. Completely natural. It was impressive.

Judging from the soft-looking silky glow of her skin—up close he'd been better able to appreciate it—she undoubtedly used her own products. He'd never made particular note of a woman's skin before, but Sophie's was especially luminous. It seemed to shine as though illuminated through some sort of inner light, one that he was unaccountably drawn to.

Had she not been his only suspect—though intuition told him she was not his thief—her avoiding him would have probably been best for both of them, Jeb thought grimly. For whatever reason, he suspected Sophie O'Brien—or better still, his mind-bogglingly severe reaction to her—was a game-changer.

And didn't have the time nor the inclination to play.

Gratifyingly, though, he thought he'd isolated why she'd been so determined to avoid him and it was the same reason he'd been so curious about her—good old-fashioned sexual attraction.

While her mind had been formulating a retreat, her body had been betraying her. Those lovely eyes had darkened further as her pupils had dilated and the rapid pulse hammering at the base of her equally lovely neck were hard and fast clues to what was really going on with her. Add to the fact that she'd swallowed several times—dry mouth, another

sign—and had been covertly checking him out...
It was a no-brainer.

Evidently—for reasons as fascinating as she was, ones he would *have* to learn—she didn't *want* to be attracted to him. Jeb grimaced.

He felt her pain.

And, courtesy of Ranger Security and the job he had to do, he grimly suspected that they were both about to get even more uncomfortable. He was here for the duration and staying away from her was out of the question.

Because, even if she wasn't the thief, he didn't think he was going to be able to help himself.

4

"AH, THERE you are," Cora said happily, peering through the wrought iron gate. "I've been looking all over for you." She frowned. "What are you doing out here? You know this is Marjorie's private Garden of Contemplation. She'll pop a blood vessel if she finds you out here."

"I got special permission," Sophie told her.

Cora's carefully drawn on brows furrowed thoughtfully. "I'd never thought to ask." Looking more than a little intrigued, she lifted the latch and took a tentative step into Marjorie's forbidden area as though she were trespassing on holy ground. She glanced around, taking in the water garden, flowering plants, shrubs and bird feeders. Water gurgled from a nearby fountain and the tinkling of wind chimes sounded on the breeze.

"Wow, this is nice," Cora murmured. "So quiet, so peaceful."

Yes, it was. Or it had been, Sophie thought with

a rueful sigh. Much as she loved Cora, Sophie had hidden away here because she'd wanted to be alone. Due to a last minute cancellation—Jeanie Wilson's vertigo was acting up again—she had an hour between appointments and it wasn't like she could just dash home and come right back. Wisteria Grove was a thirty-minute drive from Twilight Acres. She'd no sooner get there than she'd have to turn around and come right back.

Better to cool her heels here and wait, but considering the fact that Jeb—when had she started thinking of him as Jeb instead of Foy's Grandson?— managed to magically *friggin'* appear everywhere she went, citing a headache, she'd prevailed upon Marjorie to let her use the garden. If he was going to flirt with her—and she was going to stupidly flirt back—then, clearly, hiding was her only option. She snorted inwardly. Work the knots out, indeed.

Her whole body had become a knot after that little exchange.

At any rate, the director had relented, albeit reluctantly, then purposely shut the curtains across the French doors which led into her office. Honestly, Sophie thought. She hadn't been interested in spying on her—at least not right now, anyway—she'd just wanted a few minutes to herself, particularly after this morning's run in with the handsome irritant. She glanced at Cora and swallowed a sigh.

An effort in futility, it would seem.

Seemingly enchanted, Cora flitted from bloom to

bloom like a starstruck butterfly. "She must really have the touch," she said. "Some of these roses are temperamental. And rare," she said bending down to peer more closely at one bush. She straightened, then turned to Sophie and smiled. "No wonder she won't let anyone back here. I wouldn't either, if I was her."

"You said you were looking for me?" Sophie prompted.

Cora's eyes rounded. "Oh, right. Yes," she said, beaming. "Guess what we're having tomorrow night?"

She couldn't begin to imagine, but a sense of dread had descended all the same. "I don't know. What?"

"A dance!" Cora enthused. "Marjorie has given her approval and the party planning committee is on top of everything. Good food, good wine, and dancing. We're calling it the Fall Ball."

Uh-oh. She had a feeling she knew where this was heading. The community was notorious for hosting themed parties, which she'd always been able to avoid by playing the old I-don't-have-any-thing-to-wear-card, but that excuse was likely wearing thin. "I'm sure you'll have a wonderful time."

"I'm sure you will, too, because you're coming."

Sophie winced regretfully. "Sorry, I can't. I'm busy tomorrow night."

Cora scowled at her. "Watching reruns of The Office doesn't make you busy, Sophie."

That was a matter of opinion, but as it happened… "I hadn't planned on watching reruns of The Office."

"Watching old episodes of All Creatures Great and Small doesn't make you busy either."

Dammit, she should have known better than to tell Cora about those. "But they make me happy," she countered. "And that's what's important."

"Piffle. You can watch those any time."

"That may be true, but—" She hesitated, feigning disappointment. "—I wouldn't have anything to wear. No formal gowns lurking in the back of my closest, I'm afraid."

Cora's smile became uncomfortably triumphant. "No worries, dear. I've already bought you a dress."

She blinked, stunned. "What? When?"

"Two actually, so you'll be able to choose which one you like the best. Betty is on standby to do any alterations, so I want you to scoot over to her house before you leave this afternoon. You're finished with appointments at three—I checked with Curtis—so you don't have to rush home to the farm. Betty says it'll only take a few minutes." She stood. "I've got shoes and accessories for both dresses as well, so once you've made your choice then let me know. You can get ready at my place," she said. "I'll help you with your hair and make-up."

Sophie's head was whirling. Two dresses? Shoes and accessories? Hair and make-up? And she still hadn't answered her question. "When did you buy me these dresses?"

"Immediately after the last time you wriggled out of coming to one of our parties," she said archly. Her gaze softened and she laid a hand atop hers. "I promised your grandmother that I would look after you, dear, and I take my promises seriously."

Sophie swallowed, touched. She knew and she appreciated it, she really did. But she failed to understand how coming to a dance where she wouldn't have a single person—in her generation, at least—to dance with fell into the "looking after her category." Not that she expected—

Sophie stilled as realization dawned and her gaze swung to Cora's. Oh, but she would have someone to dance with, wouldn't she?

Foy's cursed Grandson—Jeb.

Which was no doubt why Cora and her Band of Merry Matchmakers were going to such great lengths to host a *ball*, for pity's sake, at such short notice. Oh, for the love of all that was holy, she thought, equally mortified and horrified. She felt like the good-hearted but homely friend who was always tragically looked over in those teen-targeted made-for-TV movies. It was a good message for a high school girl, but pretty damned pathetic at her age. Disgusted, she glanced at Cora, who looked innocently back at her.

Sophie wasn't buying it. And she sincerely doubted that her well-intentioned but seriously misguided friend had bought those dresses months ago. She'd be willing to bet Cora had called one of the boutiques she liked to frequent and had something appropriate and in Sophie's size delivered this very afternoon. Renewed misery washed through her.

She'd become their pity-project.

One that was going to be paraded like a prized animal in front of the best-looking, most lethally attractive man she'd ever encountered in her life.

"Indulge an old woman, would you?" Cora said, smiling softly. "It would mean a lot to me."

If she'd issued the I-Could-Die-Tomorrow warning like she typically did when she was trying to get her way, Sophie might have been able to resist. As it was—her cheeks puffed as she exhaled heavily—she couldn't, because the sentiment was sincere. For whatever reason, Cora was certain Foy's Grandson was crucial to Sophie's future happiness. She'd be proven wrong soon enough, so what was the harm in humoring her?

"All right," she sighed. "I'll come."

Cora's lined face lit up. "Excellent, my dear. You won't regret it, I promise."

Sophie sincerely doubted that, but refrained from commenting. Though she didn't relish the idea of being so obviously pimped out, as it were, the ball would actually give her a chance to do a little more investigating. Though she'd spoken to both Rose-Marie and Lila, she hadn't been able to catch the other two victims—Pearl McIntosh and Nanette

Hearst—at home. Pearl had been visiting family in the city and the last time she'd dropped by Nanette's, she'd been at the salon, getting her weekly set. Neither woman, Sophie was certain, would miss the Fall Ball.

Neither would Marjorie, for that matter—she'd have to patrol the festivities, make sure none of the rules were being broken—and, while Sophie didn't suspect the administrator of any wrong-doing, she'd like the opportunity to take a peek into her office, to see how accessible those safe-codes really were. Though she didn't know at this point where Pearl or Nanette kept their jewelry, both Lila's and Rose-Marie's had disappeared from their safes. It was an incriminating common denominator, one that definitely needed investigating. Once the party was in full swing, there was no reason why she couldn't duck out for a few minutes and do a little poking around.

Once the alcohol and music really started flowing, none of the seniors would miss her, she was certain. Though she'd deliberately avoided these formal affairs, she'd been to enough of their other parties to know that inhibitions went by the wayside quickly with this lot. Foy and a couple of his cronies had done their own version of The Full Monty at last month's British Invasion party—which Cora had secretly renamed The Twig and Berries Show—and Hortensia Forsythe hadn't let the fact that she needed a walker keep her from doing a table dance. She shook her head and chuckled at the thought.

Come to think of it, Foy's Grandson was in for an eye-opening experience. No point in only one of them being uncomfortable, Sophie thought, marginally cheered. And, while she definitely dreaded going to this ill-conceived dance, a vain little part of her actually looked forward to looking good in front of him for a change. Because if Cora was going to the trouble to pull all this together on her behalf, then no doubt the dress would be spectacular.

And what girl didn't dream of having a Cinderella moment?

JEB DIDN'T KNOW what had surprised Payne more—that he hadn't gotten any further along on this case than he had, or that he'd had to abandon the cause long enough to come home to retrieve, of all things, his tux.

"Why on earth would you need a tuxedo at a nursing home?" Guy asked.

"In the first place, it's not a nursing home. It's a retirement village and let me tell you, these people take their retirement seriously," he said, chuckling darkly. "It's like Spring Break around that place year round, only better because, unlike most poor teenagers, these folks have the cash to do things up in style. Do you know what they're planning next month? They're bringing in a *snow machine* so that they tube down the south hill of the village," he said, feeling his eyes widen. "Foy said where Mother Nature couldn't provide, money and ingenuity could. A snow machine," he repeated. "To go tubing. Probably while drunk and high. And *yesterday* they decided to host a ball, which is why I'm here this afternoon picking up my tux. Black tie only, I'm told, or they won't let me in the door, Foy's notorious grandson or not."

"I'd never thought about getting a snow machine," McCann said thoughtfully, evidently intrigued. He sent a speculative look at Payne, who also, incredibly, seemed more interested in that little part of Jeb's speech than anything else. "This Foy has a point. Instead of packing up the kids and heading to Colorado next month, we ought to get a snow machine and set it up near your cabin."

"That north slope is all but clear," Payne said, his gaze thoughtful. "And there's plenty of room since I built the addition."

"We could use the ATVs to bring the kids and tubes back up the hill."

"Or install a cable. There's time, and it shouldn't be too involved. Jamie could do it, I'm sure."

McCann grinned, anticipating their new toy. "We'll need to clear it with the wives."

"Emma won't mind," Payne remarked. "She can bring the animals."

"I'll check with Julia and give Jamie a call, to see if he and Emma would be on board with a change of plans."

Had he vanished? Jeb wondered, watching the conversation play out in front of him. Granted the snow machine was a cool idea, but this wasn't exactly the reaction he'd been expecting when he'd mentioned it to them.

"Sorry," Payne said, turning back to him. "Didn't mean to get sidetracked."

McCann nodded his goodbye and retreated to his own office, presumably to nail down a snow machine.

"So, other than needing a tux, how are things going?" his boss asked.

Naturally, this was the question he'd been dreading, because truthfully things weren't *going* at all. Jeb hesitated, then rubbed the back of his neck. "Much as it pains me to admit it, not well," he finally confessed.

Jeb had never seen the point in learning how to bullshit. He'd just always figured his time was better spent making sure it wasn't necessary. On the rare occasions he could have employed the tactic, honesty still prevailed.

He settled into a chair. "On the surface going in as Foy's grandson was a good idea, but in practice… it's not really helping me all that much. I've learned family histories, medical histories, heard old stories and new stories and eaten everything that's been put in front of me for the past two days, but—" He shrugged helplessly "—that doesn't make them trust me. And the questions I need to ask aren't coming up in polite conversation."

Payne winced. "I see." He arched a brow. "What about Foy? Can he ask the questions?"

Jeb snorted. "Foy's too busy dating and playing cards and getting massages to be of any assistance. I mentioned my dilemma to him last night and his response was, 'Tough, sonny. That's your problem, not mine.'"

Then the old guy had promptly told him to get lost, that he had a date coming over and that he'd turn the porch light off when it was safe for him to come back to the house.

That damned light didn't go off until two o'clock this morning. His date—who Jeb strongly suspected got paid by the hour—had left at ten, but Foy'd forgotten the light and had only remembered when he'd needed to get up to "drain the lizard."

Sheesh.

Jeb had used the time to the best of his ability, attempting to break into Marjorie's office, but the locking mechanism required better tools than he'd had on hand—rectified now, of course—and he hadn't dared risk ruining the door and leaving evidence behind. He planned on slipping away tonight during the party and giving it another go. On the surface, everything about the director seemed above board and suspicion, but at this point he couldn't afford to strike a single person off his list.

"What about the O'Brien woman? Have you gotten a read on her?"

Not in the way Payne thought, but… "She's universally adored out there," Jeb said, which was true. "The residents treat her like an honorary granddaughter. The cook at the diner makes her favorite pie at least once a week, Foy services her bicycle—"

"Her bicycle?"

"She uses it to make home visits around the village," he explained. "It's easier to negotiate around the scooter traffic." He sucked in a breath, then released it slowly. "She's certainly close enough to everyone there to have pulled it off, but my gut says that she's not our thief. And intuition aside, on the surface I don't see any motive. She's successful in her own right. She wouldn't have needed the money."

"That's assuming the jewelry has been sold," Payne added. "This could be something else." He shrugged. "Maybe the thief just wanted the jewelry."

"It's possible." At this point, *anything* was possible. But if that was true, why take the high-end stuff? Why not take the costume jewelry? Why not target other valuables? Other people? Though the thefts had definitely been deliberate, something about it all felt odd and haphazard. Off. He couldn't quite put his finger on it yet, but he couldn't deny the suspicion all the same.

Payne was thoughtful for a moment. "If your gut says she's not involved, then odds are, she's not.

But perhaps she would be willing to help you," he finally said. "If she's universally adored, then it only stands to reason that she's universally trusted as well."

Jeb's pulse gave an involuntary leap. Under ordinary circumstances that would have undoubtedly been an excellent suggestion. Sound, well-reasoned, spot-on. But these were hardly ordinary circumstances, because there was nothing ordinary about the way he reacted to her—hell, even the *thought* of her, given how his groin was tightening right now. Were that not problem enough, there was the tiny issue of her not wanting to be within one-hundred yards of him.

Not that she couldn't be persuaded…

Strictly speaking, he didn't *want* to be attracted to her. But he was.

She might not *want* to want him. But she did.

And that universal adoration in the village was reciprocated. It was obvious that she adored them all, that she'd do anything and everything for them. If he asked for her help, he was certain that she would give it.

That Payne hadn't questioned his instincts, had even told him to go with his gut, meant more than Jeb could have ever hoped for. It was proof that he'd made the right decision, evidence that the instinct to leave the military had been spot on.

He needed to reward that trust with a positive result, and if that meant asking the most extraordinary ordinary woman he'd ever met for her assistance, one that he wanted more desperately with each breath…then so be it.

5

Unaccountably nervous, Sophie looked into the mirror and gulped.

Holy crap.

When Cora had told her that she'd bought her a dress for this evening's event, Sophie had immediately known two things. One, that it would be exquisite, because Cora's taste was faultless. Two, that it would be expensive. She'd nearly choked on her own tongue when she'd glanced at the price tag, but Cora had insisted that it was worth it.

What Sophie hadn't counted on was a third description, one that was easily the most notable about the beaded, sequined chiffon gown she presently wore.

It was *sexy*.

So sexy, in fact, that it felt a bit like false advertising. This wasn't her real body, not one she recognized, anyway. Her breasts weren't this plump, her waist this small, her hips this curved.

Cora clapped her hands together delightedly. "You look wonderful! Simply wonderful!" she enthused. "My goodness, who knew you were hiding such a lovely figure beneath those shapeless scrubs?"

"My scrubs are comfortable," she said, feeling duty-bound to defend her practical, serviceable clothing. She smoothed her finger over the delicate beading, turned this way and that as the sequins caught the light.

"Maybe so, but they're criminally unflattering. Of course, it would help if you'd buy the right size. They're too big and boxy. They give you all the dimension of a kitchen sponge." She thrust a small purse into her hands and dropped a black, fringed shawl over her shoulders. "Come along, we need to get going."

"I need to be able to move," Sophie told her as Cora quickly herded her out the front door. A gust of cold wind scattered leaves across the porch, making her long for a more substantial coat. "I do a lot of bending and stretching. I'd be miserable in tight clothing."

"We'll take the golf cart tonight and save our feet for dancing," Cora told her. "And being tight and fitting are two different things, dear. No worries." She started the cart and backed out of the driveway. "Now that I know your proper size, I'll have some made for you."

"What? No, I—"

"I knew when I saw that dress it would be the one you'd choose," Cora said. "The peacock design is especially gorgeous, isn't it? And those colors look fabulous with your skin."

She didn't know about the colors and her skin—skin was skin, wasn't it?—but the dress was definitely stunning. It was a black halter-style design with jewel-toned beaded peacock feather embellishments which snaked over the bodice and down over her right hip. The lower half of the gown was accordion-pleated chiffon with a ruffled, flirty hem. The dress feathered around her feet with every step she took and felt good against her legs.

True to her word, Cora had insisted on doing her hair and make-up. Rather than loading her hair up with a lot of goopy spray, her fairy godmother had rolled it on huge rollers to give it a little extra body, then let it fall loosely around her shoulders. She'd gotten a little more dramatic with the make-up—had insisted the dress deserved it—but, rather than forcing every feature to make a bold statement, she'd focused most of her attention on Sophie's eyes. "It's eyes or lips, dear," she explained. "Never both."

Sophie had known a little dart of panic when she'd watched Cora whip out the green eye shadow, but she had to admit that the finished effect was noticeable, but not garish. She should have known not to worry, she thought, darting a glance at her older friend, a wry grin curling her lips.

Cora might be willing to hastily host a dance to

put her on display for Foy's Grandson—she got the sudden mental image of Cora leading her around a rink with a leash attached to her neck, feeding her chocolate treats every time she did something right, just like a dog show she'd watched recently, and smothered a laugh—and buy her a tasteful but sexy dress, but ultimately she'd draw the line at tacky or inappropriate.

And it was hard to stay annoyed with her when Cora so clearly thought she was being helpful. So determined to find her a man. Come to think of it, she'd been particularly relentless about it since Gran died. That, and making sure that she was safe. Gran had confided in her about the "family" problems and Cora had insisted on alerting the guard at the front gate after the incident with her animals. It meant a lot.

Sophie cleared her throat. "Thank you," she said. "For all of this." She gestured to the dress, feeling suddenly awkward.

Cora grinned. "You are more than welcome, dear." She pulled up to the community center and, ignoring the "No Parking" signs nearest the door, did just that.

"Cora, Marjorie will—"

"Some rules beg to be broken, dearest." She shrugged, unconcerned. "I'll leave the keys in the ignition and if she's that upset about it, she can move it herself." She glanced at the doorway and gasped delightedly. "Doesn't that look lovely? Joy and Martha have certainly outdone themselves."

They had, Sophie thought, following her gaze. Corn stalks wrapped with twinkle lights stood on either side of the door and a swag of Indian corn, mums and black-eyed Susan's hung in an arch above the entrance. Music and laughter rang from inside, indicating that they were fashionably late, just as Cora had planned.

"Never go anywhere without making an entrance," she'd said.

Though she'd been relatively indulgent of Cora's mechanizations up to this point, Sophie suddenly found herself very nervous. Her empty stomach fluttered with unease and her hands trembled, betraying her anxiety.

"You look absolutely beautiful, Sophie," Cora told her. "You're going to knock him dead."

Him. Jeb. Foy's Grandson. The man whose bottom lip she wanted to suck. He was inside and they were making an entrance. And she had on green eye shadow and a sexy dress. *Oh, sweet heaven.* What the hell had she been thinking? She couldn't do—

Cora snatched her arm an instant before Sophie would have dug in her heels, dragging her forward. Though the room didn't stand still when they walked inside, several appreciative glances turned in their direction.

His, of course, was the one she felt most keenly. It slid over her body like a caress, lingering along her neck, her breasts, the curve of her hip. Though she knew it was insane, she could practically feel that blue heat, felt a rush of color burst beneath her skin everywhere his gaze touched. It was unnerving. Thrilling. Terrifying. Electrifying. If he glanced at her crotch, she'd undoubtedly embarrass herself with an immaculate orgasm, Sophie thought, her sluggish blood pounding through her veins.

She resisted the almost overwhelming urge to look at him and followed Cora deeper into the room. The tables had been draped with gold and plum colored table clothes and candlelight glittered behind hurricane lamps. Fall flowers and stalks of wheat tied with satin ribbon decorated the food and beverage tables, and the scent of mulled cider hung in the air. The only discordant note was the band, which was currently playing Adam Levine's "Moves Like Jagger."

Badly.

And none of the participants on the dance floor possessed the skill to move like Mick, but what they lacked in proficiency, they made up for with enthusiasm. Especially Foy, Sophie thought, watching him work a walking stick like a microphone.

"It's disturbing, isn't it?" Jeb said, materializing at her side. She jumped a little and her heart stuttered. How the hell had he done that? "You don't want to watch, but you can't look away."

She smiled in spite of herself, her pulse racing

through her veins as desire and adrenaline flooded her system. "Sort of like a train wreck, you mean."

He leaned closer, still seemingly mystified. "And he knows every word. Watch him," he said, gesturing with his glass at Foy. "He doesn't miss a single syllable. I don't know what's worse—that his hips actually move like that or that he's more acquainted with popular music than I am."

"Look at it this way," she said. "You know exactly what to get him for Christmas."

He chuckled, the sound warm and deep. "Yeah. An iTunes gift card."

She shrugged negligently, feigning a nonchalance she didn't feel. "Or Maroon 5 tickets."

A startled laugh broke up in his throat and his mouthwatering shoulders shook with humor. She knew because his shoulder was so close to her head. She'd realized that he was tall, but this close his size was particularly noticeable. At five foot four inches, she was of average height and wasn't used to feeling short, but next to him she felt positively petite. Even in these heels. She rather liked it.

And naturally, he looked fabulous, she thought, covertly studying him. The tuxedo he wore was obviously not rented, further confirming her suspicions about his clothing. Clearly it had been custom made, tailored precisely to accommodate his glorious frame. The material draped flawlessly over his massive shoulders, down his trim middle and his trousers hit the tops of his gleaming shoes at that difficult but magical point to prevent bunching.

"You're right," he said with a sigh. "No doubt he'd like the tickets better."

The song drew to a close, much to the chagrin of Foy and his audience, and another slower one took its place. Lady Antebellum's "Just a Kiss." A quick glance toward the band revealed a hastily retreating Cora, who'd obviously just made a request.

No doubt everyone in the room had noticed it as well and they were all looking on at the pair of them with expectant smiles.

Sophie felt more heat creep up her neck, heaved an inward sigh and tapped the dwindling reserves of her patience.

Left with little choice, Jeb turned to her and, smiling, offered his hand. "Would you like to dance, Ms. O'Brien?"

"Yes, thanks. Better to go ahead and get it over with, I suppose." With as much reluctance as anticipation, she carefully put her hand in his—there it was again, that almost crippling sizzle—and, wobbly-legged, followed him out onto the parquet floor.

His smile didn't waver, but something in his gaze shifted as he pulled her into his powerful arms. "I'm sorry?"

Sophie clamped her mouth shut to keep from moaning aloud. He felt *wonderful*. Big and hard and muscled and warm and the scent of him flooded her senses, that woodsy, musky fragrance. A hint of something else reached her—oranges, maybe?—but the impression fled as others filled her. Tendrils of heat wound through her middle and spread vine-like through her limbs, settling hotly in her womb. The only thing that kept her from nuzzling his neck was physics—she couldn't reach it. She should have worn the higher heels, Sophie thought absently, feeling his chin brush the top of her head.

"I only meant that we wouldn't want to disappoint everyone," she finally explained.

"Disappoint everyone?" He drew back and looked at her, his gaze brooding and slightly confused. "I'm afraid I don't follow."

She could tell by the tone of his voice that "not following" wasn't something he was accustomed to and admitting it even more so. For whatever reason—insanity, probably—she found that oddly endearing.

She grinned, pleased, then gestured covertly toward the rest of the room. "They're all watching us," she said. "And, as I'm sure you've figured out, this crowd never misses the opportunity to throw a party, but this? This is a little much, even for them."

Though he didn't visibly look around the room for confirmation, she felt his muscles stiffen when realization hit. "No," he said disbelievingly. "Surely they didn't— Foy, er…Gramps told me this dance had been in the works for months."

Sophie chuckled. "Gramps lied. This party was manufactured out of thin air because Cora and her

Party Planning Posse are in full-throttle match-making mode, and the men are going along with it because there's food, alcohol and the potential for mischief. Like pieces on a chess board, we've been well-maneuvered."

"Matchmaking? Us? But I…" He glanced around again, as though needing additional confirmation. Cora and her group were all huddled together, looking on with self-satisfied smiles. Foy danced by, waggled his brows meaningfully at the two of them, and then winked at Jeb.

"Don't worry," she said. "Asking me to dance was enough. I don't expect a proposal."

He drew back once more, looked at her again with that shockingly blue gaze as though she were some sort of foreign entity or a riddle he couldn't quite figure out. "You're teasing me."

It was a statement, not a question.

Ah, Sophie thought, as pleasure warmed her chest. Something else the badass former Ranger wasn't accustomed to. "About the proposal? Yes. The matchmaking bit and this party being hosted solely for our benefit? No." She winced regretfully. "That's all true, I'm afraid."

"I'm…shocked," he said, giving his head a small shake.

She rolled her eyes. "Hang around a little while longer. You'll get used to it."

Heaven knows she could get used to this, Sophie thought, feeling his masculine thighs brush against her body as they swayed to the music. Despite the just-a-kiss theme of the song, Sophie concluded she must be more slutty than she'd ever realized, because at the moment she'd be monumentally disappointed with just a peck. Anything less than a proper back-against-the-wall, legs-around-his-waist screaming orgasm would leave her heartbroken and miserable.

And the kicker? She'd never been a sex-against-the-wall kind of girl. She'd always been a clean sheets and controlled lighting kind of girl.

Of course, she'd never been this attracted to a man either. She'd never felt so consumed with awareness that it had literally infected her, made her itch for the remedy. Fantasize about the cure. Crave it. Be her own best friend, as it were.

He chuckled softly. "Thank you."

Sophie frowned, perplexed. "For what?"

"You said I smelled good."

She did? Out loud?

Evidently seeing her confusion, he laughed again and humor lit his gaze. His wicked mouth tilted at one corner, making the dimple appear in his cheek. "You smell nice as well."

"It's soap," she said, mortified, sucking on the insides of her cheeks. Good Lord, how long was this song, anyway?

He hummed under his breath, leaned in and took a breath. "Ah, yes. The cherry vanilla, right?"

Shock bloomed through her and she looked up at

him. He'd been smelling her soaps? Had paid close enough attention to be able to differentiate one scent from another? That was a first. Men typically didn't appreciate her work. Though he'd never been stupid enough to say it, she'd been able to tell that Luke thought it was frivolous. That this man evidently had been interested enough to smell each one pleased her more than she would have ever imagined.

Smiling, she inclined her head. "I see you've been checking out my display in the general store."

"I have," he admitted. "I like the packaging. It's simple and wholesome and allows the product to speak for itself. I bought a bar of the citrus and sandalwood," he said, then leaned down so that she could smell him, putting her mouth in dangerous proximity to his neck. Unable to help herself, Sophie's eyes fluttered shut and she breathed him in. Her insides melted.

"I'm surprised you didn't notice," he said, his voice not quite as level as it had been a moment ago. He straightened and she felt his fingers flex against the small of her back.

"I'm so used to them," she lied. No wonder she'd smelled oranges, Sophie thought. That hint of something else had been familiar because she'd designed it. Something about knowing that his big hands had used something she'd touched—she'd made—on his wet, naked skin made her belly clench and her feminine muscles contract. Warmth seeped into her panties and she resisted the urge to squirm against him.

If she didn't get away from him soon, she was really going to embarrass herself. Hell, she'd already told him he smelled good, for pity's sake, without even realizing it. Heaven only knew what she'd say next. "I want to lick you all over." Or "You could lick *me* all over." Or even, "Why don't you bend me over that chair and take me until my eyes roll back in my head."

Her poor nerves couldn't take it and the stress of the unrelenting attraction—the seemingly endless pull of his gaze—was wearing down her resolve.

At long last the song ended and he reluctantly released her. She immediately missed his warmth, wanted him to draw her closer again.

"Would you like something to drink?" he asked, gesturing toward the refreshment table. Another smile twisted his lips and he leaned forward and lowered his voice. "Since they've gone to all this trouble on our behalf, we should probably make a good show of it. I don't mind if you don't."

Wonderful. So much for making an escape. At least one with any dignity. And now, if she said she did mind, she'd just look ungrateful and bitchy. What had happened to her plans? The one where she avoided him and lusted from afar, most specifically. Sophie heaved a resigned sigh.

But she'd pretty much thrown that plan under the bus when she'd agreed to come tonight, hadn't she?

Yes, she had. And she grimly suspected it was a

decision that was going to haunt her later, with unforeseen but far-reaching consequences.

"I don't mind at all," she lied, her mouth stretched into an unnatural too-bright smile. But... She gestured wordlessly toward the foyer, where the restrooms were located. "I'm just going to run to the..." She purposely left the sentence unfinished so she wouldn't have to tell another fib. Honestly, she'd been telling so many untruths of late she was surprised her nose hadn't started to grow.

He nodded knowingly. "Right. I'll see you in a few minutes then."

Sophie merely smiled and took off, dodging Cora with the same bathroom ruse. She might have been willing to change her Avoid Jeb plan for the evening, but she wasn't about to change the other one. Mere seconds ago, Marjorie had been dance-napped by Fred Holcolm and would easily be occupied for the next twenty minutes. Fred was a slow talker—he gave a whole new meaning to the phrase "Southern drawl"—and could turn a trip to the mailbox into a drawn out event.

This was her chance. That the timing gave her an opportunity to regroup and gird her loins, as it were, was just a happy coincidence. Right? Right.

With one last glance into the ball room, Sophie zigged toward the restrooms for appearance sake, then zagged and ran out the side door.

6

JEB WATCHED SOPHIE'S retreating back as she exited through the double doors and released an agonizingly slow breath. He felt like he'd been holding it since she walked in this evening and his stomach ached with the effort.

But how was a man supposed to breathe when she looked like *that*?

He'd known the instant she'd walked in, of course, because the tell-tale knot behind his naval had given its warning and the hair on the back of his neck had prickled with awareness. He'd only turned around to confirm it and the second he'd caught sight of her in that dress he'd damned near choked on his tongue.

Because Sophie O'Brien had a body that wouldn't quit.

He didn't know why he hadn't noticed before. How he could have possibly missed it even beneath those plain unisex clothes she typically wore?

Clearly he needed his eyes examined, because her breasts were full and lush, her waist so small he could span it with both hands—he knew because he'd done just that while they'd been dancing and he'd gone so hard he'd had to put a little distance between them to keep from embarrassing himself. And her hips... Mercy. Her hips were mouthwateringly generous and curved. Hips like those put a man in mind of how he'd fit between them, how they'd cradle him as he plunged into her silky welcoming heat.

Rather than her usual ponytail, her dark hair had been left down and loose and had brushed over the tops of her slim shoulders. Those melting brown eyes had been outlined with a smoky green, giving her an exotic, sexy look which had only enhanced her appeal.

Oddly enough, he'd never paid particular attention to her mouth before tonight—another sign he needed to see an optometrist, he thought with a dark chuckle—but one look at her ripe cupid's bow lips had left him so turned on his hands had actually begun to shake. They were a natural rosy color, pillowy soft, with a distinct extremely sexy V in the middle of her upper lip. He'd wanted to taste that V, trace its outline with his tongue.

Ultimately, though, how she looked was negligible to the way she *felt*.

Simply taking her hand to lead her onto the dance floor had left him oddly shaken. The blistering zing of awareness aside, there was something about the way her small but delicate fingers felt against his, the fleshy vulnerability of her smooth palm nestled against his bigger one that made an odd sensation wing through his chest. A curious mix of expectation, *familiarity*, of all things, and longing. That irrational urge to protect had swelled again as well, coupled with the even more disturbing need to possess.

Jeb didn't need a degree in psychology to understand the significance of these caveman-like inclinations. They were easily enough, alarmingly deduced. Had he been a dog, he would have merely pissed a circle around her, marking his territory.

That was a singularly unique development, one that had evidently reached his twin because his cell phone had vibrated in his jacket pocket. He hadn't checked the message yet, but was certain it contained a call back request.

It would have to wait.

Jeb cast a glance toward the doorway and frowned when Sophie didn't emerge back through it. She'd been gone for several minutes—typical, he imagined, she was a woman, after all—but, because he was a glutton for punishment, he wanted to dance with her again. He wanted to hold her sweet, curvy body next to his, feel her small hands wrapped behind his neck, her lush breasts against his chest. He even liked the way her hair tickled his chin, the scent of her wafting up around him.

She felt…right.

Gratifyingly, her petite frame had hummed with the same sexual energy, the same hammering need, the same helpless desperation. It had taken every atom of willpower he possessed to keep from leaning down and kissing her, tasting the desire on her tongue.

Because he knew it wouldn't be enough. He wouldn't be content with just a kiss. He'd want to devour her. Taste every part of her—the arch of her neck, the curve of her hips, the swell of her belly, the fluted edge of her spine, the dimples in her lower back, the plump crowns of her pouting nipples, the soft moist skin between her thighs. And when he'd finished feasting on her, he'd want to take her so hard that their resulting release would tilt the friggin' world off its axis.

For a start.

Jeb felt his lips quirk, exhaled mightily, then shifted to relieve some of the pressure behind his zipper.

On a personal level, suggesting that they spend the rest of the evening together for the benefit of their senior citizen matchmakers probably hadn't been the wisest decision, one that was no doubt going to result in a perpetual hard-on, chronic sexual tension and the inability to relieve himself without soaking a ceiling tile, but…

If he was going to ask for her help, as Payne had suggested, then this was as good a time as any. Since the seniors were determined to matchmake, they'd undoubtedly grant him and Sophie the privacy necessary to hold the conversation.

Privacy, with her, was a tricky bit of business, but if it meant that he could get the job done, then he was simply going to have to make it work.

He knew that Colonel Carl Garrett—one of the toughest old bastards Jeb had ever had the pleasure to serve under—had recommended him for his current position. Not until he'd given up trying to get Jeb to change his mind, of course, but he could hardly blame the veteran soldier for that. The Colonel had been convinced that a promotion and the benefit of time would alleviate the damage of that bedamned mission in Mosul, but Jeb had been equally certain that it wouldn't.

Recognizing a stalemate when he saw it, the Colonel had reluctantly let him go.

While coming out of the military wasn't ever going to wash the blood off his hands—there wasn't a day that went by when he didn't think about his fallen team—Jeb had consoled himself with the fact that he'd never again have to execute orders against his better judgment. That Payne had made a recommendation instead of an edict was a monumental relief and gave him the benefit of his own judgment and experience.

And while he'd never *experienced* anything close to the myriad of feelings Sophie O'Brien's presence elicited, instinct told him that she wasn't the thief and that she was the key to solving this mystery. A single look around the ballroom—at all the trouble this group had gone to on her behalf—was only further confirmation that she was the perfect person to help him catch the perpetrator. Hell, they'd put together this event for her in less than twenty-four hours. She'd said they'd done it for *their* benefit, but Jeb certainly didn't think so. Admittedly, everyone seemed to like him well enough and he supposed that he should be flattered that they all thought he was good enough for Sophie, but this was *her* party, not his.

Which begged one important question…

Why?

Why was she still single? Why was the Metamucil Brigade doing her match-making for her? Why were they so determined to see her with someone?

"Haven't lost her already, have you, son?" Foy asked, sidling up next to him. Looking distinguished in his tux, a Mason's ring winking on his finger, his pretend grandfather pulled a small silver flask from his inside pocket and took a drink, wincing with the burn.

Jeb bit back a wry grin. "She's gone to the restroom."

Foy inclined his head. "Women," he breathed with a smile. "Aren't we lucky?"

Jeb didn't know how one related to the other, but nodded all the same.

The older man's gaze followed Mary around

the room, a fond glint in his eye. "They're soft and sweet-smelling. They can be tender and nurturing one moment, and fiery and fierce in the next. Younger men don't appreciate that," he continued. "They're too slick, determined a girl's not going to get their hooks into them, and can't see past the end of their peckers."

In the process of taking a sip of his own drink, Jeb choked.

"That's because they're weak and stupid," Foy continued, darting him a concerned glance. "Only a real man, one with an evolved mind and a firm sense of self can appreciate the complexity, the strength and vulnerability—the *sheer magnificent beauty*—of a woman." He turned to Jeb, arched a graying brow. "Have you ever witnessed the birth of a baby?"

The question took him by surprise. "No, I haven't."

"No children then?"

Jeb shook his head. Much to his parents' lament. They'd been singing the settle-down-and-give-me-a-grandchild song for several years now.

Foy's gaze turned inward and unexpectedly somber. "I have," he said. "My one and only, a boy. Back then it wasn't customary for the fathers to be in the delivery rooms with the mothers, but hell would have frozen over before they'd have kept me out of that room."

Given what he knew of Foy thus far, that seemed perfectly within character, Jeb thought.

"For hours and hours, it went on, her labor," he continued, his voice strangely even, absent of its usual enthusiastic inflection. "I have never seen anyone in my life in that much pain and never felt more helpless in the face of it. She bore it all, my Annie. She squeezed my hand so hard she broke two of my fingers."

Like a badge of honor, he held them up for Jeb's benefit. They were crooked, bent in two different angles and had obviously healed without a proper setting first.

"Limp with exhaustion, soaked with sweat, she'd smile at me between contractions—*smile*," he emphasized wonderingly, "because she'd fallen in love with our baby the instant she'd learned she was pregnant and she understood the reward waiting at the end of the agony." Foy paused, swallowed, his expression grave. "I didn't, at that point. All I could see was her suffering and, with every cry of pain, I just knew she wasn't going to survive it, that I was going to lose her. It didn't matter that the doctor told me that everything that was happening to her was perfectly natural, that she wasn't in any danger. I didn't see how her little body could go through all of that and not fail." Foy hesitated, bit the inside of his cheek, and a sense of unease slid up Jeb's spine. "She was the first to notice that something was wrong," he said. "Because he didn't cry, you see. He never made a sound."

Jeb inwardly swore. *Jesus…*

"I was too busy looking at my boy—my *son,* blood of my blood, flesh of my flesh—and falling hopelessly in love." A soft smile caught his lips and he shook his head, clearly lost in the memory. "It's true that men are visual, because I can tell you that, while I was excited about having a baby and made all the right noise and said everything that was expected of me, I just didn't get it. I didn't recognize the wonder and awe and significance of what that meant…until I saw him, and the world changed." He released a slow breath, took another pull from his flask. "All of that happened in the space of a few heartbeats, and then, in a few more, that new world crumbled." Foy glanced up, held his gaze. "It broke me," he said simply. "And my wife, whose own heart was broken, whose body was spent and bleeding, turned and held on to me so that *I* wouldn't fall to pieces. *That*, my friend, is strength." He looked away, surveyed the room once more. "They'd wanted to take him away, didn't want to let her see, let alone hold our son, but Annie wasn't having it. She insisted that they give him to her—" He frowned thoughtfully, hesitated again. "—and I'll never forget the look on her face, the bittersweet longing in her eyes as she slipped her fingers over his cheek…" Foy cleared his throat. "We named him Beau, after her father. She sang him a lullaby, thanked the Almighty for the privilege of carrying him, then dressed him in the clothes we'd bought to bring him home in so that he could be properly buried. They're side by side now, the pair of them, and my name has already been cut into the stone." He shrugged, blew out a breath. "All it's waiting on is for me to die. She made me promise to live until then—*really live*—so that's what I'm doing. I never broke a promise to her and I never will."

Jeb swallowed. "She sounds like an amazing woman."

Foy chuckled, inclined his head. "That she was," he said fondly. "Let me tell you, any man who thinks of them as the weaker sex is a fool, and any man who thinks he doesn't need one is an idiot. We weren't designed to live alone. There's a reason Tab A fits into Slot B."

Er… While Jeb appreciated that Foy had shared his story with him—it certainly gave him more insight into his pretend grandfather—he sincerely hoped this wasn't going to segue into the birds and the bees discussion. Admittedly, Foy had the benefit of wisdom and experience when it came to women and relationships, but when it came to sex Jeb was confident that he didn't need any direction. A subject change was in order.

"Sophie tells me that this ball was only set into motion yesterday. That it hadn't been in the works for months."

"She's right. I lied."

Jeb blinked, stunned that he'd admit to it so read-
ily. "Why?"

"Because Mary told me to."

That's it? Really? "Did Mary tell you why she
wanted you to lie to me?"

"No, and I didn't ask. These ladies know how to
put on a party and Mary gets frisky when she's been
into the sangria." He grinned up at him. "If I can
get the band to play some John Legend, it's going to
be a win all the way around for me." He leaned in
as though sharing a secret. "Word of advice. Don't
just dance to the slow songs. Get out there on the
floor and put a little hip action into it." He gave a
little swivel of his own for demonstration. "Do a
little advertising, if you get my drift. You save the
slow tunes for the end of the evening, when it's time
to close the deal."

Before Jeb could formulate a reply—not that he
could think of one off the top of his head—Foy
waved at Mary and took off. Determined to live.
Keeping his promise.

Another look around the room confirmed that
Sophie still hadn't returned from the ladies' room.
He frowned. Granted her clothing probably made a
trip to the bathroom more time consuming than it
did for him, but he really would have assumed she'd
be back by now. A thought struck.

Had she left? he wondered. Had she changed
her mind about staying for the evening for appearance's sake?

Given the way she'd been dodging him, it was entirely possible, Jeb thought grimly, a dart of disappointment mushrooming in his chest.

Feeling suddenly ill at ease and twitchy, he walked out into the hall, looked in both directions and, while there were several people huddled in clusters of conversation, she wasn't among them. He didn't want to linger outside the bathroom door like some sort of pervert, but at this point he didn't know what else to do. As luck would have it, Lila emerged from the ladies' room.

"Evening, Lila," he said, smiling at her.

She inclined her head, eyes twinkling. "Jeb. I hope that you're enjoying yourself. I couldn't help but notice that you were dancing with Sophie earlier," she said. "Sweet girl, our Sophie. And so pretty, too."

"Yes, she is," he agreed, recognizing another sales pitch. He looked pointedly at the restroom door and hesitated awkwardly. "She, uh... You didn't happen to see her, did you?"

Lila frowned at first, then finally took his meaning. Her eyes rounded. "No, I didn't, sorry. It's empty."

He straightened, smiled, though it felt weird on his face. "Right."

She'd bolted.

Left him here horny and miserable, in a tux, the lone actor in this two-person play they'd been forced to perform. The idea of going back into that room, alone and pitiable—an odd sound emerged from his own head and he realized it was his teeth grinding against one another—while the rest of the attendees got hammered and paired off made him want to howl. He could cheerfully throttle her, Jeb thought, stunned at how quickly his irritation surfaced and how ineffectual his attempts to tamp it down were.

Ordinarily he didn't allow himself to get worked up over things he couldn't control. Emotion was the number one enemy of common sense and could cloud judgment faster than the blink of an eye. When life or death decisions were on the line, one learned to ignore those impulses and soldier on.

Literally.

It was only years of practice that allowed him to nod politely at Lila, take a quick look into the ballroom to confirm Marjorie's whereabouts, then get about the job he was here to do.

And if he cursed under his breath all the way to her office and kicked a stray ear of Indian corn that had fallen into his path, then by damn, he'd earned it. His cell vibrated again and, with a grim "Not now, Judd," he plucked it out of his pocket and hurled it into a nearby pond where it landed with a satisfying plunk.

Shit, he thought, eyes widening in shock as he stopped short. That wasn't his phone. It was Ranger Security's phone.

In a fit of temper, he'd just destroyed company property.

Him. Jeb Anderson, decorated soldier, former Army Ranger, West Point graduate. Nicknamed Shades in Jump School because he'd been so cool and enigmatic. Unreadable, he'd been told. The ultimate poker face.

And he'd let *her* do this to him. Wind him up so tightly that all he could do was spin. He felt his expression blacken.

It was intolerable.

Women might be strong, they might be able to endure much more than he'd ever realized, they might be kind and nurturing, fierce and fiery. Hell, they might be everything Foy had said about them.

But they were also trouble.

And only a fool wouldn't realize *that*.

He rounded the corner, noting the golf cart parked near the fence as he passed, then silently opened the gate into Marjorie's courtyard. The Forbidden Garden, as Foy liked to call it. Jeb had just put the pick in the lock on one of the French doors leading into the director's inner sanctum when a flash of light from inside made him still. He lowered himself to the ground, nearer to a gap in the curtains, and peered in. A small pen light hovered over an open filing cabinet, putting off little helpful illumination, but the large aquarium nearest the intruder was much more accommodating.

Jeb blinked, certain his eyes had deceived him. Shock detonated through him.

A shimmer of black chiffon, a wink of turquoise beading...

What in hell was she doing in there? What possible reason could she have for breaking into the director's office? Could he have pegged her that wrong? Could his instincts be that off?

No, he didn't think so. But clearly a little reconnaissance was needed.

SWEARING SOFTLY UNDER her breath, Sophie carefully slid the filing drawer closed and moved on to the next one. Like its predecessors it, too, revealed nothing out of the ordinary and certainly no easily accessible safe codes. Marjorie's computer was password protected and, though she'd tried a few possible codes—drill sergeant, task master and boss woman, just for kicks—she knew she wasn't going to be able to gain access.

In all probability, if the codes were on file in this office, then they were on the hard drive.

The only other possibility was a locked drawer in the bottom of her desk. Sophie had crawled up under it and tried to access the locking mechanism from the back, but with no success. Other than a questionable bottle of nail polish—blood red, which was hardly Marjorie's style—and a pop-on clown nose under her credenza, she hadn't found anything of note at all in the director's office.

Unsurprisingly, she kept good records, notating every last detail about each resident. Trips to the doctor's office, which prescriptions they were on, any allergies, family relations, religious and political affiliations, even their likes and dislikes. At the bottom of Lila's file she'd written "Loves salt water taffy."

Residents who'd passed away were put into a separate drawer, their folders marked with a pretty sky blue heart. Sophie had gotten a little choked up when she'd come across her grandmother's file and had run her finger across the beloved name.

Theodosia Grace O'Brien. Friends and family called her Dozie. She'd been a wonderful woman, her grandmother. The kindest person she'd ever known, with a heart for people and animals alike. She never passed a person in need without offering to help and she never noticed a stray without taking it in. Her lips quirked sadly.

Like her. She'd been the ultimate stray.

Marjorie had marked "estranged" next to her father's name on her grandmother's file, along with "Needs a pet," and "Excellent gardener." Both were very astute observations.

In addition to the files on the residents, Marjorie also kept files on all the employees. Hank, who manned the barber shop, each of the beauticians at the salon, even the onsite postal worker. Sophie learned that Hank was a medium who hosted ghost tours in downtown Atlanta on the side, that one of the grounds crew was a recovering alcoholic, and that Ethel had "coulrophobia." She made a mental note to look that up.

Naturally, she'd taken a minute to review her own file as well. Marjorie had denoted all the primary stuff—name, age, date of birth, business on site, the relation to her grandmother. "Works well, universally liked, poor taste in clothes and men." Honestly, she'd pegged her with the poor taste in men comment, but was beginning to get a bit of a complex about her scrubs. Didn't people understand the concept behind her work wear? She didn't select them for their style, dammit. They were comfortable.

Her cheeks puffed as she exhaled and, with one last look around to confirm that she hadn't left any evidence of her visit behind, Sophie stood, blew a kiss to Marjorie's beloved Kissing Fish, Emma and Mr. Knightley—Lizzie and Mr. Darcy had tragically gone to the big aquarium in the sky last year—and made her way quickly back outside.

The codes had been a long shot, but they'd at least given her a starting point. Now she wasn't certain what she'd need to do next. Find a way to get Marjorie's computer code? Break into Marjorie's house and search for the jewelry?

Eek. She was a soap-making goat farmer who moonlighted as a masseuse—she wasn't a cat burglar. Before she committed any additional crimes, she needed to talk to Pearl and Nanette. She needed to know exactly how their jewelry was stolen and, more importantly, where it was stolen from. If—

and this was a big if—their items had been removed from their safes as well, then she'd be left with no other choice than to take a closer look at Marjorie.

But if that meant she might be able to recover Lila's necklace and Rose-Marie's brooch and whatever else had been taken, then so be it.

Sophie had no idea how long she'd been gone, but knew that it had been longer than the traditional bathroom visit. With any luck, Jeb would have been too occupied by everyone else to notice anything remarkable about her absence.

Anticipation spiked as she drove the golf cart back across the grounds, off the lighted paths, of course. A flash of white caught the corner of her eye as she rounded the big elm tree nearest the pond, but a closer look revealed it was only a swan. Her face chilled from the speedy drive, she pulled the cart right back into position near the door—silently thanking Cora for leaving the keys in the ignition—and snuck back into the recreation center.

Foy, Clayton Plank and several other of the men were on the dance floor reenacting Lady Gaga's Bad Romance—hilariously well, actually—and Hortensia Forsythe was more than halfway through her table dance. She was down to her slip and heels, and Martin Howard was standing in front of her, wolf-whistling and shouting "Take it off, Teensy!"

Cora and a group of her friends were huddled together in the corner of the room, giggling like school girls, a suspicious cloud of aromatic smoke drifting up above their heads. No doubt they'd have the munchies soon, Sophie thought, with a chuckle.

Looking exhausted and past caring, Marjorie was slouched in a chair near the band, drinking champagne directly from the bottle.

Clearly she'd been away much longer than she'd realized, Sophie thought, scanning the crowd for a head and shoulders which would stand well above the others. Her own shoulders drooped dejectedly when her search proved futile.

He'd left.

It was just as well, she told herself. Really. There was no reason for her to be upset, for her to even care that he'd given up on her and made his exit. It wasn't like they'd made a real date. It had only been for the benefit of everyone else, right? Isn't that what he'd said?

So why was she suddenly so depressed? Why did she feel like she'd been shown a present only to have it snatched out of her grasp when she reached for it? Why, for the love of all that was holy, was she on the verge of tears?

She knew why.

Because, at one point, while they'd been dancing, she could have sworn she saw the same raw and ragged desire that had been tearing her up for days, clawing at him as well. The tension in his touch, that brooding inscrutable gaze...

Hope, that easily kindled insidious builder of expectation, had sprouted.

Clearly she'd been mistaken. Once again.

Sophie swallowed tightly, laughed as Foy and his crew reached the "zombie shuffle" portion of the iconic dance, then smiled her goodbyes at everyone and pushed back through the double doors out into the night. The music and laughter faded and the silence closed in around her, making her even more keenly aware of being alone.

A weak, resigned chuckle bubbled up her throat and she shook her head. *That's* what Marjorie should have written at the bottom of her file, Sophie thought.

"Will die alone."

7

Hidden behind a massive magnolia, Jeb watched as Sophie left the party. She'd barely stayed five minutes upon her return and, though he hadn't been able to clearly see her face, everything about her body language suggested that she was unhappy. Her shoulders were rounded, her step slow. He heard her chuckle, but there was no humor in the sound. It rang hollow, almost defeated. Then she'd shaken her head, tightened the wrap around her shoulders and, rather than take the cart again, began walking toward Cora's.

Cold and confused—an admittedly unfamiliar state for him—and plagued with the irrational urge to comfort her, to right her wrongs, Jeb frowned into the darkness, trying to make sense of what had just happened. Was she disappointed that she'd missed him? he wondered. That he'd left? Was that the reason for the sudden onset of unhappiness?

But if she'd wanted to spend the evening with

him, then why in the hell had she snuck away? Why had she left? Better still, what had she hoped to find in Marjorie's office? What had she been looking for? The jewelry? Was it possible that she knew there was a thief among them? Yes, he thought, his stomach clenching. Who knew this group better than Sophie? Who interacted with all of them? It was entirely possible that she was aware that something was going on.

But if that was the case, then why look in Marjorie's office? There certainly wasn't any high-end jewelry in there, Jeb thought. The director wasn't the type and a quick look into her financials had revealed a frugal spender and faithful saver. Big purchases were planned, not impulsive. In fact, other than the cost of those exotic fish he'd spotted in her office and the garden attached to it, Marjorie didn't splurge for anything.

He glanced at Sophie again, watched the lovely swing of those heavily rounded hips and felt another stab of desire land below his belt. Moonlight gleamed off her dark hair and a gentle breeze teased at the ends, lifting them away from her creamy neck. He swallowed thickly, his mouth parching as he appreciated the sheer feminine perfection of her body, the achingly sweet slope of her cheek, the ripe fullness of her mouth. How in the hell had he ever thought her ordinary? he wondered, his chest suddenly tight, when she was clearly the most beautiful woman he'd ever clapped eyes on.

Though he didn't know when he'd made the conscious decision to continue following her, Jeb found himself doing that all the same. Careful to stay hidden behind various trees and shrubbery along the way, he stayed close enough to reach her quickly if needed, but far enough away to prevent detection. Against all reason and better judgment, irritation had given way to curiosity and the insatiable need to figure her out. To find out why she'd abandoned him to break into Marjorie's office.

As soon as she'd climbed into her vehicle, he'd dashed a block over to Foy's, slid behind the wheel of his Jeep and, staying a few car lengths away, fell in at a comfortable distance behind her truck. Fifteen minutes into the drive, traffic thinned and streetlights vanished. Withering Kudzu creeped along the embankments and he narrowly missed a deer.

Finally, she made a right turn onto Shady Springs road, drove along another mile, then stopped at a gated entrance to a long graveled driveway. With the beam of her headlights, he saw the gate swing open—remote access?—then he purposely drove past the entrance to her farm. Still puzzling over the gate, he waited until he was certain she'd had time to go inside, then backtracked and killed his headlights. He pulled past her entrance once more and parked in the driveway of an old barn.

Though it was pitch black without his headlights, his eyes soon adjusted to the darkness and he made his way toward her farm. The gate was ground level, easily ten-feet high, with slats too narrow to wiggle through and the surrounding fence proved just as impenetrable. Just as high as the gate, it was clearly custom designed, a cinderblock wall which had been covered in stained and textured concrete stamped to look like an old rock wall. He whistled low.

This wasn't a fence devised to keep things in—it was erected to keep things *out*.

He frowned, staring at it, and wondered who or what had frightened her to the point that she felt like she needed it. Who or what was she afraid of? Because one didn't go to the trouble and expense to build something like this without good reason. He'd come here looking for answers and so far he only had more questions. A cursory glance revealed that any trees or limbs close to the fence had been cut away, obviously to prevent someone from finding a way over. The only thing that stood in his favor was his training, otherwise he wouldn't have been able to clear it without a ladder.

Thirty feet inside he encountered another fence— barbed-wired—which he'd completely missed in the darkness. He toppled end over ass, felt the metal bite into his skin and tear his clothes and landed flat on his back with an undignified grunt. Stunned, he laid there for a minute, in what he gloomily suspected was goat shit, and felt a laugh swell in his chest. Unbelievable, he thought, wheezing quietly as his shoulder shook. Could he possibly Barney Fyfe this anymore?

He feared the answer to that question.

With a small grunt, still in his tux, he stood and dusted himself off, then dropped into a crouch and made his way into the low valley below her house, which sat on a small knob overlooking a pond. He could hear the occasional bleat of a goat, the rustle of feathers. Lights burned from the front porch and several windows downstairs, casting a decent glow across the front yard.

Lots of flowers bloomed from various planters around the yard, and whimsical whirly-things made out of multicolored metals dangled from the bare tree branches and swirled in the breeze. Obviously a fan of metal artwork, a red pig with a pink snout and blue wings stood next to her front door. He smiled and shook his head. Before he could move any closer, an unexpected noise registered and he immediately froze.

Oh, hell.

Jeb didn't need extensive Army training to recognize the tell-tale, dreaded sound that emerged roughly ten feet behind him. He was Southern, after all, and any born-and-bred Georgia boy worth his salt would recognize the distinct metallic click and slide of the cock of a twelve gauge shotgun. And given the decided assuredness and rapidity of the action, he knew whoever had him in their sights was familiar with the gun and knew how to use it.

"On your feet and hands where I can see them," she ordered. He had to hand it to her. Sophie O'Brien was cool as a cucumber. Her voice was smooth and steady, not betraying the slightest bit of fear. Which, irrationally, irritated him. He was a strange man trespassing on her property—she ought to be afraid, dammit. Granted, he didn't wish her any harm, but how was she to know that? Why hadn't she stayed in the house and called 911 like a normal woman would have done?

Oh, right, he thought sarcastically. Because she wasn't a *normal* woman. When compared to other women he'd met, anyway. She was kind and confident, fiendishly clever and sexy as hell. Mother Earth and Rosie the Riveter all wrapped up in a lushly curved '50s pin-up era body.

He wanted her.

And the hell of it? Aside from the conflict of interest and tiny matter of her name at the top of his suspect list?

She didn't like him. Or didn't *want* to like him. All arrogance aside, that was novel. And galling.

"Move," she said again, her voice firmer. "I'd rather not shoot you—my ice cream is melting—but I will if you don't do as I say."

Beautiful, Jeb thought, feeling extraordinarily stupid. He'd been an Army Ranger, one of the fiercest soldiers among Uncle Sam's finest…and he'd been bested by a goat farmer with an Annie Oakley complex. One that, to add insult to injury, was more concerned with her melting ice cream than finding a man lurking in the bushes outside her house.

With a sigh dredged from the depths of his soul, he did as she asked and flashed a grin at her. "Evening, Sophie. Your shrubs need mulching."

She gasped, betraying the first bit of surprise. It was ridiculous how much that pleased him. "You?" she breathed, her eyes wide. "What the hell are you doing out here?"

He pasted a reassuring look on his face and gestured to the gun still aimed at his chest. "Would you mind lowering your weapon? It's a bit unnerving."

She did as he asked, bringing the barrel down until it was aimed directly at his groin. "There," she said, a smirk in her voice. "Feel better?"

"Not particularly, no." She was still in her evening wear, but had obviously taken off her shoes because a pair of purple and black muck boots had replaced her strappy pumps. Between the shotgun, the dress and the boots, she looked like a beauty queen gone rogue. The thought startled a chuckle out of him.

"You think it's funny that I've got a loaded gun pointed at you?" she asked.

"No, I don't think it's funny at all—I used to get shot at for a living." He shrugged, his gaze tangling with hers. "But when you've been a target for as long as I have it loses the power to scare you."

Some of the starch left her spine and she swallowed, the delicate muscles in her throat working.

He glanced pointedly at her feet. "I was laughing at your shoes. They don't exactly match the dress."

She started, blinked and then a smile bloomed over her lips and she lowered the gun. "They were by the door. I didn't have time to color coordinate."

He shoved his bleeding hands into his pockets, looked out across the pond, watched the water ripple in the moonlight. "All right," he said, because he had to know. "What gave me away?"

Satisfaction clung to her grin and she cocked her head toward the edge of the property. "There are height sensors near the inside of the primary fence. I don't have anything here taller than I am, so anything above six feet trips an alarm."

He nodded consideringly. Smart and sophisticated. Given the breadth of the fence he should have anticipated something like that. "Any particular reason you've erected a fortress around your house?" he asked lightly. "Or why there's another fence inside of that one?"

A shadow shifted fleetingly behind her gaze, but she merely lifted an unconcerned shoulder, then turned and walked toward the house. "To keep people out, obviously," she said, her voice droll. "Come on. I'm looking forward to hearing why you were skulking in my shrubs."

As an enemy captured behind the lines, as it were, he'd expected an interrogation, but he had a few questions of his own he wanted answered first. "In my line of work we don't call it skulking, Ms.

O'Brien. We call it surveillance." He mounted the steps. "And I'll be happy to tell you why I'm monitoring your behavior as soon as you tell me what you were looking for in Marjorie Whitehall's office tonight."

SOPHIE FELT HER eyes round and bit back a curse. He'd seen her? But how? Why? Surveillance, he'd said. Dread ballooned in her belly. Had she been under surveillance this whole time? Was that why he'd been conveniently popping up everywhere she went? Why she hadn't been able to make a move without practically running into him? Why he'd been...so attentive? Flirty, even?

Ah... Her chest squeezed. Of course, it had. And she'd been so blinded by her uncustomary, ridiculously potent attraction to him that she'd missed it.

Right.

And to think she'd been relieved when it had been him she'd caught. For a moment she'd been terrified that one of her so-called family members had gone crazy enough to risk going to jail.

Feeling like she'd been kicked in the gut, Sophie squared her shoulders and pushed through the door. Her kitty, Boo—named for Boo Radley, of course—yowled and wound around her legs. He cast a haughty look at Jeb, his yellow eyes unblinking, then rather than bow up and hiss like he'd done upon meeting Luke, he strolled over to Jeb and sniffed tentatively at his leg.

Traitor, Sophie thought, scowling at her beloved pet.

"Ah," Jeb said, seemingly delighted. "Who's this?"

Sophie toed off her boots and returned the gun to the cabinet. "Boo. He's had diarrhea lately, so I'd be careful if I were you."

Predictably, Jeb grimaced. "Oh. Bad luck. I hope it's nothing serious."

"It's not." Because it was a lie. Her patience at an end, her nerves frayed to near-breaking, she turned and crossed her arms over her chest. "Listen, this is my house, so we're going to have this conversation on my terms. Any questions you have for me are optional. The ones I have for you are not. Why the hell have you been following me and what the hell are you doing trespassing on my land?"

He'd scared the hell out of her. She'd always lived by the adage better safe than sorry, so she was prepared for anything, but she'd grown so tired of living, constantly looking over her shoulder, that she'd been trying not to do it anymore. Being afraid had felt too much like a victory for them, a loss for her. She wanted the power back.

But she'd realized tonight that she was much more frightened than she'd ever realized. It was unnerving.

In the process of shrugging out of his coat— clearly he'd meant to stay awhile—Jeb paused and shot her a wary look. She didn't know how she knew it was wary—naturally, nothing about his expression shifted, but she could feel the difference, almost like an atmospheric change.

Suddenly Heathcliffe cried from the front porch and Jeb's eyes widened in shock. He jumped as though something had bitten him, and whirled around. "Bloody hell," he breathed. "What was *that*?"

Sophie was too busy convulsing with laughter to tell him. Watching GI Joe meets James Bond spin Matrix-style around her living room looking for the boogey-man because of a bird was simply... priceless. Eyes streaming, her sides heaved and she couldn't catch her breath.

Jeb glared at her. To her delight, his cheeks actually turned pink. She'd be willing to bet that didn't happen often.

"Yeah, yeah. I'm sure it was funny. You didn't run for your gun, Annie Oakley," he drawled. "So I can assume we're not in any immediate danger."

Still chuckling, she shook her head and wiped her eyes. "Ah, wow. I needed that," she said. Poetic justice.

He shrugged a mouthwatering shoulder, his expression droll. "I live to entertain."

"It's good to have goals."

Seemingly weary, he dropped onto her couch and started loosening his tie. It was such a man thing to do, she found herself momentarily dumbstruck.

"Are you going to tell me what that was or not?"

Have a seat, Jeb. Make yourself at home, Jeb.

Take off your shirt, Jeb. Wait, no... She gave herself a shake. It was then that she noticed the state of him. His coat was covered with dirt and debris and tiny tears rent his shirt. Blood oozed through the linen from a couple of cuts on his chest and visible gashes marred his hands.

She frowned, seized with the irrational urge to nurse those minor injuries. "What happened to you?"

"Fence number two. Stupid me, I left my night-vision goggles at home." He lifted his hand, inspected the damage, then grimaced as though it didn't signify. "It's nothing. The noise?" he prodded.

"It was Heathcliffe, one of my peacocks." She arched a brow. "You've never heard one cry before?"

The corner of his sulky mouth twitched with a grin and he cut a look at her with that bright blue gaze. "Obviously not."

"It takes some getting used to."

He snorted. "It's creepy as hell."

That, too, but she'd grown to like it. She snagged her ice cream from the table and settled into her chair. "Your tux is ruined."

He laughed softly, watched her spoon a bite of ice cream into her mouth. "So is my pride, but I'll recover." He heaved a dramatic sigh. "I don't want anything to drink, thanks."

She smiled unrepentantly. "I'm only polite to invited guests."

He tsked. "What would Emily Post have to say about that?"

"Nothing I'd care to hear, I'm sure. Please tell me what you're doing here."

He sighed softly, the sound seasoned with dread, then he looked up at her, that bright blue gaze pinning her once more. "Were you looking for me when you came back to the ball?"

Sophie opened her mouth, closed it. What an odd question. Why would he want to know that? What difference did it make to anything? She licked her lips. "I… Does it matter?"

He leaned forward, resting his arms on his knees, his hands dangling between them. He studied her carpet, then gave a little resigned laugh, as though the answer surprised him. "It does."

She couldn't imagine why, but rather than dance around half-truths and lies, it was time for a little honesty. She'd give it with the hope that he'd reciprocate. She released a small breath. "I was," she admitted. "I'd told you that I would come back, and I happen to appreciate that old antiquated notion that people should do what they say they will. But by the time I'd gotten back, you'd already left." She purposely avoided looking at him, swirling the melted ice cream around the bottom of her bowl. "So I left, too."

"But why did you leave to start with?" he asked. "Why did you go to Marjorie's office?"

Oh, no. She'd answered a question. Now it was

his turn. She set her bowl aside, then looked up. "Why have you been following me? Either you tell me or you leave. The choice is yours."

"It's part of my job," he said.

She felt her forehead wrinkle and renewed fear washed through her. "You're being paid to follow me? Who hired you?" Surely to God her father hadn't— Or her mother— But why? What could they possibly want? Beyond making her miserable? She absently rubbed her arm, struggling to control the irrational panic. She was an adult. She was protected. She didn't have to be afraid. She could take care of herself, dammit.

Evidently something in her expression caught his attention. Concern lined his otherwise smooth brow, reflected almost tenderly in his gaze. "Sophie? Are you all right? Nobody hired me to follow you, specifically," he said, still staring at her. "You just got swept up in the net of my investigation, that's all."

Swept up in the net? His investigation? What did that mean? She nodded, the rush of adrenaline spent, making her insides tremble. Geez. She couldn't take much more of this.

"Right," she said, trying to sort it out amid the mess in her head. "But you obviously suspect me of something, or you wouldn't have been following me, you wouldn't have danced with me, and you wouldn't have come over my fence," she persisted. She arched a brow and might have whimpered. "Could you please just stop talking in cryptic circles and tell me what's going on?"

He released a heavy breath. "Okay, let's get something straight. I haven't *followed* you anywhere until tonight, after I caught *you* skulking around Marjorie's office. Up to that point, I have been conducting an investigation, which like it or not, you've been a part of. Because I don't think you're the person I'm looking for and because you are so well-liked and trusted in the village, I'd planned on asking for your help. Tonight. At the Fall Ball. Then you left and didn't come back and you broke into Marjorie's office and, well—" He laughed darkly. "—for obvious reasons, that sort of changed things."

"If by 'changed things,' you mean 'moved to the top of your list,' right?" Wonderful. Just brilliant. Several things suddenly clicked into place. "Listen, I know damned well that you aren't who you say you are—Foy doesn't have any children, so a grandson is pretty much out of the question. You've spent more time wandering around the village, visiting with other people than you have spent with your so-called grandfather, so it's obvious to me that you are investigating something or someone related to Twilight Acres. Here's a thought," she said, sarcasm rising right along with her temper. "Why don't you just ask me if I've done what you think I've done? Just ask me, Sherlock, and I'll tell you the truth. I won't lie."

He shrugged, then shot her a sardonic grin. "That simple, eh?"

"You're the one making it complicated."

"How am I supposed to know whether or not you're lying?"

She lifted her chin. "If you were following me so that you could eliminate me as a suspect and then ask for my help, then you're already half-convinced that I'm not the person you're looking for."

His gaze searched hers and that Petri dish sensation commenced again. She resisted the urge to squirm beneath that probing stare, that singularly intense, unwavering regard.

"Tell you what," she said. "In a show of good faith, I will tell you what I was doing in Marjorie's office first, then you can decide whether or not you want my help."

He blinked, seemingly surprised. "That's…generous. You had me on the ropes. Why are you backing down?"

She chuckled low. "Oh, I'm not backing down. I'm showing mercy. Sometimes that takes more courage, wouldn't you say?"

Jeb grinned, the dimple appearing in his cheek. Seemingly impressed, his gaze drifted across her mouth, making her lips tingle. "All right. Show me what you've got, badass."

Mercy. If he looked at her again like that, more than her lips were going to be tingling.

Time to put up or shut up. She released a slow

breath. "Over the past couple of years, several of our residents have supposedly misplaced some of their valuable items. Four, that I'm aware of. Losing things is common enough among the residents of Twilight Acres. It comes with the territory." She hesitated, bit her lip. "But losing stuff from their *safes* isn't. Two of the four who have supposedly 'lost' their valuables had them go missing from their in-home safes. I believe someone is stealing from them, taking advantage of them," she said, her voice hardening with anger. "And I want to know who."

A slow grin had begun to spread across Jeb's face—which he tried unsuccessfully to smooth away with his hand—and his eyes twinkled with knowing humor. Almost like she'd confirmed a suspicion.

Sophie paused, lifted a brow. "What?"

"Nothing," he said lightly. "Please continue."

Why did she get the sensation that he knew as much or more about this than she did? She shot him a wary look. "These safes were installed when the complex was built and new codes are programmed when a new resident moves in."

His smile faded and he leaned forward. "Who has access to the codes?"

"Other than the resident, only Marjorie."

"I see."

No doubt he did. "Personally, I don't think Marjorie is guilty of anything—she's utterly devoted to the residents and the village."

That blue gaze sharpened. "Then why did you break into her office?"

"Because I wanted to see how accessible the codes were, to see if perhaps someone could have looked at them without her knowledge."

"You're a whole helluva lot better at this than I am," he muttered grimly.

"Sorry?"

"Nothing. Go on. Did you find anything?"

She winced, shook her head. "Not the codes, anyway, which was what I was looking for. Her computer is password protected and there's one locked drawer in the bottom of her desk, which I couldn't get open. It's possible that the code file is in there, but I doubt it. In all probability, it's on the computer, but the likelihood of someone knowing her password is slim to none." Boo leapt into her lap and she stroked his silky fur. "She keeps good records though," Sophie added. "She's got detailed files on everyone."

He made a moue of agreement. "That could come in handy."

"That's what you're doing here, isn't it?" she asked, wondering why it had taken her so long to put it together. "You're investigating the thefts."

He nodded, gave his head a small wondering shake. "I am. Rather poorly, it would seem." He passed a hand over his face. "Geez."

"Ah, I doubt that," Sophie told him, eying him

consideringly. "You'd never tolerate a poor performance, most especially out of yourself."

He glanced up, a hint of surprise lighting his gaze. He studied her again, his eyes narrowing slightly in bewilderment, as though he was not only interested in trying to figure out what was going on in her head, but that it was somehow imperative. Necessary. "What makes you so sure?"

She lifted her shoulder, didn't just meet his gaze, but held it. "Intuition. I'm good at reading people."

A beat slid to three. "I've been told I'm not easily read."

Ah. So that was it. *She* was getting into *his* head and he wasn't used to it. For whatever reason, that little bit of insight settled warmly around her heart. She hummed under her breath. "Perhaps the person who told you that didn't speak the right language."

There, Sophie thought. Chew on that.

8

"SO, AM I still at the top of your list?" Sophie asked, absently stroking the cat sprawled across her lap.

He envied that cat.

Jeb swallowed a sigh, suddenly exhausted, still disturbed by her speak-the-right-language comment. What did she mean? That he'd just never met anyone capable of understanding him? That couldn't be right, because even Judd couldn't always get a bead on him. Granted it was rare, but it did happen. He winced, remembering his phone, and made a mental note to call first thing in the morning to get a replacement.

Was she still at the top of his list? she wanted to know. She, of the double fence and sexy dress and melting eyes and hot mouth.

"No, not that one, anyway," he said, resting his head against the back of her couch. She'd never truly been there to start with, but now didn't seem like the time to tell her that. Her house smelled like cinnamon and yeast and a low fire burned on the hearth, crackling merrily.

"Oh? There's more than one list?"

"You've been officially moved to the top of my pain-in-the-ass list, but you are no longer the prime suspect in my investigation." Eyes closed, he laughed softly. "Happy now?"

"I was the prime suspect? Really?" she asked disbelievingly. "Why?"

"Because in the preliminary search, one of our agents found a complaint about you in an online review of the community. The reviewer accused you of taking a piece of jewelry from a resident."

She inhaled sharply.

He turned his head and cracked one eye open. "You don't ever Google yourself?" He winced. Shit, that sounded dirty. "I didn't mean… Er…"

Her ripe mouth curled into a wide grin and her eyes twinkled with humor. "My grandmother would threaten to wash your mouth out with soap."

"You know what I mean," he said.

"I do," she admitted. "And no, I have never Googled myself," she said, giggling. Her face fell. "But clearly that is something that I need to start doing if there are slanderous allegations against me being reported in cyber space."

"They didn't say that you'd *stolen* it, only that you'd *taken* it," he pointed out.

Her shrewd gaze narrowed. "Ah. Accepted it, you mean?" She sighed. "Well, in that case, I am guilty. Cora gave me a cameo pendant. It had been a gift from her husband, one he'd bought her during their honeymoon in Rome. I suspected that her family didn't like it, but since it wasn't theirs and Cora wanted me to have it, I couldn't refuse."

Jeb smiled. "I can see where that would have been difficult. She doesn't seem like the type to take no for an answer."

She snorted. "I'll say. How the hell do you think I ended up in this dress?"

Jeb let his gaze drift slowly over the dress in question and, by default, the body beneath it. Naturally, his own body reacted accordingly. Heat flooded his groin and his fingers itched to touch her. "I can't fault her for that, I'm afraid. You look beautiful."

He could see the pulse hammering in her throat from where he sat, watched her gulp, her gaze sliding along his thigh. "Thank you," she murmured. A frown suddenly marred her brow and she winced, then nudged the cat off her lap and stood. "I'd better put some antiseptic on that," she said, nodding at his fingers.

He shook his head. "Nah. Don't trouble yourself. I'm fine." He'd had much worse. *Much*, much worse, as a matter of fact, but was touched that she seemed so concerned. He wasn't used to having anyone make a fuss over him—anyone except his mother, of course—and it felt odd…but nice.

"It's no trouble," she said, heading toward the

door. Just as she would have went through, she grabbed the jamb, stopped short, wheeled around and looked at him. A sheepish smile tugged at her lips. "Can I get you something to drink, Jeb?"

He grinned, chewed the inside of his cheek. So he'd been upgraded to guest status then? Sweet. "Do you have any liquor?"

"Johnny Walker."

He lifted a brow. Annie Oakley knew her scotch. "Red?"

She nodded haltingly. "I've got Red. I've also got Blue."

He whistled low, pleasantly astonished. Blue was as legendary as rare. "You're willing to waste your good scotch on a trespasser?"

She lifted her chin. "I'm willing to *share* my good scotch with a partner."

"You'll help me then?" He'd assumed that she would since she'd already taken it upon herself to look into the thefts, but he hadn't officially asked her yet.

"In any way I can," she told him, determination ringing in her tone. "This person isn't just taking a piece of jewelry, they're taking a memory. Lila's father had given her that necklace for her coming-out party. She's heartbroken that it's gone and she suspects her daughter, which has undoubtedly caused resentment."

"Do you think the daughter took it?"

Sophie considered the question before responding, which he liked. "I don't know. Lila said Monica had only been concerned with the monetary value of the piece, but that it had been insured." Her brow puckered. "She never said if Monica knew the necklace was insured."

"That's something we're going to need to know."

"I can ask her."

Jeb grinned at her. "I'm counting it on it."

She returned his smile, then disappeared into the other room. While she was gone, he put a few more logs on the fire, pleased when the timber took flame. He liked that she'd opted for a working fireplace instead of gas. Gas might be more user-friendly, but there was nothing so satisfying as the scent and sound of a real blaze.

A cursory glance around her living room revealed a good deal about his new "partner." She had a keen eye for good electronics, comfortable furniture—some of it repurposed, like the antique traveling trunk that doubled as her coffee table—and vintage prints. Some he recognized—the Parrish's, for instance—but others he couldn't place.

A handmade quilt lay folded over the back of the couch, suggesting she spent a lot of time curled up with a blanket, and a stack of books rested on the end table. Everything from the classics to current popular fiction. He browsed her DVD collection and felt his lips twitch. A fellow Dr. Who fan.

A fellow Dr. Who fan with a double fence around her place, who'd looked momentarily terrified when she thought he'd been paid to follow her, almost as if he would have done her harm. And she knew her way around a rifle. He'd also noticed that she'd absently rubbed her arm, or more specifically the five inch scar on the inside of it. Up until this point she'd been wearing long sleeves, so he hadn't caught a glimpse of it until tonight. It was faded, which indicated she'd had it awhile and it would have hurt. The unconscious reaction coupled with the fear told him that it hadn't been an accident—it had been deliberate—and she was terrified of the person who'd given it to her.

The urge to protect had been plaguing him since he'd met her, but it was a living, breathing thing inside him now. He wanted to pummel the hell out of whoever had hurt her. He wanted to make them afraid. He wanted to pay them back in kind for what they'd put her through.

Though he desperately wanted to probe her about it, to ask more questions, he couldn't bring himself to do it. Some pains were too difficult to share, a fact he knew all too well himself. Some burdens weren't lifted with a conversation, they were lanced, like a boil.

He couldn't ask that of her. Wouldn't.

She returned to the living room then, the first aid kit under one arm, the whiskey beneath the other, and a pair of crystal tumblers in her hands.

He hurried forward. "Here, let me help you with that," he said, rescuing the whiskey first.

"Thanks," she murmured. She set everything else down on the trunk.

He gestured to the bottle. "Mind if I pour?"

She shook her head, her lips twitching. "Not at all. You're really excited about this, aren't you?"

"'Pleased' is the word I think you're looking for," he said. "I've never had the Blue."

"Then you're in for a treat. It was my grandmother's favorite," she said. "She was Scottish. A war bride. She was only seventeen years old when my grandfather brought her over here. She said she was willing to leave her country for him, but she wouldn't give up her name." A sigh slipped through her lips. "And she never did. She was an O'Brien until the day she died."

"So she was your maternal grandmother then?" Jeb took the top off and carefully distributed the liquor into their tumblers, then handed one to her.

"No, paternal." She raised her glass and clinked it against his. "To a new start."

Paternal? Wouldn't Sophie have taken the grandfather's name then? After all, it would have been the same as her father's. How could she be an O'Brien. Unless she'd chosen to be...

His gaze tangled with hers. "To a new start," he repeated. He lifted the glass to his lips without ever taking his eyes off of hers. Anticipation spiked as the whiskey settled smoothly on his tongue, smokey and sweet. Just like her, he thought, watching her savor the rich amber liquid.

He hummed appreciatively, winced as the fire sizzled pleasantly down his throat. "Nice," he murmured. "Thank you."

"You're welcome." She smiled, almost shyly, then gestured to the couch. "Take a seat and I'll work on those cuts."

He did as she asked, shifting his tumbler to his other hand. She settled in next to him, opened the first aid kit, then reached for his hand, wincing as she inspected the gash in his palm. "I'll try not to go too Nurse Ratched on you," she said, her small fingers inspecting his damaged skin.

He stared broodily at her, unable to help himself. "Hey, I'm just glad you didn't shoot me."

Her lips twitched. "Me, too. Mild abrasions are within my scope, but a gunshot wound is beyond my talents." She carefully cleaned the negligible wound, chewing absently on her bottom lip while she worked.

He wished she wouldn't do that. Her mouth was distraction enough, without her sinking her teeth into it. And watching her mouth while she was touching him, even if it was only to bandage a few shallow cuts, was…provoking.

"Was being Foy's grandson the only untrue part of your cover story?" she asked.

Firelight brought out the red in her hair, Jeb noticed, and cast a warm glow over her face. This close he could see a series of ginger freckles across her pert nose and he found them strangely adorable. He was a freckle man. Who knew?

"Depends," he said. "What did you hear?"

Finished with one injury, she moved onto his fingers. "That you were former military. A Ranger."

"What do you think, Nancy Drew?" he drawled, interested in her response. What did she see when she looked at him? Aside from those disturbing bits of insight she'd already exhibited.

She nodded at his glass, indicating that he should move his drink to his other hand. He did, and shifted closer to her on the couch, so that she could more easily reach him. "Oh, I never doubted that part," she told him. "I was just looking for confirmation."

He took another drink, felt the warmth of the alcohol burn through his blood. "It's true," he said. "I came out a few months ago and went to work for a private security company in Atlanta. Rose-Marie Wilson's family hired us and I was assigned to the case. It's my first, as it happens, so I'd like to make a good impression."

"I'm sure you did or they wouldn't have hired you." She made a nonsensical noise under her breath, then frowned at his hand. "This one is worse. I'm going to have to put a bandage on it."

He was past caring. At this point he would have let her wrap his whole damned arm in gauze if it meant she'd keep touching him. Funny how something so seemingly innocuous could elicit such a strong reaction.

But her fingers were cool and tender, her profile achingly sweet, and every bit of desire—every last fiber of this unholy attraction—seemed to boil up from beneath his skin. Heat slithered into his groin, tightening his balls.

"There," she said, looking up at him. She stilled at his expression and her smile faltered. "All d-done."

No, he was the one who was done, Jeb thought fatalistically. No doubt he'd been done the day he met her. He'd just been too ignorant to realize it.

SOPHIE'S HEART SKIPPED a beat in her chest and, though she'd finished tidying up those scratches, she still kept Jeb's hand in hers. She should probably let it go—and had intended to, really—but when she'd glanced up and caught him looking at her like *that*...

No man had *ever* looked at her like that.

Like he wanted to lay her out like dinner on the ground and lick her up with a spoon. Like he wanted her as much as she wanted him. Like every depraved thought that had flitted through her mind the last couple of days hadn't been original at all, because he'd thought of them first and more often.

Impossibly, it made her hotter.

Longing twisted through her, tying her up in knots, and her mouth watered while the rest of her body had decided to liquefy and simmer. She longed to touch more of him, to slide the tip of her thumb across the slope of his brow, to taste the skin on the highest part of his cheek, where she knew it would be the softest.

She had never, ever wanted a man more than she did him right now.

Ever.

And she instinctively knew she never would again. He had some sort of mystical power over her, an appeal that called to her on a purely visceral level. Not that she didn't find him fascinating, because she did. She liked being able to predict those inscrutable faces—the man behind the mask, as it were—and she especially liked that she appeared to be the only person who could do it. Take now, for instance. For all intents and purposes, he still looked every bit as lethal and intimidating as always.

But she could tell that the alcohol had mellowed him out, easing some of the tension from his shoulders and his eyes—that purely remarkable shade of blue—had gone all heavy-lidded and sultry-looking. Combined with that perpetual sulky, sensual mouth he looked especially hot...wicked, even.

And if he didn't stop looking at her like that, she was going to be in serious trouble.

"It's getting late," he said, his gaze dropping hungrily to her mouth.

"I'm sure Foy is worried about you."

He snorted, a chuckle startled out of him. "Foy locked me out of the house until two a.m. last night. He had a guest over," he drawled. "And he was especially hopeful about Mary and her inability to hold her sangria tonight."

Sophie grinned, not the least bit surprised. "Foy is definitely the resident Romeo."

He passed a hand wearily over his face. "Foy is a pain in the ass."

She grinned. "But he's not at the top of your pain-in-the-ass list, is he? Cause that's my spot. Undeserved," she said with a feigned, wounded shrug. "But what can a girl do?"

He hesitated, arched a hopeful brow. "A girl could give me her couch for the night."

The idea of him spending the night at her house made her belly clench. Too much temptation, too easily accessible. Too close. But the idea of saying no never occurred to her. It *was* late, and it was a thirty minute drive back into the city. For him to make the trip not knowing whether or not Foy was going to let him into the house seemed absurd when he was already here.

"You're welcome to the couch, but I've got a guest bedroom upstairs."

He released a sigh. "You're an angel of mercy."

More like a glutton for punishment, Sophie thought, but warmed at the compliment all the same.

"An angel of mercy with excellent taste in alcohol," he added, gesturing to the bottle. "And one who knows her way around a twelve-gauge shotgun." His twinkling gaze snagged hers and he grinned. "If you can fry an egg without letting the edges get all crispy and gross, you'd be a top contender in The Perfect Woman contest."

"Ah, I see why you've asked to spend the night," she said. "You're drunk. Off three inches of scotch."

"I'm not drunk," he said, smiling. "I'm…warm. A couple of ticks behind buzzed maybe, but not drunk." He inclined his head. "That's good stuff."

She was "warm" too, but could only attribute a minor portion of it to the alcohol. Of course, she hadn't finished hers, so…

"Come on," she said. "Let me show you upstairs." She released his hand, immediately missing its warmth, then stood and headed toward the hall. A thought struck and she shot him a look over her shoulder. "Shouldn't you call Foy and let him know not to expect you?"

"Can't," he said matter-of-factly. "My phone is in the pond."

Sophie felt her eyes round, started mounted the stairs. "What? Why? How did it get there?"

"It's not important," he said. "It wasn't my finest moment. But if I could use your phone to send a text, I'd appreciate it. Judd's going to flip a bitch if he doesn't hear from me soon." His tone was a bit grim and held a degree of certainty.

Sophie opened the bedroom door, ushering him inside. "Who's Judd? Your boss?"

Jeb glanced around the room, made a moue of approval. "My twin. This is nice, thanks. I've been sleeping on a futon at Foy's."

Another jolt of shock moved through her. "You're a twin. There are two of you?" she asked faintly. She gulped. That was hardly fair to the world, was it?

He grinned. "We're not identical," he said, humor lighting his gaze. "But we're closely bonded."

"A twin connection, you mean?"

He nodded, didn't elaborate further.

"That's cool," she said. "So you're close?"

A dark chuckle emerged from his throat. "Uncomfortably, at times."

She envied him that. Her brother was two years older, but she never remembered being anything but afraid of him. He'd been the perfect blend of the worst of her parents, a sociopath with a violent streak.

Sophie nodded, unable to contribute. "Right," she said. "There are clean linens on the bed. You can use the hall bath—I've got my own—and there are towels and washcloths in the linen closet and a spare toothbrush in the drawer next to the sink. Let me just go and grab my phone. And I'm going to lock up while I'm downstairs. I'll only be a minute."

By the time she'd arrived back upstairs, he'd removed his shoes and socks, set the heels against the wall and had stripped off his shirt. He stood, barechested, his slacks unbuttoned, but not unzipped, and was in the process of hanging his shirt on the bedpost when she walked in. Lamplight glowed over his gleaming skin, casting shadows over the muscled planes of his body. He was glorious, a living, breathing testament to the ultimate male form. There were scars, too, of course—evidence of war—and she ached to kiss each one, to thank him for bearing them for their country.

A tattoo encircled his right bicep, which at first glance looked almost tribal, but a closer peek revealed it was the sign of the Gemini, repeated over and over. She felt a grin curl her lips.

"I'll have to tell Cora," she said, handing him her phone.

A question appeared in his gaze as he accepted it, the muscles rippling beneath his skin. Her stomach clenched and heat flooded her womb. "That you've got a tattoo," she added a bit unsteadily. She shook herself, blinked, determined to look at something besides his splendid abs. "She said you've have ink," she explained.

He glanced at the tattoo, as though he'd forgotten that it was there. "Right. Yes. Judd has the same one, but it's on his left arm. We got them after we graduated Jump School." He keyed in a few lines of text, sent it, then handed her phone back over.

"He was in the military as well?"

"He's still in the military," he said, an odd shutter falling over his gaze. He glanced away—so that she couldn't see his face?—and smoothed a finger over the coverlet. "He's on leave right now, in Crete, which is why he's had access to a cell phone, otherwise communication is spotty."

She winced, wondering what had made him

suddenly shut down. The wall had come down so quickly, she'd nearly recoiled. "That must suck."

He met her gaze once more. "It does," he said, expelling a breath. "But it is what it is. We'll adjust."

Meaning they hadn't yet. Interesting. Jeb had told her earlier that he'd come out of the military a couple of months ago and gone to work for a security company. At the time it had seemed like such an innocuous statement, one that didn't signify…but it clearly did. Why had he come out of the military? Why had he abandoned what should have been a life-long career? Particularly when his brother—his twin—was still serving?

Something horrible had happened, Sophie thought, studying him. Because only something substantial would have made this man switch course mid-stream. She knew it as well as she knew that the world was round, that the sky was blue, the grass green.

To her surprise, he took a step forward, lessening the distance between them, putting his bare skin within arm's length of her fingers. Too close. Startled, Sophie swallowed.

"Do you remember the song we danced to tonight?" he asked, his voice low, a little rough and unsteady. He sidled a little closer. Or had she moved? She couldn't be sure. Either way she could feel the heat coming off his skin, could smell the tang of the orange in the soap he'd used.

"I—I do."

His gaze slid hungrily over her face, along her cheek, her eyes, lingered on her mouth. "Remind me of the title, please."

She moistened her lips, her own gaze dropping inexplicably to his mouth. Her knees wobbled. "Just a Kiss."

"I agree," he said, closing the distance between them. He framed her face with both hands, his thumbs sliding over her jaw, then drew her to him and lowered his mouth to hers. Sophie went up on tiptoe, vibrated like a tuning fork, then looped her arms around his neck and…melted.

A tornado of energy, of sensation, whirled from the bottoms of her feet to the top of her head, wrapping her in an eye of unparalleled joy, infinite desire. Longing bubbled up inside of her, bittersweet and curiously sacred, and she clung to him, feeling the power in his touch, the desperation in his lips. His were soft against hers, but firm and his tongue expertly probed the inner recesses of her mouth.

A low moan hummed against her lips and she smiled when she realized that it was his. He seemed to tense against her, almost as though he'd been shocked into stillness—in awe—then he'd pushed his hands into her hair, angled her head and deepened the kiss. Like he was drowning. Like he couldn't breathe. Like he needed her. He tasted like good scotch whiskey, spring rain, a new beginning…familiar. Hauntingly so, which was impossible and yet..the sensation was there all the same.

Warmth flooded her womb, tingled hotly in her nipples, made her breasts heavy with longing. Her stomach fluttered, the backs of her thighs quaked with a shiver and she could feel the pulse beat hammering between her legs.

Jeb wrapped her closer, one massive hand on her face, his thumb sliding reverently over her cheek, while the other hand slid down her back and settled hotly on her ass. He gave a little squeeze, lifting her up so that the evidence of his arousal rode high on her belly.

He was...

That was...

Oh, sweet heaven.

His fingers trembled against her face, proof that she affected him as much as he affected her. He groaned softly, the sound ringing with regret, then slowly ended the kiss and rested his forehead against hers.

His brooding gaze burned with longing, a hint of futility and something else, something she couldn't quite decipher. Wonder, maybe?

"Just a kiss," he murmured, his breath and tone equally, gratifyingly, unsteady. "For now."

Quivering from one end of her body to the other, Sophie nodded.

Because that sounded like a promise.

9

DESPITE THE FACT that he'd been wound tighter than a spool of thread, Jeb slept like the dead in Sophie's guest bedroom. Sleep had eluded him for a couple of hours after she'd retired to her own room—probably because he'd imagined he could hear the whine of the zipper when she'd removed her dress—followed by the sound of her shower starting immediately thereafter. The hard-on he'd been fighting delivered a knock-out punch with that one, because he couldn't think about her being in the shower without thinking about her being naked. And wet.

He shifted and continued his trek to her barn. Though he hadn't heard her get up or go out of the house—mildly disconcerting, all things considered—she'd left a note taped to the coffeepot citing her whereabouts should he wake and find her gone.

That kiss must have done more than scramble his loins—it must of fried his brain as well. Honestly, he'd been thinking about kissing her for days—looking at her mouth, longing for the taste of her. He'd wanted it with an intensity that had left him nothing short of baffled.

But nothing could have prepared him for the act itself, or more significantly, the feelings it would provoke. The instant he'd touched her lips to his, felt the sweet slide of tongue into his mouth, that jerk behind his naval had given a massive yank he'd felt to the soles of his feet…then the knot he'd been carrying around in his belly—the one that had grown tighter every time he'd clapped eyes on her—suddenly loosened and unfurled, relaxing with a release so achingly perfect he'd felt the relief of it all at once. It was like his middle had slipped an unknown tourniquet and the feeling of happiness and contentedness, desire and need had welled up within him, filling him so completely he was hard pressed not to collapse beneath the weight of it.

If merely kissing her did this to him, then he couldn't imagine what it would be like when he finally bedded her. And, he would. He had to. It wasn't a matter of exercising restraint or using good judgment or even the power of his baser instincts.

He needed her. He *needed* to get inside of her, to hold her and taste and feel her greedy little body beneath his. And every beat of his heart, every determined, rhythmic push of his blood through his veins, only intensified the sensation, only heightened his awareness of it.

It was terrifying.

Other than failure, Jeb had never been afraid of anything in his life. He'd walked into battle a dozen times over, had been as close to death as anyone was capable of being just as often and yet, he'd never been afraid. Wary, maybe. Careful? Always. Hell, he didn't have a death wish. But one didn't join the military without coming to terms with their own mortality pretty damned quick. Fear could get you killed.

That he was afraid of this woman—this extraordinarily ordinary, gun-wielding, soap-making, goat farmer—was nothing short of inconceivable. He released a pent-up breath.

But there it was.

Jeb smothered a laugh and shook his head. Clearly he'd lost his mind. Rather than lingering on that thought, he took a moment to survey her property with the benefit of daylight. Ducks, geese and swans glided along the top of the large pond in front of her house and chickens clucked from a nearby pen. Farther down the lane nearest the barn, half a dozen goats gobbled feed from a trough, while a lone one struggled to get its head out of the fence.

Not the brightest of animals, goats, Jeb thought. Tsking under her breath, Sophie emerged from behind the pen, a cup in her hand. Dressed in a long-sleeved flannel shirt, a pair of jeans and her now infamous muck boots, she looked adorable. Her cheeks and nose were pink from the morning chill and a pink camouflage hat covered the top of her head.

"Come on now, Jenny," she called. "I don't have time for this."

"Why not?" Jeb asked, setting a foot against the fence railing. "Are we in a hurry?"

She started and her gaze found his. A smile slid over her lips, lighting her whole face. Something in his chest squeezed almost painfully.

"Not particularly, but she does this every morning. She's not as smart as the other goats and they pick on her. That's why she won't eat with them." She bent down and carefully angled the goat's head back through the fence, then put the cup up under its nose and rubbed its head. "Here, sweetheart," she cooed indulgently. "Fight back today, would you? Give 'em hell."

Jeb grinned. "I didn't know being a motivational speaker came along with this job."

She shrugged, gave the animal one last pat. "I'm always a cheerleader for the underdog."

Because she'd been one? Jeb wondered. Because she had firsthand experience of the inequity? Or, like him, was she just wired that way? Possibly both, he imagined. He cast a sweeping glance around her farm, noting the tidiness of everything. No weeds, no debris, no downed trees or old stumps. A pair of peacocks—one male and one female—walked slowly by, pecking at bits of leftover grass in their path. Despite their "cry"—he suppressed a shudder, remembering—they were truly beautiful birds.

"You've got a lovely place here," he said. It was warm and inviting, nice and lived in.

"Thank you," she said, coming over the fence. "It's a lot of work, but I enjoy it and it's home. I couldn't imagine living anywhere else."

"You're awfully isolated out here," he remarked, scanning the front edge of her property, eyeing the fence.

She peeked into the cup in her hand, to avoid looking at him, he suspected. "I've got everything I need to take care of myself."

"The fence—both of them—look relatively new." He was fishing and she knew it.

"I put them in after Gran died. Some of the family wasn't happy with the terms of her will." She arched a brow and smiled. "I see you found the sweatshirt I left out for you." Her lips twitched. "It almost fits."

Ah, yes, he thought, poking a tongue inside his cheek. The sweatshirt in question was John Deere green, with the infamous logo on the breast. It was a large. No doubt it would have swallowed her, but it was admittedly a little tight on him. Paired with his tuxedo pants and dress shoes, he looked ridiculous. But his shirt was ruined and without another to go under the equally torn tuxedo coat, he'd no doubt look like a male stripper.

He'd elected for ridiculous instead.

And as a diversionary tactic, bringing it up had worked well. It had almost made him forget that she'd actually revealed something. Some of the family wasn't happy with Gran's will? And that had required this sort of fortification? A fence inside a fence. The first fence he could understand—it was the first line of defense, designed to keep people out. The motion sensors were a brilliant touch. They alerted her to an intruder and gave her ample time to either ambush them—like she had him, which still boggled the mind—or to alert the authorities and lock herself out of harm's way.

He'd noted the locks on all the doors and windows—the sensors there as well—and the loaded gun cabinet next to the door this morning. She was ready. She was prepared. And she was clearly determined *not* to be a victim.

But from who? A member of her family? An image of her rubbing that scar suddenly emerged in his mind's eye and his stomach tightened with dread. She'd taken her paternal grandmother's name, had presumably changed it from that of her father's. A tingling eddied through his fingers, across the back of his neck.

Her father? That's who she was afraid of? It was and he knew it. Every bit of intuition he possessed told him that it was true. Shock and anger rocketed through him and bile tickled up the back of his throat. He'd already asked Charlie to do some deeper study into her background, but she'd been looking under the wrong name. No wonder she hadn't found anything that threw up a red flag. As soon as he went in this morning to get a new phone, he'd update her and see what she could find out. He had to know why Sophie was this spooked, what had happened to make her so afraid of the one man who was supposed to love and protect her. He couldn't imagine the betrayal, couldn't wrap his head around it.

But he knew this—nobody was going to lay a finger on her on his watch.

Hadn't he felt it all along? The vulnerability? The baffling urge to protect? It's because she needed it. Desperately.

"I did find it, thanks," he said, pulling at the shirt in an attempt to stretch it a bit more. "An old boyfriend's?" he asked, dreading the answer to that question. The idea of her kissing anyone else—he couldn't push his mind past a single kiss, because it flatly refused to go there—made him want to tear his hair out by the roots and howl.

She shot him a look. "No," she told him. "Come on, I need to get a few things from the shop." She gestured toward a building behind her house. A miniature version of the house, it sat roughly thirty feet from her back door. Convenient, but separate. "They gave me the sweatshirt when I bought my tractor," she explained. "Large and Extra Large were my only choices."

He winced. "I would have preferred Extra Large."

Her lips twitched. "I'll bear that in mind next time."

"You know how to drive a tractor?" he asked, shoving his hands into his pockets. Why was he not surprised? "You just scored another point in The Perfect Woman contest."

"I try," she said, laughing softly. She pushed through the front door of the little building and the scent of citrus and vanilla immediately rose up to meet him. A quick look revealed a showroom of sorts, with lots of different soaps and lotions arranged around the room, grouped according to scent. Sophie slid behind the desk at her computer, clicked through a few screens, then the whine of the printer reached his ears. "Right," she said. "Feel free to take a look around." She picked up a basket. "I've got to pull a few orders together."

Taking advantage of the chance to learn more about her, he strolled around the room, then made his way to the back, where the actual work took place. Soaps in different stages of production filled large square molds, little round molds and a big knife, similar to a paper cutter sat in the middle of one table. Bits of precut fabric, satin ribbon and her label on another, obviously where the finishing work happened. Various ingredients lined shelving attached to one wall, lots of essential oils and things he didn't recognize. A stove and refrigerator rounded out the room and her iPod docking station sat on the window sill. There was no chair, even at the finishing station, indicating that she was on her feet for the entire process. It was much more labor intensive than he'd realized, obviously, Jeb thought, impressed.

"This is incredible," he told her. "You do everything yourself, from start to finish."

She nodded, seemingly pleased. "I do," she said, then darted him a sheepish look. "It's the only way to ensure quality control."

He smiled and inclined his head. "Ah, I see. Control issues, huh? Is it because you're the only one who can do it right or because you don't want to let anyone else help you?"

She considered him for a minute, her melting brown gaze fixed on his. Reading him. Seeing things no one else could see. "Hmm. Do I detect the voice of experience in that question?"

Unnerved, a bark of laughter rumbled up his throat. She *had* to quit that. "It's vaguely familiar," he said, rubbing the back of his neck.

She laughed, the sound low and knowing. "Oh, I don't think so. *Hauntingly* familiar, more like. Taking orders must have been sheer hell for you," she said, her tone thoughtful. "I'm honestly a little surprised that you ever went into the military at all. But where else are men with honor, a sense of duty and the belief in the greater good supposed to go, huh?" The corner of her ripe mouth lifted in a grin, as if it was a foregone conclusion.

As if she hadn't flipped his world on its end.

In a couple of sentences, after having known him for three days, she'd just summed up his entire military career, as well as his motivation for pursuing it.

He was so stunned, his feet turned to lead and panic punched his heart rate into overdrive.

Was nothing safe from her? Was she going to be able to read every insight into his soul, every carefully locked down secret, every unformed thought that flitted through his head?

Because if that was the case, more than his sanity was in trouble. Gut instinct told him his heart was as well.

SOPHIE WASN'T EXACTLY sure what she'd said that had rooted him to the floor, but clearly she'd rattled him. "Jeb?"

He blinked, seemingly coming out of stupor. "Sorry," he said, his smile strained. "I was woolgathering."

She set the basket on her hip and reached for the door. "Come on," she told him. "I'll fix a little breakfast and we can talk strategy."

"Strategy?"

"For catching the jewel thief," she went on. He closed the door to the shop for her, then beat her to the back door so that he could open it for her, ever the gentleman. In his too small John Deere sweatshirt and tuxedo pants, she thought, stifling a snicker. He should have looked ridiculous—like a proper fool, to tell the truth—but, naturally, he didn't. His shoulders were mouthwatering beneath the too tight fabric and now that she'd seen them bare, in all their muscled glory, she didn't think he could ever look anything short of perfect to her.

She'd relived that kiss a million times since last night, still shivered when she thought about it now. And while he might have been talking to her because she'd been an initial suspect in his investigation, that's *not* why he'd been flirting with her.

She didn't know when anything had ever pleased her more.

This glorious specimen of masculine flesh, this honorable, duty-bound, sweet, funny, frustratingly inscrutable former Ranger wanted...*her*.

She'd be lying if she said she wasn't surprised.

Sophie knew her own worth—she knew that she was a catch, that she was hardworking and clever, devoted and loyal to those she loved, honest and trustworthy. She had many good qualities. But those good qualities and her mind—probably her best one—were packaged beneath a completely ordinary face. She owned a mirror. She knew what she looked like. She was passably attractive, her eyes being her best feature.

But men didn't look at her and swoon, they didn't whistle when she walked by, and they certainly never looked at her and lusted.

But Jeb had.

And it thrilled her to her little toes.

She set her basket on the counter, offered him a

seat and quickly set to work on their food. "Tell me what you know so far," she said. "What have you been able to find out?"

She felt his brooding gaze as it followed her around the kitchen. The back of her neck prickled beneath that unwavering regard. "Not much," he said. "We know from Rose-Marie's family that her brooch was taken from her safe, so that's in keeping with what you've told me about Lila. That pattern holds with Nanette Hearst as well. I was able to talk to her yesterday and, though it took a little bit of effort—she had me looking at every picture she'd ever taken of her cat—" he drawled with a wry smile "—she finally revealed that she'd been certain that the piece had been in the safe."

"Were you able to get a picture of it?" she asked. "So we'll know what we're looking for."

"Not of hers, no. I have one of Rose-Marie's."

Sophie flipped the bacon, then began cutting up a bit of melon. A quick check of the eggs revealed they weren't quite ready. "I don't have a picture of Lila's, but it would be easy enough to get. She's wearing it in one of the photographs on her mantle. I would know it if I saw it again."

"It should be easy enough to snap a picture of it with a cell phone," he said. He released a breath. "That still leaves Pearl McIntosh. Unfortunately, I haven't had any luck finding her."

"She's been visiting family in the city. She's supposed to be back today. Her book club is meeting and she's not going to miss that."

"Do you think you could talk to her?"

"I can." A thought struck. "Does Foy know about all of this?"

"He does," Jeb told her.

"I'm surprised he didn't offer to help you."

Jeb hesitated. "I'm not convinced that he actually believes that anything has been taken."

"You should have told everyone that you were his nephew," she said. "It's pretty much common knowledge that he and Annie didn't have any kids."

He winced. "Actually, they did. A boy, but he was stillborn."

Shocked, Sophie turned to look at him more fully. "What?" she breathed. "How do you know that?"

"Because he told me. Last night, while I was waiting for you." He swallowed, then gave his head a regretful shake. "Sad stuff. Tragic."

She'd known Foy for years, considered him one of her closer friends at Twilight Acres and, though she'd heard many stories about his Annie, the one he'd shared with Jeb, obviously, was one she'd never heard. She didn't think anyone else on site had heard it either. Foy was the reigning king of Twilight Acres. News about him travelled fast. Tragic news would have travelled faster.

Jeb arched a brow. "You didn't know?"

Sophie shook her head, bit her lip. "No, I didn't, and I doubt anyone else does either."

Her handsome guest mulled that over. "Oh. Wow."

"Yes, wow. He must have had a reason for sharing something so personal, something he hadn't confided in even his closest friends."

"Would Marjorie know?" he asked.

Sophie chewed the inside of her cheek. "I don't think so. It wasn't in Foy's file."

He grimaced. "I really need to get into her office."

"That's how you caught me, isn't it?" she breathed. She hadn't thought about it last night, but clearly he'd been coming to Marjorie's office for the same reason she had.

He grinned, shrugged. "Yes. When you didn't come back to the dance, I decided that, rather than waste the rest of the evening, I should try to do something proactive, something I was actually getting paid to do. So I left and went over there." He leaned forward, considered her. "How did you get in exactly?"

"Through the French doors in her garden. There's a hide-a-key rock next to the fountain." She grinned at him. "How were you going to get in?"

He sighed softly, eyes twinkling, and shook his head. "By picking an unlocked door, evidently."

"We can go back tonight, if you'd like."

He nodded. "When does Marjorie normally leave?"

"Not until around six, usually," Sophie told him.

"Why don't we grab a bite to eat at the diner?" he suggested lightly. "Then when we leave together, everyone will assume that I'm coming home with you and my absence at Foy's won't seem so notable."

His plan made perfect sense, logical and well-reasoned, but she couldn't help but feel like he was angling for an invitation to spend the night. A thrill whipped through her, swirling around her middle, that "for now" promise ringing in her ears.

She smiled, then turned back to the stove. Ah, the eggs were ready. "Be sure to bring an overnight bag. You can follow me through this gate this time instead of coming over the fence."

"Right," he said, chuckling. "I wouldn't want to risk another injury that required a Band-Aid." He held up his hands, gesturing to the Disney princess one across his knuckle. "I've got to take this off before I get back to Foy's. He'll revoke my Man Card."

Sophie chuckled, plating their food. "Hey, that's all I had on hand. I love Mulan. She's a warrior, too. Carried a sword. Defeated the Huns. I thought she was appropriate."

"Bullshit," he said. "You thought it would be funny to put a girly Band-Aid on my hand."

Sophie laughed, outed, and slid his plate in front of him. She'd already set butter and jam, salt and pepper on the table. "That might have a teensy, insignificant part of my motivation."

"Ha."

She sat down, draped her napkin over her lap and

added a smear of butter to her toast. She peeked over at him, noting the grin on his face with a hefty dollop of satisfaction.

"You made eggs," he said. "With no crispy, gross edges."

Yes, she knew. "The trick is to cook them slowly."

"That settles it. You are The Perfect Woman."

Pleasure bloomed through her chest, pushing a smile it took effort to contain over her lips. "Oh, I doubt that. Perfection is too hard to live up to. I'd rather be ordinary, but skilled."

"Trust me," he said. "You're not ordinary. You're...remarkable," he said, his voice strangely thick, a hint of unmistakable wonder and admiration.

Sophie blushed to the roots of her hair. "I'd argue with you, but that would be stupid. So thank you." She swallowed a bite of fruit. "I think you're pretty damned remarkable, too."

She did. And if the tightness in her chest and the happiness tripping through her veins were any indication, she was half in love with him already.

So much for swearing off men, Sophie thought with a fatalistic sigh. It had been a bad idea from the start, one doomed to failure. And if she was going to fail, better it be *spectacularly* with him than with anyone else.

10

"HERE YOU GO," Payne said, handing over a new cell phone. "What did you say happened to yours again?"

"It got wet." True enough, if not completely accurate. He arched a brow. "Is Charlie around?"

"I think she might be in her office. If not, then you can look for her at the bakery down the street. Raw Sugar. Her sister-in-law, Mariette Martin, owns it and she and the baby spend a good bit of time down there." He leaned back in his chair. "Any progress?"

"Yes, a bit. I've talked to Sophie and she's going to help me," he said. He felt a smile tug at his lips. "She was actually investigating the thefts on her own. I caught her in the director's office last night."

Payne's gaze sharpened with interest. "Really? What was she looking for?"

Jeb explained briefly. "She's going to talk to Pearl today, secure a picture of her missing jewelry, and find out if her necklace was taken from her safe. If so, then that narrows things down a bit."

"Yes, it does," Payne said. "And the director is the only person who has access to the codes?"

"Other than the resident, yes, that's the way it looks."

"I'm sensing a but."

Jeb released a small breath and winced. "But I don't think she's guilty," he admitted. "The village is her life. She's intimidatingly efficient. I can't see her rolling through a stop sign, much less stealing jewelry from her residents."

"Is it possible that someone has gotten access to her codes?"

"That's what Sophie was looking for last night, but she didn't find anything. The codes are not easily available, but it's not impossible that someone has managed to get to them. We suspect that the file might be on her computer, but it's password protected."

"Charlie should be able to help you with that." He chuckled darkly. "We all changed the passwords to our computers recently—I changed mine to pure gibberish—and she still managed to get into each one. I had an electronic post-it on my desk top when I turned it on the following morning. 'Nice try, but no cigar, Chief,' she'd said."

Jeb chuckled. Actually, that wasn't why he'd wanted to talk to Charlie—he wanted to talk to her about Sophie—but Payne had an excellent point. "I'll find her."

"Keep me posted."

Jeb promised to do just that, then left Payne's office and went in search of Charlie. Luckily, she was in. He knocked on her doorframe. "Do you have a minute?"

"Sure," she said, smiling in welcome. Married to one of the other agents, Jay Weatherford, and being the first female non-Ranger hired on by the company, Charlie was an interesting woman, one they all seemed to respect. "What can I do for you?"

"Remember how I asked you to dig a little deeper into Sophie O'Brien's history?" he asked, settling into a chair in front of her desk.

"I do," she said, hesitating smally. "I've got to tell you, there just isn't that much to go on. From everything I can tell, she's squeaky clean. She's never even had a traffic ticket."

"That's what I wanted to talk to you about. I've found out a little more about her myself and…I wondered if you could do a little more poking around for me."

"Of course," she told him.

Jeb leaned forward, trying to find the right words to explain his request. "She's clear of any suspicion as far as my case goes," he explained. "In fact, she's helping me."

Charlie's eyes widened. "Oh."

"This would strictly be for my own benefit." He

cleared his throat, feeling heat climb his neck. "It's personal."

Impossibly, her eyes rounded further and when she "oh'ed" again, no sound emerged from her mouth.

"I think she's in some sort of danger, only I can't get it out of her," he added. "Every time I ask her a question, she finds a way to avoid telling me anything. I don't want to press her, but—" He shook his head. "—something's not right. She's afraid of someone. Her father, I think, quite honestly." He told Charlie about the scar on her arm, the double fence, the near panic attack when she thought he'd been hired to spy on her. "She told me last night that her grandmother had kept her maiden name and that she'd taken it. The grandmother she's talking about was her paternal grandmother, so—"

Understanding dawned in Charlie's eyes. "So she purposely abandoned her father's name." She nodded once. "Right. I'll look into it and get back to you."

He breathed a small sigh of relief, caught her gaze once more. "Thanks. And I'd appreciate it if you wouldn't mention this to—"

"Mum's the word," she said. "I could blackmail every one of y'all if I was a dishonest woman. There isn't a man working here who hasn't had me do something similar." She smiled and waved him off. "Don't sweat it."

"There was one other thing," he said. "I need to

get into a password protected computer and I was told that you were the woman to see about that."

"Piffle," she said. "It's child's play." She reached into her desk and handed him a simple USB drive. "Plug this little baby in and it'll do the rest."

He whistled low. "Really?"

"Really. I wrote the program myself. You can even save the files you're looking for onto it."

He looked at it once more, then glanced at her and smiled. "You're a little scary, you know that?"

She preened. "Thanks."

Confident that things were finally moving in the right direction, Jeb left the building and made his way to his truck. Because he knew he couldn't put it off much longer, he decided to go ahead and let his brother know that he was fine. He punched in the number, called up the message screen.

Other phone is dead. New number. I'm fine. He paused, winced. Swore.

It's a woman.

There, Jeb thought with a smile. That ought to explain everything.

And it wasn't just any woman, either. It was possibly *the* woman. Because he grimly suspected that she was going to ruin him for anyone else, that after everything was said and done, she was going to be the one he wasn't going to be able to let go.

He'd just shifted into reverse when his cell phone rang. "Dammit, Judd, I don't have..." He frowned, not recognizing the number. But it wasn't Judd. "Jeb Anderson," he answered.

"Yes, yes, I know!" Foy snapped. "I called you, didn't I? Why wouldn't I know who I was calling?"

Foy? "But I just got this—"

"Phone," Foy finished. "I've been trying the other number for hours, but you didn't ever answer, so I just called your boss and got the new number from him."

Brilliant. "What did you need, Foy?"

"I need you to get over here and figure out who has stolen my Annie's engagement ring out of my safe, that's what I need! It's gone." Panic and despair made the older man's voice break. "Gone," he repeated. "Someone's taken it. Someone's taken her ring."

Jeb felt his expression darken. "Have you told anyone, Foy?"

"No," he said. "I thought it was best to talk to you first."

"That's right. Keep it to yourself and let me do my job. Sophie's helping me now and we're going to get to the bottom of this."

"Do you have any idea who it might be?"

"Not yet, no," he admitted, unwilling to lie. "But I know who it's not and sometimes that's more important. We'll get Annie's ring back, Foy. I promise."

"You shouldn't make promises it's not in your

power to keep, son," Foy told him, his tone weary. "It only makes you feel helpless when you break it."

"I have no intention of breaking it," Jeb said determinedly. "I'm on my way. Stick around the house because there are some more questions that I need to ask you."

Foy sighed heavily, the sound laden with heartache. "I'm not going anywhere."

He wasn't either, Jeb thought, until he'd nailed this bastard to the wall.

UNABLE TO EAT, Sophie pushed her food around her plate and kept glancing toward Marjorie's office, waiting for the lights to go out.

"Looking every few seconds isn't going to make her leave any faster, Sophie," Jeb told her, shooting her an indulgent smile.

She grinned, tucked her hair behind her ear. "I know. I'm just impatient."

She still couldn't believe that Foy had been a victim. Everyone knew and loved Foy and more importantly, everyone knew how much he'd loved his late wife. It was a shameful thing to take her engagement ring from him. Utterly horrible. She glanced around the diner, took in the beloved faces around her and realized with a sickening since of dread that, more than likely, one of these people was responsible.

Looking more than a little pleased with herself, Cora strolled up to their table. "Evening, Sophie, Jeb."

Sophie nodded at her, returned the grin. "Evening, Cora."

"Y'all are looking like quite the pair," she remarked. "I couldn't help but notice that both of you left the dance a little early."

Sophie was surprised Cora had been able to notice anything at all from last night, all things considered.

"We did," Jeb said. "We ended up at Sophie's place so that we could have a proper chat." He made "a proper chat" sound wicked and depraved, as though they'd done things Cora had only ever read about.

Cora's brows winged up her forehead and she shot a knowing look at Sophie. "*Really?*" she drawled knowingly. "Well, isn't that nice?"

Jeb glanced across the table at her, his gaze so hot she felt her skin scorch. It might have been for Cora's benefit, but it was sending her heart into arrhythmia. "Oh, it was," he remarked, his voice rife with innuendo. "I don't know when I've enjoyed an evening more."

Though there was a hint of truth in that last statement, Sophie nevertheless grinned and kicked him under the table. He grunted with pain and his eyes widened. "It was harmless, really."

"I spent the night," Jeb confided, evidently to punish her for the kick to his shin.

Before Cora's eyebrows completely disappeared, Sophie quickly interjected, "In the guest bedroom.

He spent the night in the guest bedroom and I slept in my own room. We did not sleep together, at all."

Her older friend's expression fell, clearly disappointed. "Oh."

Jeb gestured to Cora, who leaned down and he whispered something in her ear.

Cora gasped delightedly, drew back and shot him a wink. "Atta boy," she said. "I knew you had it in you."

Smiling happily, Cora grinned at her and then twinkled her fingers in goodbye.

"What did you say to her?" Sophie asked suspiciously, her smile taking the heat out of the question.

"That's between me and Cora," he said. "It's a secret."

"You told her you were spending the night again tonight, didn't you?"

His blue eyes twinkled with devilish humor. "I might have said something like that."

She lifted an unconcerned shoulder. "Oh, well. I might have told your brother the same thing, so it's all good."

He choked on his tea. "What?" he wheezed. "My brother? Why are you talking to my brother?"

"Strictly speaking, we're not talking." She popped a fry in her mouth. "We've been texting."

His expression went comically blank. "You've been texting my brother. But—" His eyes widened as understanding dawned. "I texted him from your phone," he said with a resigned nod. "Right."

"He's concerned about you," she told him, eyes twinkling. "He says he's been picking up some weird vibes."

Jeb chuckled darkly. "Oh, he did, did he? Wonderful. Brilliant. I appreciate that."

"I couldn't ignore him," Sophie protested. She withdrew her cell phone from her purse and held it up so that Jeb could see. "See? He even sent me a picture. Isn't this gorgeous?" she said. "That's the view from his apartment. Look at that water. It's so blue. It reminds me of your—" She stopped short. *Oh, hell.*

Naturally, he hadn't missed the slip. A grin tugged at both corners of his lips, making that increasingly dear dimple wink in his cheek. "It reminds you of my what?" he asked.

She took a sip of her drink, looking at a speck on the table. "S'not important."

"What?"

Oh, geez. "It's not important."

"That's cruel," he said. "I sense you were on the verge of paying me a very sincere compliment and now you're refusing." He tsked under his breath, as though he was heartbroken.

"Oh, please," she said with an exasperated sigh, feeling the tops of her ears burn with humiliation. It was a constant state where he was concerned. "I was just going to say that the color of the ocean there reminds me of your eyes." She met his gaze, drawn in, as usual. "You have the bluest eyes I've ever seen." Her breath thinned in her lungs. "They're quite...compelling."

He swallowed. "See? I knew it. A compliment." He looked away and drummed his fingers on the table, almost as if he was embarrassed. "Thank you."

She leaned forward, studied him a little closer. A hint of pink stained his cheeks, confirming her suspicions. For whatever reason, that little bit of color cheered her, made her feel like she wasn't alone in *this*—whatever it was—happening between them. If she could make this badass former Ranger blush with a little compliment about his pretty eyes, then anything was possible, right?

"Can I get you anything else?" Ethel asked, her plump face wreathed in a smile. She looked particularly happy for them, as though she, too, had been a part of the match-making scheme. "A slice of cake? A cup of cobbler?"

Jeb shook his head. "Nothing for me, thanks. I'm fine." He glanced at Sophie and lifted a brow. "Would you like something?"

Sophie shook her head. "No, thanks."

Ethel frowned at her, put a hand against her forehead, checking for a temperature. "You all right, Sophie? You're not getting sick, are you?"

"Er...no," she said, mortified. "I'm just full." Geez, it wasn't like she'd *never* turned down dessert before. Granted, it wasn't often, but it wasn't such a damned phenomenon either.

"But you love my chocolate cobbler," she persisted.

Jeb's lips twitched with humor, the wretch. "I do," Sophie admitted. "But I'm going to pass tonight, all the same."

Ethel tsked. "Nothing to share, even? I could bring two spoons."

"How about an order to go?" Jeb suggested, an odd gleam lighting his gaze. It was almost...wicked. A shiver slid down her spine as his gaze fastened on her mouth and lingered. Remembered heat bloomed on her lips, the taste him of him on her tongue.

"Excellent," Ethel enthused, beaming. "I'll fix that right up for you."

Sophie shook herself and considered him for a moment, her gaze narrowed in thought. "You like chocolate cobbler?" she asked.

He shrugged a single massive shoulder. "I don't know, I've never had it."

She grinned. "Then why did you order it?"

"Because I like chocolate. It reminds me of your eyes," he confided, leaning forward so that he could better look at them. "Melting and sweet and a little sinful."

Holy hell, Sophie thought, feeling her jaw go marginally slack. She blinked, almost drunkenly, taken aback at this description, then dredged her vocabulary for some sort of response. She finally settled for, "Oh."

"It was one of the first things I noticed about

you," he said. "They're quite lovely. And so expressive."

She cleared her throat. "Thank you."

"You're welcome. Do you know what else I noticed about you?" he asked, lowering his voice. It was a little rough and foggy and sexy as hell.

She tried to respond, but squeaked instead.

"Your skin. It's beautiful," he said, his gaze tracing her face. "It practically glows with an inner light, one that's just yours. And it's *so* soft," he added, issuing a soft masculine growl. "It makes me wonder what the rest of you feels like, if there are bits that are even softer."

She was going to drool all over herself if she didn't close her mouth, Sophie thought, feeling suddenly under the influence of…something.

Him, she realized. *This* is what he did to her. With a few words, he'd turned her body into a puddling pool of heat, her brain to mush.

Need contracted her muscles, vibrated along her nerve endings and warmth mushroomed in her belly, spread up into her breasts, making her nipples tighten behind her bra and her feminine muscles clench. She squeezed her legs together in an effort to alleviate some of the mounting pressure, the desire to squirm.

"Oh," she managed to say again.

Looking entirely too pleased with himself, masculine humor clinging to his grin, he reached across the table and took her hand, pressing a lingering kiss

into her palm. Who would have ever thought that
was such a sensitive area, that it would have been
mysteriously linked to her core? Certainly not her,
she thought, sinking her teeth into her bottom lip
as sensation flooded her.

"Guess what?" he asked.

Probably, she didn't care. She moaned a little,
squeezed her eyes shut, then opened them in a vain
attempt to regain some sort of control. "What?"

"Marjorie left five minutes ago."

11

JEB WATCHED AS she blinked the desire out of her eyes, then chuckled as she started and gave her head a shake. "Come on, then," she said. "Let's go."

"Ethel still hasn't brought my to-go order." More to the point, he couldn't get up without everyone noticing that he was...*up*. He should have known better than to taunt her, that it would only result in his own frustration, but he just couldn't seem to help himself.

It was just too damned easy.

And knowing that she wanted him, that he made her hot, that he made her lose control, was so damned powerful it was difficult to ignore. Impossible to resist.

"Forget the to-go order," she said, sliding out of the booth. "Let's go."

Thankfully, Ethel arrived and handed over his container. "Here, darlin'," she said. "If you've got a little ice cream to add to it, then all the better."

Grinning his thanks, Jeb left enough cash to cover the bill, plus a generous tip, then followed Sophie's lead and exited the booth. He was still hard enough to upend the table, but he tugged his sweater down and prayed that no one would notice.

Naturally, she did.

Her eyes dropped below his waist, rounded, then she visibly swallowed. "Oh," she said. "I see."

He chuckled grimly. "Just walk in front of me, would you?"

Seemingly unable to tear her gaze away from his crotch—which, naturally wasn't helping matters—she nodded distractedly and licked her lips. "Right. Sure."

He groaned. "Sophie, you're killing me."

She gave herself a little shake, then blushed. "Sorry. I'm just— That's—"

He wheeled her around and nudged her toward the door. "—distracting," he finished. "Believe me, I know," he added drolly.

Having already agreed upon a strategy for getting into Marjorie's office, Sophie had parked her car close to the director's building in order to make it look like they were simply getting ready to leave. At the last minute, they veered off the lighted path, then snuck into the garden.

Sophie went unerringly to the hide-a-key rock, slipped it from the bottom of the enclosure, then carefully opened the door. She dropped down into a crouch once they were inside the office, then he closed the door, locked it behind him and adjusted the curtain until there wasn't any discernible opening anyone could see through.

"All right," Jeb said. "First things first." He withdrew the USB device he'd gotten from Charlie and plugged it into Marjorie's computer. The screen immediately glowed to life, prompted for the password, then a series of asterisks streaked across the text box and, like magic, they were in. The home screen loaded, revealing a picture of the Twilight Acres sign. He clicked through a few desktop files, grimacing when they revealed nothing.

"Well?" Sophie asked. "Do you see anything suspicious?"

The light from the aquarium glowed touched the side of her face and she was so close, her sweet breath whispered across his ear. "No," he said, trying to concentrate on the task at hand. "Nothing yet."

He loaded her documents and scrolled through them, then felt a smile curve his lips. "Ah," he said. "Bingo."

Finding a file marked simply "Benchmark," which was the name of the safe company, he clicked on it, his anticipation spiking. It withered, deflated, when he was once again prompted for a password.

"Shit," he said. "This file is password protected."

"The little thingy won't work?" she said gesturing to the device. Her terminology made him grin.

"I don't know." He was tempted to remove it, then

install it again just to see what would happen, but was afraid that it would shut the whole computer down, or at the very least, alert Marjorie to the fact that she'd been hacked. The director was obviously very concerned about protecting her privacy and that of her residents, but something was beginning to feel off. Why password protect the document? He attempted to open another file, only to have the same thing happen again.

She protected *every* file? But why? It was almost overkill. Everything couldn't be sensitive, right?

Jeb released a breath. While they were here, he might as well give it a go. He closed out of that screen, launched the document files once more, then removed USB, waited for the tell tale ding, then plugged it back in, opened the file and held his breath.

Once again the little asterisks did their thing and the document materialized on the screen.

Sophie squeezed his shoulder. "Wow, that's handy."

Jeb grinned. Yes, it was, he thought, making a mental note to thank Charlie. He immediately saved the file to the drive, then looked for others that might prove useful.

"I'm going to try to get into this drawer again," she whispered.

He nodded distractedly. "Okay, I'm going to keep poking around in here."

Sophie dropped to her hands and knees, then

crawled up under the big desk, nudging his legs over in the process. His gaze dropped to her luscious rump, displayed to mouthwatering perfection in a pair of worn jeans. Muttering something about Cora and her scrubs, she'd opted for a different outfit today, one that was infinitely more feminine and flattering.

Trying to ignore the sudden flash of heat in his loins, he determinedly directed his attention to the task at hand. He clicked through a few more document files, then on a whim, moved to her pictures. A file called My Happy Place caught his attention. It, too, was protected, but thanks to Charlie's little miracle of technology, it was no match for him.

The first picture loaded and Jeb felt his eyes bug and his jaw go slack. "Holy mother of…"

Sophie stilled. "What?" she asked. "Did you find something?"

"Er…you could say that." He was going to need some bleach for his eyeballs and some sort of memory modification charm, like you'd find in a Harry Potter book.

She abandoned the drawer and wiggled back out from under the desk, then popped and peered at the computer screen.

She inhaled sharply. "Is that…"

"It is," he confirmed tonelessly. "It's Marjorie. In a leather corset, fishnet hose and thigh high boots."

Sophie peered closer, her eyes squinted in confusion. "She looks like she's in some sort of...dungeon."

"Well, the guy she's with is in chains, attached to a wall," Jeb said.

"And she's got a leather riding crop in her mouth." She swallowed, released a sigh. "That explains the red nail polish, anyway."

Jeb clicked through a few pictures, each one more graphic than the next, showcasing Marjorie as an enthusiastic and competent dominatrix. "What nail polish?"

"I found a bottle of red nail polish under her desk last night. It's not anything I've ever seen her wear. Around here, anyway." She blinked owlishly. "Clearly she wears it...other places."

"In her happy place," Jeb told her. "That's the name of the file."

"Wow. I would have never suspected her of something like this. It's..." She shook her head. "I can't even wrap my mind around it."

"And if you didn't imagine she could be a dominatrix, then what does that say about whether or not she could be a thief?"

She paused, shook her head. "I still don't—"

Suddenly a noise from the foyer reached them, a distinct sound of the door opening. Sophie gasped and they shared a look. Jeb gestured under the desk, where she quickly scrambled, then killed the power to the computer. He grabbed the USB, then crowded in under with her, dragging the desk chair into place just as the door swung open.

If that was Marjorie, then they were screwed. And she'd probably beat them, Jeb thought, stifling the inappropriate need to chuckle.

Feeling him shake, Sophie turned her head toward his and shot him a questioning look. He could just make out her perplexed expression and it made him want to laugh all the more. She glared at him significantly, then put her hand over his mouth.

"Stop it," she mouthed silently.

He kissed her hand again, this time touching his tongue to its center.

She stilled, went a little boneless and smothered a moan.

But whoever had come into the office clearly wasn't Marjorie. They didn't turn on the light and didn't come near the desk. Instead, humming lightly under their breath, the person opened the cabinet beneath the aquarium and the sound of lightly splashing water resonated like thunder in the quiet room.

"Hello, my lovelies," the person trilled. It took a second to place the voice—Ethel.

Sophie noticed it too, her gaze finding his once more in the dark. A frown marred her brow, suggesting that it wasn't Ethel's job to clean Marjorie's aquarium.

It would be easier to focus on that little tidbit of information if her breasts weren't pressed right up against his chest. Plump and ripe, the sensual weight of them sizzled through him, making another part of his anatomy take notice.

It swelled accordingly.

She noticed.

Jeb shrugged helplessly. What could he say? He wanted her. He'd made that plain enough over the past few days. Him having a hard-on, particularly when she was nuzzled so closely up against him, shouldn't come as any real surprise.

She bit her bottom lip, smothered some sort of noise, then dropped her head against the curve of his shoulder. Her warm breath fanned over his neck, eliciting another burst of reaction and he felt his dick stir against her, seeking her like some sort of carnal divining rod.

To his everlasting joy and torment, she scooted up and slid her nose along his throat, breathing him in, then pressed her lips against him, tasting his neck. And the hell of it? He couldn't move, not without making a sound or knocking something over. He had to lay there and take it, and the she-devil knew it.

Jeb bit back a curse as she slipped farther up along his body, but somehow managed to get an arm around her, then slip his hand up under her sweater, touching her sleek, warm skin.

So soft… Softer than he'd dared to imagine.

She answered him with another retaliation of her own, sliding her hand along his jaw, then turning his head and pressing her lips against his. Her kiss was slow and thorough, laced with an undercurrent of desperation and urgency. Her entire little body hummed with it, vibrated like a struck piano wire. She shifted, drawing herself more closely to him and ran her hand down over his chest, then lower still as she cupped him through his jeans.

He would have come up from beneath the table if she hadn't held him down, stilling him with a deeper kiss. Stroking him through his jeans, she sucked his tongue into her mouth, mimicking a more intimate act, and he felt an ooze of pleasure leak from his dick, a warning of what was to come.

Literally.

It seemed impossible that Ethel was in the room with them, messing around with that damned aquarium, but the periodic hum or splash of water would confirm it.

It was mind-boggling. But strangely thrilling, he had to admit.

Not content to merely touch him through his clothes anymore, he felt Sophie's hand at the button on his jeans, felt it give. She couldn't lower the zipper without it giving them away, but she'd used the silent breath he'd sucked in as an opportunity to slide her hot little fingers over the head of his penis, coating him with his own cream.

Jeb set his teeth so hard he feared they would crack.

She was trying to kill him, he decided. Trying to make him have a heart attack.

Rather than let her torture him, Jeb decided a little torment of his own was in order. He carefully nudged her onto her back, then followed her down with a kiss. She tasted like French fries and sweet tea, like seduction, like heaven and he wanted to sink into her so desperately his hands shook from the effort of holding back. He wanted to slide his dick deep into the heart of her, nestle his own hips into the perfect cradle of her wider ones and slake his lust in her soft, welcoming body.

He just *wanted*.

He found the hem of her shirt, then edged it up, pushing his up over her warm, silky skin until he found the lacy edge of her bra. He expertly popped the clasp in the middle, silently thanking the brilliant designer who'd thought of that plan, then felt the cup give way and snag on her nipple.

A brush of his fingers and it was out of the way and her plump, lush breast was in his hand, the beaded nipple thrusting against his palm. He ached to taste it, to feel it rasp across the roof of his mouth.

From the dimmest recesses of his mind, he heard the office door close, felt the silence close in around them once more. They both stilled, then looked at each other. Waited. Heard the exterior door whoosh shut, the tumbler in the lock click into place.

Then he was on her.

Jeb shoved Marjorie's desk chair out of the way,

rolled into the space behind the desk, taking her with him.

She shrugged out of her shirt, removing the bra in the process, then lifted her hips so that he could get her jeans off. Good Lord, she was beautiful. Full, lovely breasts, crested with rosy crowns, the sweet curve of her belly, a thatch of dark curls nestled between her thighs.

He didn't know where to start, which part he wanted to taste first. Rather than wait on him to figure it out, she leaned forward and drew the shirt over his head, then bent forward and pressed her hot mouth against his chest, licking a path along the upper ridge of his right pec. She hummed appreciatively, slipped her greedy hands over his belly and around his back.

Jeb groaned, lowered his zipper and shucked his pants and boxers. She moaned when she saw him, a tiny little mewl of feminine affirmation, of desire, and something about that sound tripped an internal trigger.

"I'm healthy," he breathed, sliding a hand down the middle of her belly, dipping his fingers into the honey pot between her thighs, gratified when she inhaled sharply and arched up into him. He palmed her right breast, then bent and pulled her into his mouth. "You?" he whispered blowing over it, making her shiver.

"Clean and protected," she said, spreading her legs, a silent, desperate invitation.

Jeb nudged her weeping folds, found her gaze and fastened his on it. "Look at me," he said, his voice raw and broken. Every muscle in his body was clenched and ready, bracing him for the unknown. Because this coupling was different—she was different—and every iota of understanding and intuition he possessed told him that when he took her, when he made her his…that was it.

He'd be lost. There'd be no him without her.

Her melting brown eyes caught his and clung. Desire, hunger, fever and something else, something tender and gentle—affection, maybe?—glinted back from him, reflected in her gaze. A soft smile shaped her lips and she sighed as she arched up and pushed herself against him.

"I need you," she said, her voice anguished, desperate. "Please."

I need you…

Not just want, but *need*.

And need he understood, because he needed her as well. He had to have her. It wasn't optional. It never had been.

With a guttural groan and a sigh of relief, Jeb pushed into her, slid home, burying himself to the hilt in her heat. Sensation rocked through him, the balls of his feet tingled, his stomach shook, every hair on his body stood on end and his chest squeezed so tightly he could scarcely draw a breath. The world dimmed to black and white, then zoomed back into colors so bright he wondered if he'd ever really seen them before.

She tightened her feminine muscles around him and rocked up, drawing him farther into her body. Her breasts grazed his chest, her soft hands slipped over his back, greedily eating up his skin, and she bent forward and kissed him, her mouth soft and inviting.

She was gorgeous, simply, heartbreakingly beautiful. And above all else, she was *his*.

12

OH, HALLELUJAH, Sophie thought as Jeb, hovering above her like a Greek god, poised at her center, the silky head of his penis sliding against her weeping folds. *At last.*

Though it had only been a few days, it felt like she'd been waiting forever for this moment, that her whole life had hinged on the next few seconds, the instant his body met hers.

His tortured gaze bored into hers, pinning her thoroughly. Desire had dilated his pupils, making his eyes a glorious midnight blue and the way he was looking at her, the possessiveness she saw in his gaze as he stared down at her as though she were the most beautiful woman he'd ever seen…

It was enough to make one a little emotional and she found herself blinking back tears, her throat tight.

She'd begged. She'd said please.

And she wasn't ashamed.

With a low moan that sounded as if it had been wrenched from his soul, he pushed into her...and the rest of the world faded away. Sophie sucked in a breath, instantly tightening around him, holding on to him.

He felt magnificent. Right. *Huge*. She arched her hips, meeting his torturously slow, rhythmic thrusts, savoring every thick inch of him as he invaded her body. He bent his big blond head and suckled her breast, pulling at her nipple with his lips, licking it with his tongue. And with every determined sensual assault against her breasts, he plunged into her, seemingly trying to sever the invisible chord that ran between the two.

"You have damned near driven me crazy," he said, thrusting into her over and over again. She could feel the rug at her back, his hot body at her front and her breasts bounced on her chest, absorbing the impact of his magnificent frame as it slid repeatedly into hers. "I've wanted you since the instant I saw you," he confided, as though it were somehow her fault. "Then the want turned to need and I knew—I *knew*—that I wouldn't be able to help myself. That nothing would keep from taking you, having you."

She wrapped her arms around him, bent forward and licked his male nipple, anchored her legs on his hips so that he could come closer, hold her tighter. "I've wanted you, too," she said. "Needed you, too. I looked at you and...melted," she said, laughing softly. "I wanted to lick you from head to toe, fantasized about sucking on your bottom lip."

He moved faster and faster, pistoning in and out of her, his tautened balls slapping against her tender flesh. "Do it now," he said, lowering his head so that she could do just that. She pulled that sulky lip into her mouth, slid her tongue over the soft, plum-like skin and sighed with satisfaction as another wave of sensation bolted through her.

Fire licked through her veins, burning her up from the inside out and she bucked frantically against him. She could feel the first quickening of release as it sparkled deep inside her and every thrust of his body acted like a bellows, fanned the flame, building it higher. She clung to him, arched into him, whimpered and thrashed as she came closer and closer to the inferno that waited for her. And then, without warning, the blaze swept through her, sucking the oxygen out of her lungs, tearing a long, keening cry from her throat as she convulsed around him.

Jeb pounded into her, milking the release, drawing every bit of pleasure from her body. His lips peeled away from his teeth, his beautifully muscled chest heaved and then suddenly, she felt him tense, felt every muscle in his body atrophy as his seed flooded her womb. It pulsed inside of her, spasm after spasm, triggering belated delight deep in her core. He angled deep, held steady, his shoulders shaking as the orgasm broke over him.

He bent and kissed her, his eyes soft, his smile sated and her heart gave an involuntary little squeeze.

"Definitely the perfect woman," he said. He carefully rolled off of her, grabbed a few tissues from the top of Marjorie's desk and handed one to her. Decidedly moist, she appreciated it and did a quick clean-up job, then tossed it into the trash can conveniently located near her head.

The thought made her chuckle.

"What's funny," he asked, dropping down beside her. He propped up on his elbow and peered at her through the darkness.

She gestured to where they were. "Just this," she said. "It's not far off from how I imagined we'd, you know," she trailed off.

She could see his eyes twinkling in the faint light, the dimple in his cheek. "Really? How did you imagine the first time?"

"With my back against the wall, dress around my waist, your pants around your knees, at the dance last night. I kept thinking about it the whole time we were dancing. How I just wanted you to grab hold of me and take me until my eyes rolled back in my head." She rolled her head toward him, smiled and lifted a brow. "Turns out I'm a proper slut."

He swallowed, his jaw a little slack. "You are not a slut," he said. "You just find me irresistible, that's all."

She laughed. "Oh, is that all?" she said drolly.

"It is," he said. "But don't worry, because I'm suffering from the same affliction. While you were thinking about me pinning you up against the wall, I was thinking about dragging you under one of the tables. I'd say that makes us about even, wouldn't you?"

"It makes us crazy," she said. She turned and peeked at him beneath lowered lashes. "But I kind of like it."

"Do you know why I really wanted that chocolate cobbler?" he asked, his hand coming up to play with her breast. He circled her nipple with his thumb, making goose-bumps pebble over her skin.

Sophie released a faltering breath. "Why?"

"Because I want to paint you in it and lick it off. I want to put it here," he said, circling her breast. "And here." He slid a line down to her belly button. "And here," he added, sliding a finger down her cleft, over her still-sensitive clit. His gaze tangled with hers. "Any objection?"

She shook her head, quivering in anticipation. "N-none at all."

THANKFUL THAT HE'D put his phone on silent, Jeb checked the display and shook his head.

Atta boy. My spidey senses are telling me this one is special. Really special. My congratulations, brother. I like her.

He'd missed another message as well, this one from Charlie. A simple "Call me ASAP." Evidently she'd found something, Jeb thought, wondering what sort of information would require an "as soon as possible" response. His gaze slid to Sophie, who was bent over putting her shoes back on.

Good Lord, had anything else felt as wonderful as being inside her? Had anything ever made him feel more powerful? More alive? More…everything.

She was utterly and completely remarkable. She was sweet and kind, full of fire and loyal, hardworking and…adorable.

This one is special, his brother had said.

Mild understatement.

This one wasn't just merely special—she was a game-changer. She was it. His undoing. He couldn't imagine taking another step forward, ever again, without her by his side. Was he in love with her? Honestly, he didn't know. He'd never been in love before, so he had nothing to compare it to. He only knew that he needed to breathe the same air she did. He needed to be near her. He needed to hold her. To protect her. To ensure her happiness.

She looked up and caught him staring and a slow smile slid over her kiss-swollen lips. "What?" she asked.

"Nothing," he lied. "I just like looking at you."

"You've got to quit saying stuff like that," she said. "You're going to ruin me for other men."

"Good."

She blinked, seemingly startled.

"It's only fair, don't you think?" he asked. "You've ruined me for other women."

Another one of those refreshing blushes painted her cheeks. It was mind-blowing, genuinely remarkable that she didn't recognize her own appeal. That she didn't know how astonishingly fabulous she truly was. Humility was a little thin on the ground these days, but Sophie O'Brien had it in spades.

Or was it doubt? he wondered, his belly tightening. Had her father done such a number on her that she was incapable of seeing her true value? Had her confidence been undermined to the point that she didn't know that she was the most amazing creature he'd ever clapped eyes on?

"Did you want to look at anything else here before we go?" she asked.

Jeb shook his head. They'd already gone through the files she'd reviewed last night and made pictures with his cell phone of everyone's pertinent details. To his surprise, she'd even started a file on him. She'd noted his name, his "adoptive" relationship to Foy, who had evidently explained things to her with that little white lie, that he was a former Ranger, but present employment was unknown. She'd notated his social style, his affable ability to start a conversation and his height, which she'd dubbed "substantial," along with the added note, "Would look good in my happy place."

Jeb had about choked when he'd read that little

tidbit and Sophie, to his delight, had become quite annoyed on his behalf.

"How dare she think she could chain you to a wall and whip you and do…other things," she'd finished, unable to go on.

"You going to shoot her?" he'd teased.

"Please," she'd said, rolling her eyes. "I'm not going to jail for a man, even one as hot as you."

Careful to make sure that they'd destroyed any evidence of their visit, Jeb took one last look around the office. The desk was tidy, the USB tucked safely away in his pocket, her chair was in its place. All of their clothing was on and accounted for, though there had been one frightening moment when Sophie hadn't been able to find her panties and they'd discovered them hanging from a low branch of an artificial ficus tree.

They were thongs. Who knew?

Satisfied that everything was as it should be, he made his way over to Sophie, who was staring at the aquarium, a line furrowed on her brow.

"What's wrong?" he asked.

"Something's different," she said. "I can't put my finger on it, but something isn't right."

Jeb glanced at the aquarium. He'd never looked closely at it before, so he couldn't say whether anything was different or not, but he knew enough about instincts and heeding them, to give her a minute to let her take a proper look.

"Ethel's not supposed to clean this either," she

added. She bent down, looked closer. "Marjorie has a company that comes in to do it for her. I've seen their van here before."

That's right, Jeb thought. He'd seen the notation on her financials.

"Do you know what coulrophobia means?" she asked.

"Not off the top of my head, but I can look." He withdrew his phone, loaded the dictionary app. He chuckled. "It's the fear of clowns," he said. "Why?"

"Because Marjorie had noted it on Ethel's file. And…" She was thoughtful, considering.

"And what?"

"And I found a red clown nose under Marjorie's desk when I noticed the nail polish."

Jeb cocked his head. "What would one have to do with the other?"

"I don't know, but it's too odd to be a coincidence, don't you think?"

Yes, he did. He just didn't know how they could possibly be connected. He bent down and watched the fish circle the tank, their pale pink bodies glimmering in the artificial light. Water bubbled from an air filter in the back and ornamental grasses swayed with the current. Coral formations provided cover should the pair wish to hide and a white castle and bubbling treasure box rounded out the décor.

Jeb's gaze narrowed as something caught his eye. His stomach clenched and his fingers tingled as he drew closer, peered at the treasure chest. It had been moved recently, the gravel beneath it disturbed and it hadn't closed properly, because something had gotten in the way.

"Sophie, could you describe Lila's necklace to me please?"

"Sure," she said, shooting him a look. "It's a diamond and sapphire choker. Each little piece is set like a flower, a pansy, I think, and very closely set."

Jeb chewed the inside of his cheek, pointed to the treasure chest. "Like that, you mean?"

She started, her eyes rounding, then bent down and followed his finger. "What?" She inhaled sharply. "Yes," she said. "Exactly like that. Oh, my goodness," she breathed. "Look at that. I bet it's all in there."

He'd bet it was, too. Jeb found a long glove in the compartment below the aquarium—wet from recent use—and pushed his hand into it so that any germs that were on his skin wouldn't get into the water and harm the fish. He reached in and snagged the treasure chest, then carefully opened it up.

Sophie's breath caught. "Lila's necklace, Rose-Marie's brooch, Nanette's diamond earrings, Pearl's string of pearls." She held up the last item. "Annie's ring. Oh, Jeb," she sighed, disappointment weighting her shoulders. "Why would Ethel do such a thing? Why would she take these things and then plant them in Marjorie's office?"

He didn't know, but it was past time to find out. "Let's call Marjorie," he said.

"Call Foy, too, and let him know that you've got it. We can alert the others after we've talked to Marjorie, but Foy..." Her face crumpled with sympathy.

Jeb nodded. "You call Marjorie and ask her to come down here. Tell it's urgent, but nothing else. I'll call Foy."

The old man answered before the end of the first ring, indicating that he'd been waiting by the phone. "Jeb?"

"I've got it," he told him. "It's safe. I've got to tie up a few things here first, then I'll bring it to you."

"You've found it? You're sure?"

"Positive. And we've found everyone else's things as well."

"Well done," Foy told him, his gruff voice thick. "I knew you had it in you."

"Thanks, Foy," Jeb told him, though he didn't feel like he'd actually done all that much. It was pure dumb luck that they'd come back tonight and heard Ethel in the aquarium. Had they not broken back into Marjorie's office, it could have been weeks, possibly months, before they'd had any sort of significant break in the case.

His gaze slid to Sophie, who just ended the call with Marjorie. A wondering smile slid over her ripe mouth as she stared at her friend's jewelry and something about that smile hooked him right in the heart. He felt it snag in his chest and tug. This was good, right?

Only his excuse, his ticket into her world, was disappearing. It was over.

So now what? Jeb wondered, his cheeks puffing as he released a breath. What sort of reason was he going to have to manufacture to keep her in his life? Because he grimly suspected that she'd just become the center of his universe.

13

NOSTRILS FLARED, eyes blazing, Marjorie marched into her office, sniffed delicately, obviously noticing the scent of sex in the air, and narrowed her gaze.

Sophie wanted to fall through the floor, but ignored the heat rushing into her cheeks and held her ground.

It helped that her ground was next to Jeb's.

"I want to know just what in the hell you think you're doing in here," she demanded. "This door was *locked*. My computer was *off*. You've got exactly three seconds to tell me or I'm—"

"Going to nail us with your riding crop, Ms. Whitehall?" Jeb asked, his lips quirking dangerously.

She gasped and all the color drained from her face. "Now, listen here. I—"

Jeb strode forward. "I'm Jeb Anderson with Ranger Security," he told her. "And I am *not* Foy's grandson. I was hired by Rose-Marie Wilton's family to investigate the theft of her vintage Tiffany brooch, as well as several other missing pieces of jewelry from other residents on site, most recently a diamond engagement ring that had belonged to Annie Wilcox, Foy's late wife, which was stolen from his safe this afternoon."

Marjorie blanched. "What? But—"

"The missing jewelry—all of it—was found hidden in the treasure box of your aquarium."

Looking as if she might be ill at any moment, Marjorie's disbelieving gaze darted to her aquarium, then she gripped the edge of her desk. "I didn't take it," she said. "I swear, I have no idea how it got there. I—"

"We know how it got there," Jeb told her. "Because we were here when the engagement ring was put into the box tonight." He arched a brow. "Do you have any idea why anyone would want to frame you for these thefts? Anyone holding a grudge against you? Anything at all you'd like to share before the authorities get here?"

She swallowed, pressed a hand against her throat. "You know who did it?"

Jeb nodded. "We do. The 'why' of it is still a bit of a mystery. We were hoping you could enlighten us."

She glanced up, her gaze darting nervously between the two of them. "How did you know about—"

"Your happy place?" Jeb asked. "I hacked into your computer," he admitted. He lifted a shoulder.

"You were a suspect in my investigation. It was necessary to clear you." He arched a brow. "She found out, didn't she? And you retaliated by using her phobia against her."

Sophie blinked and swiveled to look at him. When had he figured that out?

"She was blackmailing me," Marjorie finally admitted. "I've always kept a decent supply of cash put aside, but she was determined to drain me dry, to take it all, just because something in my personal life isn't precisely in character for a director of a retirement home." Marjorie swallowed. "How dare she. It's no one's business but mine. And Twilight Acres is my home. These people, as infuriating as they can be," she admitted with a significant eye roll, "are my family."

Sophie certainly understood that. She felt the same way about all the residents here.

"How did she get the codes to the safes?"

Marjorie grimaced. "Undoubtedly the same way you did," she said. "By figuring out my password."

"I didn't figure out your password. I used a customized program that did it for me. I wouldn't think Ethel would have access to something like that."

"Could she have figured out your password?" Sophie asked.

"She could," she said. "She knew my other name. My handle. The Whippet." She squeezed her eyes shut. "Stupid," she muttered. "I should have changed

it. I just never suspected she'd do anything so heinous."

The Whippet? Really, Sophie thought. Like the
dog? She got the "whip" part, but... Oh, she thought,
understanding dawning. Female dog. Bitch. Whippet. Double meaning. Quite clever, actually.

"Any idea why these specific people were tar-
geted?" Jeb asked.

Marjorie rubbed a line from between her brows.
"Any person who ever had anything negative to say
about her cooking could have been a target," she
said. She frowned. "Foy's ring went missing today?"
she asked.

Jeb nodded. "It did."

"Cora had mentioned that Ethel was having a tan-
trum today because Foy had suggested her mashed
potatoes didn't have enough salt." She rolled her
eyes, looked up at them. "Did you recover all the
missing items?" she asked.

"We did," he said.

"Then I'd like an opportunity to handle this in-
house," she said. "You can ask them all first and I'll
abide by whatever they decide. But I can fire her for
this with the threat of going to the authorities if she
ever harasses any of us again."

And she'd have the leverage to get Ethel completely off her back, not that Sophie could blame her
for wanting that. Granted pain was not part of her
pleasure process, but to each his own. If Marjorie
got her jollies by beating the crap out of people who

liked it, then who was she to judge? Hell, she'd just had sex with a man right here under her desk. She certainly didn't have the right to hurl any stones.

Jeb considered her request. "I'll talk to everyone and get back to you. In the interim, change your safe codes and your passwords and don't let her know that we're onto her."

"You saw her, you say?" she asked, lifting a brow.

"We did."

"But she didn't see you?"

"We were hiding," Jeb told her.

Her eyes twinkled with knowing humor. "I'll just bet you were." She glanced at Sophie. "Your sweater's on inside out, sweetheart. Might want to correct that before you leave."

Sophie felt her eyes widen in alarm, glanced down at her shirt and winced. "Damn."

"And if you ever find you can't keep him in line, let me know," she added. "I've got a few toys I could lend you."

Sophie cleared her throat. "I don't think that'll be necessary, thanks."

Marjorie merely shrugged, then predictably settled down and got to work.

"Do you think they'll go for it?" Jeb asked her. "Do you think Foy and the rest of them will let Marjorie handle Ethel?"

Sophie chuckled darkly. "Oh, I think they're definitely going to be more in favor of Marjorie meting out justice than anyone else."

Jeb slung an arm around her shoulder and pressed a kiss against her head, the treasure chest in his hand. "Come on," he said. "Let's go give these people their belongings back."

She grinned. "I like the sound of that."

"And then we're going to go to your house and I'm going to do some finger painting. With chocolate. And you're going to be my canvas."

Sophie grinned. She couldn't think of a better way to end the day.

"WHAT DO THE letters ASAP mean to you?" Charlie asked Jeb the next morning when he finally got around to returning her call. They'd returned the jewelry last night, confirmed that Marjorie would be responsible for Ethel's punishment, then gone back to Sophie's and played paint by number with chocolate cobbler on each other's bodies.

It had been wonderful. The best. He'd awoken this morning to her sweet rump squashed against his aching groin, her plump breast his hand and a smile of bone deep contentment on his face. For the first time since he'd left the military, since that horrible business in Mosul, he felt…hopeful about the future.

Guilt had accompanied it, of course, but admittedly it wasn't as debilitating as it had been before.

"Sorry," he said. "I haven't had time."

"Are you with her?" she asked.

He watched as Sophie threw feed out to her

chickens. "I am, but she's not right here with me at the moment so I can talk, if that's what you mean."

"Yes and no," she said, letting go a breath. "Listen, I'm not even sure where to start, so I'm going to give you an abbreviated rundown, okay?"

Unease nudged his belly and he felt his attention narrow. "Okay."

"Sophie's family is as screwed up as they come. With the exception of both grandparents, who are both deceased, she doesn't have a single relative who isn't certifiably crazy. Seriously. Her father never attended a school he didn't get kicked out of. He stabbed a kid in Kindergarten through the hand with a pencil and that's the least violent thing on record, although certainly not the least disturbing. His teacher's note said, and I quote, 'The boy scares me. There's a darkness in his eyes, a pure lack of remorselessness that makes me fear for my safety as well as the other children's.'"

Jeb whistled low. "Damn."

She laughed grimly. "And that's not even the half of it. He met Sophie's mother in reform school. Her mother had already been diagnosed with Borderline Personality Disorder, with an unnatural predisposed hatred of other members of her sex. So the sociopath meets and marries the psychopath and they have a boy, whom they adore. But when Sophie came along…"

"Oh, geez," Jeb said, passing a hand over his face.

"They terrorized her, Jeb. I widened the net to

a three state radius and found hospital records that would break your heart. The last one I found was right here in Cobb county. She'd been six, taken to the hospital by her grandmother. Multiple cuts and bruises and a gash inside of her right arm that required twenty-four stitches to close. She took her grandmother's name less than a month later, but the grandmother kept a restraining order against her son until the day she died. Sophie has been renewing one for both her parents and her brother every six months for the last two years. She's called the police department several times, reporting disturbances around her house, crank calls and vandalism to her car. They even poisoned her animals. Bastards."

Ah, Jesus. He lowered his head, stared at the porch decking beneath his feet. The fence inside the fence—it had been to protect her animals. Anger tightened his fingers, made them ache and he had to unclench his jaw in order to respond.

"Do you know where they are now?" he asked.

"That's why I'm calling," she said. "They're holed up in a cheap hotel less than three miles from her address and they've been there for three days. I don't know what they want or what they're planning, but she needs to be on guard. They're dangerous."

Yes, they were, Jeb thought. And they were going to play hell trying to get past him. "Thanks for everything, Charlie. I appreciate it."

"Keep her safe," she said. "I don't know her, but I like her already."

Smiling, her cheeks pink from the cold, her muck boots on her feet, Sophie mounted the steps to the porch. Her expression faltered when she saw his face.

"What's wrong?" she asked.

What to say? He knew she was going to be angry that he'd asked Charlie to dig around in her past, but her family, who seemed hell-bent and determined to hurt her, were an immediate threat. She needed to know. And, unfortunately, it was his job to tell her.

"That was Charlie," he said. "Our resident hacker, remember?"

"The one who designed the password breaker program?"

He nodded. "One in the same." He hesitated, trying to find the right words, or if not the right words, then at least the ones that would piss her off the least.

She frowned, concerned. "Jeb, what it is?"

He looked up, caught her gaze. "Your father, mother and brother are in a motel less than three miles from here. They've been there for three days."

She stilled and a flash of fear raced across her face. "How do you know this?" she asked faintly. She frowned. "I don't understand…"

"I know because I asked Charlie to look," he said. "I knew that you were afraid of something, I knew that you'd built a fortress around your house and kept a cache of loaded weapons next to your door." He paused, swallowed, glanced at her arm. "I knew that someone had hurt you. Badly," he added. "But I didn't realize, until you'd made that comment about some family members being unhappy with the terms of your grandmother's will, that it was by someone who was supposed to love and protect you."

She sank down onto the top step. "They've been there for three days?" she asked. "That's unusual. They usually never stay here that long." Her tone was wooden, lifeless, but the fear was unmistakable all the same. "They'll breeze through for a day, make a crank call or slash my tires, or try to poison my animals, or taunt me from the distance allowed by the protection order," she said. "But they never stay. They leave."

It was heartbreaking to watch her, to see the sadness round her shoulders, the fear make them tense. "When was the last time you saw them?"

"A couple of weeks ago. In the parking lot of the grocery store. They told me they were going to get me. Called me a 'thieving bitch' because Gran left me everything. She raised me," Sophie said. "She wasn't just my grandmother. For all intents and purposes, she was my mother. She nursed me through childhood illnesses, she braided my hair, she taught me how to cook, helped me with my homework." She swallowed, her voice cracking. "She was all I ever had."

Jeb pulled her into his arms. "I wish I could have met her. She sounds like another perfect woman," he said, giving her a squeeze.

The comment had the desired effect and she managed a wan smile. "She was," she said. She nodded toward the end of the driveway. "He left me there," she said. "At the end of that drive. Bleeding, bruised, scared, no shoes. In the middle of December. I was six."

Bile rose in the back of his throat. "He's not right, Sophie. He's sick. They all are."

"I know that now," she said. "And I guess a part of me knew it then, but I still wondered what was wrong with me, why was I so hard to love?"

She was killing him, Jeb thought. Absolutely killing him and her pain made him want to pummel the ever-loving hell out of her father.

She slid a finger over the scar on her arm. "My mother did this," she said, shocking him. "He brought me here and left me to keep her from killing me. I should thank him for that."

"You don't owe any of them anything."

"They're coming for me," she said. "They wouldn't have hung around otherwise."

Jeb tilted her chin up and stared into her woefully familiar eyes. "They won't get near you, sweetheart. I'd die first."

Her chin trembled and she leaned forward and pressed a kiss against his lips. "Don't you dare," she said fiercely, her voice cracking. "Don't you dare."

Jeb swallowed the lump that formed in his throat. "I know all of your secrets," he said. "It's only fair that you know one of mine."

14

Sophie stilled, then turned to look at Jeb. "You don't have to do that," she said. "You haven't found out anything that I wouldn't have eventually confided. It would have taken more time, because it's painful, but I would have told you."

His gaze searched hers. "I want to tell you. I *need* to tell someone," he said, his voice strained. He hesitated. "You pegged it when you said you didn't know how I ever stood being in the military because I liked being in control. It was a struggle, I'll admit. But I liked the sense that what I was doing made a difference, that I was part of something bigger than myself, that I was doing my bit for Uncle Sam."

"I can understand that," she said, snuggling in closer to his side. She loved the way he felt next to her, as if this niche inside his arms had been made expressly for her.

"I've always had good instincts and, when I've

followed them, they've never let me down. Not once."

She had a terrible suspicion she knew where this was going.

"Six months ago I took a team into Mosul. I felt like something was off, wrong, and that I didn't need to move forward." He paused, his gaze turning inward. "I conveyed my feelings to my commanding officer, who was sitting safely back at base, maneuvering us like pieces of a chess board. He told me to press on. To follow orders."

Ah, Sophie thought. She'd been wrong. His instincts had been right, not wrong. And he'd ignored them.

"I did," he said. "And even though I led my men in, when the bullets started flying, I was the only one who survived."

Sophie's heart squeezed and she wrapped her arm around his waist. "Oh, Jeb, I'm so sorry."

"That's why I came out," he said. "That's why I pulled the plug on my career and found a new one. I decided that I was never going to follow another order that put me at odds with what I felt was right."

"I don't blame you," she said. "You were on the ground, in front, in the line of fire. That officer should have listened to you. Should have trusted your instincts." She grimaced. "No wonder you couldn't stay," she said. "How could you after your commanding officer showed so little confidence in you? Especially since ignoring your expertise resulted in the death of your friends."

He turned to look at her, that wondering expression on his face once again, the one that said she'd just taken another peek inside of his head and he'd been unprepared for it. "That's unnerving," he said. "You…get me, you know it? You really do."

Sophie grinned. "Do you know what I'd like to do right now, soldier?" she asked, arching playful brow.

He chuckled low. "What?"

"Get *on* you."

"I CAN'T TAKE this waiting," Jeb told Payne days later. "And it's wearing on Sophie's nerves too. She's constantly looking over her shoulder and is taking a pistol with her everywhere she goes." He blew out a breath, rubbing the bridge of his nose. "I'm sick of it. Sick of watching her suffer."

"What are you going to do?"

"I'm going to go scare the hell out of them," Jeb said. "I'm going to frighten them so terribly and threaten them so thoroughly that they'll never look cross-eyed at her again, much less violate the protection agreement."

At this point, the issue of Sophie's family was common knowledge, as were Jeb's feelings for her. He'd known the first day that she'd walked into the diner that she was special. He'd felt it in his gut.

She was it.

His.

"Wait for us," Payne told him. "I'll get Jamie and Guy and we'll be there in less than half an hour. No point in going in alone and, between the three of us, I think we'd make a formidable team."

Touched, Jeb swallowed. He wouldn't have asked, but sincerely appreciated the offer. Had Judd been here, Jeb knew his little brother would have had his back. It was heartening to see that these men would, too.

"Thanks," he said. "I appreciate it."

Thirty minutes later, dressed in black swat outfits and packing enough artillery to level a small town, the four of them burst into Sophie's family's dingy motel room and went Special Ops on their ass.

Her father had scrambled from the bed and curled into a ball against the wall, her brother had literally pissed himself and her mother had screamed like a wild woman and launched herself at Payne, who'd held up his gun and coolly informed her that it had been awhile since he'd gotten to shoot someone and she'd do as good as anybody.

"Leave immediately," Jeb had told them. "Don't call her, don't send her any letters, don't look at her, don't come within a hundred miles of her. Stay the hell away from her, or make no mistake, I'll hurt you." He meant it. "And believe me, I know how. I can make you feel pain you've never imagined in your worst nightmares. Do you understand?"

"Fine," her father snarled. "The bitch isn't worth it."

Jeb drew back and slammed his fist into his jaw,

knocking him out cold. "Don't you talk about my future wife like that," he said.

The four of them sat in the parking lot and waited for the three to load up their stuff and leave. Looking appropriately frightened, they had, spinning gravel as they aimed their car away from her farm.

"You're going to marry her, huh?" Jamie asked, stuffing a snack cake into his mouth.

"What?"

"In there," he said. "You told her father not to talk about your future wife like that."

He blinked. "I did?"

The three of them chuckled and shook their heads. "You did. Sounds like a Freudian slip, doesn't it, boys?" Guy remarked.

Payne arched a brow. "Do you want to marry her?"

Jeb felt a bemused smile slip over his mouth, tugging the corners of his lips. He did. Sweet heaven... he did. He laughed, shook his head. "Yes, I do."

"Well, get on with it then," he said. "Didn't that group host a ball in less than twenty-four hours? A wedding is even more romantic. I'll wager they could pull one of those together in half that time."

A spark of an idea formed and he nodded, feeling the rightness of it settle over him.

"I've got to go," he announced, pushing from Payne's car and heading to his own.

"I imagine you do," Jamie called out. "Let us know when and where and we'll be there."

Jeb grinned. "You got it," he said. "And brace yourselves, boys, cause these senior citizens know how to party."

"Sophie, someone's here to see you," Carl called.

She frowned and checked her appointment book. She didn't have anyone down. How could she have missed…?

Jeb ducked into her massage room and smiled when he spotted her. "Hey," he said. "You owe me a working over, remember?"

She chuckled softly. "I seem to recall something like that. Get undressed and get on the table."

He did, revealing the body she'd come to think of as hers, the glorious muscles, the sleek skin. Her living playground. She warmed the oil and dropped it on his chest, then swirled it over his slickened skin.

He groaned. "Oh, that feels good. You really know what you're doing."

"Did you ever doubt it?" she asked, smiling as her heart rate tripped into over-drive. Her breasts grew heavy with want, hungering for his touch. Her womb flooded with a familiar heat and soaked into her panties, readying for him.

"You know what would make this massage even better?" he asked.

She bit her lip, trailing her fingers down the front of his thighs, watching his dick leap to attention. *Hers*, she thought. *All hers.*

"What would make it better, Jeb?"

She took him in hand, had the pleasure of watching his back come off the table, a hiss of pleasure move between his clenched teeth.

"If you'd get naked and get up on this table…and slide around on top of me."

Unable to resist him, Sophie did just that. She threaded her fingers through his, frowning when something didn't feel right. She drew back.

"What happened to your hand?" she asked, staring at the bruised knuckles.

"It ran into your father," he said, his gaze searching hers. "They're gone, Sophie. And they're never coming back. Ever."

Her heart skipped a beat and she blinked, confused. "What?" she breathed.

"Me, Payne, McCann and Jamie went over to the motel and explained things to them," he said. "They could leave and never bother you again, or we were going to show them what would happen if they didn't." He cracked his knuckles and grinned.

"What?"

"It wouldn't have come to that, but as bluffs go, it worked well. Bullies only respond to force. We were forceful."

Her chest squeezed and emotion clogged her throat. "You did that for me?"

"I would do that and a whole lot more for lesser reasons," he said.

She melted, resting her forehead against his.

"How am I supposed to resist you when you say things like that?" she asked helplessly.

He drew back, smiling. "I didn't know you were trying to resist me."

"Well, not very hard, I'll admit," she said, "but I should be trying. I shouldn't be so damned easy."

"Why the hell not?" He grabbed her bare rump, lifted and pushed up into her, making her eyes roll back in her head. "It's working brilliantly for me," he said. "God, you feel good. I feel like I'm going to die every time we're together like this and still, I look forward to it."

She tightened around him, leaned back and put her hands on his chest, undulating her hips. His big hands anchored either side of her waist and he pushed up, meeting her as she rode him, catching her rhythm and going with her for the ride. He leaned forward, pulled a nipple into his mouth. "Marry me," he said, thrusting harder.

She started, certain she'd misunderstood him, felt the flash of impended release boiling up inside her. "Marry me, Sophie," he repeated, his voice raw, desperate. "I need you." He bit back a curse, then groaned as she clenched around him once more. "Marry me. Please. I love you."

She came, hard. Her neck went boneless, too weak to support her head, and a long cry of release ripped from her throat, happiness permeating every cell.

Her release triggered his and he joined her there,

his glorious body quaking beneath hers. "Marry me," he repeated, those blue eyes beseeching. "Say yes. Be mine."

Sophie smiled, melted against him. "I've been yours since the day I met you," she said.

"Then let's make it official. Cora's got your dress."

She straightened and pulled away from him. "What?"

"She's got your dress and the church is ready," he said, grinning like a fool.

Her fool.

"You're joking."

"Do I look like I'm joking? You're the one who said they could host a party in no time at all. Why would a wedding be any harder?"

"They're all waiting? Right now?"

"Every last one of them." He stood, retrieved a small box from his pants pocket and withdrew a ring. "Here," he said, his hands trembling. "Let's make it official, shall we?"

A lump welled in her throat. "It's Annie's ring."

"It was," he said. "Foy wanted you to have it. He's giving you away. Threatened to plant a conker on Clayton Plank if he had a problem with that."

She chuckled, her eyes welling with tears. "I can't believe you did this," she said. "I don't know what to say."

He tipped her chin up and kissed her. "'I do' will suffice."

Thirty minutes later, dressed in a designer gown she couldn't have been more happy with had she picked it herself, surrounded by her surrogate family and friends, Foy walked her down the aisle and he and Cora gave her away.

Cora gave her a squeeze, her eyes brimming with tears. "Your grandmother would have been so happy to see you today," she said. "She made me promise that I'd see you settled, and I have," she said. "I never break a promise."

Sophie's throat clogged with emotion and she hugged her dear friend. "Thank you, Cora. For everything."

"Love you, sweet girl," Cora said. "He's a lucky man."

Sophie turned to Jeb, who stood waiting patiently for her. Those vivid blue eyes glowed with happiness and pride and, God help her, love.

He loved her.

With his brother serving as best man via the face-time feature on his phone, the preacher officiated the service, then asked the all important question.

"Do you, Sophie, take Jeb to be your lawfully wedded husband, to love and to cherish, to have and to hold, in sickness and in health, for richer or for poorer, for as long as you both shall live?"

Her gaze tangled with his and her chest ached with joy. "I do."

He breathed an audible sigh of relief, much to the merriment of their guests.

"I love you," she whispered, because she hadn't said it yet. "You're the winner of my Perfect Man contest."

* * * * *

DO YOU NEED A COWBOY FIX?

New York Times bestselling author
Vicki Lewis Thompson
returns to Mills & Boon® Blaze® in 2013
with more

Sons of Chance

Chance isn't just the last name of these rugged
Wyoming cowboys—it's their motto, too!

Saddle up with:

Long Road Home

Lead Me Home

Feels Like Home

Take a chance…on a Chance!

Dear Reader,

This is a sappy, sentimental love letter to all of you who've welcomed me back to the Mills & Boon® Blaze® line and taken the Sons of Chance miniseries into your homes and your hearts. Thank you for all the funny and appreciative emails and for your continued support of my books, whether you're reading them in paperback or on your ereader. You rock!

Because you've embraced the SONS OF CHANCE with such enthusiasm, I'm going to keep writing books about them! So get ready for another summer of gorgeous cowboys coming at you in 2013. I have you and my wonderful editor, Brenda Chin, to thank for it, and I'm thrilled! Life at the Last Chance Ranch has become part of me, and I didn't want to say goodbye to all those folks I've come to love.

But I'm getting ahead of myself. We're still at the beginning of 2013, and you're holding book nine in your hands. While I hope you've read all the others, you might have missed some. I realize that and I try really hard to make each book stand alone. So whether you're a frequent visitor to the Last Chance Ranch or a newcomer, I have a feeling that Rafe and Meg, best man and maid of honor at a traditional ranch wedding, will touch your heart and make you smile.

Be sure and pay attention to the epilogue, though, because it'll give you a hint about book ten!

Continuing to be yours,

Vicki Lewis Thompson

FEELS LIKE HOME

BY
VICKI LEWIS THOMPSON

First published in Great Britain 2013
by Mills & Boon, an imprint of Harlequin (UK) Limited,
Eton House, 18-24 Paradise Road, Richmond, Surrey TW9 1SR

© Vicki Lewis Thompson 2012

ISBN: 978 0 263 90291 4
ebook ISBN: 978 1 408 99651 5

14-0113

Harlequin (UK) policy is to use papers that are natural, renewable and recyclable products and made from wood grown in sustainable forests. The logging and manufacturing processes conform to the legal environmental regulations of the country of origin.

Printed and bound in Spain
by Blackprint CPI, Barcelona

New York Times bestselling author **Vicki Lewis Thompson**'s love affair with cowboys started with the Lone Ranger, continued through Maverick and took a turn south of the border with Zorro. She views cowboys as the Western version of knights in shining armor—rugged men who value honor, honesty and hard work. Fortunately for her, she lives in the Arizona desert, where broad-shouldered, lean-hipped cowboys abound. Blessed with such an abundance of inspiration, she only hopes that she can do them justice. Visit her website at www.vickilewisthompson.com.

With thanks to Tony Horvath for creating such
fabulous covers for the Sons of Chance.
I'm blessed!

Prologue

August 23, 1980
from the diary of Eleanor Chance

I THINK MOST FOLKS IN Shoshone, Wyoming, would say that I'm a nonviolent sort. In fact, ask anyone in the entire Jackson Hole area who knows me, and they'll tell you I'm a calm woman not prone to outbursts of rage.

So these same people might be shocked to learn that I could, given the opportunity, twist Diana Chance's head right off her scrawny neck. I've never been so fired up in my entire life, which includes the time that my dear husband, Archie, forgot my birthday AND our anniversary in the space of a month.

If I had Diana in my clutches, nothing would save her except a promise to stay and be a devoted mother to my sweet little grandson, Jack, and a wife to my son, Jonathan. But the irresponsible piece of baggage has LEFT. She's abandoned both my son and my grandson, and for that I will never forgive her.

I hated the fighting between Jonathan and Diana, but I hate this more. No child should have to grow up knowing that his mother didn't love him enough to stick around. I will do all in my power to make it up to this poor little boy, but he's not even two. How can he be expected to understand?

All he knows is that his mother is gone. Her note tells us not to try and find her. Believe me, I've considered it. I have a little money put away, and I could hire a P.I. to track her down, but then what? Other than twisting her head from her neck, what do I want with her?

I want what I can't have, which is for her to be a good mother to my grandson and a good wife to my son. It's not possible. Archie tells me to let it go, that dwelling on it is useless and will make me even more miserable. I suppose he's right, but what I wouldn't give for two minutes with that sorry excuse for a mother.

_1_

Present day
Last Chance Ranch

SO THIS IS THE HOME MY MOTHER left more than thirty years
ago.

With a sense of foreboding, Rafe Locke turned into
the circular gravel drive that fronted a two-story log
ranch house, climbed out of his rented Lexus and pock-
eted the keys. He hoped the car's shocks were okay.

The luxury sedan might not have been the best choice
for driving over the rutted dirt road leading to the main
house, but trucks were his twin brother Wyatt's style,
not his. Wyatt operated a wilderness trekking company
and loved long, arduous hikes. Rafe gave financial advice to high-profile clients and worked out at a gym.

Although Wyatt had offered to meet his plane at the
Jackson airport, the guy was a busy bridegroom with
things to do. And things on his mind, like whether their
mother, Diana, would risk returning to face her oldest
son, Jack, in order to attend Wyatt's wedding.

Whether Diana showed up or not, Rafe wanted to be

in charge of his own transportation during the week of
wedding festivities. Once their dad, Harlan, arrived,
he'd also appreciate having the Lexus at his disposal.
He didn't like driving trucks, either.

As Rafe surveyed the house with its wide porches
and country ambiance, he had no trouble imagining
his mother's objections to the lifestyle. The structure
represented home and hearth, not the sleek sophistication Diana craved.

She would sneer at the rockers lining the porch and
the horseshoe knocker on the massive front door. She'd
think the multicolored flower beds on either side of the
porch steps lacked design and restraint. She'd hate the
wrought-iron boot scraper anchored in cement beside
the steps.

The house had quite a bit of square footage, though,
and Wyatt had said the acreage was considerable, too.
Rafe hoped the Chance family had a good financial
advisor. Considering property values in a resort area
like Jackson Hole, they were likely sitting on several
million in assets.

Wyatt seemed oblivious to that, which was so like
him. Instead he'd rattled on about the family history,
and how Archie Chance and his bride, Nelsie, had built
the center section themselves during the Great Depres-
sion. Later two wings had been added at an angle that
made them look like arms reaching out to welcome
visitors.

Or ensnare them. His mother had said she'd felt
trapped at the Last Chance. Escaping to San Francisco
and marrying financier Harlan Locke had been her so-
lution. Except her marriage to Harlan had come apart
eighteen months ago, and Rafe knew she wouldn't look

forward to socializing with her ex, especially when they'd be prominently showcased as the mother and father of the groom.

But that issue paled in comparison to her confronting Jack, the son she hadn't contacted since she'd left, the son who Wyatt, Rafe and Harlan hadn't found out about until after the divorce. Wyatt had chosen to visit the ranch and meet his half brother. He'd discovered that Jonathan Chance, Jack's father and Diana's first husband, had died, but he'd left two more sons, Nick and Gabe, and a widow, Sarah.

Wyatt had fallen in love with Jackson Hole, the Chance family and Olivia Sedgewick. Rafe wished to hell Wyatt had agreed to marry Olivia somewhere else, anywhere else. But she was local and Wyatt wanted the wedding to take place at the ranch, which he considered his new home base.

Rafe suspected Wyatt also had an agenda that included Diana finally making peace with Jack. Wyatt had bonded with his half brother and wanted the old wounds healed. Knowing softhearted Wyatt, he had dreams of the Lockes and the Chances becoming one big happy family.

Although Rafe was also Jack's half brother, he had no such dreams. He'd do his job as best man because he loved his twin, but Wyatt was the outlier in the Locke family. Diana, Harlan and Rafe were dyed-in-the-wool San Franciscans used to their sushi bars and lattes. Whooping it up in cowboy country wouldn't be their idea of a good time.

Thinking of urban conveniences reminded Rafe that he hadn't checked his cell phone reception since turning off the main highway. Monday was a busy trading day and he'd been AWOL for a good part of it. Time to play catch up before he announced his presence to anyone inside.

After tucking his Wayfarer sunglasses in his shirt pocket, he reached inside the car, pulled his iPhone from the holder on the dash and tested the internet connection. Amazingly, it worked.

Absorbed in checking end-of-trading stock prices, he lost track of his surroundings until the sound of rapid hoofbeats made him whirl in alarm. A horse and rider bore down on him. Swearing, he dove into the car to avoid having himself and his iPhone smashed to bits.

Instead of stampeding past, the rider pulled up right next to the car. The horse snorted loudly and stretched its nose toward the Lexus. The beast could be breathing fire and brimstone for all Rafe knew.

"Did I scare you?" The voice was decidedly female. "Sorry about that."

Rafe tossed his phone on the seat and slid carefully out, giving the brown-and-white horse a wide berth. "I wasn't scared. I was startled." He glared up at the rider, whose red hair curled out from under the brim of a brown cowboy hat. "Anybody who sees a horse running straight at him would—"

"Cantering. Spilled Milk and I were just cantering toward you."

"Looked damned fast to me."

"I was trying to catch you before you went inside. I saw the car and realized you must be Rafe, and I wanted to introduce myself." She swung down from the saddle, dropped the reins to the ground and held out her hand. "I'm Meg Seymour, Olivia's maid of honor. We'll be in the wedding together on Saturday."

So this was Meg, and she wasn't at all what he'd expected, but she had a warm, firm handshake. Now that she was on the ground, he estimated her height at around five-eight. The boots added another couple of inches, and the hat a couple more, which made her seem almost as tall as he was.

"I thought you were from Pittsburgh," he said. Wyatt had told him that, and Rafe had held out the vain hope that Meg would be a kindred spirit who wasn't into the jeans and boots routine. Instead, here she was decked out like a certified cowgirl.

"I am from Pittsburgh."

"Have you spent a lot of time out here?" Rafe eyed the horse, which kept stretching its neck toward him as if wanting to take a bite. Rafe edged back.

"Nope. My first time. Hey, don't worry about Spilled Milk. She's just curious. You can rub her nose. She likes that."

"Uh, no thanks." Although he kept his attention on the horse, he managed to get a quick glimpse of Meg's green eyes and the light dusting of freckles across her nose. She was cute enough, but thanks to her he was too damned close to an animal who wanted to eat him. Meg had dropped the reins as if abandoning all responsibility.

She shrugged. "Okay. I guess you're not much into horses."

"Not really. Shouldn't you be holding on to her?"

"She's trained to stand still when I drop the reins."

That was all well and good, but from where the horse stood, she could easily reach him with those big teeth. "Is she trained not to bite?"

"Absolutely, but if she's making you nervous, I can—"

"I'm not nervous, but I don't want to get bit, either." Great. Now he looked like a wuss.

"Let me back her up some." Turning to the horse, she picked up the reins. "Back, girl. That's it. A little more. Good."

Rafe breathed easier, which allowed him to pick up a cinnamon scent that he'd guess belonged to Meg and not the horse. When she'd turned to move the animal back, he also couldn't help noticing the great fit of her jeans. He wasn't into the country look, but snug jeans showed off a woman's ass to good advantage, and hers was worth admiring.

Keeping herself between Rafe and the curious horse, she faced him again. "Better?"

"It's just that I live in the city." That wasn't much of an excuse. She lived in the city and she was totally at ease with this animal. "Where did you learn so much about horses?"

"I'm no expert, but I ride English back home. I had to adjust to a Western saddle when I arrived, but I've about accomplished that, so tomorrow I can start learning how to rope."

"You want to learn to rope this week?"

"I do."

"Why?"

"Because it's something I've never tried and being on the ranch gives me a golden opportunity. I really love it here." She smiled.

And Rafe's breath caught. Earlier he'd thought she was cute with her freckles, her shamrock-green eyes, and her red curls peeking from under her hat, but that smile of hers turned cute into beautiful. Her beauty was all the more impressive because he couldn't see a trace of makeup.

She studied him for a moment. "You know, Wyatt said you didn't look like him, and you sure don't."

"We're fraternal twins, not identical."

"He said that, but still, I expected some similarities. Instead of being on the fair side like Wyatt, you're a *GQ* version of Jack Chance. Same dark hair, same dark eyes. Dress you up in Jack's trademark black shirt, jeans and boots, and you could pass for him."

"I doubt it. There's not an ounce of cowboy in me."

She gave him another once-over. "Then you'll have to fake it for the wedding."

"I'll follow the dress code when I have to, but not until then."

Her eyebrows rose. "You didn't bring jeans and boots?"

"Don't own any."

"Oh, that's no problem. I'm sure you'd fit into Wyatt's clothes, or Jack's for that matter."

The idea of wearing jeans and boots was bad enough, but wearing borrowed jeans and boots was worse. "Thanks, but I really don't need them until the wedding and I'll pick up the required outfit for the ceremony later in the week."

Her look of confusion was almost funny. "But... how can you try riding if you don't have any jeans and boots?"

"I can't, which is fine with me. Wyatt promised me I wouldn't have to get on a horse, and I'm holding him to it."

She stared at him, apparently at a loss for words.

"The thing is, Wyatt and I not only look different, but we have totally different personalities. He's the rugged outdoor type, and I'm the urban professional type. I'm crazy about the guy and wish him well in whatever he does, but we have almost nothing in common."

"Yes, but you're not in San Francisco now. You're *here*. Why wouldn't you want to take advantage of what the Last Chance has to offer?"

A tiny voice in the back of his head murmured *because I don't want to make a fool of myself.* He wasn't ready to acknowledge that voice to himself, let alone to the maid of honor. "Because riding and roping and mucking out stalls, or anything that's involved with ranching, doesn't interest me."

"Then what will you do all day?"

"I have my iPad and my iPhone. When Wyatt doesn't need me for wedding stuff, I'll work remote."

"Ah." She nodded. "He said you're involved in the financial world somehow."

Trust Wyatt to be vague on that point. His twin had never quite grasped what Rafe did for a living. "I'm a financial advisor."

"And I'm sure you're good at it, too."

"I hope so. I have clients who depend on me being good at it." He even managed some investments for Wyatt, who gave him carte blanche to do whatever he thought was right.

Her green gaze became serious. "Please take this next comment in the spirit of friendly advice."

"Okay."

"The Last Chance is an amazing place. In the few days I've been here, I've heard stories of lives being changed by contact with this ranch and the people on it. I'd hate for anyone to waste that privilege."

"Meaning me."

"Yes."

He thought her earnest advice was sweet, even if it was misguided. "The thing is, I don't want my life to change."

"Well, then." She gave him a look filled with pity. "I guess it's a good thing you brought your iPad and iPhone." She mounted up. For a moment she hesitated, clearly still thinking about his response and whether to say anything more. Then her expression closed down. "See you at dinner."

"Sure. Nice meeting you."

"Same here." With a wave, she turned Spilled Milk around and urged the horse toward a large, hip-roofed barn about two hundred yards to the right of the house.

Rafe didn't have to be a mind reader to know that Meg was disappointed in his attitude. But damn it, he hadn't come here to attend cowboy school. Or to change his life.

Most guys would give their eyeteeth to live the way he did. He made decent money, rented an apartment with a view of the bay and dated sexy women. He was only twenty-nine, and although his twin had decided to tie the knot, he felt no similar urge.

After watching his parents' marriage dissolve and the messy financial entanglements of that dissolution, he'd vowed to be very sure before he made a commitment. If he should find the perfect woman in the far distant future, he'd want her to be a successful business-woman in her own right, someone who was as happy with a San Francisco lifestyle as he was. And there would definitely be a prenup.

In any case, he was in no hurry to get to that stage. He liked his present status just fine, and if Miss Meg Seymour wanted to dive into ranch activities and see about changing *her* life, she was welcome to it. But she could leave him out of that program, thank you very much.

2

MEG FROWNED AT HER REFLECTION in the mirror. She'd
tried on every pair of earrings she'd brought to Wyoming, plus the long and dramatic ones in turquoise and
silver that she'd bought during a shopping trip in Jackson with Olivia. She'd also changed clothes three times.

This was not like her, and she was angry with herself because she knew the cause of it all. She wanted
to look stunning for Rafe Locke when she came down
to dinner. What a ridiculous goal that was.

One glance had told her that he dated skinny women
in designer dresses and up-to-the-minute hairstyles who
had exotic jobs in the art district. That was so not her.

She'd never been skinny or willing to shell out for
designer clothes or an expensive salon cut. She was a
brainy engineer who worked for the City of Pittsburgh
designing traffic-control systems in areas of urban
growth. She had her hair cut at the same Pittsburgh
salon where her BFF Olivia had worked until a year
ago, when she'd moved to Wyoming.

But Rafe had snagged her attention. He claimed
not to be interested in ranch life, but she sensed he

was more wary than uninterested and possibly afraid of looking foolish doing something he wasn't good at. His apparent reluctance to step out of his comfort zone posed an irresistible challenge to her.

She knew from personal experience that breaking through self-imposed boundaries created a life full of excitement. Rafe's attitude implied that the Last Chance would be a blip on his ultrasophisticated radar, a place to tolerate until he could satisfy his duties as best man and return to the rarified, and possibly stifling, air of his San Francisco existence. Shaking him out of that self-satisfied rut would be good for him and tons of fun for her.

His well-toned body tempted her, too. Those broad shoulders and narrow hips would look great in cowboy gear. She could picture his dark eyes shadowed by a tilted Stetson. Oh, yeah.

At least once during their meeting this afternoon she'd caught a flash of interest in his expression. Building on his initial interest might be a way to lure him into tasting cowboy life. He really did look like a younger version of Jack Chance, and almost every woman in Shoshone agreed that Jack was sexier than hell. He was also taken.

Rafe was not, and he had the makings of a hero. After all, he was Wyatt's twin and Jack's half brother, so a cowboy's soul could be hiding under that urban exterior and just waiting to be turned loose. Meg figured she had first crack at him, at least for the week of the wedding. Wasn't that the prerogative of the maid of honor when the best man was single? If it wasn't in the wedding party rules, it should be.

This dithering had made her late, though. She'd heard

Olivia and Wyatt arrive at least twenty minutes ago and the sound of laughter and the clink of glasses from downstairs told her that drinks were being served in the living room. In late August the weather was nippy enough for a fire in the evenings and she could smell cedar smoke. All the Chance family would gather tonight because welcoming Wyatt's twin, who was also Jack's half brother, was a big deal.

Rafe would be down there trying to keep everyone in the family straight in his mind. Meg felt a little sorry for him having to deal with it after a day of traveling. And he didn't fit into this ranch crowd at all, which wouldn't help.

Meg felt totally comfortable here and had a good memory for names and faces. Even so, she always mentally reviewed the players before jumping into a large gathering. Jack, the oldest Chance son, was married to Josie, who owned the local tavern Spirits and Spurs. Their baby son was named Archie after his great-grandfather.

Next oldest was Nick, a large-animal vet who'd married Dominique, a talented photographer. They were plowing through the paperwork to adopt Lester, a thirteen-year-old boy in foster care who'd been part of a work program for disadvantaged youth held at the ranch for the first time this summer. Nick and Dominique, along with everyone at the ranch, had fallen in love with Lester and had decided they'd be more than happy to start their family with him.

The youngest son, Gabe, was married to Morgan, a redhead. Meg and Morgan had bonded over the joys and problems of having red hair. Morgan and Gabe's little toddler, Sarah Bianca, had inherited the red hair, so Meg felt right at home with those two.

The sixtysomething ranch foreman, Emmett Sterling, would probably be at the gathering because he'd worked at the ranch for years and was considered part of the family. He actually might become part of the family if he and Pam Mulholland, who ran a nearby bed-and-breakfast, ever got married. Pam was Nick Chance's aunt, and she'd be there, too.

Sarah Chance, the matriarch of the group, had finally found a new love after the untimely death of her husband several years ago. Peter Beckett, her fiancé, would be in attendance. A philanthropist, he'd funded the ranch's summer program for young teens.

It was a lot to take in and, unlike Wyatt, Rafe didn't seem eager to embrace the Chance family. That would throw extra tension into a situation already filled with drama.

Meg liked and admired the Chance family, but her personal obligation was to Olivia and Olivia's sweetheart, Wyatt. By extension, Meg felt some loyalty to Rafe, and he'd have a much easier time of it if he'd get that burr out from under his saddle, as they said out here in the West.

"Meg?" Olivia's voice floated down the hall. "I've been sent up to check on you."

"I'm in here." Meg shook her head and made the silver-and-turquoise earrings dance. They went well with the black dress she'd settled on, the simple little black dress that every woman was supposed to have hanging in her closet. Knowing her limitations in the fashion department, Meg had clung to that advice.

Olivia, looking radiant in a dark green dress, ap-

peared in the doorway of what was still referred to as
"Roni's room." The Chances had taken Roni in when
she was a runaway teen. Now she worked as a mechanic
on the NASCAR circuit and had married a guy on her
racing team.

The decor hadn't been updated since the days when
Roni had been obsessed with NASCAR. But it was the
only upstairs bedroom with an attached bath, so it was
usually assigned to any single female guest. Meg quali-
fied and was grateful for the privacy.

"Oh, Meg, those earrings are spectacular with that
dress." Olivia beamed at her.

"And you look terrific, as always." Meg glanced lov-
ingly at her friend. Olivia constantly experimented with
her hair, and recently she'd colored it in various shades
of red and blonde. For tonight's event she'd created an
arrangement of upswept curls and dangling ringlets that
inspired Meg's awe.

"Thank you." Olivia smiled. "Being crazy in love
helps."

"I don't have that going for me, unfortunately. I wish
I'd asked you to come early and do my hair. It just sits
there, a curly red blob."

"Is that what's keeping you?" Olivia crossed to the
dressing table, picked up a tube of gel and squeezed
some into her palm. "I can fix that in a jiffy."

"The hair, the dress, the makeup, the jewelry. I've
been a mass of writhing indecision." Meg's anxiety level
dropped significantly as Olivia massaged hair gel into
her misbehaving curls.

"Sounds serious." Olivia finished with the gel and
picked up a brush and a hair dryer. "You're usually the
calmest one of the bunch."

"I think it's having Rafe here."

"He does change the dynamics." She turned the dryer on low and began to work. "He's a different kind of guy and he doesn't quite fit in at the moment, but I'm counting on the fact he's Wyatt's twin. He'll be fine. It'll all work out."

"I hope so. He seems sort of…" Meg hesitated to label him and risk offending his future sister-in-law.

"So you've met him?"

"I introduced myself this afternoon. He thinks I tried to run him down while I was on Spilled Milk."

Olivia met Meg's gaze in the mirror and laughed. "So did you?"

"No! Of course not!"

"Just wondering, because speaking for myself, I have the strongest urge to mess with him."

Meg grinned, relieved she could be honest. "Livy, he's ridiculously uptight. He told me he has 'no inter-est' in participating in the activities of the ranch. Won't dress in jeans and boots until forced to. Plans to spend the week checking in to work on his iPad. How crazy is that?"

Olivia nodded. "That's what he said just now, too. He seems to be holding the ranch and the Chance family at arm's length. Poor Wyatt doesn't know what to do."

"Well, that sucks. For Wyatt and you, but for Rafe, too. He has no idea what he's missing. It's a crime to come to this beautiful ranch and stay cooped up with an iPad."

"I agree." Olivia used the brush and hair dryer to ar-range Meg's hair in soft, layered curls that framed her face. "There, how's that?"

"Incredible." Meg turned her head to view the results. The earrings swung rhythmically as she moved. "Now I feel gorgeous enough to take on Rafe Locke."

Olivia smiled. "And do what with him?"

"You know, I think, deep down, he might *want* to loosen up, but he's afraid to. He needs some help."

"Well, if anyone can help him overcome those fears, it's you." Olivia stood back. "Go get him, girl."

RAFE WAS HOLDING UP, but just barely. The shock of seeing his doppelganger—Jack Chance—walk into the room had largely worn off, but keeping the names and faces of the Chance clan sorted out had taken its toll. Fortunately no one had asked him the million-dollar question—whether Diana was coming to the wedding.

Even if they had, he wouldn't have been able to give them an answer. He realized his mother was taking rudeness to a new level by waiting this long to reply, but surely a family rift that had lasted thirty-two years gave her some dispensation from the Emily Post crowd. He didn't condone her behavior, either now or thirty-two years ago, but he didn't want to see her humiliated, either.

He was trying to figure out a way to ditch the whole dinner plan and head upstairs to bed when Meg walked down the curved staircase looking like a queen at her coronation. He stared, then caught himself and glanced away.

But the image stayed with him. She'd abandoned the cowgirl look for a slinky black dress that showed off cleavage he hadn't imagined existed when she'd worn a T-shirt. Her curly red hair now fell in soft waves around her face, and dangling earrings caught the light as she moved.

Dressed like this, she could walk into any nightclub in San Francisco and turn heads. She was turning them here, even though every man in the place except Rafe was spoken for. After an hour in the company of these guys, Rafe knew they all adored their wives, or fiancée in Wyatt's case. But a man would have to be dead not to notice Meg tonight.

The only male who dared say something was thirteen-year-old Lester, a foster kid who would eventually be a part of the Chance family when Nick and Dominique formally adopted him. Lester gazed up at Meg with reverence in his eyes. "Wow. You clean up real good."

That brought a laugh from everyone, including Meg. "Thanks, Lester." She touched the lapel of the boy's new Western shirt. "You're pretty stylin' yourself."

"This is new." Lester stuck out his skinny chest to show off his shirt. "Boots are new, too. Ropers."

"Very nice. I'll bet you and Nick went shopping today."

Rafe covertly watched the interchange and wished he'd had the presence of mind to compliment her instead of allowing Lester to take the lead. The boy was small for his age, but apparently he had a gift for working with horses. Of the eight boys who'd spent the summer months at the ranch, Lester had been the standout according to Sarah. Nick and Dominique couldn't stop talking about how much they enjoyed having him as part of their family.

Gazing at Lester, Rafe thought about what Meg had said this afternoon about the Last Chance changing lives. Here was a perfect example and Rafe applauded the effort. The ranch was a lifeline for a boy like Lester, but Rafe didn't happen to need saving.

Wyatt walked over to stand beside him. "I saw your reaction when Meg came down, bro." He gestured in her direction with his beer bottle. "It's the most animated you've been since you arrived."

"She's a good-looking woman." Rafe took a sip of his red wine as he watched Meg fuss over Lester.

"She's also really special to Olivia."

Rafe glanced at Wyatt. In the two months since Rafe had last seen him, Wyatt had become a cowboy, both in dress and attitude. It suited him. "That sounded like a warning. Are you saying I should keep my hands off Meg?"

"That's not my place. Meg is a big girl, and she makes her own decisions. I've come to respect that about her. I'm just saying that you shouldn't... Hell, I don't know what I'm saying."

"I do." Rafe usually could tell what his twin was thinking, even if Wyatt couldn't put it into words. "You're telling me not to cause a problem for your fiancée's best friend. I promise not to do that."

"Thanks. I appreciate it." Wyatt squeezed Rafe's shoulder. "Looks like Sarah's herding us all into the dining room. I think you'll enjoy the food."

"I'm sure I will. The ranch is great, Wyatt."

"Yeah, it is." Relief shone in Wyatt's gray eyes. "I'm glad you see that."

Rafe felt like a first-class jerk. He'd known Wyatt desperately wanted his approval of the place and the family. That had been plain ever since Wyatt had announced his engagement. Yet Rafe had been reserving judgment, holding himself slightly apart. As his twin, Wyatt had sensed Rafe's attitude and had been troubled by it.

Rafe would rather cut off his arm than hurt Wyatt, and his behavior was doing exactly that. "I've been thinking," he said as they walked down a hallway lined with family photos. "Maybe I should take a shot at riding a horse while I'm here."

Wyatt laughed. "You don't have to do that, buddy. I know it's not your thing."

"That's true." He remembered what Meg had said this afternoon. "But when am I ever going to have a better setup than this?"

"That's true. I'd take you out tomorrow, except Olivia and I are having a final meeting with the caterers in the morning, and we're double-checking the flower order in the afternoon, but the next day I could probably—"

"Don't worry about it. I'm sure there are a million people around here who could teach me the basics." He immediately thought of Meg, but discarded the idea. She intrigued him far too much, and things could get messy. He'd just promised his brother not to create a problem.

Wyatt nodded. "You're right. I'll check with Emmett. He'll know who has some spare time tomorrow."

"Great. You know, this house is huge."

"It is." He gestured to the large room they'd entered. Although it held four round tables that could each seat eight, they weren't set for dinner. "They use this area at lunch and all the hands eat here along with whatever family members are available."

"Sounds like good PR." On his right, through a set of double doors, was a smaller dining room furnished with one long table, the kind that could be expanded or contracted as needed. Gleaming silverware and faceted goblets sparkled in the light from a hammered metal chandelier.

"It's more than PR," Wyatt said. "It's the way the Chance family does things. There's not a bit of snobbery in them."

Guilt pricked Rafe again. "I'm sure that appeals to you."

"Yeah. Don't get me wrong. I love Mom. But she's a terrible snob. And I hate to say it, but so is Dad."

Rafe sighed. "He is, and damn it, I was acting like a snob when I first got here. I'm sorry about that. It's just so...different from what I'm used to."

"I know." Wyatt grinned at him. "That's why I like it here."

Rafe could tell. He was happy for his twin, and he vowed he would do his best to fit in for the short time he was part of Wyatt's new world. As they all filed into the dining room, he hesitated, unsure of where he was supposed to sit.

Sarah glanced his way. "Rafe, why don't you—"

"He can sit here, Sarah." Meg patted a chair next to her. "We're the two who don't have kids or spouses, so we might as well hang out together."

Sarah looked pleased. "That works."

Rafe took the offered chair. "Thanks." Sitting next to her at dinner wasn't the same as making a play for her, so he felt okay with it. He also thought a polite compliment was in order. "You look really nice."

Her cheeks turned slightly pink. "Thank you. I don't get dressed up very often."

That made him wonder how she earned a living. "Where do you work?"

"I'm an engineer for the city. I specialize in traffic

control." She gazed at him steadily, as if to assess his reaction.

"Huh. I've never met someone who did that." So she had brains, too. She intrigued the hell out of him, and he'd just promised Wyatt not to get involved.

"My job doesn't usually make for fascinating dinner conversation."

He laughed as he unfolded his napkin and laid it in his lap. "Mine, either."

"So what shall we talk about?"

"Well…" He couldn't resist telling her of his latest plan, especially after the way she'd goaded him earlier. "You'll be happy to know I'm going to try riding tomorrow."

Her green eyes grew wide. "You *are?*"

"Yep. I decided that you're right. I'll never have a better chance than now, so why not?"

Her smile dazzled him. "That's fabulous. Congratulations."

"Thanks. I'll probably fall off, but what the hell?"

"You won't fall off."

"I might. I don't know the first thing about riding a horse." He picked up his water glass and took a drink.

"It's easy. What time do you want to start?"

He nearly choked on his water. "Start? What do you mean?"

"I mean, after challenging you to experience life on a ranch, I think it's only fair that I be the one to teach you to ride. The hands are all busy and I'm relatively free. So what time?"

"I—" He cast around for a way out of this. He'd be terrible in the beginning, and he didn't relish the idea of looking bad in front of her.

"I suggest eight-thirty. I'll meet you down at the barn." She smiled again. "You're going to love this, Rafe."

"If you say so." He had plenty of misgivings about having her teach him to ride, but the plan had one positive side. Given his lack of experience with horses, the time spent together had zero chance of being romantic.

3

MEG ARRIVED AT THE BARN ten minutes ahead of schedule the next morning. Rafe hadn't shown up in the kitchen for breakfast or even for a cup of coffee, so maybe he'd blow off this lesson. She hoped not. Teaching him to ride would satisfy several objectives.

Olivia and Wyatt would be much happier if Rafe participated in ranch life instead of staying aloof from it as he'd originally planned. Plus Meg enjoyed pushing people out of their comfort zones, and she wouldn't mind getting to know Rafe better. But she couldn't force him to do this.

If he didn't keep their appointment, she'd back off, way off. She valued those who made agreements and kept them. Anyone who couldn't do that moved several notches down in her estimation.

After petting Butch and Sundance, the two dogs lying on either side of the barn's double door, Meg stepped inside and breathed in the welcome scent of hay, oiled leather and horse. She truly loved it in Jackson Hole, and specifically at this ranch. After only four days, she was already questioning whether she wanted to stay in Pittsburgh or consider a move to Wyoming.

Her two older brothers had moved away, one to Connecticut and the other to Indiana. Although her parents still lived in Pittsburgh, they'd started making plans to retire in Florida. She really had nothing holding her except a job and friends.

The job was no problem. She could find something out here. And her friends would simply come visit. The more she thought about the idea, the more she liked it.

Besides, she was already making friends here, like the foreman, Emmett Sterling. She found him oiling tack, which explained why the tangy scent had been so strong when she'd first come into the barn.

At their initial meeting she'd told him that he reminded her of Tom Selleck, especially with his graying mustache. Emmett had blushed. He was an old-fashioned cowboy, a modest man with a strong work ethic, and she admired that.

He glanced up with a smile when she walked into the barn. "Hey, there. When do you want to schedule that roping lesson?"

"I'm not sure yet, Emmett. I don't know if you've heard that I volunteered to teach Rafe how to ride, assuming he hasn't changed his mind since last night."

"I did hear that from Wyatt." He gave a nod of approval. "Great idea."

"If he comes. Maybe he's decided not to."

Emmett looked over her shoulder. "I think you're in luck."

She turned and tried not to let her jaw drop. For a second she thought Jack had walked into the barn, but the stride was different and the jeans were blue denim, not the black that Jack favored. No telling where Rafe had dug up the jeans, shirt, boots and hat, but they fit him well.

A little too well, in fact. Yesterday his dress shirt and slacks had partially disguised his build, but this outfit disguised nothing. The snug jeans showed off his muscled thighs and the shirt emphasized his broad chest.

The borrowed hat was black. By accident or design, Rafe had tilted it at the right angle to make his dark eyes sexy and mysterious, exactly as she'd imagined they would be when shadowed by a hat. He looked amazing.

He came to a stop in front of her and spread out his arms. "Will this do?"

She had the inappropriate urge to move right into those outstretched arms in the hope he'd wrap them around her. "You should wear clothes like that more often." Whoops. She'd said that out loud. "I mean, yes, that'll do fine."

"Sarah rounded them up for me this morning."

"Did you eat any breakfast? I didn't see you in the kitchen."

"I never eat breakfast. I grabbed a cup of coffee before I came down here. That's all I need."

She didn't think so. He might get away without breakfast when he sat in an office clicking computer keys, but his morning routine was about to shift dramatically toward fresh air and exercise. She decided against mentioning his need for real food because he probably wouldn't believe her.

Instead she turned to the foreman, who was watching them with thinly disguised amusement. "Emmett, which horse do you recommend for Rafe?"

Emmett didn't hesitate. "Destiny."

"I was thinking that, too."

Rafe shifted his weight and looked apprehensive. "'Destiny' sounds like the devil horse you put green-horns on to test them."

"We wouldn't do that, son." Emmett clapped him on the shoulder. "You've come here with an honest desire to learn how to ride. If you'd bragged about your riding skill when we knew you didn't have any, *then* we'd bring out the devil horse."

"Trust me, I have nothing to brag about when it comes to horses. I can deconstruct a stock offering in no time flat, but when it comes to mounting up and riding off into the sunset, I got nothin'."

Emmett reached for a halter hanging on the wall. "It's not a bad place to start. You're a blank slate with no bad habits. Meg, if you want to lead out Spilled Milk, I'll fetch Destiny. Rafe, you come with me. I'll show you how to put this on him."

Meg watched the two men head down the row of stalls. Emmett ambled along with the slightly bow-legged stride of a guy who'd spent most of his life in the saddle. Rafe moved with the grace of an athlete, but there was no cowboy in his walk yet. Even so, the view of a jeans-wearing Rafe from behind was outstanding. Life at the Last Chance had just become more scenic.

DESPITE BEING ASSURED that Destiny wasn't a powder keg ready to explode, Rafe studied the large brown-and-white animal from outside the stall. He wasn't eager to get into a confined space with him.

"Come on in, son. He won't bite."

Rafe edged into the stall. "How much does he weigh?"

"Around a thousand pounds, give or take."

"He must be pretty strong."

"Yes, but he's trained to cooperate with you. Come closer so you can see how to halter him. You put this on in order to lead him out of the barn. Later you'll take the halter off and replace it with a bridle, which provides your steering mechanism. Don't worry. He's used to all this, so he won't put up a fuss."

"Right." Taking a deep breath, Rafe approached Destiny. As Emmett put on the halter, Rafe ignored the enormous teeth and concentrated on Destiny's deep brown eyes. He could see himself in the reflection there, and he *looked* like a cowboy, even if he didn't feel like one.

"See how that's done?" Emmett finished with the halter, snapped a lead rope to a metal ring and handed over the rope. "Go ahead and lead him outside."

Before Rafe could object that he didn't know enough yet, he found himself tramping back down the aisle between the stalls, towing a horse behind him. Emmett walked along, too, probably to make sure Rafe didn't do anything stupid.

"How long has Destiny been at the ranch?"

"Let's see. I guess it's about twenty-four years, now."

"Yikes! I didn't mean you had to give me a geriatric horse. Can he handle my weight?"

Emmett chuckled. "Twenty-four's not so old. Horses can live to be forty or more. Destiny was born when Jack was around ten, and he came up with that name for him. Thought it was real dramatic."

"So this is Jack's horse?"

"Not really. He's a little too tame for Jack these days. Jack rides a black-and-white stallion named Bandit."

"Destiny isn't a stallion?"

"Not anymore."

"Oh." Rafe was torn between relief that Destiny was a pushover and humiliation at being consigned to a horse with no balls, one that wasn't spirited enough for Jack Chance.

"Destiny's a good starter horse," Emmett said. "He has one bad habit, though. If you're out on the trail and decide to climb off him, you'd better tie him up real good. He likes to work himself loose and head on home."

"I'll remember that. But I think maybe I should just stay in the corral today, don't you?"

"Maybe for the first ten minutes, until you get the hang of it."

"I don't think ten minutes will do the trick."

"You'll be surprised at how fast you pick it up, son. Once you're comfortable in the saddle, you and Meg should take 'em out and admire the scenery. We have a lot to look at around here."

"Yes, you do." Rafe couldn't argue with that. Coming out of the house this morning he'd been greeted with a spectacular view of the snowcapped Grand Tetons. Funny that his mother hadn't mentioned the amazing scenery when she'd described the ranch. Lining rockers up on the front porch made a lot more sense when a person could sit and look at those mountains.

When they emerged from the barn, Meg was already at the hitching post with her horse, the one he remembered from yesterday.

"Just tie Destiny up next to Spilled Milk," Emmett said. "I'll get you a blanket, saddle and bridle."

"Thanks, Emmett." Rafe walked the horse in a semi-circle so he could approach the hitching post from the right angle and do a decent job of parallel parking next to the other horse.

After tying the lead rope to the post, he stepped back. "So far, so good."

Meg settled a patterned blanket over her horse's back and glanced at Rafe. "Looks like you and Destiny are making friends."

"I figure he's just putting up with me."

"Just think of him like one of those dogs over there." Moving with calm efficiency, she put a saddle on top of the blanket. "Emmett said he was treated like a pet when he was young, so in some ways he's more dog than horse."

"If I'd ever had a dog, I could relate to that analogy."

"You've never had a dog?"

"Nope."

"You don't like them?" She leaned to tighten the leather strap running under the horse's belly.

"I don't know if I do or not. We didn't have dogs when I was a kid, so I never got used to having them around. With my work schedule, it makes no sense to have a pet, anyway."

"I know what you mean about that. I decided not to adopt a dog right now, either, considering the hours I work. I have a fish tank, but it's not the same. I get my horse and dog fix when I go out to the stables back in Pittsburgh."

She straightened and pointed to the strap under the horse. "It's a good idea to tighten it, then wait for the horse to let out some air, then tighten it again."

"Good to know."

"Okay, now I'll tighten it again." She went back to

her task, which gave him a chance to watch her without her being aware.

This morning she'd returned to her cute and wholesome look. Knowing that she could be all sunshine and daisies during the day and transform into a seductress at night fired his blood. He wondered which persona she'd have naked. Probably both.

"Rafe?" Emmett tapped him on the shoulder. "You okay?"

Rafe turned toward him. "I'm fine. Why?"

"I told you a couple of times that I'd brought out your tack, but you were staring into space like you didn't hear me."

"Sorry." He tugged his hat lower and hoped Emmett wouldn't notice his embarrassment. "Lost in thought, I guess."

Emmett's slow smile indicated he knew exactly where Rafe's mind had been. "Be careful," he said in a low voice.

"I will." He knew neither of them were talking about horseback riding. Meg had at least two male protectors, and Rafe wouldn't be surprised to find more. She'd made friends in the short time she'd been here, and they didn't want her to get hurt.

Well, neither did he. Wyatt knew that he wasn't in the habit of treating women poorly, but Emmett couldn't know that. In any case, Rafe would leave well enough alone when it came to Meg. Yes, she intrigued him, but pursuing that interest wasn't worth the risk.

"I'll leave you both to carry on with the program," Emmett said. "Holler if you need any help, though."

"Thanks, Emmett," Meg said. "We should be fine."

Giving her horse one last pat, she walked over to Destiny. "Let's get this guy saddled. I'll let you do it."

"All right." Rafe put the blanket on the way she had. Then he made sure the stirrups and the leather belt thing were lying on top of the saddle before he swung it up to Destiny's broad back.

"Good job. You must have been watching very closely."

"I was." Good thing she didn't know how closely.

"Then cinch it up."

"With the belt thing?"

"Yes. It's called a cinch."

"Good to know." He managed to knock his hat in the dirt while he dealt with the cinch.

She picked up his hat, dusted it off and hung it on the saddle. "This hat doesn't have a string to hold it on."

"No. Sarah mentioned that." He grappled with the leather cinch while Destiny stomped his front foot. That startled him, but he soldiered on as if he had no thoughts of that hoof crushing his skull like a melon. "Can horses smell fear?"

"Why, are you afraid?"

"No, no. Just wondered."

"I'm sure they can tell when someone's afraid of them. Then they try to take advantage."

"They do?" He managed to get the cinch buckled and stood up again. "Like how?"

"Like not minding you, walking you under a tree branch to scrape you off, things like that."

"Good thing I'm not afraid of this horse, then." And by God he wouldn't be. He didn't relish the idea of being knocked off by an overhanging branch. "Now we wait for him to let out air, right?"

"Right." Meg gazed at him. "I'm trying to imagine growing up without animals in the house. We had dogs, cats, gerbils, hamsters, you name it. Was someone in your family allergic?"

"No. We had very expensive furniture and my mother didn't want it ruined."

"Ah." For a brief moment sympathy flashed in her green eyes. Then she glanced away, as if she knew that he wouldn't appreciate seeing that emotion coming from her.

She was right. He didn't want her sympathy. "It was more of a hardship for Wyatt than for me. I didn't really feel deprived."

"I guess it's all in what you're used to."

"Exactly. So is it time to tighten the cinch on this hay-burner?"

She laughed in surprise. "*Hay-burner?* Where'd you get that, from some old Western?"

"Probably. It just popped into my head. Hanging out at the old homestead must be affecting my vocabulary."

"Next thing you know you'll be saying things like 'howdy, partner' and 'don't you fret, little lady.'"

"God, I hope not. If you hear me start saying dorky things like that, give me a kick, okay?"

"I will." She grinned at him. "And I won't be the only one. Cowboys don't talk like that in real life."

"Do they say 'hay-burner'?"

"They might, among themselves." She leaned closer and lowered her voice. "But if I were you, I'd avoid that one, too. The Chances are proud of their breeding program and their registered Paints. They might be offended."

"Point taken." He savored the cinnamon scent that

wafted from her skin when she was this close. Her mouth looked delicious, and that's why he had to move back and forget about it. He put distance between them, but forgetting about her pink mouth wasn't so easy.

He cleared his throat. "So, is it time to tighten the cinch on this valuable registered Paint?"

"Yes." Her green eyes sparkled. "But Destiny isn't valuable to the horse breeding operation anymore, now that he's no longer—"

"In possession of his family jewels?"

"You noticed?"

"I'm not that observant. Emmett told me. Damned shame."

"It makes him easier to pair up with other horses. Stallions can get touchy with each other, and a mare like Spilled Milk, if she happened to be in season, couldn't go on a trail ride with a stallion. Things could get complicated."

And now he had a visual that was no help in getting his mind off sex. "I hadn't thought of all that."

"Fortunately, Emmett and I did. So cinch him up, and we'll get started."

"Sure thing." Rafe was able to pull the cinch a couple of notches tighter, and while he did, he thought about the poor horse's missing sexual equipment. Rafe, however, wasn't missing any of his, and whenever he looked at Meg, his animal instincts took over.

He'd been so sure a riding lesson couldn't possibly become sexual in nature. Less than thirty minutes into the session, it already had.

4

MEG WONDERED IF RAFE had been warned not to get too friendly with her. Wyatt might have done that, and although she appreciated his big-brother, protective attitude, she didn't want him discouraging Rafe. Maybe he hadn't, but Meg thought someone had issued a word of caution.

Her attempts to flirt with Rafe would spark an initial response, but then he'd tamp it down. Once they were out on the trail and away from anyone who might overhear, she'd ask him why. Maybe he had his own reasons for putting on the brakes, but she was willing to bet Wyatt was at the bottom of it.

First things first, though. She had to get him comfortable with riding so he'd agree to take one of the ranch's many trails. Each one was beautiful, and Meg could hardly wait to show Rafe the wonders he'd been willing to dismiss yesterday.

When Destiny was saddled, she had Rafe watch her put on Spilled Milk's bridle. Then she helped him with Destiny's and explained how the bit worked to control the horse. Finally it was time for Rafe to mount up.

"You get on from the left side." She took his hat off the saddle horn and handed it to him. "You'll want the saddle horn available to hold on to while you swing up."

"Got it." He settled the Stetson on his head and instantly added a yummy factor.

She hadn't realized how sexy cowboy hats were until she'd traveled to Wyoming, where it was the headgear of choice. Now she couldn't imagine men choosing to wear anything else. Put a Stetson on a guy and his hottie quotient shot up a good twenty points.

Standing by Destiny's head, she held the horse's bridle while Rafe shoved his booted foot into the left stirrup and swung his right leg over the saddle with natural grace. Once he conquered his initial nervousness, he'd be great at this. And he rocked the denim look. Watching him mount up, which stretched the material in fascinating places, brought a little shiver of delight.

"And just like that, you're on," she said.

"So I am." Gripping the horn with both hands, he shifted in the saddle. "This isn't too bad."

"I need to adjust the stirrups, though. Your legs are longer than the previous rider's. I don't want your knees drawn up like a jockey's."

"Shouldn't I do the adjusting?"

"It'll be more efficient if I do it while you're in the saddle." She was just the girl to adjust his stirrups, too. Considering how close she'd have to be to his muscled thighs, she wouldn't delegate this job to anyone. Moving to his left side, she glanced up. "Take your left foot out of the stirrup."

He obeyed, and as she lifted the flap of leather to alter the length, she savored the flex of muscles beneath the faded jeans. The scent of minty soap, freshly washed denim and pure masculinity swirled around her in a heady combo. She would adjust Rafe's stirrups any day.

"Now the other side." Rounding the back of the horse, she repeated the motion on his right stirrup. "Okay, put your feet in and let's see."

"It feels better."

"Looks better, too. Stand up in them so I can see how much clearance you have." As he did that, she was obliged to gaze at his crotch. Mercy. "Good. You can sit again." She resisted the urge to fan her face.

"I didn't realize there was so much to the fit of the saddle and the stirrups."

"You need to be as comfortable as possible." She didn't want any of that valuable equipment getting bruised, either. Yowza. With an effort she pulled her mind away from the subject of Rafe's endowments. "You'll want to keep your heels down with your weight sinking into them to lower your center of gravity."

"Sarah convinced me to wear the boots because she said the heels would keep my feet from slipping through the stirrups. I decided I didn't want to be dragged to my death, so I went with the boots."

"You won't be dragged to your death, Rafe. I'll save you before that happens."

He smiled at her. "What a relief. I could have worn my loafers, then."

"'Fraid not. The leather shank keeps your shins from chafing. Boots aren't only for impressing women. They serve a purpose."

"Women are impressed with boots?"

"Some are." She untied Destiny's reins from the hitching post.

"Are you?"

She glanced back at him. "Depends whose feet are in them."

He nodded. "Fair enough."

"I thought we'd start by making a few circuits of the corral." She led Destiny over to the gate.

"Please tell me you're not going to lead me around like a kid on a pony ride."

"Just until I get you inside the corral. After all, it is your first time."

"You make me sound like a damned virgin."

That made her laugh. "Would you rather we started out with a wild gallop across the meadow?"

"No, I wouldn't. But I hope nobody sees this part. It's embarrassing."

"It'll be over before you know it." She unlatched the gate, led Destiny inside and latched the gate again. "Ready to take over?"

"I'm so ready."

Knotting the reins, she lifted them over Destiny's head and handed them to Rafe. "Hold these in your left hand, and keep them fairly loose. You don't want to pull on his mouth. He neck reins, so when you want him to go left, lay the reins against the right side of his neck, and vice versa." She stepped back.

Horse and rider remained stationary as Destiny quietly waited for directions.

Rafe frowned. "Where's the gas pedal?"

She realized he really had *no* idea how to ride a horse. Most people knew how to get them going at least. "Nudge him in the ribs with your heels."

He applied a slight pressure.

"Harder."

When he used more force, Destiny started off.

"Remember, reins against the right side of his neck to go left, and against the left side to go right."

"Got it." Rafe followed her instructions, and soon he was controlling Destiny's slow progress around the corral.

"Bored yet?"

"Getting there. How do I speed him up?"

"You nudge him again and click your tongue. But first sink down into your heels, because a trot is—" He was into the trot before she could finish the sentence.

He bounced uncontrollably in the saddle, lost his stirrups, his hat and his temper. He began to swear.

She struggled to keep a straight face. "Pull back gently on the reins and say 'whoa.'"

He did, and sat there catching his breath. "That was torture. What did I do wrong?"

She was impressed that he'd ask the question instead of blaming either her or the horse. "You got ahead of me. A trot isn't an easy gait to master."

"No shit." He climbed down off the horse.

"Are you giving up?" She couldn't believe it, but everyone had a different tolerance for frustration.

"Hell, no, I'm not giving up." Taking hold of Destiny's bridle, he started off at a brisk walk. "Gotta get my hat."

"Oh." She smiled to herself. She'd suspected he might have the makings of a cowboy. And sure enough, he did.

AFTER THAT DEBACLE, RAFE listened more carefully to Meg's instructions, and eventually he began to sense the rhythm of the trot. He still bounced a little, but he didn't lose his stirrups or his hat, which was progress.

Next she taught him to canter around the perimeter of the corral.

He remembered the term *canter* from yesterday. When he'd accused her of running straight at him, she'd protested that she was only cantering. Now he understood why riders would want to do that. He could canter all day long.

"That's good!" she called out. "I think you're ready for the outside world."

He thought so, too. To his surprise, the corral had started to feel confining. He wouldn't claim to be a natural at riding, but he'd caught on a lot faster than he'd expected.

Meg opened the gate. "Wait here by the corral while I get Spilled Milk. Then we'll be off." She gazed up at him. "You're doing great. Really wonderful for your first time. How do you feel?"

"Terrific." It was the God's truth. He'd ridden motorcycles, but this was better, more...real. He liked the view from the back of a horse, the sense of partnership he felt, and the visceral thrill of going fast in tandem with this powerful animal.

"You'll be sore tomorrow, but maybe not too bad. I recommend a soak in a hot bath later on."

"I'll do that. You haven't led me astray so far."

"Give me time." She winked at him and sauntered away.

What the hell? He stared after her, his brain buzzing with what had obviously been a suggestive remark. And in case he'd been too dense to pick up on it, she'd followed it with a wink.

Digging his cell phone out of his jeans pocket, he speed-dialed his brother.

Wyatt answered immediately. "What's up, bro?"

"What if Meg has the hots for me?"

"She does?"

"I think she might, yeah."

Wyatt let out a gusty sigh. "Figures."

"Look, I don't want to cause— Whoops, gotta go. Here she comes." He disconnected and shoved the phone back in his front pocket. He'd thought of leaving it behind, but the jeans fit tight enough that he wouldn't lose it, and he was used to having his phone with him at all times.

Her eyes narrowed as she approached on Spilled Milk. "Keeping up with stock prices?"

With a sense of shock, he realized that he hadn't thought of his job once since waking up this morning. Normally he'd have checked the market several times by now. "No. I had to ask Wyatt about something."

The disapproval faded from her green eyes. "Best man stuff?"

"Yeah, kind of."

"I know the preparations are important, but could I ask you a big favor?"

"Sure."

"Would you mind turning off your phone during the ride? We have a bright, sunny day to enjoy some gorgeous scenery. I hate to think of it being interrupted by a cell phone chime."

"I can do that." He took out the phone and noticed there was a text message from Wyatt. He'd read it later. Turning off the power, he tucked the phone away again.

"Thank you."

"You're welcome." He met her gaze. Her eyes glowed with happy anticipation. She was looking forward to this ride, looking forward to spending time alone with him. Wyatt and Emmett might be worried about a potential involvement, but she seemed to have no such fears.

He allowed himself to imagine what it would be like to kiss her, and fire licked through his veins. Wyatt had said she was a big girl who made her own choices, and for some reason, she'd chosen a private ride.

Unless he was mistaken, and he rarely was when it came to a woman's interest, she was giving him the green light. Only a fool would ignore that kind of opportunity. Rafe's body warmed to the possibilities as his expectations shifted. He was no fool.

"I'll lead because I know the path, but if you have any problems at all, sing out. I'll keep tabs on you from time to time."

He grinned. "To make sure I'm not being dragged to my death?"

"Yeah, stuff like that. Let's ride." Turning Spilled Milk, she started away from the barn at a brisk trot.

Rafe enjoyed the sight of her ass rising and falling in sync with her horse. Although he was glad she wasn't babying him, he hoped the entire ride wouldn't be a trotting marathon. He still bounced. Even with the bouncing, though, he was filled with elation at the prospect of riding out into the open field...and what might follow once they were truly all alone.

The sun warmed his shoulders and the mountains thrust pristine white peaks into a sky so blue it looked painted on. To think he'd planned to spend the day working. Tightness in his chest that he hadn't realized was there began to loosen.

They stopped briefly so Meg could deal with a gate that led to the wide-open spaces.

"Do you know if all of this is Chance land?" he asked as she leaned down from her horse to fasten the gate behind them.

"Yes, it is." She moved past him so she was once again in the lead. "Archie Chance won it in a card game in the thirties."

"That sounds like a myth. Things like that don't really happen."

"I guess they do in Wyoming. Ready for some cantering?"

"You know it."

"Then let's go!" She urged her horse forward.

Destiny didn't need any nudging as he set off in pursuit of Spilled Milk. A gust of wind nearly took Rafe's hat, and he used one hand to anchor it. At first he held the reins and the saddle horn with his other hand, but as his body adjusted to the horse's rhythm, he let go of the horn and held the reins like a real cowboy would.

He was riding! If he hadn't been worried about spooking the horses, he'd have let out a whoop of delight. What a rush. He couldn't believe he'd gone twenty-nine years without experiencing this. Sharing it with a sexy woman like Meg made it even better.

Before he was ready for the canter to be over, she slowed her horse, and Destiny fell back to a trot, and eventually a walk.

"That was fun," he said. "I could do that again."

"I'm sure you could." She swiveled in her saddle to glance back at him. "But I don't want to overdo it on your first ride. You might feel great now, but you could end up being miserable tonight."

"If I recover okay tonight, do you think we could come out here again tomorrow?"

She smiled at him. "So you really like it that much?"

"Yeah. It's much better than I imagined it would be."

"So maybe you're not totally a city boy."

He shook his head. "I'm still a city boy. Just because I'm enjoying the hell out of this doesn't mean I wouldn't like to find a coffee shop over the next hill."

"No coffee shop. Are you getting hungry?"

He hesitated to admit it after announcing that he never ate breakfast. "A little."

"We can go back."

"Not yet." No way was he going back until he'd had a chance to find out exactly what that wink of hers signified.

"Then we'll keep going." She faced forward again. "It is spectacular, isn't it? According to Sarah, the wildflowers will be gone soon. By September or October, they could have snow."

"I know Wyatt didn't want to wait any later to have the wedding because he was worried about weather."

"I'd like to see this place in the winter. I'll bet it's beautiful then, too. A different kind of beauty."

"Do you ski?" Walking the horses wasn't as exciting, but it meant he could talk to her, get to know her better.

"Not yet. I plan to learn. Olivia wants me to come out here again, so if I visit her this winter, I could learn then. Do you ski?"

"Some. I haven't done it much lately, though. I always seem to be working." The comment made him sound like a drudge, and he wasn't. But he owed it to his clients to keep up with the markets and emerging trends. That required constant vigilance. Today was a rare break in his routine.

"Jackson Hole is a fantastic place to ski."

"So I hear. Wyatt's already said something about celebrating Christmas here, but I don't know..."

"We could visit at the same time and you could teach me to ski! That would be a nice trade, don't you think?"

"It would." So now she was suggesting that they coordinate visits. If that wasn't an indication of interest, then he knew nothing about women.

He liked the prospect of seeing her again in December. He liked it quite a bit, assuming he could do some work while he was here. Many of his clients were shifting assets around at the end of the year, so he was usually busy.

"Of course, there's always the possibility I'll be living here by then."

"Living here?" He had trouble keeping up with her whirlwind approach to life. "You'd move?"

"I'm seriously considering it. I've fallen in love with the area. All I need is a job. Shoshone's a one-traffic-light town, but Jackson might be able to use me in some capacity."

"And you've been here how long?"

"Four days. Five counting today."

"Don't you think you need more time before making a major decision like that?"

She shrugged. "Not really. I grew up in Pittsburgh, and I like it okay, but something about this area just feels like home, you know?"

"Not exactly." He'd never thought in those terms. His parents' house had been a showplace, but not what he'd call a *home.* His own apartment worked for him and had that outstanding view, so he supposed it was home, although he'd never called it that.

"Well, my philosophy is that life's short. You have to grab the good stuff while you can. Speaking of that, there's a pretty little creek up ahead. Let's stop and rest awhile. I didn't think to bring water, so the horses can get a drink and so can we."

"Okay." He tried to decide if he was dealing with a certified flake. Meg was fun to have around and he was sexually attracted to her, but if she'd pull up stakes and switch locations in the blink of an eye, then…then so what? Did it matter?

Even if they got cozy with each other during the week of the wedding, it would be a no-strings affair. Her life decisions wouldn't affect him in the slightest, except that if she moved, she'd be around in December if he made the trip back to Jackson Hole.

But who knew if they'd even like each other at the end of the week if they did become involved. They'd only met yesterday. There might be strong chemistry between them, but until he'd at least kissed her… He almost laughed at his typical caution. Kissing her would be outstanding, and he damned well knew it. The sex would be even better.

Meg pulled her horse to a stop beside a bubbling rivulet of water about two yards wide. "There's a flat rock over there we can sit on."

He liked the idea of the rock, but not the lack of trees. "There's nothing to tie the horses to. Don't forget that Destiny likes to wander."

"I haven't." She dismounted and led her horse to the stream. "But Spilled Milk is trained to be ground-tied, which means if I drop the reins to the ground, she won't go anywhere, so if we tie Destiny's reins to Spilled Milk's saddle horn, we're golden."

"Sounds good." He was perfectly willing to bow to her expertise, especially if it meant being able to spend some time with her on that rock. He felt a few twinges in his muscles as he climbed down. Too bad the ranch didn't have a hot tub on the property, one he could share with Meg tonight.

Copying her actions, he led Destiny over to the water and watched the horse plunge his nose into it. "Here we are watering our horses, just like a scene out of a Western movie."

"Fortunately I don't expect any bad guys to ride up and ambush us."

"If they did, I'd save you. You may know riding, but I know karate." He hadn't practiced in a while, though, so he was glad he wouldn't be put to the test.

She glanced over at him. "We are so trading lessons. I want to learn karate."

"It takes years."

"Oh, I know. I'm not expecting to become an over-night expert, but you could get me started and I could go from there."

"Is there anything you don't want to do?"

"Yes. I don't want to miss anything."

He gazed at her as that statement hovered between them. Did she include him in it? He hoped she did.

She might be a flake, but she was a fascinating one. He'd never met anyone who had such a voracious appetite for life's many experiences. Her enthusiasm was contagious. He'd smiled and laughed more this morning than he had in the past month. If she treated sex the way she did everything else, he was about to become a very lucky man.

5

MEG SENT RAFE OVER TO SIT on the sun-warmed rock while she tied Destiny and Spilled Milk together. Theoretically her plan should work, but she hadn't dealt with Destiny's little quirk. She'd make sure to keep an eye on the horses so she could stop them if they began to wander off.

Once she'd finished, she left the horses and joined Rafe. "Have you had any of the water yet?"

He smiled at her. "I was waiting to see how you planned on doing it. Maybe you're going to drink out of your hat. That's how it's done in the movies."

"I'd rather not." She made a face. "Sounds unsanitary and might ruin my hat." She dropped to her knees. "I'll just scoop it up in my hands, like this." She proceeded to demonstrate the technique she'd used last time she was here.

She'd forgotten that she'd dripped water down the front of her shirt in the process. When she'd been alone it hadn't mattered. She'd sat in the sun until it dried.

But today she was not alone. With an audience making her self-conscious, she got some of the water into her mouth, but most of it ran down her chin and soaked her shirt. She didn't have to look to know that it was plastered to her body and her nipples stood out in sharp relief. She could feel them tightening from the cold.

"Interesting." His voice vibrated with laughter.

"I didn't mean to do that." Winking and flirting was one thing. Setting herself up as a wet T-shirt model was a little over-the-top, even for her. She pulled her shirt away from her body, but the minute she let it go, it clung to her breasts like plastic wrap.

"I'm not complaining."

She cast him a sideways glance, and sure enough, he was frankly admiring her breasts. "A gentleman wouldn't look."

He shoved his hat back with his thumb in a very cow-boylike gesture. "I never claimed to be a gentleman. Besides, weren't you the one who wanted a chance to lead me astray?"

She swallowed. Yes, she'd thought she was quite clever to make that flippant, offhand remark. But now that they were completely alone, she felt the full force and heat of his sexuality. He was one potent guy. She might have bitten off more than she could chew.

Keeping his gaze locked with hers, he took off her hat and laid it on the rock beside her. Then he put his next to it.

Her heart thundered. "Don't you...want a drink of water?"

"I think you scooped enough for two of us." Cupping her cheek in one hand, he leaned forward, his attention on her mouth. "Let's see."

Closing her eyes, she waited, quivering, for what she

guessed would be one of the most outstanding kisses of her life. She wasn't disappointed.

He touched down lightly, sipping the moisture from her lips. His tongue traced the outline once, and again, more slowly. He cradled the back of her head with his other hand and held her still as he continued to explore the contours of her mouth with calm deliberation.

His leisurely approach was at complete odds with her wildly beating heart and the coiled tension she felt coming through his fingertips. She envisioned a small flame licking its way along a fuse to a stick of dynamite.

His breath caught and he swore softly as he pulled back.

Opening her eyes, she looked into the inferno raging in his. "Rafe?"

"You scare the hell out of me."

Dazed by the emotions swirling between them, she could barely speak. "Why?"

"Because I want you so much." With that, he captured her mouth with a ferocity that made her gasp.

Gone was the easy, unhurried caress, the almost lazy attention to her lips. Something raw and primitive seemed to drive him as he thrust his tongue deep with a moan of frustrated desire. She clung to his broad shoulders to keep her balance as the world began to spin.

Her response built quickly. Joy surged within her as she drank in his passion. At last. A man who matched her intensity. He kissed her with the kind of single-mindedness she'd always dreamed of and had never found.

The world narrowed to this connection. Nothing else mattered but kissing Rafe, drawing a quick breath, and kissing him some more. He was ambrosia and nectar of the gods. He was skydiving and parasailing. He was shooting the rapids in a bright red kayak. She couldn't get enough of his mouth, his tongue…

A loud whinny threw her right out of the sensual pool she'd been drowning in. Pulling back, she glanced over at the horses about the time Spilled Milk whinnied again and bared her teeth at Destiny. The gelding was up to his old tricks of trying to walk away, and Spilled Milk was having none of it.

Meg leaped up. "We need to separate them before she completely loses her cool. You untie Destiny while I calm Spilled Milk." She ran over to the horses without waiting to see if Rafe had followed.

Fortunately, he was right behind her. "What happened?" he asked as he untied Destiny's reins from Spilled Milk's saddle.

"I'm guessing that Destiny's been tugging on her and trying to get her to leave. Spilled Milk, being a well-trained horse, stood her ground. The more he pulled, the madder she got. She wasn't going to let him lead her astray."

"As I was trying to do to you?"

She looked over at him and smiled as she stroked the mare's neck. He was one yummy guy. "You could never lead me where I don't want to go, cowboy."

He glanced up. "You do realize that Wyatt warned me to stay away from you."

"I was afraid he'd made me off-limits."

Rafe finished untying Destiny, but he kept a firm grip on the reins. "He told me how special you are, which is something I can see for myself. He seemed to be afraid that I'd somehow cause you problems."

"How?"

He shrugged. "The usual, I suppose. Make passionate love to you and then leave you to cry your eyes out."

"Wyatt's a little too old-fashioned." She held his gaze. "I'm capable of making passionate love without the crying-my-eyes-out routine."

His expression grew serious. "Just so we're both clear on this, I'm not ready to settle down."

"So what? I'm not ready to settle down, either."

"Does Wyatt know that?"

That made her chuckle. "I haven't discussed my relationship plans with Wyatt. I met him for the first time four days ago."

"And yet you're discussing them with me, and you only met me yesterday."

"That's because you could become intimately involved with those plans."

Desire flashed in his eyes. "Are you saying you're fine with a wild and crazy fling this week, with no promises on either side?"

"That's what I'm saying." She mentally crossed her fingers. She might have finally found a man with the same capacity for joy that she had. She never would have guessed it, given his attitude when she'd first met him, but that kiss...that kiss had told her all she needed to know.

If, under his businessman's exterior, Rafe was the kind of passionate man she believed him to be, then she wouldn't easily let him ride off into the sunset. If he truly wanted that, she'd let him go. But as he'd discovered with horseback riding, he might not know exactly what he wanted...yet.

THEIR SIZZLING KISS HAD shaken Rafe more than he cared to admit. He wasn't exactly a novice at this sexual adventure business, but he'd never experienced a first kiss that was quite so explosive. If they could generate that kind of heat with only a kiss, he wondered what would happen when they got down to serious business. He might want to keep a fire extinguisher handy.

He tried to keep his tone casual. "As it happens, we're both sleeping on the second floor, right down the hall from each other."

"Very convenient."

"I think that kind of proximity is what Wyatt was worried about."

Meg seemed to consider that for a moment. "So do you think he's worried about me getting hurt, or could he be worried about our drama interfering with the wedding?"

"Both, probably." Rafe sighed. "The situation's dicey enough without you and me adding to the tension. Everybody's concerned about whether my mother will come to the wedding, which would create one kind of problem, or whether she'll refuse to come, which would create another. Wyatt's in for it, either way."

"Yeah." She nodded as if she'd had the same thoughts. "Do you think we can have what we want without jacking up the drama quotient?"

"I'd like to believe we can." He met her gaze. "Or more accurately, I *want* to believe we can, because… you turn me on, Meg."

"Likewise." Those green eyes told him she was as eager as he was to find out what kind of magic they could create.

He grinned. "That does wonders for a man's ego."

"You're pretty good for mine, too."

"So are you ready to risk it?"

"I am. Are you?"

"With you sleeping right down the hall, I don't know if I could resist the temptation. Maybe I just need to hoist the white flag right now and say I need you in my bed."

"So it's to be your bed, then?" She gave him a teasing glance. "Are you saying you prefer a king-size mattress to a double bed in a room covered with posters of studly NASCAR drivers?"

"I could ignore the posters, but mine is definitely the party bed."

"Okay, so that much is settled. What about…"

He cleared his throat. "Don't worry. I'll take care of that."

"Don't assume you have to. I don't believe a man has to be in charge of birth control. I can run into town this afternoon and make that purchase. I'll just need to know the size."

He couldn't believe how adorable she was. "Ginormous." When her eyes widened, he couldn't help laughing. "What do you suppose a man will say when you ask him a question like that? Of course he'll tell you to get the supersize ones."

"Yes, but I wouldn't want them to fall off."

He laughed harder. "The way they're constructed, I doubt they would, but I'm going to save you the trouble of standing at the counter puzzling over which ones. I know exactly what I want, and what size, so I'm the logical person to take care of that little matter."

Her eyes sparkled. "Or big matter, as the case may be."

"The *huge* matter."

"Okay, okay, I get the idea." She hesitated. "Are we

going to text each other once we're both upstairs, or what?"

"Tell you what. You recommended a hot bath for me, right?"

"Yes."

"When you hear the water running in the bathtub, you're welcome to wander down the hall and scrub my back." Or whatever else she wanted to put her hand to... He shifted his weight as his jeans' fly started to pinch.

"So everything's planned."

"Yep." Rafe made sure he had a good hold on Destiny's reins as he walked around his horse, which was blocking access to Meg. "So Spilled Milk won't move no matter what, right?"

"That's right."

"Good. Then hold these." He put Destiny's reins in her hand.

"How come?"

"I need one more for the road." Sweeping off his hat, he pulled her close and gazed into her green eyes. "Don't let go."

"Rafe Locke, are you about to be a bad boy?"

"Yes, ma'am, I am." Dipping his head below the brim of her hat, he settled his mouth firmly over hers, and once again, the world caught fire.

Except this time the flames licked through his entire body as she wound both arms around his neck and pressed against him. Sweet heaven. He deepened the kiss and she arched forward, sending her hat sliding down her back.

With a groan he cupped her bottom and brought her as close to his aching cock as layers of denim would allow. The dampness from her shirt seeped into his, reminding him of the way her breasts had looked outlined by wet fabric.

Operating with blind desperation, he managed to hook his hat on her horse's saddle so he'd have his other hand free…free to slide under her shirt and cradle her breast in one hand. She shivered and moaned softly.

He longed for bare skin, but now was not the time. Stroking his thumb over damp lace, he caressed her taut nipple as he thrust his tongue deep into her mouth. Tonight. Tonight he'd know the full wonder of making love to her. And it would be so good. So very good.

One of the horses snorted, bringing him back to reality. He lifted his mouth from hers. "Tonight."

"Yes."

What a sweet word that was. He wanted to hear her say it over and over while he gave her all the pleasure she could stand. Groaning, he released her. Tonight. Somehow he'd find the patience to wait until then.

6

_____

MEG'S SHIRT WAS DRY BY the time they brought the horses in, but her pulse still skyrocketed every time she glanced at Rafe. Several of the hands were working around the barn, cleaning stalls and grooming horses, so she didn't look at Rafe very often as they unsaddled Destiny and Spilled Milk, because she didn't want to give herself away.

She showed Rafe how to use a brush on Destiny's glossy coat and they worked side by side, grooming their mounts. Every accidental, or not-so-accidental touch sent a jolt of sexual awareness through her. Rafe was probably affected, too, but he acted totally calm.

"Perfect morning for a ride," he said conversationally. "Couldn't have been better."

A devil took possession of her tongue. "I don't know. I thought it was a little warm out there."

He coughed and cleared his throat. "Personally, I like it on the hot side."

"Then you'll be pleased to know it will stay that way while you're here."

"I'll admit that makes me a happy man. Nothing like working up a sweat doing what you enjoy."

He'd turned the tables on her quite effectively, and now she could barely breathe as she imagined what would happen in that big bed upstairs tonight.

"You're awfully quiet over there, Meg. Cat got your tongue?"

She did her best to calm her racing heart. "I...uh... just remembered I have some things to do up at the house." She put the brush into a bucket and untied her horse from the hitching post. "I'm finished here anyway."

"If you are, then I must be, too." A hint of laughter ran through his words. "Should we put them back in their stalls now, or what?"

Right. She couldn't simply abandon him when he didn't know the routine.

Emmett came around the corner of the barn. "You two all done?"

"I think for now we are," Rafe said.

"I'll take those two and turn 'em loose in the pasture for you. Did you have fun?"

"Sure did." Rafe untied Destiny and led him over toward Meg. "I wouldn't mind a repeat tomorrow."

"There, see?" Emmett clapped him on the shoulder. "I knew you'd take to it." He glanced at Meg. "You look a little flushed, girl."

Meg swallowed. "I'm fine."

Rafe handed Destiny's lead rope to Emmett. "You do look flushed, Meg." He glanced over at Emmett. "She was just mentioning that she thought it was quite warm out there."

"Honestly, I'm fine." Or she would be, once she got away from the major heat source in the black Stetson.

"Even so, you'd better head on up to the house for a cool drink." Emmett gave her a fatherly smile. "Don't want anyone falling by the wayside before the big day."

"That's for sure." Rafe slung a casual arm over her shoulders. "Come on, you. Let's get you cooled off." He gave her a little push toward the house before letting his arm slide free.

She tingled everywhere he'd touched her. "It's your fault, you know," she murmured.

"Yes, but you started it," he said in a cheerful tone. "And for your information, I'm a writhing mass of frustration inside."

"I don't believe you. Emmett didn't mention that you looked flushed."

"My reaction takes place a little lower. I've been struggling to keep my pride and joy under control so I can walk."

"Well, for your information, I have a reaction going on a little lower, too."

"Good. I'll take full responsibility for your damp panties if you'll take full responsibility for my pinched penis."

She nearly choked on a laugh.

"You okay?"

She nodded and cleared her throat. "Listen, we need to stop this or we'll never make it through the day."

"You're not having fun?"

"I didn't say that, but what if I snap and drag you upstairs in broad daylight?"

"That would give everyone something to talk about

besides the problem of my mother. For all you know, we'd be doing them a favor by creating a diversion."

She looked over at him and grinned. "Interesting idea, but if it's all the same to you, I'd rather not be the main topic of conversation around the ranch."

"I'm just sayin'. So if you happen to lose control and haul me upstairs, it wouldn't be all bad."

"I'll keep that in mind."

"But if you're not feeling inclined to do that right this minute, I think I'll turn on my cell phone."

She gave a guilty start. "Good grief, by all means. I hope you weren't waiting for my permission."

"Well, no. It's the damnedest thing. When I'm with you, I forget all about work." He pulled his phone out of his pocket. "I can't say that happens very often."

"I'll take that as a compliment."

"I guess it is, but that also means you could become a liability." He powered up the phone.

Her happiness ebbed a bit. "That doesn't sound nearly as nice."

"Don't worry." He scrolled through his messages. "I won't let that happen."

Happiness gave way to irritation. "I wasn't worried. I was insulted. What do you mean, I could become a *liability?* You make me sound like a bad investment."

He frowned and glanced over at her. "Sorry. I didn't catch all that."

"Never mind." Nothing like a guy mesmerized by the information coming through his iPhone to kill the mood. She started up the porch steps, unwilling to compete with technology for his attention.

"Meg, wait." He caught her arm. "You're upset. What's the matter?"

She turned. A step above him, they were eye to eye, nose to nose. Also mouth to mouth, but she wasn't in a kissing mood. "You said I could become a liability. I don't appreciate being told that."

He winced. "Yeah, that was a bonehead thing to say. I didn't mean it like it sounded."

"How did you mean it, then?"

"It's the way financial types talk. Everything's viewed in terms of assets and liabilities. If something boosts the bottom line, it's an asset. If it doesn't, then—"

"Spare me the economic lecture, Rafe. I know about assets and liabilities. I want to know why you're so ready to dump me into the second category."

"Because you're so vibrant and sexy that when I'm with you, I forget everything else. That's good, and I really like the way I feel when I'm with you, but it's also a little scary."

She blinked. He'd actually admitted that he was afraid? That was progress. He must be venturing outside his comfort zone for him to say something like that.

"The thing is, if I'm going to do my job, I can't afford to zone out on a regular basis. I only meant that if I allowed myself to focus on you all the time, I'd be in danger of letting my work suffer."

Time to calm his fears. "In what world would I monopolize your time? Or allow you to monopolize mine? This week is an aberration for both of us. Normally I'm working, too, plus I have friends and family and plenty of my own interests. Furthermore, I respect your time and your work. I would *never* suck up chunks of your life to the point I'd become a *liability*."

He looked stunned. "No, of course you wouldn't. If I'd taken time to think, I would have realized that. It *was* an insulting thing to say, and you have a right to be angry. I'm sorry."

He looked so miserable that the anger leaked right out of her. In truth, he had paid her a huge compliment. Apparently not much came between Rafe and his precious work.

But she had, for one golden morning. Although she'd meant what she'd said about not sucking up chunks of his life, she wouldn't mind freeing him from his shackles once in a while. If not her, then who?

"It's okay." She smiled at him. "Go ahead and check your stock prices and whatever else you need to do. I'm going to take a quick shower before lunch." She started to leave.

"Wait. The message I was reading was from Wyatt. He and Olivia have a break between appointments, and they wanted to know if we'd meet them for lunch at the Spirits and Spurs. He said it might be the only time the four of us could get together before things get crazy."

"Sure. I'd love that."

"Good." He seemed immensely relieved that she wasn't upset with him anymore. "I'll text him that we'll be there in..." He glanced up. "How soon?"

"Thirty minutes."

"Great. I'll tell him."

"That should give you a little time to check in at work."

He grimaced and shook his head. "I have a feeling I'm going to regret that liability remark for a long time."

"Nah." She touched his hand. "You can make me forget everything else, too, including bonehead remarks." Leaving him to mull that over, she ran up the steps and into the house.

RAFE GOT READY QUICKLY while ignoring the fact that Meg was right down the hall in the shower. Now was not the time for fun and games. They were due in town, and besides, he felt a little off balance after their last exchange. So he freshened up and waited for her at the bottom of the winding staircase that connected the first and second floors.

While he waited, he tapped the borrowed Stetson against his thigh as he replayed their flare-up. The conclusion was obvious—he'd been an ass and she'd called him on it.

Fortunately she seemed willing to forgive him and let the subject drop. Fine with him. They had so little time to enjoy each other that he didn't want to waste any of it on arguments.

No question that he was in uncharted territory with Meg. After one morning with her, he realized how superficial his relationships with women had been up to this point. She was the first one to get under his skin, and in trying to explain that, he'd almost blown his chance to be with her.

She was so different from the women he usually dated. He'd gravitated toward a cool exterior, someone who didn't get too excited about anything, someone who skimmed over the top of life and avoided emotional depths. Pleasant women. Undemanding women.

He hadn't demanded anything of them, either. No wonder he hadn't considered marrying any of them. He'd never bothered to get to know who they were, and vice versa.

Two days ago that kind of life had made perfect sense. Now he wondered what it said about him that he'd been satisfied with such tepid encounters. He'd never thought of himself as a coward, and yet…

"Let's go!" She came bouncing down the stairs in a crisp white blouse tucked into a fresh pair of jeans. Instead of boots, she wore sneakers with daisies all over them. She'd also ditched the Western hat in favor of sunglasses perched on top of her head, and she had a denim purse slung over her shoulder.

Apparently she liked to come at life from many angles. He'd met the cowgirl and the seductress. This afternoon she was the girl next door. Her mop of red curls and sunny smile filled his heart with joy. "You look terrific."

"Thanks." She joined him at the bottom of the stairs and gave him a once-over. "So do you. How many spare outfits did Sarah have?"

"Only two." He walked to the door and opened it for her. "After this I'm back to my slacks and dress shirts."

"Noo."

He laughed at her exaggerated distress. "If it makes you that unhappy, I could find out where the washer and dryer are in this place."

"You could." She glanced over her shoulder at him as she walked out the door. "Or we could go shopping."

Shopping for his clothes sounded a little too domestic and intimate. "Nah, I'll just wash what I have." Closing the door, he followed her down the porch steps.

"But don't you need to buy some dressy Western wear for the wedding?"

"So Wyatt said." He led the way toward the Lexus that was still parked in the drive. Maybe he ought to move it when they came back. "At some point I'll go to Jackson and pick up what he suggested."

"That makes sense." Some of the cheer had left her voice. "Didn't mean to push."

He blew out a breath as he opened the passenger door for her. "You weren't pushing, Meg." He might have to officially admit that he *was* a coward, scared to death of letting someone get too close. "What would you say if I told you I've never shopped for clothes with a woman I'm dating?"

She glanced up at him as she slid onto the leather seat. "I'd say you're a very private man. I'll keep that in mind."

In that instant he could see the wall going up between them, a very familiar and comfortable wall for him. He didn't think it would prevent them from having sex and enjoying some good times this week. But it would stop him from getting to know Meg on a deeper level, because if he held back, so would she.

As he closed the door and rounded the car to the driver's side, he realized that this was how he reacted with every woman. They'd reach a point where he would have to make a choice to be open or build a wall. He'd always chosen the wall.

What if he made a different choice this time? What if he used this week to find out if he could have a relationship that didn't involve a wall? If he ever planned to risk it, now seemed like a good time, and Meg seemed like the right woman, open, flexible, giving.

Climbing behind the wheel, he started the car, turned on the air and pulled out of the gravel driveway. "I think it's possible for a man to be too private," he said.

"Oh?" Caution echoed in that single syllable.

He hated hearing that note of hesitation and knew he'd put it there. "If you're offering to go with me to

Jackson this afternoon, I'd be honored to have you. I think it'll be boring as hell, but I—"

"Boring? No way!" The smile was back in her voice. "I *love* helping a gorgeous guy pick out clothes. I have all the fun, and you spend all the money. What could be better than that?"

He glanced over at her, and her face was alight with enthusiasm at the prospect. To think he'd almost deprived her—no, almost deprived *himself*—of the experience. And he wouldn't soon forget that she'd labeled him gorgeous. "I'm sorry I didn't take you up on the suggestion right away. I just—"

"Hey, it's not the way you usually operate. I get that. Knowing I'll be the first woman you've ever taken clothes shopping makes me feel special. I'll do my best not to be annoying."

"I can't imagine you being annoying."

"Trust me, I can be. Now that I know how good you look in this Western stuff, I'll be trying to get you to load up on it."

"And then what?" Rafe winced as the Lexus took a beating on the rutted road leading to the highway. "I can guarantee I won't be dressing like a cowboy in San Francisco."

"Are you sure you couldn't find times to wear jeans and boots? Not every guy wears jeans like you do."

"What, they put them on backward?"

"You know what I mean. You have a great butt, Rafe. You should show it off more."

That made him grin. "I'm not sure that's a good idea in San Francisco."

"Okay, maybe not," she said with a laugh. "Anyway, you'll be in possession of the credit card, so you can rein me in anytime. I don't think it would hurt to have a few extra outfits, though, now that Wyatt's moved here."

"So these would be my Wyoming vacation clothes." He stepped on the brake pedal as they came to the two-lane highway leading into the small town of Shoshone. After glancing both ways, he pulled out.

"Exactly," she said. "You want to fit in when you're here, and now that you're a horseback rider, you really need the right clothes."

"I'm not sure I can call myself a horseback rider yet."

"Sure you can. You were awesome for your first time. After a few more outings, you'll be— Rafe, look out!"

"Shit!" A red pickup was in their lane, coming straight at them.

7

MEG SCREAMED AND COVERED her face with both hands. *Not again. Please, not again!* She braced for the impact, the sound of grinding metal and breaking glass, followed by pain, incredible pain.

The car jerked violently, throwing her against her seat belt. Every muscle in her body tensed, and then... nothing. Gradually she became aware of Rafe beside her, gasping for air.

"It's okay." He drew a shaky breath and his arm came around her shoulders. "We're okay, Meg."

She dared to take her hands away and open her eyes. The car was tilted to the right, off the road, and the engine was still running. She felt light-headed and did her best to breathe, even though she felt as if a giant hand squeezed her chest.

Someone rapped on Rafe's window. She watched in silence as Rafe powered it down to reveal a teenager's agonized stare.

"God, I'm sorry! Are you okay? Is anybody hurt? I have a cell phone. I can call someone. Jesus. I'm so sorry."

Rafe heaved a sigh and shut off the motor. "I think

we're all right." He turned to look at Meg. "Meg? You okay?"

She nodded, unable to speak.

"I don't know what happened!" The kid seemed semihysterical. "When I checked before, the road was deserted, but then, suddenly, there you were! Thank God you have good reflexes, man. Listen, do you need a tow? I have rope. I can get you outta there."

"That might be a good idea." Rafe gave Meg's shoulder a quick squeeze. "Hang on. I'll supervise getting us hitched up to his truck, and then I'll be right back."

"My girlfriend is directing traffic so we won't get run over doing this. Man, I am so sorry."

"Things happen." Rafe unsnapped his seat belt and opened his door. The kid held it while he levered himself out. Once he was standing, he leaned down to give Meg a reassuring smile. "You might want to give Olivia a call and tell her we're running late."

Meg nodded again, although she couldn't call. She didn't want to admit that she'd tightened every muscle for fear that if she relaxed a single one, she'd start shaking uncontrollably. After three years, she'd imagined herself over the shock, but obviously she wasn't.

To be fair, she hadn't been tested until now. A couple of near-misses in a parking lot and having a driver stop suddenly in front of her—those minor close calls didn't count. They'd been nothing like this. She'd been convinced they would die.

Rafe and the kid, who wore a straw cowboy hat and looked no older than eighteen, worked together to attach a rope to the front of the car and the back of the pickup. Meg watched them and tried to keep herself together.

She longed to crawl into bed and curl up in a ball, but that wasn't an option.

Rafe opened the door and eased back inside the car. Then he started it up. "Once we're on the road again I'll be able to tell if there's any damage. The kid's insured, so no worries there." He looked over at Meg. "Were you able to get in touch with Olivia?"

"Not yet."

"She's probably turned off her phone. Did you leave a message? Whoops, here we go." He gripped the wheel as the rope tightened and the car gradually edged up the small embankment and back on the road. Rafe set the emergency brake and got out of the car again.

While Meg watched Rafe and the teenager disconnect the rope, exchange information and shake hands, she began to quiver. Apparently the shakes were going to take over, whether she wanted them to or not. Her teeth began to chatter.

When Rafe came back, he put the car in gear without looking at her and started down the road. "That's that. Or at least, I hope it is. I'll know in a few minutes if we have an alignment problem. Maybe not, but wow. Too close for comfort, huh?" He reached over and took her hand.

Once he touched her, he glanced sharply in her direction. "Meg? Good God, you're not okay, are you?"

"N-not r-really."

"There's a dirt road up ahead. I'll turn off there." He kept giving her worried looks as he approached the road, drove down it and shut off the engine. "What is it? Whiplash? Should I take you to a hospital? Hell, I don't even know where the nearest one is. Screw that. I'll call 9-1-1." He took his phone off the dash.

"No!"

He paused, his finger hovering over the phone. "Meg, you're scaring me. If something's wrong, then I want to get help."

"I j-just need s-somebody to hold m-me."

He was out of the car in a flash and came immediately around to her side. Opening her door, he reached in and unfastened her seat belt, then scooped her up and deposited her in the backseat. He climbed in after her, tossed his hat into the front and pulled her onto his lap.

"Y-you're so w-warm."

"And you're cold as ice." He held her tight. "And shaking like a leaf. I should have realized it sooner."

She clung to him and burrowed against his solid chest. She couldn't seem to get close enough.

"You're okay." He stroked her back and kissed her hair. "You're safe, Meg."

Slowly her tremors subsided, and once they had, she took a shaky breath. "Better."

"Good." He continued to stroke her back. "Take your time. We're in no rush."

"But Livy and Wyatt…"

"I'll call them in a little while, just so they won't worry."

"The thing is…three years ago…I was in…a very bad accident."

Rafe groaned. "No wonder you're a mess." He rocked her gently. "Poor Meg."

"No, *lucky* Meg. I should have died. But I didn't, which everyone said was a miracle."

His arms tightened around her. "That's scary."

"This was the first close call I've had since then. I lost it. Sorry."

"Don't be. You had a perfectly logical reaction. I wish it hadn't happened, but life's unpredictable."

"Exactly. But I didn't always understand that. The accident changed me." Resting her cheek against his chest, she listened to his steady heartbeat and thought how precious that sound was.

"I can imagine it would."

"I'd always been a fairly positive person, but when I realized how easily life can be snuffed out, I vowed to make the most of still being alive, against all odds."

"Which explains why you're so ready to try new things."

"You don't know the half of it. I have a list."

"A bucket list?"

"Sort of, but I'd rather think of it as my celebration-of-life list."

He kissed the top of her head. "Would you show it to me sometime?"

"Sure. But it's not a set list. It's always changing. Some things drop off after I've done them, and other things are added as I think of them."

"I see."

Shifting position, she gazed up at him. "For instance, you're on it now."

He looked into her eyes and smiled. "And exactly how am I on it?"

Her pulse quickened. "I'll bet you can guess."

"I sure hope so. Will I get checked off tonight?"

"I suppose that's possible." She reached up and traced his mouth with her finger. "But I have a feeling once won't be enough."

"I have the same feeling." Leaning down, he captured her lips in a slow, sensuous kiss.

She kissed him back, enthusiasm mingled with gratitude that they'd survived. The kiss quickly heated up and he'd started unbuttoning her blouse when both of their cell phones belted out simultaneous ring tones.

He lifted his head, his gaze hot. "Later."

"It's a date." She climbed off his lap and they both reached into the front seat for their phones so they could assure the bride and groom that all was well.

RAFE WASN'T SURE WHAT haunted him more—the harrowing experience on the road today or the knowledge that Meg had nearly died in an accident three years ago. As he pulled into the dirt parking lot next to the Spirits and Spurs, he admitted that Meg's decision to fully embrace life made a lot of sense.

As he switched off the engine, she unbuckled her seat belt and reached for her door.

"Will you let me help you out?" he asked.

She paused and turned to him. "I'm really fine. You don't have to baby me."

"That's not why I want to do it. I think of it as a gesture of…caring. I realize you're capable of getting out of a car by yourself, but then I lose the chance to be gallant."

She smiled. "You were very gallant when I went through that meltdown."

"I hope so. I never gave it much thought before, but gallantry appeals to me. Some women object to it on the grounds that I'm not treating them like an equal."

She took her hand off the door. "I won't. I'm secure in my equality."

"Good to know." He couldn't help chuckling. She was such a fascinating combination of spunkiness and vulnerability.

"The longer I'm around you, Rafe, the more I think you really are a cowboy underneath that sophisticated exterior."

"City boys can be gallant, too, you know."

"I'm sure, but it seems to go with the life out here, somehow. To me, cowboys are the modern equivalent of knights in armor, and when I think of gallantry, I think of knights."

"In that case, I'll be as much of a cowboy this week as I can manage, given my limitations." He climbed out of the car and walked around to her side feeling happy to be alive. Meg helped him keep his priorities straight.

When they walked into the Spirits and Spurs he had the unwelcome thought that his mother would hate it there. His father might, too. It was old, and the tables were scarred from years of hard use. The overriding smell indicated that beer was more popular than any other beverage.

A few days ago, Rafe probably would have turned up his nose at the idea of having lunch in a cowboy beer joint. Yet now he could hardly wait to slide into a booth and order up a pitcher and some eats. It suddenly seemed like the most fun he could have, short of taking Meg to bed. And he looked forward to enjoying that tonight.

The place was full of lunch patrons enjoying exactly the kind of meal Rafe had in mind—a juicy burger and a big pile of fries. His parents would roll their eyes, but they weren't here, and he was enjoying a sense of liberation. Wyatt and Olivia waved from a booth across the room, and he put his hand in the small of Meg's back and guided her over to them.

Olivia jumped up and gave Meg a hug. "How awful for you, sweetie! I hate that you went through that."

Wyatt slid out of the booth and held his hand out to his brother. "Thanks for getting here safe and sound, bro. I wonder if we need to haul that kid into traffic court. He shouldn't have—"

"It was a rookie mistake," Rafe said. "He looked terrified, and I doubt he'll try anything like that again without checking and double-checking. I think he'll punish himself enough reliving that moment when we almost crashed."

Olivia shuddered and glanced at Meg. "I can only imagine what went through your mind."

"You probably can. You were there to get me past the trauma three years ago."

"I was." She looked over at Rafe. "Did she tell you she had a near-fatal accident?"

"Yeah." And Rafe was so grateful that she had told him. If their positions had been reversed, he wondered if he would have been that willing to share. He had much to learn from Meg.

Wyatt studied his brother and his gray eyes twinkled. "Nice duds there, Rafe. Did Sarah fix you up?"

"As a matter of fact, she did."

"Well done." Wyatt gestured to the table. "As you can see, Olivia and I started on a pitcher, but let's get another one and have some food. What sounds good?" Then he hesitated. "Or maybe we should rustle up a bottle of wine. I'm sure they have—"

"Beer's fine," Rafe said. "In fact, beer and a burger would be perfect for me, but I can't speak for Meg."

Wyatt looked surprised, but he didn't make a comment.

"I'd be very happy with a burger and a beer," Meg said. "At this point, I could use some comfort food."

"Coming up." Wyatt signaled a waitress and gestured for Rafe and Meg to have a seat. After the waitress took their order, he glanced across the table at his brother. "How was the ride this morning?"

"Good." Rafe nodded. "It was good."

"Rafe was amazing," Meg said. "He picked up on the basics in no time. I think we have a cowboy on our hands."

"Really?" Wyatt raised both eyebrows. "I never would have figured that."

"Meg's exaggerating. I had beginner's luck. Besides, they put me up on Destiny, the old man of the barn. I couldn't go wrong."

Olivia laughed. "I've heard tales of that horse from when Jack was teaching Josie to ride a couple of years ago. Isn't Destiny the one who likes to head on home if his rider gets off and doesn't tie him up good?"

"That's the one." Meg grimaced. "I tied Destiny to my horse, and before we realized it, Spilled Milk was ready to lay into Destiny because he was trying to drag her away from her station."

Wyatt looked amused as he glanced from Meg to Rafe. "So, brother-of-mine, you didn't notice that the horses were getting snippy with each other?"

Rafe gave Wyatt the evil eye. "We were admiring the spectacular scenery. It's easy to get caught up in the view when you're in this part of the country."

"So it is." Wyatt picked up his mug of beer and took a sip while unsuccessfully hiding a grin.

"Are the caterers all set for Saturday?" Meg asked.

Rafe could recognize a change of subject when he heard one, and he followed her lead. "Yeah, how's everything going? As the best man I need to know these things."

"The caterers are all set," Olivia said. "We'll double-check on the flower delivery after lunch to make sure what we ordered will actually be here."

"I feel as if I should be doing more," Rafe said. "Are you sure you don't want me to organize a bach-elor party?"

Wyatt shook his head. "Olivia and I would ten times rather have a party here for everyone Thursday night. This tradition of separating the men and women doesn't work for us."

"So I might as well cancel the stripper." Rafe sighed as if bitterly disappointed.

"Maybe not." Olivia shared a glance with Meg. "Did you hire a man or a woman?"

"He didn't hire either one," Wyatt said, "because I told him not to." He paused. "You didn't, right?"

"No, I followed your instructions, but from the way the female contingent is looking at me, maybe we need to rethink this. Ladies, do you want a male stripper at the party Thursday night?"

Olivia leaned forward. "Could we have a guy wear-ing tight jeans and chaps?"

"And shirtless, but with a leather vest," Meg added. "And spurs on his boots. I want him to jingle when he walks."

"Yes!" Olivia and Meg exchanged high fives across the table.

"Ooo, and leather gloves with fringe, right, Livy?"

"You have such good taste, Meg. You can create my fantasy cowboy any day."

Wyatt groaned. "Pay no attention to them, Rafe. They have a warped idea of what looks good on a man."

"It's what looks good coming *off* a man that's important," Meg said.

"Keep talking." Rafe pulled a napkin out of the dispenser. "If someone can loan me a pen, I'll make some notes so I get this right."

Meg turned to him. "For Thursday night?"

He winked at her. "That, too."

8

ALL THE KIDDING AROUND at lunch helped Meg relax and forget about the incident on the road into town, but once she and Rafe were headed for Jackson on another two-lane road, she tensed up again. Not good. This week would involve lots of time riding in cars and trucks.

"A leather vest with no shirt, huh?" Rafe glanced over at her. "That's what it takes?"

"It's a start." She tried her best to sound upbeat and teasing. Maybe Rafe wouldn't notice that she wasn't quite into it.

"I don't know about the chaps, though. That might be overkill."

"Possibly so." She'd conquer this case of nerves. She had to.

His response was a couple of beats late, and he'd switched topics on her. "I'm really curious about this list of yours. Can you tell me more about what you've already done?"

That brief hesitation and change in topic told her he'd guessed that she was nervous about being back on the road. Instead of asking her about it, he'd decided to subtly remind her of moments she'd been strong and brave. That kind of empathy didn't come along every day.

"I tried hang gliding last year when I was in San Diego for a traffic control conference."

"Did you like it?"

"You bet. My job takes up too much time, so I haven't gone back to it. If I change jobs and move here, I'm looking for a less time-consuming position so I can build in breaks for things like that."

"You might have to take a pay cut."

"That's okay. I don't need a lot of money." She watched with some apprehension as they came up behind a slow-moving semi. No doubt Rafe would want to get around the truck. Well, she'd just take a deep breath and keep calm.

"I've always wanted to try hang gliding. There's this guy named Hutchinson out of San Francisco who makes amazing videos of sports like that. Have you seen any of them?"

"I have, as a matter of fact. Did you know he was born in Shoshone and his dad runs the feed store there?"

"Huh. Small world."

"He's good friends with Jack Chance, and I'm pretty sure he'll be at the wedding. If so, you can meet him."

"I'd like that." He made no move to pass the truck. "So what else have you done?"

"Rafe, you don't have to poke along behind this truck. I'll be fine if you want to pass."

"We're in no rush."

"No, but we're doing ten miles under the speed limit. The truck's put on his left-turn signal twice to let you know you can go around."

"You're sure?"

"Yep."

He let out a breath. "Thank God." Easing out to check traffic, he tromped on the gas and the powerful car zoomed around the eighteen-wheeler and back over to the right side of the road. "I could tell you were still a little freaked out, so I didn't want to make it worse."

"I know, and I appreciate that." She gazed at him. Besides being the hunkiest chauffeur she'd ever had, he also looked relaxed and confident behind the wheel. The last of her tension drained away. "But I'm fine now."

"I believe you." He gave her a smile before returning his attention to the road. "I can hear it in your voice."

"You were smart to get me talking about my list."

He shrugged. "I just hated to think of you white-knuckling it all the way to Jackson. It's not your style."

Warmth flooded through her. "That might be the nicest thing you've said to me. It's *not* my style, which is why I hated falling apart like that. But you've been great about it. No wonder clients trust you with all their money."

"And that might be the nicest thing you've said to me."

"I'm worried about you, though, Rafe."

His eyebrows lifted. "Me? Why?"

"I have a bad feeling you're all work and no play."

"No, I'm not. I go out to dinner. I catch a movie now and then."

"That's all fine, but I mean something exciting to get your blood pumping."

His smile was incredibly sexy. "I didn't think it was appropriate to mention *that* kind of excitement, considering the plans you and I have tonight."

"Oh, for heaven's sake. I didn't mean sex. I meant like taking a sailboat out on San Francisco Bay."

"I've done that."

"When?"

"Um, maybe ten years ago. My friend who had a boat sold it." He passed another slow-moving truck. "Would you like to go sailing on the bay?"

"Is that an invitation?"

"Absolutely. If you ever come to San Francisco, I'll take you sailing. Give me some advance warning, and I'll brush up my skills. You'd love it."

And so would he, she thought. The next part wasn't easy to say, but she made herself say it. "You don't have to wait for me to come to San Francisco. I'll bet there are plenty of women who would be thrilled if you took them sailing."

"I'd rather wait for you."

"Why on earth would you wait? It might be a year or two before I show up. And I can tell you want to do it."

"With you, yeah, but not with some random woman who might or might not get a kick out of going. I have no doubt that you would eat it up with a spoon, and we'd have a great time."

He was so cautious and guarded. She didn't know all the reasons why, but she could guess from things Olivia had said. Rafe and Wyatt's self-absorbed mother hadn't given them much attention and their workaholic father hadn't, either. Rafe seemed to have modeled himself after his dad, maybe hoping for approval from at least one parent.

She decided not to push the issue anymore. Obviously work and a familiar routine had been his shield for many years. If it lacked exhilarating highs, at least it didn't have devastating lows, either.

But she wouldn't give up on him. Their successful horseback ride told her that he still had the capacity to cut loose, and his kiss told her that a passionate man lurked under his careful exterior. Tonight she'd find out exactly how passionate he could be, and she could hardly wait.

RAFE TURNED THE CONVERSATION back to Meg's list, and she allowed him to do that. He found out about her hike through the Alps, and her future plan to walk the Great Wall someday soon. Her list ranged from spending an entire day at the Louvre in Paris to bungee jumping in Queenstown, New Zealand.

He was relieved that she'd seemed to give up on her campaign to inject some excitement into his San Francisco life. She might have a demanding job with the City of Pittsburgh, but he doubted she could imagine the pressures he faced every day, knowing the financial effect his recommendations could have on his wealthy clients. Planning a sailing date with someone he didn't know well would only add to his stress.

Still, as he listened to her describe the things she'd done and those she planned to do, he got caught up in her excitement. He wouldn't mind tagging along on some of those trips. Finding the time would be a challenge, but her enthusiasm was infectious.

He decided not to mention his interest, though. Such plans were more of a pipe dream than a reality for him. If she thought he wanted to go, she might start counting on it, and he couldn't promise that.

They finally arrived in Jackson, a town crowded

with cars bearing out-of-state plates. He had to circle the square twice before a parking spot opened up. But when it did, he pulled in right in front of the store he was headed for. Wyatt had told him which one would carry clothes suited to the wedding plus anything else he decided to buy for his own use.

Although he'd balked at taking Meg with him at first, now he was glad she'd suggested coming along. What would have been a boring trip to buy clothes he didn't actually want could turn into a great afternoon. Meg had a gift for making everything seem special.

She waited for him to help her out of the car, but once she was out, she was in bouncy tour-guide mode. "In that far corner of the square is the vintage clothing shop where Olivia and I found our dresses for the wedding. Next to it is Silver Reflections, the jewelry shop where I bought the earrings I wore last night."

"I liked those. I wonder if you need another pair." The idea of buying her jewelry was much more appealing than shopping for his clothes.

"Not really. I don't dress up that much." She pointed across the square. "Over there in the middle of the block is the gallery that carries Dominique's photography. If we have time after buying your stuff, we should go over."

"She's Nick's wife, right?" He hoped by the day of the wedding he'd have all the vitals of this family down.

"Right. It was pictures of Nick in cowboy mode that launched her career in Jackson Hole." Meg looked him up and down. "Has Dominique seen you in those clothes yet?"

"If she's the tall one with short brown hair…"

"That's her."

"Then, no. In the kitchen this morning I met the redhead and her little girl."

"That's Morgan, Gabe Chance's wife, and little S.B., aka Sarah Bianca. Anyway, I'll bet Dominique would love to get some shots of you in full garb. She's been after Jack to do it, and he won't, but you look so much like him, she might pounce on you instead."

Rafe shook his head. "She'll have to keep hounding Jack. I feel like enough of a fraud wearing this stuff without having pictures of me on display somewhere."

"I doubt Dominique will take that as a valid excuse, but you can try." She turned back toward the Western clothing store. "Ready to put a dent in your credit card?"

"I don't mind that part. But let's make this as quick as possible. Even if you don't get dressed up much, I'd like to check out the jewelry shop."

She smiled at him. "You don't have to buy me jewelry, Rafe."

"I know. But I'd like to."

"So I'll think of you when I wear it?"

He blinked at the accuracy of her statement. That was exactly what he wanted, although he hadn't realized it until she'd said so. He didn't want to fade out of her memory at the end of the week.

"I'll think of you whether you buy me jewelry or not," she said softly. "So save your money for other things, like a ticket back to Jackson Hole at Christmas."

"I can afford both."

She gazed at him and finally her green eyes began to twinkle with laughter. "So be it. If you want to throw your money around on jewelry for me, I'd be a fool to turn it down."

"I'm glad you've seen the light. Maybe we should do that first."

"No." She laced her fingers through his and tugged. "Come on, Rafe. Take your medicine like a man."

"All right." He sighed and walked with her toward the store. "But I want to start with the leather vests."

She paused and glanced at him. "Are you serious?"

"Isn't that what you said turned you on?"

"Yes, but I didn't think you'd actually be willing to buy one."

"Hey, now that you've confessed one of your fantasies, I might as well work it."

She grinned. "I like your attitude. You'll have to try it on without a shirt so I can tell if it's the right look. Will you do that?"

"*No.* For God's sake, Meg. I'll buy the vest, but I'm not parading around in the store wearing a vest and no shirt underneath. I'll look like an idiot."

"Then if you won't come out of the dressing room wearing the vest, I'll have to come in."

He stared at her. "I don't think so."

"If I did, I could check something else off my list."

"What?"

"Making out with a cute guy in a dressing room." Her cheeks were pink with excitement. "It's number fourteen."

He recognized a challenge when he heard one. She was daring him to go along with her crazy idea. And the more he thought about it, the more turned on he was. Maybe this shopping trip wouldn't be so boring, after all.

Squeezing her hand, he reached for the door. "First we have to find out if they have any vests that you like."

"If they don't, maybe you'd model some chaps without your—"

"That's where I draw the line, toots."

She laughed as they walked into a store that he instantly recognized as exclusive. Exclusive stores often had full doors on the dressing rooms. He began to anticipate getting Meg alone in one of them.

Glancing around, he noticed that the place catered to manly men. One wall held nothing but boots and belts, and the scent of oiled leather permeated the store. Jeans and shirts were neatly folded on planks supported by oak barrels. Any vacant wall space had been filled with coiled ropes, spurs and branding irons.

Rafe counted about six people shopping and at least two sales ladies. One of them, a middle-aged woman wearing a sparkly Western shirt and red jeans beamed as she walked in their direction. "May I help you?"

"I need something for a wedding at the Last Chance this weekend," Rafe said. "I'm the best man."

"Yes, of course. That would be the Locke-Sedgewick wedding."

"That's right. Meg is going to help me pick out something."

"Perfect." The woman started toward the back of the store. "If you'll both follow me, I'll show you the jackets first."

"Thanks." He stroked his thumb over Meg's palm. "Oh, and by the way, do you happen to carry any leather vests?"

"We do, but a leather vest worn under your Western jacket will get quite warm this time of year. If you want the look of a vest, I suggest fabric."

Meg spoke up. "The leather vest is for...another time."

"Ah." The woman glanced over her shoulder at Meg. "So you're also interested in some articles that aren't specifically wedding-related."

Meg nodded. "We are. In fact, if you'll point me toward the leather vests, you and Rafe can discuss jackets."

"They're on the far left wall hanging below our display of hats."

"Be right back." Meg slipped her hand from his and with a saucy little wink went in search of vests.

Rafe watched her go. He didn't hear the saleswoman's question until she tapped him on the arm. He turned to her and felt heat rising up from his collar. "Sorry. You were saying?"

"What color jacket are you interested in?"

"The groom said I should look for something in dove-gray."

"Excellent choice. Let's see what we have in your size."

Rafe managed to pay attention long enough to give her his coat size and pretend interest as she handed him three different jackets on sturdy wooden hangers.

"And you'll need Western dress slacks to go with that. Those are over here." The woman started moving toward a different section of the store.

"Wait a sec. I don't want to lose Meg."

The saleswoman chuckled. "Oh, I'm sure she'll find you."

Of course she would, but he didn't want her to go hunting all over the store. That would waste time, and he could hardly wait to find a way to slip into one of the dressing rooms and…

"Waist and inseam?"

He focused on the saleswoman again and gave her his measurements. Then he scanned the store, looking for that bright mass of curls bobbing around somewhere in the aisles. And there she was, coming toward him with an armful of leather vests and a triumphant grin that made him want to laugh out loud.

He'd never shop for clothes again without thinking of her smug expression as she brought him the makings of her cowboy fantasy. He hoped to hell he could live up to the image she carried in that creative mind of hers.

9

MEG WALKED WITH RAFE OVER to the hallway that led to a row of dressing rooms, but she didn't want their ever-helpful sales lady to guess her intention. She piled the vests on top of the clothes Rafe already held in his arms. "Go ahead and try everything on," she said. "I'll be out here if you want to show me anything." Then she sat primly in one of the two leather wing chairs near the dressing rooms.

"I'll just put you in number three," the woman said. "My name is Clara. Let me know if you need any different sizes."

Rafe cast a quick glance at Meg. "Thanks so much, Clara. I'm sure something out of this pile will work." Then he walked into the dressing room and closed the door.

While her pulse danced a jig, Meg counted to sixty. Then, making sure nobody was watching, she walked quickly to Rafe's dressing room and turned the knob. He'd locked it.

Rapping softly, she lowered her voice. "It's me."

The door opened immediately and he pulled her inside. "Sorry. Habit." Then he crushed her against his chest and brought his mouth down on hers.

Rafe had the sort of kiss that demanded her full attention, and yet as she wrapped her arms around him, she realized that his were bare. And he was wearing one of the leather vests.

Although she couldn't see him, her roving hands provided enough tactile evidence to visualize her fantasy, and she moaned softly as she wiggled closer. The scent of leather and aroused male released a flood of happy hormones into her system.

He lifted his mouth from hers. "Is this what you had in mind?"

"Oh, yeah." She kissed his chin, moved down to the sexy hollow in his throat, and kept on going. Spreading the lapels of the vest aside, she licked her way to each flat nipple as she stroked his soft chest hair.

"Meg." His voice was strained. "Maybe you shouldn't do that."

"Yes, I definitely should. You're delicious." She used her tongue to trace a moist path to his navel and felt him shudder.

When she dropped to her knees and reached for his zipper, he closed his hand over hers. "I don't think—"

"Right. Don't think." Pushing his hand away, she drew the zipper down. Blood pounded in her ears. She'd never been so bold with a man in a public place. Then again, she'd never been so inspired to be bold.

He might have protested, but he was more than ready for her. When she dipped her hand inside the opening of his briefs, his erect cock surged forward. She took a moment to caress and admire the beauty of it.

If he really wanted to stop her, he could do it now.

But instead he trembled and thrust his fingers through her hair. She took him into her mouth.

He tasted of forbidden pleasures and untamed lust. Her heart raced as she measured the length of him with her lips and tongue. He was magnificent, and tonight he would be all hers.

This was only a short preview, and she couldn't take long or someone would suspect. Hollowing her cheeks, she applied pressure right where she knew it would accomplish the most good. His fingers tightened against her scalp, and he gasped once before his hot, salty essence filled her mouth.

Swallowing what he'd given her, she remained still for a moment as he fought to get his breathing under control. Then she slowly released him, tucked him back into his briefs, and zipped his fly. Then she rose, nibbling her way back up his body until she finally reached his lips.

He kissed her deeply before drawing back, his dark eyes smoldering and his voice husky. "That was amazing."

"Glad you enjoyed it."

A sharp rap sounded on the dressing room door. "Finding anything you like?" called the saleswoman.

Gazing down at Meg, Rafe smiled. "Sure am."

"Good! Let me know if you need anything."

"Thanks, but this should do it."

Meg leaned back to survey the vest, which had been her favorite of the ones she'd found. But she didn't dare speak until the saleswoman was gone.

"You chose well," she said at last, keeping her voice low. The leather was dark brown and supple, the design simple and slightly retro. It showed off Rafe's magnificent chest and sculpted arms to perfection.

"You don't want to see how the others look?"

She shook her head. "This one already has a very good association for me. I'd love to see it on you again."

"With that kind of reaction, I'll wear it any time you want. Sadly, now I have to pick out the boring stuff."

"I know. I'll be outside in the chair, ready to give my opinion."

He touched her cheek. "So, did we take care of number fourteen?"

"Fourteen *and* fifteen."

He laughed softly. "I really need to get a look at that list."

She fully intended to show it to him, but before she did, she might add a few things. Being with Rafe was expanding her horizons.

RAFE WASN'T SURE WHAT HE bought besides the vest. He was too blissed out from Meg's dressing-room treat to care what else went on his credit card. He suspected she'd used his mellow mood to talk him into more jeans and shirts than he would ever need.

Eventually they'd stashed the bags of clothes in the trunk of the Lexus and he put enough brain cells together to remember about the jewelry shop. "I still want to get you some earrings." Taking her hand, he started walking around the square.

"It's liable to cost you. Silver Reflections only sells Native American pieces and none of them are cheap. I splurged on those silver-and-turquoise ones."

"I feel in the mood to splurge."

"You may not realize it because you were sort of

catatonic back there in the Western-wear store, but you already splurged. You might want to pull out your sales slip and reconsider a trip to the jewelry store."

He shook his head. "That was all for me. I want something for you."

"The vest was for me."

He flashed back to the moment she'd slid to her knees in the dressing room. "Maybe so, but I made out like a bandit on that vest deal. I think we could have a long argument as to who benefited the most from it."

"Do you think the saleswoman had any idea what was going on in there?"

"If she did, she's too good a salesperson to let a little thing like oral sex in the dressing room interfere with writing up a big order."

"Aha!" She glanced up at him. "So you did realize that we ran up a sizable bill in there. I thought maybe you were oblivious."

"Oblivious to the type and amount of clothes." He smiled at her. "But finances are my game. I'm incapable of ignoring the bottom line, so believe me, I saw and registered the total."

"You could have objected."

"Nope. That was the best shopping trip of my life. If I end up giving half of those things to charity, I don't care. I don't have a list like yours, but if I did, I'd put getting a blow job in a dressing room right near the top."

"Woo-hoo!" Meg let go of his hand and threw her arms in the air. "Progress in the having-fun department!"

"Don't get cocky. This doesn't mean I plan to take some unidentified woman sailing on San Francisco Bay."

"About that."

"You can talk until you're blue in the face, Meg, but I'm not doing it. I now have a mental picture of taking you out there, and I'm sticking with that scenario. It's you or nobody."

"That suits me fine."

"It does?" He recaptured her hand. "I thought you were determined to get me out on a boat, with or without you."

"I suggested that because I didn't want to hold you back, but…it turns out I don't want you taking some other woman sailing."

"Oh?" He couldn't help feeling really great about that.

"I'm not proud of myself for saying so, Rafe. A true friend would want you to enjoy yourself, even if she couldn't be there."

"Correct me if I'm wrong, but I think we've gone a few steps past friendship. Not that we can't be friends, too, but what happened back in the dressing room adds another layer of meaning, don't you think?"

"It wouldn't have to. We could write it off as one of those thrilling little moments that is here and gone."

"Some people might be able to do that, those who skate along on the surface of their emotions." The way he'd been accustomed to doing until he'd met her. "You don't strike me as that kind of person."

"Well, I'm not, but on the other hand, we both agreed we're not looking for anything permanent."

He wondered if she was trying to convince him or her. "Right. No strings, no obligations. But the sailing date was your idea, so I'm reserving that experience for you and me. Does that work for you?"

She smiled up at him. "Perfectly. It's simple, really. Any activity we discuss doing together is reserved for us."

"Like me giving you skiing lessons this winter?"

"Precisely. And if you want a hang gliding buddy, I'm your girl."

His girl. The thought made his breath catch, but in a good way. He wondered if they were both kidding themselves about the future of this relationship. One of them might get invested, after all, and he had a funny feeling it could be him.

Yet if he knew she didn't want that, he could put on the brakes if he had to. Maybe everything would work out the way she envisioned and they'd meet at various times to sail, ski, hang glide and make love, all without a commitment of any kind.

It was an interesting concept and the only one that made sense considering his schedule. He'd have to juggle his work in order to find time for those activities, but he'd do it. The prospect of seeing Meg several times a year was worth crunching his other obligations.

Silver Reflections was a small shop, but dense with shiny stuff. Rafe hadn't been inside many jewelry stores, but he was used to cases of gems like diamonds, rubies and emeralds. This place didn't deal in precious stones.

Instead the cases included gold and silver decorated with turquoise, mostly, although there were other opaque stones in various colors. Rafe noticed a few ornate necklaces that seemed almost old-fashioned compared with the beautiful simplicity of others.

The shop was empty of customers when they walked in. The man behind the counter wore a Western shirt along with a bola tie containing a piece of turquoise as big as a hen's egg. He looked Native American, and his lined and weathered face could belong to a man of fifty or eighty. Rafe couldn't begin to guess his age.

He smiled. "Welcome."

"Thank you." Rafe expected more—an offer to sell them something, a suggestion about jewelry for the pretty lady—but the man said nothing else. Instead he simply watched them with polite interest.

Meg walked forward and held out her hand. "Hello, Samuel. I'm Meg. You probably don't remember, but I was in here a few days ago with my friend Olivia. We each bought earrings."

The man's face creased in a wider smile as he took her hand in both of his. "Now I remember who you are! Your friend is getting married."

"She is. On Saturday. This is Rafe Locke, the best man."

"Glad to meet you, Samuel." Rafe shook the man's hand and noticed he was also wearing a watch with a turquoise-studded band and a couple of elaborate turquoise rings.

"Samuel's a silversmith," Meg said. "He's made many of the pieces you see. Like that, for instance." She pointed to a dramatic necklace in the glass case.

"I noticed that when we came in." Rafe had never seen anything quite like it. A strip of polished silver about half an inch wide had been shaped to fit the back of a woman's neck and then spiral forward into an elegant coil that ended in a green stone the exact color of Meg's eyes. "I'd like to see what that looks like on."

Meg laughed and shook her head. "No, you wouldn't. It's way too expensive."

"I'm not saying we'll buy it, but I'm fascinated by the design. Samuel, would you mind if Meg tried it on?"

"Of course not." He unlocked the case and tenderly withdrew the necklace. "I remember you looked at this one last time, Meg, but you didn't ask me to show it to you." He took the tag off before handing the necklace to her.

"No point in that." Meg turned the necklace so it caught the light. "It's out of my price range. This is the sort of necklace Harrison Ford would buy for Calista."

Samuel nodded. "Harrison did look at it, as a matter of fact. But he couldn't decide, so it's still here, waiting for you."

"Not for me, but it's fun to think I'm trying on a necklace that Harrison Ford considered." Pulling aside the collar of her white shirt, she fit the molded silver end of the spiral around the back of her neck. "I love the idea that it doesn't need a fastener of any kind." She settled it against her breastbone, where it nestled as if made to rest there.

Rafe had known he'd buy the necklace for her the minute he'd seen it, but now that she had it on, he was even more convinced. "You need to undo one more button of your blouse to show it off."

"How scandalous." She winked at him and unfastened the button. "The silver feels cool on my skin."

"It'll warm up as you wear it," Samuel said. "Looks good on you. You're the right one for malachite."

"So that's malachite?" Rafe took a closer look at the stone, which had faint bands of black running through it. "I know nothing about these things, but I like it."

Samuel glanced at Meg. "When's your birthday?"

"Not for months, if you're thinking I need a birthday present, Samuel."

"No, I wasn't thinking that. I just wondered the day."

"November fifth. Why?"

Rafe blinked. His and Wyatt's birthday was November third.

Samuel looked pleased with himself. "*That's* why the necklace is so right for you. I had a feeling about you from the beginning. Malachite is your birthstone."

"I thought my birthstone was topaz."

"It can be, but so is malachite, and I personally think that's a more interesting choice."

"So do I," Rafe said. "We'll take it."

Meg's eyes widened. "We most certainly will *not* take it." She started to remove the necklace.

Rafe put a restraining hand over hers. "Meg, it's perfect on you." He glanced toward Samuel for backup. "Isn't it?"

"Yes." Samuel gazed at Meg. "I thought so the first time you came in the store, but then you left without it."

"For a very good reason. It's beyond my means."

"I understand that, but when I create a piece of jewelry, I always imagine who will wear it. You'll probably think I'm making this up, but it's the truth. When I worked on that necklace I imagined a woman with fiery hair and green eyes, a woman born in November who had a zest for life." He spread both hands. "And here you are."

"That's a lovely sentiment, but the necklace costs too much." She cast a pleading glance at Rafe. "Don't let yourself get carried away."

"You heard the man. He made the necklace for you." Rafe had listened to plenty of sales pitches in his life, and he recognized Samuel wasn't making one. The guy was an artist who wouldn't push his creations on those who didn't want them.

"We came in here for earrings," Meg said. "I'll accept a pair of earrings from you, Rafe, but this…"

Samuel pulled a small booklet out from under the counter. "Meg, what do you know about this stone?"

She turned back to the counter. "Only that it's pretty."

"It's more than pretty." He thumbed through the book. "Here we are—'malachite is a stone for the adventurous spirit, a risk-taker who yearns to live more fully and find unconditional love.'" He closed the book and gazed at her.

"Wow." She swallowed and placed her hand over the green stone. "That's…that's me."

Rafe felt a little shaky. That certainly described his brother, but he'd always thought he and Wyatt were polar opposites. Still, those words struck a deep chord in him, as well.

Maybe he wasn't so different from Wyatt, after all. He'd tried hard to be Wyatt's opposite, and…this was hard to admit, but he'd done it mostly to please his father. What had started out as the purchase of a beautiful piece of jewelry for Meg was turning out to be much more significant than he'd planned on.

"You notice I designed the necklace so it doesn't need a clasp," Samuel said.

Meg nodded.

"That wasn't just a random decision, or me trying to leap ahead of the pack with some clever innovation." His voice grew soft and slightly roughened with emotion. "I made it open-ended to signify freedom—

freedom to live and freedom to love. It needs to go to the right person."

"I don't think there's any doubt that Meg's the right person." Rafe pulled his wallet from his back pocket. "That's your necklace, Meg."

"But—"

"Furthermore, unless you object strongly, you should wear it out of the store." He took his credit card out and gave it to Samuel.

"Meg." Samuel looked at her. "Call me a crazy old man if you want, but I believe it's bad luck to refuse such a heartfelt gesture."

"Oh, I don't think you're crazy," Meg said. "But I'm not so sure about my friend Rafe, here."

Rafe wasn't convinced of his sanity, either. Buying a necklace, expensive or not, because the stone and the design had special significance wasn't typical of the Rafe Locke who'd arrived in Jackson Hole. The cost of the necklace hadn't bothered him at all and he'd have paid twice that to see Meg wearing the glorious spiral of silver.

But it wasn't the purchase of a high-end necklace making the ground shift beneath his feet. It was the growing suspicion that the woman wearing it had the power to change his life forever.

10

MEG KEPT TOUCHING THE necklace all the way back to the car. "I've never had anything this beautiful in my life," she said. "I don't know how I'll ever thank you."

"This would be the right time for me to make all kinds of lewd suggestions as to how you can thank me, but I won't, because I already have my thanks just looking at you wearing it."

"I wanted to scoff at his story about picturing someone like me as he made it, but..."

"I believe him. I'm sure he does that all the time, and when it works out, he's excited like he was today. I'm sure customers come in who aren't right for a piece he's made, but he has to sell it to them anyway. That must be a little frustrating."

"I feel like a princess wearing this."

He glanced over at her and smiled. "You'd be beautiful without it, but I have to admit I'm taken with how that bit of malachite directs me straight to your cleavage."

"And I thought you liked the malachite because it matches my eyes."

"That, too. Incidentally, Wyatt's and my birthday is two days before yours."

"Really? Then malachite is your birthstone, too."

"Guess so."

She thought about what Samuel had read out of the book he kept under the counter—*malachite is a stone for the adventurous spirit, a risk-taker who yearns to live more fully and find unconditional love.* "What did you think of that stuff Samuel read to us?"

"I'm still mulling it over."

She'd just bet he was. "Those things aren't always accurate." But she thought it described the person he could become, even if he wasn't there yet.

"I know." He looked over at her. "But it fits you to a T."

"I thought so, too. It was eerie. I was drawn to that necklace when I first saw it, but I figured it was the artistry of the design that pulled me in. It's so different. But I knew nothing about malachite or the properties he claims it has. Now I want to learn more."

"Your wish is my command." He pulled his iPhone out of his pocket as they reached the car. Leaning against the fender, he tapped on the screen. "I'll look it up on Google."

"I didn't think about it, but your phone hasn't rung once this afternoon."

"Kind of hard for it to ring when it's off."

"You turned it off? When?"

"When we got to the Spirits and Spurs. I didn't want anything interrupting our lunch, and then I didn't want to have it ringing while we drove up here."

"You didn't have to turn it off." She was amazed that he'd made that decision. "I wouldn't have minded."

"I would have minded. I wanted to talk to you, not to someone in San Francisco."

"Thank you." She admired how good he looked leaning against the fender in his jeans, boots, Western shirt and hat. A pickup truck would have suited the image better than the Lexus, but he seemed comfortable with the luxury car.

She didn't doubt that he made good money and the necklace hadn't been as damaging to his budget as it would have been to hers. That didn't mean she felt totally okay with his purchase. Yet Samuel had made a good point. When someone truly wanted to bestow a gift, it would be ungracious to refuse, even if she didn't believe it was bad luck as Samuel seemed to think.

Rafe glanced up from his phone. "Are you ready for the scoop on malachite?"

"I am." She touched the stone, which seemed warmer than it had when she put it on. It had probably soaked up some sun in addition to her body heat.

"Besides what Samuel told us, malachite is a stone of transformation."

"Is that so? Am I going to become a werewolf or something?"

He chuckled. "I don't think that's the kind of transformation they're talking about. They mention breaking outworn patterns and…oh, I like this part. It's supposed to release inhibitions." He glanced up from the screen and waggled his eyebrows at her.

Meg laughed. "So it will transform me into a wild woman?"

"I guess we'll see, won't we? And speaking of that, it's time to head back home via the drugstore."

"The drugstore? Why do we—" And then she remembered. "Oh, yes. The *drugstore*."

"And it's getting late. I'm sure Sarah expects us for dinner."

"She does. I had hoped we'd have time to stop at the gallery and take a look at Dominique's photographs, but we should probably skip that. I didn't expect to spend so much time in the jewelry store."

"I'm really glad we did, though." He shoved his phone back in his pocket and pulled out his car keys. "That necklace looks terrific on you."

"If malachite is your birthstone, shouldn't you be wearing it, too?"

"Sorry, but that necklace just doesn't go with my outfit." He opened the passenger door and ushered her in.

She rolled her eyes at him as she slid onto the leather seat. "I didn't mean the necklace, but something else, like a belt buckle with a piece of malachite on it."

"Now that *would* be a total waste of money. I might wear the jeans we bought on weekends, and possibly even the shirts sometimes, but there's no way in hell I'm walking around sporting a Western belt buckle like some urban cowboy."

"Okay, but don't be surprised if you end up being all inhibited because you resisted the power of the malachite."

Leaning down, he gave her a quick, hard kiss. "Something tells me if you lose your inhibitions, I'll give up on mine, too. We sort of proved that today in the dressing room. Now buckle up. We have to make tracks for the drugstore."

Meg had no idea where the nearest one was, but Rafe pulled up MapQuest on his phone and soon had them parked in front of what Rafe was now referring to as the "condom outlet."

"I'm sure people depend on this store for other things besides condoms," Meg said.

"I can't imagine what." He turned off the motor and unlatched his seat belt. "Want to come in with me?"

She thought about it for all of two seconds. "Yes, I do. I've never tagged along on a condom shopping trip."

"Don't tell me that's on your list."

"No, but maybe it should have been."

Rafe sighed and shook his head. "I'm not planning to linger over the selection, but if you want the experience, I'm not about to deprive you."

Moments later, Meg stood in front of the display while Rafe searched for the type he preferred. "It's been a while since I've looked at these," she said. "I had no idea there were so many different kinds."

"This is an especially well-stocked store," Rafe said. "Ah, there they are." He unhooked a package from a metal display rod.

"What did you get?" She glanced at the package. "Those don't look very interesting. Don't you want ones with ribs?"

He glanced at her with a grin. "I don't. Do you?"

"I'm not sure." She lowered her voice. "I've never had ribs before. At least I don't think I have. Are ribs a good idea?"

"Once again, I'm the wrong person to ask. They aren't going to do anything for me, but apparently they're supposed to provide an extra thrill for you. If you want me to get ribs, I will."

"Nah." She linked her arm through his and drew him

away from the condom display. "We'll save that for another time, after the regular ones become too boring."

He choked on a laugh. "If I have anything to do with it, the regular ones aren't going to be boring."

"I believe you'll have a great deal to do with it."

"I plan to, although we can't count out the malachite. In fact, from a scientific standpoint, we shouldn't add in another variable like ribs when we're testing the influence of the stone."

She paused, and since they were linked arm in arm, he had to stop, too. "Exactly how do you think the malachite is going to influence things, by the way?"

"Isn't it obvious?"

"Not to me."

"If you wear the necklace while we're having sex, then—"

"You want me to do that?"

He gazed down at her. "I've been imagining that ever since you put on the necklace. I thought you'd probably figured that out."

"No, I didn't." But now that he'd introduced the idea, she found herself becoming aroused by the mental picture he'd painted. "So this necklace isn't strictly for me, after all, is it?"

"No. It's along the lines of the vest you wanted me to buy."

She blew out a breath. "I feel *so* much better about accepting it now. Here I thought you were just buying me expensive jewelry, but you really wanted an accessory for your sexual fantasy."

He frowned. "That's not my *only* motivation. Once Samuel explained how he'd made the necklace for someone like you, I thought it would be a crime if you didn't own it."

"That's nice, too, but knowing you're thinking of some hot sexual scenario connected with it takes away my misgivings. In a sense, this necklace is as much for you as it is for me."

"Yeah." His gaze traveled from her mouth to her throat, down to the necklace, and beyond, to the cleavage she'd revealed by unfastening one more button.

The heat of that gaze made her shiver with longing. "Too bad we have to go through the whole dinner ritual."

"I know. I'm way hungrier for you than I am for food right now." And that hunger was obvious in his expression. "But we're here because of a family wedding, and that has to take priority over everything else."

She nodded as they continued up the aisle toward the cashier. "So let's get ourselves back to the ranch and be sociable. I'm trying to remember who's supposed to be at dinner tonight."

"A smaller group than we had last night, according to Sarah." Rafe paid for the box of condoms as nonchalantly as he might pay for a package of Life Savers.

Meg was impressed with his sophistication. She didn't know many guys who would be comfortable taking a woman in with them while they shopped for birth control. Rafe might have balked at the idea of buying clothing when she was along, but he had plenty of confidence when it came to anything sexual. She found that very arousing.

As they started back to the ranch, she began to count the days they'd have left before the wedding consumed all their time. "When's your dad flying in?"

"Thursday. I'm picking him up at the airport, which is one reason I rented the Lexus. He's partial to this make of car."

She sensed the eagerness to please in Rafe's voice. He wanted his father's approval and wasn't always sure he'd get it. "And Thursday night's the party at the Spirits and Spurs. Will he come to that?"

"I suppose. It's not going to involve strippers and raunchy movies, so he'll probably go."

"That's good. We'll have drinks and dancing. He should enjoy it."

"What kind of dancing?"

"Oh." She realized that it might not be quite the type his father would want. "Country, I'm afraid. The first night I was here, we all went into the Spirits and Spurs because they had a local band playing. It was a lot of fun, but it's definitely country music, and country swing is popular around here. Line dancing, too."

"He won't do any of that."

Meg took note of the finality in Rafe's statement. "You're sure? I mean, maybe if we get a couple of drinks in him, and one of the women who's really good at it coaxes him out on the floor, he'll—"

"It's not going to happen, Meg. Fact is, I don't know how to dance that way, either. I'll probably sit it out with my dad."

"I certainly hope not!"

He glanced at her in obvious surprise. "What's so wrong about that?"

"You're the best man, Rafe, so you can't just sit it out, even if your dad chooses to. Besides, the party is only the beginning. They'll have a DJ playing country music at the reception, too. It's part of your job to be out there on the dance floor."

"I hadn't thought of that. And Wyatt didn't say a word."

"I'm sure it's not one of the main things he's worried about, but I happen to think it's important. And if I have to appeal to your competitive instinct, I will. The Chance men have a reputation for being great dancers."

Rafe groaned. "This is not a hurdle I anticipated. Do you know anything about country swing or line dancing?"

"Some. But the best dancer in the family is Jack. If you really want to learn how to—"

"Are you seriously suggesting I ask Jack to teach me to dance?"

"I don't know. Maybe. Yes, I think I am. In fact, it would be excellent if Jack taught you to dance." She looked over at him and his jaw had tightened along with his grip on the steering wheel. "But you don't think so, do you?"

"Not so much."

"How much dancing experience do you have, exactly?"

"I...um...you know. Dancing at clubs."

"You mean where you get out on the floor and gyrate around without actually touching your partner?"

"Like that, yeah. I've done a little ballroom dancing, too."

She knew this would be a tough sell, but if she could convince him, he'd be much happier during the wedding festivities. "That's not quite the same thing. But I promise you, if you take on this challenge and master the Texas Two-Step and a couple of line dances, you'll be a hero."

"I will?" He sounded a little more interested.

"Guaranteed."

"I'm not saying I won't try, because I see your point. It's part of the festivities, and it'll look bad if I don't participate, but...Jack? Couldn't I learn from someone else?"

"You could, but after all, he is your brother."

"Half brother."

"Half brother, then. But let's say you get someone else to teach you, somebody on the ranch, maybe even Sarah. I've seen her dance with Jack and she's very good."

He nodded enthusiastically. "I'll ask Sarah. We get along great. She's a very kind woman, and besides, she is, in fact, a *woman.* Learning to dance from somebody of the opposite sex would be a plus."

"Yes, but think of the result. You'll show up at the party Thursday night with some skills you've learned from Sarah. But everyone knows Jack is the ultimate authority on country dancing, and they'll realize you wimped out and chose Sarah. You didn't go to The Man."

"I don't want to go to *The Man,* okay?"

"I'm telling you, Rafe, you'd score more points if you did. Jack's the best, and if you acknowledge that by asking for his help, he'll be proud of what you accomplish. You'll have an ally out on the floor instead of a competitor."

His jaw tightened again. "I don't care if Jack's an ally or not. I didn't come to the Last Chance to kiss up to my half brother."

Men. "I know you didn't! But can't you play the game, just for this week?"

"I'm still trying to picture me going up to Jack and asking if he'll teach me to dance. How am I supposed to do that with a straight face?"

"I'll go with you. I'm fairly sure that Jack, Josie and little Archie are coming to dinner tonight. It'll be your perfect opportunity."

"I don't know, Meg. Sounds like a disaster in the making."

"Rafe, if you'll take this on, I promise to dance with you a whole lot, both on Thursday night and Saturday night."

He was silent for a few seconds. "I hadn't thought of that. I don't want you out there dancing without me."

"Of course you don't, especially if I'm wearing this necklace and feeling all uninhibited."

He groaned. "All right. If Jack is there, I'll ask him. Jesus. I can't believe I just agreed to do that."

"You won't be sorry."

"I'm already sorry."

Meg smiled to herself. This week was turning out to be the most interesting one of her life.

11

RAFE PRAYED THAT MEG had been wrong and Jack wouldn't be coming to dinner, after all. But his luck didn't hold out. Jack, Josie and their seven-month-old son, Archie, sat down at the family dining table, along with Josie's brother Alex, who was the marketing director for the ranch, and his wife, Tyler, who organized seasonal events for the town of Shoshone.

Rafe was glad to meet Alex and Tyler, who hadn't made it the night before. He could see the family resemblance between Alex and Josie, who were both tall and blond. Tyler was a little brunette firecracker who used to work as a cruise ship activities director.

Tyler would be another good candidate as a dance teacher, Rafe thought. In fact, almost anybody would be better for the job than Jack Chance, in Rafe's opinion.

As they all gathered, Sarah explained that Nick and Dominique, along with Lester, were working on a framing project for Dominique's new show opening next week and couldn't take time to come up to the house for dinner. Wyatt and Olivia were in town visiting Olivia's father, an inventor who had a new gizmo to show them. Sarah's other daughter-in-law, Morgan, thought that she was catching a cold, so Gabe was home feeding her chicken soup and making sure little Sarah Bianca didn't get sick, too.

Rafe didn't wish sickness on anyone, but he wouldn't have minded if Jack had caught a cold instead of Morgan. While Rafe listened with half an ear to the dinner chitchat, he pictured Jack doubling over in a fit of laughter when he heard Rafe's request. That malachite stone Meg wore must have messed with his brain or he never would have agreed to this.

Everyone at the table admired the necklace, of course, and Rafe could feel speculation coming from all quarters. This family would understand what a necklace from Silver Reflections was worth, and the fact he'd bought it for Meg made a definite statement about how he felt toward her. He hadn't factored that in, but he still didn't regret buying it.

No, he only had one regret at the moment, and that was his idiotic promise to ask Jack to turn him into a twinkle toes on the dance floor. Sheesh. If only he could hit the delete button on that part of today's conversation with Meg.

She wasn't likely to let him off the hook, either. After only knowing her a short time, he realized that she was one determined woman. But he procrastinated all through dinner in hopes that maybe, after a glass of wine, she'd decide not to force the issue. Dessert was nearly over, and he was beginning to think maybe he'd avoid this humiliation, after all.

Then Alex, who was once a DJ and would perform that job during the reception, turned the conversation in a direction that was sure to cause Rafe trouble. "I'm still working on the playlist for Saturday night," Alex said. "I'm going for a mix of tunes because we'll have all ages there, and I've already consulted with Olivia and Wyatt on their favorites. But I'll take requests from this group, too."

"I hope you'll play 'Electric Boogie,'" Meg said. "The Electric Slide is the one line dance I've totally figured out."

"Already included," Alex said. "It's a classic and a crowd pleaser. Anything else?"

"'This Kiss' by Faith Hill," Josie said. "I love dancing with Jack to that song."

"Speaking of that," Meg said.

Rafe held his breath. *Here it comes.*

"Rafe and I were talking about the whole dancing thing, and it turns out he isn't all that familiar with country dancing. Jack's the expert in the family, so—"

"So," Rafe said, interrupting her, "I'd appreciate it, Jack, if you'd give me some pointers." If he had to do this, he might as well man up and ask the question himself.

For a split second everyone at the table was completely silent. In that split second Rafe began to sweat bullets.

"Be glad to," Jack said. His eyes crinkled at the corners as if he wanted to laugh, but to his credit, he didn't. "No time like the present." He pushed back his chair. "Let's head for the living room and move some furniture. I suggest we start with the Electric Slide."

At that moment Mary Lou, the ranch cook, bustled into the dining room with a carafe in her hand. "Who needs more coffee?"

Jack stood. "You know what, Mary Lou? Instead

of coffee, Rafe and I could use a six-pack of beer. I'm about to teach him to dance."

The cook stopped in her tracks. A fiftysomething woman with flyaway gray hair, she'd recently married a ranch hand who went by the single name of Watkins. "Let me get Watkins," she said. "He's gotta see this."

"No bystanders," Jack said. "Anybody who shows up in the living room has to dance."

Rafe sent Jack a look of gratitude. A lesson would be tough enough without an audience.

Mary Lou grinned. "No problem. Watkins is one hell of a dancer."

"I can do the footwork while I'm holding Archie." Josie extricated the baby from his high chair. "Is that good enough, Mr. Dance Instructor?"

Jack smiled at her. "You bet."

"That's great," Josie said, "because I wouldn't miss this for the world."

"I'm in," Alex said. "And, Rafe, buddy, I feel your pain. I didn't know squat about this stuff when I came here from Chicago two years ago."

Jack laughed. "And despite our best efforts, he still resists adopting the country way."

"Alex is an awesome dancer," Tyler said. "He just marches to a different drummer."

"Yeah." Josie winked at her brother. "I think it's that Animal dude from *The Muppet Show*."

"Nice, sis." Alex made a face at Josie.

Rafe glanced across the table. "Take heart, Alex. There's a new city boy in town."

"You'll be fine," Jack said. "Especially if Mary Lou remembers to bring us some beer."

Ten minutes later, a space in the living room had

been cleared of chairs, end tables and lamps. Music was arranged with help from a set of speakers out of Sarah's bedroom, and Josie contributed her downloaded tunes.

While Sarah and Josie searched for "Electric Boogie" on Josie's iPod, Rafe accepted the beer Jack handed him and took several healthy swallows.

"I have to say, I admire your guts," Jack said. "It's not easy to come into this situation as a greenhorn."

"Thanks, and no, it's not."

"Wyatt warned me that this kind of life isn't your style and you might be standoffish."

Rafe met his gaze. Each time he looked at Jack, he had the eerie sensation he was looking in a mirror. "To be honest, that was my original plan. It hasn't worked out that way."

Jack glanced over at Meg, who was practicing some line dancing steps with Tyler. "Women have a way of changing things."

"Yeah." Rafe drank some more beer.

"That's a nice necklace you bought her."

Rafe shrugged. "Well, like she said at dinner, it's her birthstone." He knew that was a really lame excuse for such an extravagant purchase, but he wasn't going into any more detail with Jack.

"Hey, I'm not questioning the decision. I've made a damned fool of myself over Josie plenty of times. Once you feel that connection, it's all over."

Rafe shook his head. "It's not like that with us."

"Not like what?"

"Neither one of us is looking for anything permanent."

"I see." Jack took a sip of his beer before glancing over at Rafe. "Let me get this straight. You're not interested in a commitment, but you bought her a valuable necklace that she'll cherish for the rest of her life. I have to tell you, that's…"

"Stupid?"

"I wasn't going to say that, but it makes no sense whatsoever."

"I know."

Jack laughed and clapped him on the back. "At least you admit that you're totally screwed. Come on, let's dance."

After one more fortifying swig of his beer, Rafe lined up between Meg and Tyler, with Alex on Tyler's far side and Mary Lou beside Alex. Jack, Josie, Sarah and her fiancé, Pete, stood in front of them, along with Mary Lou's new husband, Watkins, a barrel-chested guy with a handlebar mustache.

"We'll walk it through without music first," Jack said. "Rafe, copy what I do when you can see me, but there's turning involved, so sometimes you'll have to be copying Meg or Tyler."

"Don't copy me," Meg said. "I've been responsible for several Electric Slide train wrecks."

"That information does nothing to raise my confidence." Rafe tried not to anticipate disaster as he listened to Jack's instructions. Then he stumbled his way through something called a grapevine step. The forward and back part wasn't too bad, and eventually he had a general idea of which way to pivot and when to stomp and clap. But when Sarah switched on the music, everything he'd learned disappeared from his brain.

Watching Meg move through the steps and wiggle her adorable ass didn't help his concentration, either. Bumping into her and then slamming into Tyler was bad enough, but colliding head-on with Jack so that they practically embraced was damned embarrassing. Before the song was over, he'd managed to step on every set of toes within range at least once.

"Well, that wasn't too bad," Jack said. "Let's take a beer break and try it again."

"Great idea." Rafe located his beer and drained the bottle. When he came up for air, there was Meg, smiling at him.

"See? You're doing it."

"If you mean making a fool of myself, then yes, ma'am, I certainly am."

"No, you're not. You did great for your first time. One more run-through and you'll have it."

"You sure look good out there. You have a great sense of rhythm." He was trying desperately not to imagine how that would translate to sex. That thought had the power to derail him completely.

Her pink cheeks turned even pinker. "Thanks, but I still have to think about every step. I'll be glad when it's automatic and I can just go with the music."

"Everybody back in line," Jack called out. "We have a lot more work ahead of us."

Rafe took his position and mentally reviewed the steps the way he used to when he was first learning karate. As he did that, something clicked in his brain. Suddenly the movements fell into a logical pattern, one he could execute with barely a misstep, just as he'd done with karate.

When the music ended, Jack stuck his thumbs in his belt loops and surveyed Rafe with obvious satisfaction. "Either I'm a hell of a teacher, or you're a hell of a pupil. That's the fastest I've ever seen anyone learn a line dance."

Rafe couldn't help smiling. "Thanks."

"Don't go getting all full of yourself, though. That was the easy part. Next you're going to learn the Texas Two-Step, and that's a whole other ball game."

Sarah glanced at Jack. "Want me to be Rafe's partner?"

"No." A look of pure devilment lit Jack's eyes. "He'll learn faster if I'm his partner."

Rafe's smile faded. "I think I need another beer."

MEG HAD BEEN IMPRESSED with Rafe's willingness to stumble through a line dance until he caught on, but she'd expected him to balk at Jack's plan to partner him in the two-step.

Instead he took a couple of swallows of beer and then walked over to stand in front of Jack, arms spread. "I'm all yours."

"Lucky me." But Jack looked at Rafe with a new gleam of respect in his dark eyes. Meg had the feeling he was testing his half brother to see what he was made of.

"Okay, here's how we'll do it," Jack said. "I'm going to take the woman's part and you'll take the man's. Have you done any ballroom dancing?"

Rafe nodded. "Some."

"Then you know how that works. You lead and I follow. Here's your basic step." He moved through it as Rafe watched his feet. "Got that?"

"One more time."

Jack repeated the steps. "Okay?"

"Yep. Got it." His expression was completely deadpan as he gazed at Jack. "May I have this dance, you gorgeous thing?"

Jack grinned. "Just keep your hands where they belong, cowboy. I may be gorgeous, but I'm not easy. Mom, start the music."

Sarah was laughing so hard she had trouble getting the music going, but eventually a country tune filled the living room. Meg stared in fascination as Rafe placed his right hand at Jack's waist and Jack rested his left hand on Rafe's shoulder. Then they joined their right and left hands together and began to dance.

By rights, Rafe should have had to look down at his feet, but instead he kept his attention on Jack's face as the two men moved smoothly around the room.

"Woo!" Josie called out. "Sign these guys up for *Dancing with the Stars*."

"Hey," Alex said. "That looks like fun. Can I cut in?"

Jack started to laugh. "Dream on, Alex."

"Now I'm feeling jealous," Watkins said. "You've never asked me to dance, Jack. For all you know, I could be your ideal partner."

"Back off, you guys," Rafe said. "Jack's with me."

After that comment, Jack totally lost it. The two men staggered away from each other doubled over with laughter. Then Alex started dancing with Watkins, and the women paired up, too. By the end of the song, everyone was gasping for breath and wiping tears from their eyes.

Meg ended up dancing with Tyler, and after the music stopped, Tyler gave her a hug. "That was hysterical. You put Rafe up to that, didn't you?"

"I suggested he might ask Jack to teach him, but I never envisioned Jack actually dancing *with* him."

"Didn't surprise me at all. When I first met Jack he was kind of a stick-in-the-mud, but everyone told me he used to be a real character. He seems back to his old self these days."

"Obviously. I think I'm in love with this family."

"How could you not be? I thank my lucky stars that I met Alex and then had the good sense to give up the cruise business and settle down here with him."

"Do I remember right that you two have a house on Chance land?"

"We do." Tyler's dark eyes sparkled. "Sarah thinks of Alex as one of her sons, and she insisted that we should live out here, especially because Alex is such a big part of the marketing end of the business. I wasn't about to object to having a house built here. It's beautiful, and it's almost like our own little community since Jack, Gabe and Nick all have houses on the property, too."

Meg checked to see if Sarah was within earshot. "Olivia said Sarah wanted to deed some land over to Wyatt, but he said no."

"Yeah, that's right. I can understand it. He's so afraid someone will think he came here to cash in on the Chance money. Besides, Olivia has that cute little house in Shoshone, and her dad's right around the corner. I think she wants to stay in town."

"If I were in her shoes, I'd want to be out here," Meg said. "There's something magical about this ranch."

"I agree."

"And yet Rafe and Wyatt's mother—Jack's mother, too, come to think of it—couldn't wait to give it up." Meg shook her head. "I don't understand that."

"So have you heard anything? Is she coming to the wedding?"

"I don't think Rafe knows. I don't think anyone knows. I hate that she's holding everybody hostage like this."

"From what I've heard, she's not a very nice person."

"And yet her sons are terrific." Meg glanced over at Rafe, who was drinking beer and laughing with Jack. "I don't know what's for the best, but everyone's getting along so well. It almost seems better if she doesn't show up. I can picture her ruining everything."

12

Despite having a great time with Jack and the others, Rafe kept thinking about his plans for tonight, which didn't include anyone except Meg. But they had to wait for the evening to wind down. They couldn't exactly announce that they were going upstairs…together.

After all the talk about the necklace, especially his conversation with Jack, Rafe didn't have any illusions about what the family suspected. Nobody would be the least bit surprised to know what Rafe had in mind once everyone retired for the evening. He didn't really care if they knew.

But he kept thinking about Jack's response to the situation. Jack was convinced that Rafe and Meg were headed for some kind of happily-ever-after. Glancing around the room, Rafe could see why he would think so.

Everywhere Rafe looked were happy couples—Jack and Josie, Alex and Tyler, Mary Lou and Watkins, Sarah and Pete. The Last Chance seemed to foster healthy, loving relationships, except in one significant case. His mother had not been blissfully happy here.

Rafe couldn't regret that, because if she'd stayed with

Jonathan Chance, he and Wyatt wouldn't exist. Still, he wondered what would happen if Diana, who was extremely high maintenance, descended on the festivities. Sad to say, he couldn't see a good outcome.

At long last, the gathering began to break up. Alex and Tyler left first. Then Jack and Josie started gathering Archie's baby stuff. Sarah asked to hold Archie one last time, and Jack walked over and held out his hand to Rafe.

"You've been a good sport." His grip was firm. "I had my doubts about you when you drove up in that fancy-dancy car, but I think you're going to be okay."

"Thanks. And thanks for being my dance instructor tonight."

Jack grinned. "That will go down in the annals of the family history, my friend. Just so you know, I've never danced with a guy before in my life."

"Couldn't prove it by me. You seemed totally relaxed about it."

"I wanted to see what you'd do if I suggested it."

"And?"

"And you called my bluff. That always gets my attention." He clapped Rafe on the shoulder. "Welcome to the family, little brother."

To Rafe's surprise and embarrassment, his throat closed up with emotion. He coughed to cover it. "I'm glad to be here."

"You haven't heard anything from Diana, right?"

"Nothing."

"You'll tell me if you do, I hope."

Rafe nodded. "You'll be the first to know. No, cancel that. You'll be the second to know. If I hear something, I have to make sure Wyatt's aware."

Jack sighed. "In some ways I'd like her to show up and get the drama out of the way. But it could be a real rodeo if she does."

"Not if I have anything to say about it."

Jack's eyebrows lifted. "You'd run interference?"

"Of course."

"Good man." He gave Rafe's shoulder another squeeze. "See you at the party Thursday night. Wear your dancing shoes." With a wink, he turned to walk with Josie out the front door.

"That's about all the fun Watkins and I can take for one night," Mary Lou said. "We have a little tidying up in the kitchen, and then we're off to bed."

Sarah yawned and stretched. "I think Pete and I are ready to pack it in, too." She glanced over at Rafe. "You were terrific tonight. I haven't seen Jack laugh that hard in a long time. It did my heart good to see you two getting along so well."

"The credit belongs to Wyatt," Rafe said. "He's the one who broke the ice and made sure that we got to know our half brother."

Sarah's expression softened. "He did, at that. He's a very special guy. He and Olivia have a bright future."

"They do." As Rafe said that, he felt a pang of envy. Wyatt had found a woman who wanted to spend a lifetime with him and they were about to start that journey together.

A couple of days ago, before Rafe had met Meg, he had thought settling down was a long way off for him. But since then he'd experienced life in a whole new way. Instead of being constantly focused on his career and the bottom line, he'd started thinking about how he would spend the money he was accumulating.

He'd had no particular plan other than becoming wealthy enough that he wouldn't have to worry about his future. But besides being a rich man, how did he visualize that future? He realized now that he'd never created a detailed picture of what he wanted. Or who he wanted to be there with him.

His attention wandered, as it had all evening, to Meg. She was so full of life. Anyone lucky enough to spend time in her presence would find her a constant source of energy and inspiration. Yeah, she threw him off balance a lot, and he was learning to enjoy the slightly dizzy feeling that came from taking crazy chances.

"I think it's wonderful that you and Meg have discovered that you're kindred spirits," Sarah said. "That makes it very convenient, doesn't it, since Meg and Olivia are such good friends?"

Rafe thought of contradicting Sarah's assumption the way he'd contradicted Jack earlier. He couldn't bring himself to do it. "It does make it nice," he said.

"You have very good taste."

"You mean the necklace?"

"No, the woman." Sarah gave him a hug. "Be happy, Rafe. Oh, and turn out the lights before you go up to bed, okay?"

"Sure."

With one last smile in his direction, she linked arms with Pete and they walked down the hallway toward her bedroom.

Rafe watched them go. He couldn't remember the last time his mother had hugged him. Sarah had known him a very short time, and yet she'd embraced him with warmth and affection, as if he were a long-lost son. For the second time tonight, Rafe found his chest tightening with emotions he wasn't used to feeling.

"Looks like everyone's going to bed."

He turned around at the sound of Meg's voice, which held a soft purr of sensuality that made his blood sing.

She stood a couple of feet away looking incredibly beautiful. The lamplight on her fiery hair created an angelic halo, but her expression wasn't the least bit angelic. Her green gaze burned with earthly lust.

"How about you?" Heart thumping, he eliminated the distance between them and drew her close. Her heat fueled his fantasies. "Are you ready for bed?"

She smiled and wrapped her arms around his neck. "I've been ready for bed for hours."

He welcomed the warmth of her arms at the back of his neck. "Me, too. I thought the evening was going to last forever."

"Same here." She wiggled closer. "But it was good, even if I was impatient to be alone with you."

His breath caught as she aligned her body with his. He tightened his grip, and allowed his gaze to travel downward, past the polished silver and malachite to the shadowed treasures beyond. The return journey brought him back to her incredible eyes. "It *was* good. Thank you, Meg. If you hadn't challenged me to try the whole dance thing, tonight wouldn't have turned out so well."

"I noticed that you and Jack had a few words before he left."

"We did." He savored this moment of holding her close, knowing that soon, they would be closer yet. Anticipation built, teasing him with possibilities. "As you predicted, we're allies now. And that's important considering what may happen this week."

Sympathy flashed in her eyes. "Your mother."

"Yes. But now Jack and I, and Wyatt, too, for that matter, can present a united front if she does show up. Without this wild dance lesson, I don't know if that would have been possible." He reached up and caressed her cheek. "And it's all because of you."

"No. You had to actually follow through. What you did tonight required a lot of courage. Now that it's behind you, you might not think so, but—"

"Oh, it required a lot of courage. I'm not about to minimize that. I was nervous as hell." He stroked his thumb across her cheekbone. All the lipstick was gone from her pink mouth. It looked even sexier bare. "But as I'm learning from you, these are the risks worth taking, aren't they?"

"I think so."

"Proud of me?"

"Yes, I am."

"Good." His pulse rate skyrocketed as he leaned down and brushed his mouth over her pink, smiling lips. "Because it's time for me to claim my reward."

"Finally." Spinning out of his arms, she grabbed his hand and pulled. "Come on, Locke. We have a date."

Laughing, he ran with her up the stairs. Briefly he remembered that he was supposed to douse the lights. Oh, hell, he'd do it later. A hot woman was dragging him off to bed. A guy didn't stop to turn off lights at a time like that.

She dashed through his bedroom door first, and he barely had time to kick it closed before she leaped on him. Wrapping her arms around his neck and her legs around his waist, she grinned at him. "I hope you know where your condoms are, big boy."

Cupping his hands under her perfect little ass, he carried her to the bed, kissing her cheeks, her nose, her mouth. "I know exactly where they are, sweet stuff." He'd left on a bedside lamp in anticipation of this moment. "Time to get you naked so I can use one."

"I can hardly wait."

Neither could he, and judging from the pressure under his fly, he'd have a devil of a time holding off long enough to give her a good time. But he would do it because she deserved no less.

Depositing her on the bed, he followed her down. Ah, glorious. He loved having his arms full of Meg. His feet were still on the floor, but he couldn't be bothered with taking off his boots right now. He had a blouse to unbutton. Leaning over her, he started in on that job while continuing to kiss and nibble at her plump mouth.

"Too slow," she said between kisses as she pushed his hands away. "Let me."

"Then I'll work on your jeans."

"No." She struggled for breath. "You work on *your* jeans."

His breathing wasn't any steadier than hers, and his heart hammered like a car about to throw a rod. "Bossy, aren't you?"

She laughed and gulped for air. "Horny."

"That's my good luck." The blood pounded in his ears as he unbuckled and unzipped. He had to interrupt his assignment when her jeans got stuck on her shoes. Kneeling, he pulled off both shoes and then figured he might as well finish the operation and tugged off her jeans and panties, too.

"Almost done." She whipped off her blouse, tossed

it aside, unhooked her bra, and threw it on top of the blouse. "There." She leaned back on her elbows.

He went still. She was a work of art, and no matter how bossy she tried to be, he would take time to pay homage. Her breasts were lush—round and smooth, tempting him with wine-dark nipples. They were generous in comparison to her slender torso and narrow waist. The silver necklace gleamed against her bare skin.

His cock throbbed as his gaze swept over the sweet curve of her hips, the graceful length of her slim legs and the fiery patch of curls between her thighs.

"Rafe," she murmured. "You're not moving."

"No. I'm looking."

"Me, too, or at least I'm trying to. The view is seriously obstructed. Would you please do something about that?"

"Yeah, sure." Not taking his eyes from her, he reached down and pulled off a boot, shifted his weight to the other leg and yanked off the second one, which fell with a thud to the floor.

She ran a tongue over her lips. "Your shirt."

"Right." Still watching her, he grabbed both sides of the shirt and pulled. The snaps gave way like exploding popcorn, and she laughed in a low, sexy voice that drove him crazy.

He started moving faster, dropping the shirt to the floor and shoving down his jeans and briefs. The belt buckle clattered to the floor as he stepped out of the whole shebang and kicked it aside.

She took a long, shaky breath as she gave him the same top-to-bottom scrutiny he'd given her. "Awesome." Her breasts quivered as she drew another breath. "Now bring that wonderful stuff over here, okay?" She parted her legs a fraction, in a subtle, yet tantalizing invitation. "I have a place you can put it."

He almost swallowed his tongue. Grabbing the handle on the bedside table drawer, he jerked it out with such force that the whole thing fell to the floor. He left it there, scooped up the box of condoms, and tore it open, destroying it in the process. Condoms flew everywhere.

But he only needed one, and he managed to get a good grip on it. His fingers shook as he tried to tear the foil. He'd never wanted a woman so much in his life.

"Here." She took it out of his hand and in two seconds had that little raincoat ready to put on.

He reached for it. "I'll—"

"No, *I'll*." Her gaze swept the length of his erect penis. "You wouldn't deprive a girl of dressing up something that beautiful, would you?"

"Meg, at this moment, I wouldn't deprive you of anything. If you wanted me to buy you the Taj Mahal, I'd..." He clenched his jaw as she rolled the condom on. He was so close. Too damned close.

"I don't want the Taj Mahal." Scooting back on the bed, she held out her arms. "I want you."

"That's good, because that's what you're about to get." He climbed onto the bed, grateful for the generous space that allowed them to lie across the mattress. That way he didn't have to take the time to change position.

As he looked into her eyes, he saw his urgency mirrored there. But if he responded to that, if he thrust deep as he longed to do and kept on pumping frantically, he'd come in seconds. "We're going to take this slow at first," he said.

She grasped his hips and lust blazed in her eyes. "What if I want fast and furious?"

"I can't. You've turned me on more than I can remember ever being turned on. My control is shot, and
I want to make sure that you—"

"I feel as if I could come right this minute, just looking into your eyes."

"Me, too." He drew in a breath. "Which is why we're
going to ease into the situation gradually." Bracing his
arms on either side of her shoulders, he probed her moist
heat gently with his cock.

She groaned. "You're teasing me."

"No." He fought the wave of his own climax. "I'm
trying not to come. Help me."

"How?"

"Lie still."

Slowly she relaxed against the bed. "I'm still."

"Don't move."

"I won't."

He slid partway in. So good. Too good. He closed
his eyes and slowly exhaled. There. Better.

"More." She sounded desperate.

Opening his eyes, he looked into hers and found the
control he needed. "Yes, more." With one firm movement, he thrust home.

She gasped. Arching upward, she dug her fingers
into his back. "Rafe, I'm…" With a soft wail, she came
apart, shuddering against him, her spasms stroking his
rock-hard cock.

Somehow he held on without coming, and as she
began to drift down from the heights, he withdrew
slightly and rocked forward again, making sure he
pressed against her clit. Instantly she tensed again. Her
eyes flew open and she looked up at him.

He smiled as he began a steady rhythm. "Let's try that again, shall we?"

"Oh." Wrapping her legs around his, she rose to meet each thrust. "Rafe, that's so... I can feel every... nerve ending... I..."

Gazing into her eyes, he soaked up the pleasure he could see there. Her breathless murmurs spurred him on to give her all he knew how to give. Shifting the angle slightly, he wondered if he could locate her G-spot.

When her pupils widened, he thought maybe he had. "Like that?"

"Uh-huh." She began to pant. "Certainly do. Oh, yeah. Magic..." She moaned softly with each stroke.

He pumped faster, and her moans grew in volume. He wasn't sure about the acoustics in this house, so he leaned down and covered her mouth with his. When she came again, he let himself come with her, and they swallowed each other's cries as they rode the wind together.

Gasping for breath, he lifted his head and gazed down at her in silent wonder. Making love to her had been everything he'd imagined it would be and more.

Her lashes fluttered, and she opened her eyes. A slow smile of satisfaction curved her kiss-reddened mouth. "That," she said, "was seriously good."

"Yes, it was." Her smile was contagious, and he hoped he wasn't grinning like an idiot. "So what do you think? Should we quit while we're ahead?" He thought he knew the answer, but it was fun to test her response.

"Are you insane? Now that I've got you in my clutches, I intend to wear you out."

"I was hoping you'd say that." Easing away from her, he crawled off the bed and grabbed a tissue to dispose of the condom. "Don't forget, you recommended a hot bath for my poor aching muscles."

She rose up on her elbows again. "I did, didn't I?"

"Think I'll go down the hall and run that bath right now."

"And leave me here sad and lonely?"

"Hell, no. I need someone to wash my back."

She glanced around the room. "No bathrobe."

"So what? Nobody's upstairs but us."

"Good point." Scooting out of bed, she stood beside him and laced her fingers through his. "Come along, cowboy. Let's have us some nice clean fun."

13

FORTUNATELY THE TUB WAS the old-fashioned kind, which made it almost big enough for two if they were willing to get cozy. Meg was more than willing to do that. She hoped that she wasn't being too obvious ogling Rafe's body, but he was one ripped dude.

As the water ran into the tub, she stroked a hand down his biceps. "I assume you got this way because you work out."

"Nah, I was born like this."

"Must have been rough on your mother." She'd meant it as a joke, but immediately she regretted bringing up the subject of Diana. "Sorry. Cancel that remark."

"It's okay." He pulled her into his arms. "I've had to deal with her all my life. I figured out pretty early that she wasn't the poster girl for motherhood."

Meg nestled against his sculpted chest and enjoyed the growing evidence of his interest pressing against her belly. "Let's talk about your workouts." She glanced up at him. "Judging from the evidence—" she slid her hands up his muscled back "—you're in the gym a fair bit."

"I am." He cupped her bottom and brought her in close. "I work off a lot of stress there, but now that I've met you, I can imagine a much better way to do that."

She nodded. "Sex as a stress buster. I can go along with that idea."

"In fact, I wonder if you'd be willing to act as my safety valve if this wedding craziness gets out of hand."

"That conjures up some interesting scenarios." She rubbed languidly against him. "So let's say on Thursday night, the pressure gets too intense for one reason or another. Shall we meet in the backseat of your Lexus?"

He stroked upward and moved both hands around to fondle her breasts. "On the other hand, why wait for pressure to build up? Why don't we just plan on some backseat sex during the party?"

"You're a bad boy, Rafe Locke." She leaned into his caress and closed her eyes. "How's the water level?" she murmured.

"What water level? I— Yikes, the *water level.*" Releasing her quickly, he spun toward the tub and turned off the faucet. "I'm going to drain some out. We don't want to flood the place when we both get in."

"And start splashing around."

He glanced over his shoulder. "Are you a splasher?"

"Depends on what's happening in the tub."

He gazed at her, amusement in his dark eyes. "Maybe I'll drain out a little bit more, then. I have some thoughts about what might be happening in the tub, and you might turn into a splasher, at that." He watched the water level and finally put the plug back in the drain. "That looks about right."

"Maybe you should get in by yourself for a while.

You really should soak your thigh muscles in warm water."

"That doesn't sound like any fun. I'll get in first, though, since I'll take up the most room. Then we'll work you in around me."

She glanced at the proud jut of his penis. "You'd take up less room if you could tame your friend, there."

"That's your department." He sat down in the tub, leaned back, and held out his hand. "Come on in. The water's fine."

"Just where do you intend to put me?" She'd thought they both might fit, but he really was bigger—in all respects—than she'd realized.

He drew his knees up slightly. "There's room at the far end."

"Let me take off my necklace first." She hadn't been without it since she'd first put it on this afternoon, and as she laid the silver spiral on the counter, she touched the malachite once for good luck. "Do you think I'll still be uninhibited if I'm not wearing it?"

"I don't know. Do you feel a lot different when it's on?"

She turned back to him with a smile. "Seeing you naked has a greater effect on my inhibitions than a piece of malachite ever could."

"Then we should join a nudist colony."

"Ah, but I don't want to share."

"Okay, then I'll have to remember to strip down whenever we're alone."

"Sounds good to me." She stepped into the small space he'd left her. "Okay, now what?"

"Sit down and stretch your legs out on each side of my hips."

Somehow she managed it. With her legs apart, the warm water caressed her intimately and she flushed as she felt the first tug of arousal.

"Okay, now hold my hands tight. I'm going to put my legs around you and pull you toward me. I'll do it slowly so we don't send waves crashing over the sides of the tub."

"I'm trying to imagine where this is going."

He laughed. "I'm not exactly sure. I'm making it up as I go along."

"That's not very comforting. What if we get twisted up in here and can't untangle without pulling a groin muscle?"

"I forgot to mention I was also on the wrestling team in high school. I can get us out of anything. Now slide forward. That's it. Closer, closer…there. How's that?"

"Interesting. Puts me in striking distance." She reached out and wrapped her hand around his cock, slick with water.

"Mmm." His gaze grew heavy-lidded as she caressed him. "So far, so good."

"I don't know what this is doing for your thighs."

"Who cares? And the beauty of this position is that it works both ways." Slipping his hand between her legs under the water, he rubbed his knuckle over her clit.

She drew in a quick breath as her womb twitched in reaction.

"I love watching how your eyes grow dark when you're excited."

"Who says I'm excited?"

"You're not? Then let's try this." Changing the position of his hand, he gently pushed two fingers into her slick channel, which was already starting to quiver.

His thumb rested lightly on her trigger point. Then he began to lazily stroke it back and forth as he found her G-spot with the pads of his fingers.

"Uh, that's pretty nice right there." Understatement of the year.

Then he stopped moving his hand.

"You could keep that up if you want."

"It's your turn."

"Oh." She was still holding his cock, but she'd forgotten about the caressing part. Squeezing lightly, she moved her hand up and down.

His breathing grew rougher. "If we were into delayed gratification, we could see how long we could keep this up, starting and stopping, without coming."

She continued to stroke him. "Are you into delayed gratification?"

"Maybe someday. Not tonight." He swallowed. "See if you can still do that while I…do this." He massaged her G-spot again.

The pleasure nearly made her lose her concentration, but she kept reminding herself to touch him, caress him and make him tremble the way he was making her tremble. She held his gaze. "Your eyes get dark, too."

"I'll bet." His breath came faster. "I'm getting close."

"Me, too." She slid her hand up and down faster as he increased the pace of his massage. Water sloshed back and forth, and the sound made the moment even more erotic.

"You're almost there. I can see it in your eyes."

"Yes." Her answer was breathless. "Can you…?"

"Almost. Faster. Don't be loud."

"I won't."

"That's it…good…good…now!" He pressed down on

her clit with his thumb and she came at the same moment his warm essence spilled over her hand.

As their breathing slowed and the water stopped churning, they sat there in a happy daze looking into each other's eyes, in no hurry to move. But at last she released him and he slowly withdrew his hand.

He cleared his throat. "Bet that wasn't on your list."

"No." She smiled at him. "But it should have been."

RAFE TOOK GREAT CARE in drying Meg after they climbed out of the bathtub. Then, because she'd remarked on his muscles and made him feel as if he should demonstrate his strength, he wrapped her in a towel, scooped her up and carried her back to the bedroom.

"I'm liking this." She looped her arms around his neck.

"When we get to the bed, I'm going to unroll you from the towel like Cleopatra was unrolled from a rug. Then I'm going to have my way with you, which is what a he-man does when he carts a woman off to his bed."

"Am I supposed to struggle and protest?"

He shrugged. "You can if that turns you on."

"Not particularly, but if it turns *you* on, I'll be happy to put up a token fight."

"I've never been into that. Too much work. I'd much rather have sex with a woman who's warm and juicy and willing."

"That describes me to a T."

"Then I think we're going to get along." He thought they were already getting along in a way that astounded him. It seemed as if he'd known Meg for years. He'd never put much stock in the concept of soul mates, but he was beginning to think there might be something to it.

Still, there were some inconvenient aspects to that theory. First of all, Meg had never said she was looking for a soul mate. Even if she were, he made his living, and a very good living, in San Francisco. She had talked about leaving Pittsburgh, but only because she wanted to relocate to Jackson Hole.

Maybe geography wasn't supposed to factor into this soul mate business, but he couldn't imagine having a soul mate who lived hundreds of miles away. He pictured a closer physical connection than that. Anyway, Meg had said she wasn't interested in settling down with one guy right now, so eventually he'd have to change her mind in addition to changing her location.

For now, though, she was the perfect person to help him through this wedding week, and he wasn't about to complain because he couldn't have more than that. So far his trip to Jackson Hole had turned out about five hundred percent better than he'd anticipated.

After carrying Meg into his bedroom, he shoved the door closed with his shoulder. Maybe it was a silly precaution since they were the only people upstairs, but with what he had in mind for the next few minutes, he thought a closed door was appropriate.

Depositing Meg on the edge of the bed, he grabbed the ends of the towel, pulled hard, and she tumbled out all pink and glowing from their bath and her orgasm. He wanted to keep that glow alive. Fortunately he thought he could. She was a very easy woman to please.

"I like this bed." She stretched her arms above her head.

"I like you in this bed." Lying down next to her, he

ran his hand from her throat downward, smoothing his palm over her breasts and pausing to tease her nipples until they stood erect.

"Is this what you mean by having your way with me?"

"It's a start." Rolling over so he was braced on top of her, he treated himself to some mouth-to-nipple stimulation. Sucking gently, he reached between her thighs and found her warm and juicy, just as she'd promised.

She began to moan and thrash beneath him. "I want you again. Maybe you should get another—"

"Not yet." He kissed her damp breasts and gave each pert nipple one last lick before he journeyed downward. "First I must have my way with you."

"I'm beginning to understand what you meant by that."

"Smart girl." He took his time getting to his destination. Her skin was tasty, and he loved running his tongue over it and feeling her shudder in response.

But at last he reached nirvana, the special place guarded by fiery curls. Nudging them aside, he settled in and laid siege to any last lingering inhibitions she might have had.

His first explorations were subtle. He used only the tip of his tongue and the faintest brush of his mouth. She sighed and relaxed, opening her thighs in surrender.

Excitement bloomed within him as he took advantage of that surrender. His next foray was deeper, more intense, and she gasped in reaction. But the moment to stop him had long passed. If she'd thought briefly of holding back, of denying him entrance to all that she was, it was too late.

He captured her fully then, using his tongue to lap

and thrust, his mouth to suck her juices until she grew wild with pleasure, rolling her hips so that he had to grasp them firmly and hold her still in order to love her. And when she was gasping and trembling, he loved her with even more enthusiasm, and she came in an unbidden rush, all her barriers gone as she flooded his taste buds with her ambrosia.

And because he couldn't resist, he made her come again, and when it was over, she lay spent, her arms flung out to her sides, her eyes glazed, her lips parted as she drew in quick, shallow breaths that made her body quiver and her breasts tremble.

Sliding up beside her, he pulled her against his hard body, his aroused and in-need-of-release body. But it was not the time. For now, he'd taken all she had to give, and it was enough. With a sigh, he closed his eyes, willed his erection to subside, and slept.

How long he slept, he had no idea. But he awoke to the sweet sensation of being aroused slowly and with great tenderness. She'd scooted down so she could kiss and lick his rapidly stiffening cock.

After the way he'd turned her inside out, he had no doubt she intended the same fate for him. But he wanted to love her the old-fashioned way one more time before the night was through.

Reaching down, he combed his fingers through her hair. "I need a condom."

"Not necessarily." She continued to stroke him, kiss him and fondle his balls.

He loved it, but he wanted that basic connection when he was buried up to the hilt and looking into her glorious eyes. "I want to be inside you, Meg. I need to be inside you."

She paused. "You do?"

"Yes, I do."

Wiggling up so that she could see his face, she gazed at him in puzzlement. "Why?"

"I don't know," he answered honestly. "I just need to be there."

"Okay. Hang on and I'll get a condom."

"Thank you." His groin ached for the climax she'd been working toward.

Leaning over him so that her breast dangled temptingly close to his mouth, she grabbed one of the scattered condoms from the floor.

He wanted to sample her breasts again, tuck his head between her thighs and taste the glory of her climax on his tongue. He didn't want the night to end...ever. But he knew it would soon.

Glancing down, he watched her roll on the condom. She was so earnest, so sexy, so completely right for him. He pushed that last thought away as he started to ease her to her back.

"Stay there," she murmured. "I think we can do it this way." Shifting into position, she hooked one leg over his hip. Facing him, she wiggled around and guided him in until they were locked together just as he'd wanted. "How's that?" She gripped his shoulder.

"I can't move much."

"You won't have to for my sake. I'm on this permanent sexual high. Touch me anywhere and I'll probably come."

"Really?" He spread his hand over the curve of her ass and squeezed. "Here?"

"Maybe."

Exploring this interesting connection between them, he stroked the spot right where they were joined.

She shivered.

He stroked it again as he began to pump gently into her, and she drew in a quick breath. How he loved watching her eyes as her climax hovered ever nearer. He couldn't imagine growing tired of the thrill.

Moving faster now, he put more pressure on that sensitive spot that seemed to give her pleasure.

She held his gaze and tightened her grip on his shoulders.

"Come for me, Meg."

"As if I could help it." Her breath grew ragged.

He touched her there again, and being able to feel the vibration of his cock moving in and out sent his system into meltdown, too. His balls tightened, readying for the surge of ecstasy.

She gulped. "I'm there."

"I know." Pressing hard with his finger, he drove into her and she cried out his name as she tumbled into the abyss.

One more thrust, and he tumbled with her, calling for her, needing her. He no longer cared if someone heard. All that mattered was the joy that blotted out everything. Without knowing it, he'd searched all his life for that all-consuming joy.

He wouldn't expect it to last. Nothing ever did. But for now it was his, and he would take it and be grateful.

14

MEG AWOKE BEFORE SUNRISE feeling sore but happy. No man had loved her like that since…ever. She'd never had a lover to compare with Rafe. That didn't mean she would tell him so, because he might think she was going ape-shit over him and that might scare him off.

She wasn't sure what she wanted to do about Rafe, but she definitely didn't want to scare him off. Nor was she going to get all weird on him and slip out of bed while he was still asleep, leaving him to wonder about her state of mind.

No, they would face this morning together and make sure they were both okay with everything before they headed downstairs to greet what would probably be curious stares. She wasn't too worried about that. From what she could tell, the Last Chance had seen its share of romances over the years.

Whatever was going on between her and Rafe might not be a permanent thing, but it was definitely a romance. They'd fallen asleep facing each other, holding hands. They'd both agreed that the old spooning position that seemed so popular didn't give either of them room to move around. She thought his willingness to give her space, even as they fell asleep, was significant.

During the night they'd relaxed and sought their own familiar sleeping positions. She lay on her back, gazing up at the beamed ceiling, and he was sprawled on his stomach, the pillow bunched under his head, and his eyes closed. She listened to his even breathing and remembered how that breathing changed when he was loving her. She'd have plenty of memories to keep her warm after this week ended.

"I can hear you thinking over there." Rafe's voice was rough with sleep, but tender, too.

She rolled to face him. "I couldn't tell if you were awake."

"I'm awake, and I have a blasted erection, which makes no sense after the night we had. I should be limp as a shredded bike tire, but I'm...not." With his morning stubble and the gleam of lust in his dark eyes, he looked even more like a bad boy.

"Yeah, but mornings are supposed to be a guy's best time, aren't they?"

His lips curved in a bad-boy smile. "I tried like hell to give you my best last night."

"And I have no complaints." She stroked his bristly cheek. "But since I'm still here, there's no reason for you to suffer."

"Noble of you, Nurse Meg."

"I'm only happy to serve. Roll over so I can check your condition."

"Oh, boy." He rolled to his back and displayed his stiff penis. "Doctor was always my favorite game."

"Mmm. You do seem to have a condition. Major

swelling going on." She tapped his shaft with her finger. "Does that hurt?"

"Only when you stop."

"I suggest covering it with a latex membrane to contain the swelling."

"What a coincidence." He leaned over and snagged a condom packet from the floor. "I happen to have that very thing lying around."

"Lucky for you." She ripped open the packet.

"Tell me about it, Nurse Meg."

"Now lie still while I apply the latex."

"Yes, ma'am."

"You may be a bit uncomfortable at first…"

"No kidding." He gritted his teeth as she slowly rolled on the condom. "Could you possibly speed it up a little?"

"I like to take my time with my patients."

"That's all well and good, but…ahh…whatever you're doing with your pinky fingers is not helping."

She struggled not to laugh. "Am I doing something with my pinky fingers? Oh, dear, the swelling seems to be getting worse. And your breathing is very irregular. I think you need some mouth-to-mouth resuscitation." Straddling him carefully so that she didn't touch his cock at all, she leaned down and kissed him on the mouth, with plenty of tongue.

He moaned and grasped her hips, trying to position her where he wanted her.

She wiggled free and sat down firmly on his thighs. Shaking her finger at him, she gave him a stern glance. "You're taking liberties, sir."

"And you're taking forever, Nurse Meg." He gestured

toward his condom-covered penis. "Are you going to reduce the swelling like you promised, or not?"

"Oh, all right." Sighing dramatically, she rose to her hands and knees. "Let's try some deep-tissue massage."

"Yeah, let's. The deeper the better." He bracketed her hips with both hands.

"Don't be hasty, now." Her little game was catching up with her. After so much foreplay, she wanted him as much as he wanted her. Her heart raced as she settled herself over the very tip of his rigid cock. But she couldn't resist teasing him by taking him in a millimeter at a time.

With a low growl he tightened his grip. "Enough's enough." He thrust upward, filling her in one swift movement.

She gasped with pleasure. "Sir!"

"Ah." He lowered his hips and pulled her down with him. "I feel better already."

Her body hummed with delight as the length and breadth of him touched her in all the right places. "I suppose we could try some patient-directed therapy."

His dark eyes glittered. "Such as?"

Leaning forward, she nibbled at his mouth. "Tell me how you want it, big boy."

His instructions were low and intense. "I want you to ride me, Nurse Meg. Ride me hard and fast."

Heat rocketed through her, igniting fires in every sensitive spot. "If you think you're up to it."

"I'll take my chances."

"Then here we go." She started off gradually, getting her bearings, finding her rhythm, but in seconds the power of being in control tempted her to pump faster.

He rose to meet her, his thighs slapping her bottom

with each stroke. The mattress shivered and shook as they came together in a wild frenzy of need.

He gasped for breath. "Meg...I can't wait..." With a groan, he drove into her and came.

She absorbed the spasms of his release and tightened the muscles holding him deep within her. She was close, so close. And then she felt his thumb press hard against her clit and she erupted, her climax dancing and twirling in time with his.

As the waves of pleasure subsided, she sank down onto his chest. They were both slick with sweat, and she rubbed back and forth to savor the feel of his moist chest hair lightly scratching her breasts.

He wrapped his arms around her and sighed. "I could stay in this bed with you all day, Nurse Meg."

"I must have a good bedside manner, then." She rested her cheek against his muscled shoulder.

"The best. There's no one I'd rather have tend to my swelling issues." He stroked her back. "Then again, the more I'm around you, the more swelling issues I seem to have, so it's possible you're both the cause and the cure."

"That works out rather neatly, don't you think?"

"It does, especially if we could escape to a deserted island right now."

"That does sound appealing. But there's this wedding on Saturday."

He sighed again. "I know."

"And in addition to the bride and groom, and the minister, of course, we're the other two most significant members of the wedding party."

"And maybe the most important thing to remember is this—if Wyatt hadn't decided to marry Olivia, chances are we would never have met."

"Oh." She lifted her head and met his gaze. "That's too terrible to contemplate."

"Yeah." He tunneled his fingers through her hair. "I wouldn't have known what I was missing, but I would have missed so much." He drew her toward him. "Your chin has a touch of whisker burn from your mouth-to-mouth resuscitation."

"I don't care."

"Good, because I want to kiss you once more before we climb out of this bed and get on with our day."

"Please do."

His lips found hers in the sweetest, most tender kiss he'd given her yet. She barely felt the prickle of his beard. It was the sort of loving kiss that she wished could go on much longer than it did.

When he pulled back, he looked into her eyes with the same sweet tenderness. "You're amazing," he said. "Thank you for giving me such an unforgettable night."

"I won't forget it, either," she said softly. "But I'm hoping for another invitation tonight."

"Consider yourself invited. It'll be the last time we're up here alone. My dad will be in a bedroom in your wing after that."

And maybe his mother, although she decided not to mention that possibility. "Then we'll just have to enjoy our privacy while we have it. And now, I'm heading back down to my own room." She extricated herself from his arms and climbed out of bed.

"I'm getting up, too." He left the bed and disposed of the condom.

Stooping, she gathered her clothes. "I should probably put these on before I go out in the hall, but I'd rather not."

"I dare you to streak back to your room."

She laughed. "It would probably be a very private streak. Judging from the way everyone looked at us last night when they found out about the necklace, they're convinced we spent the night together. They won't venture up here until they know we're both decent." She bundled her clothes together and decided streaking was the way to go.

He picked up his shirt from the floor. "Are you okay with everyone knowing?"

She glanced at him. "I'm okay with it. Are you?"

"Meg, I'm damned proud that you considered me worthy of being your lover. I don't care who knows it."

She smiled with relief. "That makes two of us, then. See you downstairs, cowboy." She opened the door, looked both ways and scurried back to her room.

Once she was there, she remembered leaving her necklace in his bathroom. Streaking once was one thing. Doing it twice was plain unnecessary because she was now in possession of the white terry bathrobe she'd packed.

Pulling it on, she tied the sash and started back down the hall just as Rafe walked out of his bedroom in all his naked glory. He spied her and paused, a smile spreading over his whiskered face.

She was mesmerized. At close quarters, while she'd been involved in either lovemaking or conversation with him, she hadn't been able to gauge the full impact of his athletic body. But when she had both daylight and perspective, she was struck by how magnificent he truly was. Michelangelo must have had someone like Rafe in mind when he sculpted David.

Well, except for the naughty bits. She'd always

thought David could have used a little more abundance in that department. Rafe outshone him there.

He chuckled. "So, are you planning to stand there all morning?"

"I will if you will. It's a great view."

"Flattery will get you everywhere, lady."

"I'm just telling the truth." She walked toward him. "That desert island is sounding better and better. You wouldn't ever have to get dressed as far as I'm concerned."

"No fair." Once she was within reach, he drew her into his arms and tugged at the belt of her robe. "I want my naked nurse back."

"I hear people bustling around downstairs." But when he opened her robe and pulled her close, she didn't object. She'd been admiring him from afar, and now she could enjoy the pleasure of feeling all those delicious lines and angles against her body.

"What people?" He leaned down and nuzzled behind her ear. "Aren't we the only two in the world?"

"'Fraid not." She cupped his firm buttocks and wanted him again. But the house was waking up, and although she didn't mind everyone knowing she'd spent the night with Rafe, she didn't want the family to think she couldn't tear herself away from him this morning.

"Too bad." He stroked her breast. "Your nipples are puckering up like they do when you want me."

"I *do* want you."

"Aha!"

"But I'm not going to act on it."

He continued to caress her. "So why did you come back?"

"For my necklace."

He chuckled. "What a great excuse." He started maneuvering her toward the bathroom. "Let's go get it, and while we're in there, we can—"

"Nope." She finally found the willpower to wriggle out of his arms and retie her robe. "You're quite tempting, Rafe Locke, but it's time for us to make an appearance."

He gave her a sad smile. "Can't blame a guy for trying."

"I'm thrilled that you're trying. Knowing you want me after all the sex we've had is…well, it's just very exciting."

"For me, too. I'm glad you still want me."

"I do." She took a deep breath. "And I would count it a huge favor if you'd go into the bathroom and bring out the necklace."

"Sure." He walked into the bathroom, giving her a tantalizing view of his tight buns in motion. Just inside the door he glanced over his shoulder. "Caught you looking."

"Why wouldn't I?"

"Good point. I'd do the same in your place." He continued into the bathroom and quickly returned holding her necklace. "So how about taking off your bathrobe before you walk back to your room? I wouldn't mind having that image to sustain me through the day."

She hesitated. She didn't *think* anyone would come upstairs unannounced, but she couldn't be positive.

"Come on, my uninhibited lover." He held out the necklace. "Need this for courage?"

"Maybe." She took it from his hand and settled it around her neck. The silver was cool against her hot skin, and she couldn't deny she felt different when she wore it.

A woman who wore a necklace this beautiful would have poise to spare. She'd accept the challenge of walking away naked from a man who wanted to admire her from behind. She'd revel in the power of her body to captivate him and hold him hostage to her whims.

"Take off the robe, Meg," he urged softly. "Take it off and walk away from me, knowing that I'll be devouring the sight of your bare ass every step of the way. I'll watch you go, and I'll want you desperately. If you turn to look before you go in, you'll see how much."

She lifted her chin and met his hot glance. "I'll do it."

"Is it on your list?"

"It is now." Untying her robe, she let it fall open and relished the way his eyes darkened in response. Slowly, keeping her gaze locked with his, she drew the robe off her shoulders and let it slide down.

Before it hit the floor, she grabbed the collar and held on. "See you downstairs, cowboy."

His throat moved as he swallowed. "You bet."

She took her time turning around, and then she strolled down the hall dragging the robe behind her as if it were a mink coat. She'd never been a runway model, but she'd seen the suggestive way they walked, and she was a good mimic.

Her heart thudded wildly as she put herself boldly on display for the man she'd loved so thoroughly the night before. She'd dared much with him, but always in the heat of passion. This deliberately provocative move was strictly solo, and it required a sexual confidence she hadn't thought she possessed.

At her doorway, she turned.

Rafe's soft laughter drifted toward her, and he gestured toward his rigid cock. "See?"

Gratifying indeed. "Hold that thought."

"Don't worry. I won't forget that visual for a long, long time. Now if you'll excuse me, I'm going to take a very cold shower."

"Sorry."

"Believe me, it was worth it. See you later, sweet cheeks."

"Which cheeks are you referring to?"

He laughed again. "I think you know." And then he was gone.

Moments later she heard the noise of the shower. Looping her robe over her arm, she walked into her bedroom. Strange, but she didn't feel like the same person who had left it yesterday.

15

DESPITE MISSING OUT ON another romp with Meg, Rafe was in a fantastic mood as he finished dressing in some of his new clothes. He liked the way they fit, and damned if he didn't feel a little more like a cowboy this morning.

Maybe cowboys had better sex. He wasn't opposed to making use of the fantasy this week, especially because it included having great sex with a woman he liked very much. He had several more days to be with her and find out if the magic continued. Assuming it did, he'd build more time into his schedule to be with her. And then...then they'd see.

He still had a thriving business in San Francisco and he wasn't about to let go of that. But if she was as captivated by their relationship as he was, she might be willing to make some concessions. After all, she was the one who'd already decided moving was an option.

Keeping that possibility under wraps seemed to be the best idea. No sense in stirring up opposition to the plan before he'd decided if it had value. He had one more unobstructed day with Meg. He hoped they could go riding. With that in mind, he tucked a condom in his jeans pocket. Never hurt to be prepared.

His cell phone lay on the dresser. He felt a little guilty for not paying more attention to his clients in the past couple of days. But hey, if any of them had lucked out and found a hot partner like he had, they'd do the same.

Maybe he should turn on the phone, though, and see how many messages had stacked up. He'd take a quick inventory and then go downstairs and have breakfast with Meg. Skipping breakfast had been a mistake yesterday, and he tried not to make the same mistake twice.

Fortunately, he didn't have a ton of work-related emails, but he had two missed calls from his father and finally the guy had decided to leave a message. He probably hadn't expected Rafe to turn off his phone because he so rarely did that. Rafe keyed in the message function.

Probably something about his dad's flight on Thursday. Maybe the landing time had changed by two minutes. Harlan Locke was a stickler for details, and his plane travel always turned into an elaborate schematic that probably drove his secretary around the bend.

Putting the phone to his ear, he prepared himself for an account of Harlan's exact ETA and his instructions for meeting at baggage claim. Rafe loved his anal father, but sometimes he had to shake his head at the minutia involved in Harlan's every move. Still, that attention to detail was probably one of the factors that had made his father a wealthy man.

Harlan's message had to do with his flight, but in a totally uncharacteristic move, he'd decided to change his schedule and come in a day early. Rafe was still adjusting to that news, which blew a hole in his plans with Meg for today and tonight, when his father dropped the bombshell.

"I'm switching my flight because your mother is coming to the wedding. She'll arrive on Friday, and I expect pandemonium when she gets there. I'd like an extra day to acquaint myself with Wyatt's bride before Diana blows everything apart."

Sinking to the edge of the bed, Rafe stared at his phone. So much for his happy little vision of spending the next few days getting to know Meg better. His father was arriving at noon today, and his mother would descend on them two days later. All hell was about to break loose.

He sent his dad a quick text promising to be at the airport at the appointed hour. Maybe he should ask Meg to come along. Nah, probably a bad idea.

Instinctively he knew that Meg and his father wouldn't get each other. She was full of optimism and enthusiasm for this event, while his dad planned to stoically endure the experience. Conversation might be strained on the ride home.

After pocketing his phone, he took a long, calming breath, put on his borrowed hat and left his room. Nothing had changed, really. He and Meg wouldn't have the same opportunities to be together, but after what they'd shared last night, she wouldn't give up on him because of that. They'd adjust.

He walked into the kitchen to find Meg sitting huddled at the table with Mary Lou and Sarah. Meg wasn't wearing her necklace, but that made sense if she thought they'd go riding later. The mood at the table was somber, though, and he had to believe they'd heard the news about Diana. All of them clutched their coffee mugs like life preservers.

Sarah glanced up the minute he walked in. "I don't know if you've heard, but Diana—"

"Is coming to the wedding. My dad left me a message. Has anyone told Wyatt?"

"Yes." Sarah met his gaze. "Diana did. She called Wyatt late last night, but he'd turned off his phone, so he didn't get the message until this morning. He called me a few minutes ago."

"But she won't be here until Friday," Rafe said, as if that made it more palatable.

"I don't know if that's good or bad." Sarah heaved a sigh. "She won't be here to cause problems with the advance preparations, but she'll show up when the festivities are in full swing. I won't have as much time to...to..." She spread her hands. "Come to think of it, I don't know what I'd do if I had more time. I guess we'll see what happens."

"She won't cause any problems," Mary Lou said. It sounded more like Mary Lou's personal threat than a considered opinion.

"I hope not." Rafe took off his hat, ran his fingers through his hair and repositioned the hat. "If it's any consolation, I'll do my best to keep her under control. I'm not saying I'll succeed, but I'll do my best."

Sarah nodded. "I appreciate that, Rafe. And just so you know, Wyatt seemed happy that she was coming. He's a sensitive guy, so he realized I might not be overjoyed, but...actually, I am glad. It's time."

Rafe thought about Wyatt, who of course wanted his mother to attend his wedding. The guy had a heart the size of Wyoming and hoped everyone would join hands and sing "Kumbaya" around a campfire. Then Rafe remembered the other player in this drama. He looked at Sarah. "Has Wyatt called Jack?"

She shook her head. "He hadn't when he contacted me, so I volunteered to do it. I called over to Jack's house, and Josie said he was on his way here to consult with Emmett about one of the new foals. I suppose he'll go straight to the barn."

"I'll go down there and tell him," Rafe said.

Sarah looked relieved. "Thank you. I think that's a good idea. He may have some questions I can't answer."

"There's one other thing. My dad is coming in today at noon instead of tomorrow." From the corner of his eye he saw Meg blink in surprise. "Now that my mother's arriving on Friday, my dad wants to meet Olivia before everything gets too…"

"That's fine." Sarah put down her mug. "I'll make sure his room's ready. Are you still picking him up, or is Wyatt?"

"I am." Initially he'd wanted to help ease his father's entry into country life by using the Lexus. Wyatt would have picked him up in his truck with the camper shell, or Olivia might have driven her Jeep. Neither one would have suited his dad. But maybe Rafe shouldn't be so concerned about whether his dad would feel comfortable with his transportation.

"I'll go with you," Meg said.

He hesitated. Not ten minutes ago he'd decided that wasn't a good idea.

"Unless you'd rather I didn't," Meg said.

In that instant he realized he wanted her there. If his dad had a problem with her sunny attitude, too bad.

Rafe's loyalties were shifting. "I'd love for you to go," he said. "I wasn't sure you'd want to."

"He'll be curious about Olivia. I'm her best friend, so I can tell him lots of great stories about her."

"Good. Let's leave about ten-thirty."

"I'll be ready."

Now that she was going with him, he was grateful she'd asked. The drive to Jackson would give them a chance to be alone before his father arrived. He wasn't thinking of it in sexual terms, because they'd need to keep close track of the time. But that drive might be their last opportunity to really talk.

"Rafe," Mary Lou said, "after you speak with Jack, I want you here in this kitchen for a decent breakfast. I'm not in favor of grabbing a cup of coffee and leaving, like you did yesterday. A body can't survive on that."

Rafe grinned at Meg. "You ratted on me, didn't you?"

"I might have said something." She did her best to look innocent and failed.

"That's fine." He discovered he rather liked having her look after his welfare. "I nearly starved to death yesterday after skipping breakfast. I promise to come back and eat whatever you put in front of me, Mary Lou."

She winked at him. "That's a deal, cowboy. And by the way, nice duds."

"Yes, they are," Sarah agreed. "Sorry I was so distracted that I didn't say anything. Meg, did you help him pick out those clothes?"

"Uh-huh." Her cheeks turned a becoming shade of pink.

He'd bet good money she was remembering the scene in the dressing room. And after all that, he hadn't modeled the leather vest for her last night. Now it was too late.

Or maybe not. Upstairs might not be their sanctuary anymore, but the ranch was a big place. He'd probably have to get creative, but it seemed a shame to waste the potential of that leather vest.

He touched the brim of his hat the way he'd seen other cowboys do. "Be back soon, ladies." He left the kitchen.

"Thanks, Rafe," Sarah called after him.

Walking quickly through the house and out the front door, he paused on the porch to take in the view of the Tetons. He still couldn't understand how his mother could have looked upon that view every day and yet failed to mention it as a feature of ranch life.

She must have been blinded by unhappiness. Rafe couldn't imagine being that unhappy, but then again, he wasn't convinced he knew his mother all that well. As he walked down to the barn, he tried to put himself in Jack's place. If he were Jack, how would he take this news?

Jack's outward behavior indicated that nothing would faze him. He projected strength and control. But Rafe knew through Wyatt that Jack wasn't as invincible as he seemed. His fear of abandonment, created by Diana, had taken years to overcome.

Rafe's allegiance was also shifting toward Jack, the man who had taught him to dance without making fun of him, the man who'd been willing to look like a fool while the two of them navigated through a Texas Two-Step. And yet, Diana was Rafe's mother. He couldn't turn his back on her, even if she deserved it.

What a mess she'd made for her three sons. Jack

might want to hold himself aloof from her, while Wyatt would be campaigning for a group hug. And Rafe... Rafe would be in the middle, trying to keep the drama from ruining what should be a perfectly good wedding and whatever chance he had at a relationship with Meg.

Jack's red truck was parked down by the barn. Judging from the advance billing he'd been given, Rafe would have expected Jack to drive a badass black truck. Instead he had picked out a truck that was, as he phrased it, *whorehouse-red.* Now that Rafe knew the guy a little better, he could see Jack gravitating toward a flashy truck.

Rafe wished he was headed down there to tease Jack about their dancing gig the night before instead of bringing the news about Diana. But he felt good about offering to do it. Sarah had enough to deal with.

She had been given the job of cleaning up the mess Diana had made more than thirty years ago. No telling what conflicting emotions were going through Sarah's mind right now. But she was one of the most gracious women Rafe had ever met, so he knew when the time came, she would act with dignity. He couldn't be so sure about his mother.

When he reached the open barn doors, he stopped to pet both dogs. The scent of horses, leather and hay stirred memories of his ride yesterday with Meg. Maybe if they came home from the airport early enough, they could take a quick ride before dinner. He wasn't sore, and he credited all the good sex for keeping his muscles warmed up most of the night.

Inside the barn he followed the sound of voices to a large stall where a mare and foal were stabled. Emmett and Jack leaned over the side of the stall watching mom and baby as they talked business.

Rafe couldn't help contrasting this business setting with his office back in San Francisco. He'd never expected to call the skyscraper where he worked cold and sterile, but in comparison to a barn full of beautiful horses, it was. He was a financial advisor, though, not a cowboy. He'd do well to remember how he earned a living.

Jack glanced up. "Hey, there, twinkle toes. I've never met a man who picked up the Texas Two-Step that fast. I'd say you cheated if I hadn't seen the way you stumbled through the Electric Slide when we first got started."

"Guess you're just an excellent teacher, Jack."

"Don't give me that. It was like a dance switch got flipped in your brain."

"Actually it was the karate switch."

Jack stared at him. "Come again?"

"I was into martial arts for quite a few years. At some point last night I called up the intense focus I once used for karate."

"Huh." Jack nodded. "That makes sense, then. You're like a Texas Two-Step ninja." He turned toward Emmett. "You should try dancing with this guy. He's good."

Emmett grinned. "No, thanks. But I'm sure sorry I missed the performance last night."

"Yeah, we were damned impressive." Jack looked over at Rafe. "Judging from your expression, you're a man on a mission. What's up?"

Rafe decided not to sugarcoat it. "Diana's coming to the wedding." He used her name instead of saying "my mother" or "our mother." He didn't know if Jack claimed her as his.

Shock registered for a split second in Jack's eyes before a mask of indifference obscured the emotion. "Okay."

"She called Wyatt this morning. She's flying in on Friday."

"Good to know." Jack's expression was unreadable. "Where's she staying?"

"She... I don't know. I didn't think to ask."

"Your dad's staying here at the ranch, isn't he?"

"Yes, and that's the other thing. Dad's coming in today at noon instead of waiting until tomorrow. He's decided to get acquainted with Olivia before my...before Diana arrives."

"Smart man," Jack said.

Emmett stepped forward. "Look, it's none of my business, but I wonder if maybe we should ask Pam to put Diana up at the B and B. Pam runs a nice place, and it might be better all the way around."

"Depends on whether she has transportation," Jack said. "Do you know if she's planning to rent a car? Because I can tell you right now, I'm not hauling her ass around." He glanced away from Rafe and tugged on the brim of his hat. "Sorry. I keep forgetting she's your mother."

And yours. But Rafe had a feeling Jack didn't think of her that way and might never think of her that way. Sarah was his mother in every sense except biologically.

"I'll find out if she's planning to provide her own transportation." The Lexus would hold both of his parents, but Rafe didn't want to be the one chauffeuring them in the same car if he could possibly help it. "If she's not, maybe I'll suggest it, along with the B and B option. I've forgotten the name of the place. What's it called?"

"The Bunk and Grub," Emmett said.

"Perfect." Rafe imagined his mother's reaction to staying in a place named The Bunk and Grub. As Wyatt had said, their father was somewhat of a snob, but Diana took snobbery to a whole new level. The next few days would be a real circus. Unfortunately, he felt like the ringmaster trying to control the inevitable chaos.

16

To Meg's surprise, Rafe spent a good part of the drive to Jackson asking questions about her job. He wanted to know things she never expected anybody but another engineer to care about, and he seemed interested as she described the traffic flow challenges when cities like Pittsburgh grew in unexpected ways.

As they talked, she wondered if Rafe was focusing on traffic in Pittsburgh because it beat thinking about his parents' imminent arrival in Jackson Hole. If he needed a distraction, she was happy to provide it. And it was fun for her. Most men she'd dated had avoided mentioning her work.

Rafe didn't bring up his parents until they stood side by side in baggage claim waiting for Harlan Locke to deplane. "Wyatt takes after my dad," he said. "Dad has some gray mixed in with his sandy hair, but his eyes are the exact same gray as Wyatt's. Temperamentally, though, they're nothing alike."

She glanced over at him. "I don't know if you remember saying the same thing about you and Wyatt the day we met."

"Did I?"

"You did, but personally I think you and your brother are more alike than different."

"It's the outfit making you say that. Underneath this Western shirt beats the heart of a big-city guy who loves to wheel and deal in the market. Wyatt hates that kind of thing. He'd rather climb a mountain."

"But you both crave a challenge, even if they're different challenges. I'll stick to my opinion."

He smiled. "You do that. But when it comes to my dad and Wyatt, they really are different. He— Never mind. Here he comes. You can see for yourself."

Harlan Locke strode toward them looking like a Ralph Lauren model, trim and sophisticated in an open-throated white silk shirt and tan slacks that—defying the logic of plane travel—remained crisp. He'd slung a leather computer case over one shoulder and he held a cell phone to his ear. Lifting a hand in greeting, he continued to talk to whoever was on the phone as he walked in their direction.

Meg told herself the phone call might be important, and Harlan had seen his son recently. It wasn't as if they'd been apart for months. But surely Harlan had noticed that Rafe had brought a friend. She thought he should get off the phone soon and greet those who had come to fetch him.

She hung back a little, though, wanting to give father and son a moment together before Rafe introduced her. The man continued to talk on the damned phone while Rafe stared at the floor and waited for his father to finish the call. Meg fumed on Rafe's behalf.

He'd been telling the truth when he'd said his father and Wyatt were completely different. Wyatt would never have put a phone call, any phone call, ahead of greeting someone who'd come to meet him. She had to believe Rafe wouldn't, either.

Finally Rafe turned and beckoned her to come over. Might as well. She wouldn't be interrupting a warm moment between father and son.

More time passed in which Harlan glanced at them, rolled his eyes, but kept talking. Finally he took the phone from his ear and disconnected the call. "Sorry about that. A client's favorite stock just tanked and I had to talk him off the ledge. I tried to warn him to pull out weeks ago, but he wanted to hang on."

Rafe put a hand against the small of Meg's back. "Dad, I'd like you to meet the maid of honor, Meg Seymour."

"Delighted to meet you, Meg." Harlan held out his hand.

Meg shook his hand and smiled. "I'm glad to meet you, too, Mr. Locke." She was glad, if only to understand Rafe better.

"Call me Harlan, please. *Mr. Locke* makes me feel old."

"Harlan it is, then." She guessed that age was a sensitive topic with him. With twenty-nine-year-old sons, he had to be in his fifties, yet he could pass for someone ten years younger.

"I see your bag," Rafe said. "I'll go grab it."

"Thanks." Harlan turned back to Meg. "Nice of you to come along and keep Rafe company on the airport run."

"I wanted to. Olivia and I have been best friends for most of our lives, so I'm the advance promo team for her. You're very lucky to get her as a daughter-in-law."

"That's what Wyatt tells me. I'm hoping she will convince him to get serious about this trekking business of his."

"Oh? I thought he was already quite committed to it."

Harlan shook his head. "To the work itself, I suppose, but he's blind to the growth potential. He never should have closed his San Francisco operation and moved everything here. He could have put someone else in charge up there and made this a second location. I've been advocating expansion for years, maybe franchise the concept. Colorado, Arizona, Florida, maybe even go international with it."

"I don't know. It's hard to imagine Wyatt as a tycoon."

Harlan laughed. "Isn't it, though? Rafe, on the other hand, is well on his way to making his first million. I wish Wyatt had some of Rafe's business sense."

"Got your suitcase." Rafe appeared pulling a Gucci rolling bag that probably cost the same as two months' rent on Meg's condo in Pittsburgh.

She hadn't thought to investigate what sort of suitcase Rafe had brought. Probably one like this if he could so easily recognize his father's. And he had bought her a necklace with a gasp-worthy price tag.

According to his dad, Rafe was on his way to making his first million. That was intimidating. She'd tried to push Rafe's sophisticated lifestyle to the back of her mind because it pointed up their differences. Maybe she'd be wise to remember those differences did exist.

Harlan murmured his approval of the Lexus when they loaded his suitcase in the trunk. Meg urged him to sit up front with Rafe, but he insisted on taking the backseat. As he climbed in, his phone chimed.

For most of the ride back to the Last Chance, Harlan took calls on his cell phone. Meg tried making conversation with Rafe, but she felt weird talking over Harlan so she finally gave up and rode in silence.

"He's on the phone a lot," Rafe said in a low, apologetic voice.

"So I see. Business must be good."

"Oh, it's very good. I used to think he worked hard to provide luxuries for my mother, but now that they're divorced, I realize he just likes working hard."

"Mmm." Meg had a million thoughts running through her head and couldn't voice any of them. Someone had once told her that if you wanted to see what a man would be like in twenty-five years, look at his father. Meg shuddered to think Rafe would turn out like this.

As they neared the outskirts of Shoshone, Harlan ended a call and, amazingly, his phone didn't ring right away. "So, Rafe, looks like you've gone native. Never thought I'd see you duded up like a cowboy."

"It's more practical to dress like this. Turns out I like to ride."

"Horses?"

"Yeah, it's the damnedest thing. Meg taught me the basics, and we went out on a trail ride yesterday. I enjoyed the hell out of it."

"Will wonders never cease. Just don't try to get me on one of those animals. I like my transportation to have a steering wheel and foot pedals. So this is Shoshone, huh?"

"This is it."

"Not much to the place, is there?"

Meg turned toward the backseat. "Depends on how

you look at it. For anyone who prefers the simple life, then it's perfect."

Harlan laughed. "Yeah, Wyatt's told me all about the *simple* life around here. He warned me not to expect decent espresso or full-service day spas in Shoshone. He mentioned one bar, one diner, an ice cream shop, a gas station and a feed store. Did I miss anything?"

"That about covers it," Rafe said.

"I don't know how you've been surviving, Rafe. You must be going stir-crazy."

"Actually, I haven't." Rafe glanced over at Meg and gave her a secret smile. "It's been a nice break from my usual routine."

"I doubt if I'll be able to say the same on Sunday, but I can't let my son get married without showing up and meeting the bride. I'll tell you this, though, I can see why Diana left. A wide spot in the road wouldn't suit her at all."

Rafe stopped the Lexus at the town's only traffic signal. "So, Dad, what about her parents? Did she ever tell you about them?"

"Only that her mother was a full-blooded Shoshone and her father was Anglo. Apparently they died."

"At the same time?" The light changed and Rafe pulled through the intersection.

"I think so, yeah."

"Was there a traffic accident, or what?"

"I don't know, Rafe. You'll have to ask her." His tone indicated that the subject was closed as far as he was concerned.

"It just feels strange to think that they were my grandparents, but I know nothing about them."

"Does it matter?" Harlan sounded slightly irritated.

"They won't be any good to you at this point. You had Nana and Papa Locke while you were growing up."

Meg wished she could lay a comforting hand on Rafe's arm, but she didn't want to telegraph anything about their relationship to Harlan. Rafe was asking perfectly legitimate questions, things she'd want to know in his shoes, but his father displayed no empathy at all. What a shame.

Harlan's phone chimed soon after that, and he returned to his business.

"There might be a way to research your grandparents," Meg said softly. "Do you know your mother's maiden name?"

"Not off the top of my head. But it would be on my birth certificate back in San Francisco."

"What about Wyatt's birth certificate?"

He sent her a look of gratitude. "You're a genius." He took out his cell phone and hit a button. "Hey, bro. Yeah, we have the parental unit in the car. Listen, can you put your hands on your birth certificate? I want to know Mom's maiden name."

He paused to listen. "Well, I thought I'd research our grandparents and find out...You did already? How come you didn't tell me?" His expression slowly changed from excitement to sadness. "Yeah, I can see why you wouldn't be eager to share that in the middle of happy times. But it's good to know. Yeah, thanks. See you tonight." He disconnected the phone and sighed.

"What did he say?"

"He had the same questions I did, so a couple of weeks ago Olivia helped him track down the information. He didn't tell me then because it's not all that positive, and Wyatt likes to dwell on the positive."

That made her smile because it was so true. "Will you tell me anyway?"

He glanced at her and then checked the rearview mirror. His father was still on the phone. Rafe lowered his voice. "Wyatt found somebody who actually knew them. They were heavy drinkers, and they chain-smoked, too. My mother had gone to a teenage slumber party the night her parents got drunk, as usual. They accidentally set fire to the house and they both died in the fire."

Meg gasped softly. "Oh, Rafe." She squeezed his arm, no longer caring if Harlan noticed.

"You can see why Wyatt wasn't ready to lay that on me in the middle of all the wedding festivities. I wonder if Jack knows. I have to believe he doesn't or he wouldn't be so hard on my mom. Something like that... well, it helps explain a few things."

"I'm sure." Meg had been prepared to dislike Diana even more than she already disliked Harlan, but knowing this sad tale changed her knee-jerk reaction. She'd been willing to condemn a woman who would abandon her child. But in a way, Diana had been abandoned, too.

When they reached the ranch, Sarah must have been watching for them, because she came out on the porch to greet Harlan as warmly as she might have welcomed an old friend. Fortunately Harlan didn't walk up the porch steps while talking on his cell phone. He was all charm and courtesy as they went into the house.

That irritated Meg even more. If Harlan saved his disrespect only for his nearest and dearest—and, by extension, their friends—that would be worse than if he treated everyone in the same high-handed way. It was as if his status as father and former chief breadwinner gave him the right to ignore common courtesy with his own children.

He might very well have shown the same arrogance with his wife, now his ex-wife. Once again, Meg decided she needed to reserve judgment until she'd met Diana and could get a sense of the woman. But the jury was in on Harlan Locke. She didn't like him.

"So, what do you think of my dad?"

She'd been so lost in thought that Harlan and Sarah's departure hadn't registered. She and Rafe stood alone in the living room. And he'd just asked her a question she didn't want to answer.

"It's okay, Meg," he said gently. "I didn't think you'd get along with him."

"We haven't had much time to talk." *Because he's been on the phone.*

He chuckled. "Let me rephrase that. You're from completely different planets."

She sighed in relief at being given a graceful way out of the discussion. "Yes, we are." And his father was from the Planet of the A-holes, but she wasn't going to say that out loud.

"It's funny, but I used to accept that he'd be on the phone all the time whenever I was with him, but this afternoon I saw it through your eyes. It's kind of obnoxious, isn't it?"

"Let's say I wouldn't do that."

"And I hope to hell that *I* wouldn't do that, but they say the apple doesn't fall far from the tree. I'm going to pay more attention to my phone habits from now on."

"You haven't been the least bit obnoxious with your phone since I've known you."

He trailed his finger down her cheek. "That's probably because you're such a good influence on me."

"Darn it! And here I hoped that I was a bad influence, the kind of wild woman who parades down hallways naked."

Heat flared in his dark eyes. "I'll never forget that. And just so you know, I'm not giving up on having some alone time with you. We'll go make out in the barn if we have to, but I—" He paused and glanced toward the staircase as Sarah and his father started back down. "Later."

She winked at him. "You bet, cowboy." Her heart felt considerably lighter knowing that he could accept her reservations regarding his father.

"I just talked to Wyatt," Harlan said as he made his way back over to where Meg and Rafe stood. "He'd like to meet up in about thirty minutes at that bar we passed on the way in—the Spit and Spots, or something like that. He's bringing Olivia."

"It's the Spirits and Spurs." Sarah's voice had lost some of its welcoming warmth. "My daughter-in-law Josie owns it."

"Oh. Sorry. I didn't get a good look at the sign when we drove through." Harlan turned back to Rafe. "So I said we could probably do that."

"We can." Rafe glanced at Meg. "Would you like to come along?"

"Thanks, but I really need to do a few things around here." She was moving from mild dislike to active dislike when it came to Harlan Locke, so the invitation held little appeal for her. Besides, she wanted Livy to form her own opinion without picking up negative vibes from her best friend. They could compare notes later.

Rafe looked as if he'd hoped for a different answer, but he gave her an understanding smile. "Right. I'll see you at dinner, then."

"Yes, I'll see you then. Nice to have met you, Mr. L—uh, I mean Harlan."

"Same here, Meg."

With one last glance in Meg's direction, Rafe followed his dad out the door.

Sarah let out a deep sigh. "And he's supposed to be the good parent."

Meg nodded. "And speaking of Diana, I just heard something you might want to know before she arrives."

"Let's go get a cup of coffee and sit out on the porch while you tell me about it." Then she smiled. "Archie and Nelsie sometimes added a little Baileys to their coffee when they felt the need. I'm feeling the need. How about you?"

"Absolutely, Sarah." Meg was so glad she'd stayed home instead of riding into town. "Hook me up."

_17_

AS THE HOURS WENT BY, Rafe asked himself if his father had always been such an arrogant snob and had to admit that he had. Rafe had excused his behavior because the guy worked so damned hard, but his dad seemed to believe that dedication to his work made him superior to everyone else.

That sense of superiority hadn't been so obvious in Harlan's own environment when he was surrounded by people like him. But here it stood out in stark relief. Seeing his father as the Chances surely did was disorienting.

He'd looked up to his father all his life and considered him a role model. He'd followed in his dad's footsteps, partly because he had a natural ability when it came to money management, but partly to please his dad. Harlan *was* pleased, and made sure to tell everyone at the dinner table that night how financially successful Rafe had become under his tutelage.

With every self-congratulating word out of his father's mouth, Meg's attitude grew more distant. Rafe could see it in her eyes. She didn't much like his father, and the more Harlan referred to Rafe as a "chip off the old block," the less she was going to like Rafe. He needed to reconnect with her.

As everyone left the dining table to gather in front of the fire in the living room, Rafe drew Meg aside. "Could I interest you in a walk in the moonlight, little lady?"

Her answering smile was tentative. "Wouldn't it be rude to do that when the evening's still in progress?"

"Not if I come up with an excuse. Leave it to me."

She still looked doubtful. "All right."

As everyone sought chairs and Sarah offered after-dinner drinks, Rafe spoke up. "I could be wrong, but I think there's a partial eclipse tonight. Meg and I are going out to take a look."

"An eclipse?" Wyatt frowned. "I don't remember hearing about that."

"That's because you're obsessed with wedding plans," Jack said. "I heard about it." He looked over at his wife. "Didn't you, Josie?"

"No, I—oh, wait, yes, now that you mention it." She ducked her head and suddenly became very busy playing with little Archie.

Rafe felt a surge of gratitude toward Jack and Josie. They knew he'd made up the eclipse story and were helping substantiate it.

"I heard about it, too," Olivia said. "You two go check it out for the rest of us."

"We'll do that. Come on, Meg." He hustled her outside before any more questions were asked.

"An eclipse?"

"There could be." He took her hand as they went down the steps to the gravel driveway. "You never know. Let's go see." He led her into the shadows created by two giant blue spruce trees on the far side of the drive.

She laughed. "Don't you need to be out in the open to look at the moon?"

"That's one theory." He pulled her into his arms. "We can discuss it later." Then he kissed her with the desperation of a man who'd gone too long without feeling her lips on his.

She kissed him back, but her response felt subtly different. Instinctively he knew she wasn't giving herself to the experience the way she had before. She'd injected a note of caution into her kiss.

Reluctantly he lifted his head. "Talk to me, Meg."

"What do you want to talk about?"

He couldn't see her expression very well in the shadows, but he didn't have to. He heard the hesitation in her voice. "Tonight at the dinner table I felt you pulling away. Was I wrong?"

"Rafe…"

Icicles settled in his gut. "I know my dad's been getting on your nerves, but I'm not him. I hope never to be like him."

With a sigh, she cupped his face in both hands. "I'm sure you won't, but listening to him I realized how truly different you and I are. You're focused on making money, and I'm focused on being happy. That makes our goals and values miles apart."

"What if making money makes me happy? I enjoy my work, Meg. How much I earn doing it is a way of keeping score. Is that so terrible?"

"No, it's not terrible at all. It's just different from my way of looking at things. We have different priorities. I've been kidding myself that we could extend this…whatever is going on between us…longer than this week, but—"

"We can." He drew her closer. "I refuse to believe we're as far apart as you say. I love my job and you love yours. And by the way, I can't see your job transferring to Jackson Hole, but I'm sure you could find something in San Francisco. You'd love the challenges of that city, Meg. There's heavy traffic, hills and trolley cars. You could really sink your teeth into the problems there."

She grew very still in his arms. "Is that why you were asking me about my work today? So you could convince me to give up Jackson Hole and put San Francisco in its place?"

"Not exactly. I was curious about how you planned to make that transition, and I really can't it happening easily here. But in a city the size of—"

"I don't want to move to another big city, Rafe. Living here would make me happy."

"Will you be happy if you're unemployed? Not doing the work you love? I don't think so."

"You know what? I'm not worried about how the job situation will work out. If I can't get hired in my field, I'll find something similar. I have some savings, and I can live on that until I figure out my next step. But if I can hang out in this area, ride horses, admire the mountains and learn to ski, then I'm going to do whatever it takes to make that happen."

"Wow." He took a deep breath and gazed up into the branches of the spruce towering above them. "You're more of a free spirit than I thought."

"Then you weren't listening," she said gently. She

stroked her hands from his cheeks to his shoulders. "Rafe, what we've had was great, but I think it's time to—"

"Don't say that."

"I have to say that. I was starting to fall for you, but after tonight I realize how crazy that is. I—I'll return the necklace."

"The hell you will."

"It's far too expensive a gift for a woman you spent only one night with. I don't care how well-off you are, that's a ridiculous extravagance."

His heart broke slowly and painfully into dozens of pieces. "Look, it's been a long day, and neither of us got much sleep last night. We shouldn't be having such a heavy-duty discussion right now."

Giving his shoulders a squeeze, she stepped out of his arms. "Rafe, I care for you, but I also care for myself. I'm not going to continue toying with an emotional connection that has the power to derail my plans to live a happy life. I refuse to allow you to make me miserable."

"So you don't care if you make me miserable?"

"Of course I do. But my first obligation is to myself. I know who I am and what I want out of life. It's not the same as what you want." She took a shaky breath. "I'm going in."

"Sure. Okay. I'm going...down to check on the horses." He had no idea if the horses needed checking or not. He didn't know if that was the sort of thing that cowboys did on a ranch. But the barn felt like a refuge right now, and he needed one.

Fortunately the place wasn't locked up. All he had to do was lift the bar across the double doors, and he was in. No overhead lights were on, but soft lights placed at ankle-height along the aisle between the stalls kept him from stumbling around in the dark.

So he was here in the barn, with its comforting scents of hay, horses, leather and old wood. Now what? He wandered down to Destiny's stall. Although he'd hoped for at least one more ride with Meg, that probably wouldn't happen.

Destiny looked up expectantly as Rafe leaned against the stall door. Belatedly he realized that paying a visit like this might work out better if he'd brought some carrots or apples. "I got nothin', Destiny," he said. "Sorry."

The horse came over anyway, and nudged Rafe's arm. Rafe stroked the white blaze that ran from Destiny's forehead to his wide nostrils. "She doesn't want me, horse. Simple as that. I guess she's looking for some guy who doesn't give a damn where his next paycheck is coming from."

Destiny snorted and pawed the straw with one hoof.

"I know. That's nuts, but what can I do? I'm not going to give up a client list worth seven figures so I can hang out with her in some tiny house in Shoshone." But as he said it, the pieces of his broken heart throbbed. It didn't sound so bad.

"But sure as the world, we'd be *poor,* Destiny. There's nothing noble about being happy and poor. I don't care what she says. I—" He fell silent as the sound of booted feet came down the aisle between the stalls.

"Kinda hard to see an eclipse if you're in the barn," Jack said.

"Turns out I was mistaken about the eclipse."

"I know." Jack walked over and leaned against Destiny's stall, facing Rafe. He had on his hat, which made

Rafe wish he'd worn his tonight, but he hadn't felt right doing it. Chalk one up for his dad's influence.

"I was just trying to help you out by going along with that eclipse nonsense," Jack said. "But when Meg came in alone, I figured everything had gone south."

"So you came down here to check on me?" That made Rafe feel somewhat better.

"Hell, no. I came down to check on the horses. I like doing that. There's a peaceful feeling about a barn full of horses at night."

Rafe let that stand, but he still had the impression Jack was here on account of him, not the horses. "As long as you're here, let me say one thing. My dad's a pain in the ass. I won't apologize for him because it's not my responsibility that he acts like that, but I will acknowledge it."

"The good part is, he's proud of you."

"I wish he'd keep that to himself. His bragging didn't help the situation with Meg. But then, that was probably doomed, anyway."

"How so?"

"We look at things completely differently."

"Then it's good you found that out now, before either of you got in too deep."

"Right." Rafe nodded. "Right." Maybe eventually he'd convince himself of that. But he ached for her so much that he couldn't believe the pain would ever go away.

"Incidentally, on a totally different subject, Sarah told me the story about how our grandparents died."

Rafe gazed at him. "Not pretty."

"No. I talked to Wyatt for a little while. He figured

out that Diana was seventeen when that happened. Do you remember what you were doing at seventeen?"

"Chasing girls and driving over the speed limit, mostly."

"Me, too." Jack grimaced. "Stupid stuff. I had a home and people who cared about me, not that I appreciated it. She had none of that. I guess she was in foster care for a little while, but mostly she was on her own."

"Jack, I still don't think that excuses what she did."

"It doesn't. But I see her differently now." He glanced up. "You ready to go back up to the house and grab us a couple of brewskies?"

"As long as it doesn't involve dancing."

"Nope. I'm saving myself for the party tomorrow night. If I get enough beer in me, I might ask Harlan to dance."

Rafe laughed. "I'd pay to see that."

"Yeah? How much? Lay some money on the line, and I'll be even more motivated."

"Let's just say I'll make it well worth your while."

"That's good enough for me." He clapped Rafe on the shoulder. "Word on the street is that you're loaded."

"Don't believe everything you hear."

"Okay, but if you're even half as rich as your dad says, you need to invest in a sure thing. I have this awesome stallion named Houdini, and a person could do very well with a percentage of his future stud fees."

"You're probably kidding, but I kind of like the idea."

"I am kidding. You don't want to do that. Breeding horses is a fool's game, but my brothers and I love it. The only way we'll ever get rich is by selling the ranch, and we have no intention of doing that."

Rafe remembered his first thoughts when he'd arrived here. "Do you have a good financial advisor?"

"We do, but he's getting old, about to retire. Are you volunteering for the job?"

Rafe thought about it as they closed up the barn and walked back to the house. "Yeah, I am. But let's use the barter system. I'll take over as your financial planner in exchange for room and board whenever I come to visit my brother."

"Deal." Jack stuck out his hand. "I assume you know Meg's planning to relocate here."

"So she said."

Jack nodded. "Thought so. Just checking."

Rafe told himself that his offer to be the Last Chance's financial planner had nothing to do with Meg. But in his heart he knew it had everything to do with her. In spite of their differences, he didn't want to lose touch with her, so if he kept in contact with the ranch, he'd always have a link to Meg Seymour.

THE THRILL HAD GONE OUT of the wedding plans so far as Meg was concerned. She went through the motions and tried to inject some enthusiasm into the activities for Olivia and Wyatt's sake. But every time she caught a glimpse of Rafe, she wanted to cry.

She'd told him that she wouldn't allow him to make her miserable, but...she was miserable all the same. The bachelor/bachelorette party was especially painful because she'd had such high hopes of dancing the night away with Rafe. Instead he danced with everyone else, including Jack.

At one point Jack tried manfully to get Harlan out on the floor, but it didn't work out. Meg wasn't surprised. Rafe's father didn't have a spontaneous bone in his body.

Rafe, however, threw himself into the party with gusto. No groom could ask for a more spirited best man than Rafe. As requests poured in for a repeat of Rafe and Jack performing the Texas Two-Step, they finally surrendered to the inevitable and danced together amid catcalls and wild applause.

Meg applauded as loudly as anyone. In spite of everything, she loved seeing Rafe moving out of his comfort zone and attempting things that might make him look foolish. Once he was back in San Francisco, that could all change, but at least he was able to step up for Wyatt's wedding.

After Rafe's dance with Jack, Meg lost track of him until he appeared unexpectedly at her side.

"I think it's customary for the best man to have a dance with the maid of honor," he said.

Her heart beat in triple time as she glanced up. He looked wonderful in the clothes she'd helped him choose in Jackson. He'd worn his borrowed hat tonight, and he blended in so well that an outsider wouldn't have been able to tell he wasn't one of the local cowboys.

"I think it's customary at the wedding reception," she said. "But a bachelor/bachelorette party isn't in the manual."

"So is that a no?" His voice was low, but there was a trace of raw disappointment there.

"Actually, it's a yes." Grabbing his hand, she drew him onto the floor. "But I'm probably not as good a dancer as Jack."

He swung her into his arms. "No, but you probably won't keep trying to lead the way he does."

"No, I won't." His touch made her slightly dizzy. She hadn't realized how much she'd missed him until she twirled in his warm arms and surrendered her hand to his firm grip.

He executed a turn with smooth efficiency. "Wyatt and I took a ride today."

"I heard that." She'd tried not to feel bereft that he'd gone riding without her. "How'd it go?"

"Great. That's something we'll enjoy doing together when I visit, and I have you to thank."

"I'm glad it's worked out."

"Damn it, Meg, I miss you."

She looked into his eyes. "I miss you, too."

"We had something special going on. I can't believe that it—"

"Great sex doesn't equal a good relationship, Rafe."

"It's a damned good start. Come down to my room tonight. We can talk."

She smiled, although her refusal was killing her. "We wouldn't just talk and you know it. I thought I could have sex with you and let it go at that, but I can't. I want more, and that's foolish. We're headed in different directions, you and I."

"But this is torture."

"Hang on until Sunday. Then it'll all be over." She didn't believe that for a minute. She'd be months getting over Rafe, and maybe longer. But at least once the wedding had passed, she wouldn't have the agony of seeing him every day.

18

TEN MINUTES BEFORE THE rehearsal was scheduled to begin in the ranch house living room on Friday afternoon, Diana hadn't arrived. Rafe didn't even know if she was in town yet. Her phone had been turned off for hours.

He paced the hallway between the living room and the dining area because windows all along one side gave him a view of the front driveway. He could also have waited on the porch, but he'd be damned if she'd find him standing out there waiting the way he had so many times as a kid.

When he'd sent her a message yesterday suggesting that she stay at the Bunk and Grub and rent a car at the airport, she'd replied *Fine*. That was the last he'd heard from her. Maybe the suggestions had pissed her off and she'd decided to stay home, after all.

Rafe had mixed emotions about that. Personally he'd be relieved, but Wyatt would be upset. Jack would be royally ticked off after he'd mentally prepared himself for this meeting. So would Sarah, and anyone else who'd been around thirty-plus years ago, like Emmett and Mary Lou.

So on balance, Rafe wanted to see a rental car with his mother at the wheel pull up in front of the ranch house within the next ten minutes. He glanced at his watch. Correction, nine minutes.

"Any sign of her?" Meg came down the hallway from the direction of the living room. Like everyone else today, she'd dressed casually in jeans and a T-shirt.

"No sign of her, but this is typical. She creates drama wherever she goes, so I'm not surprised."

"It must be hard on you, though." She stopped a short distance away. She'd been maintaining that physical distance recently, even though her expression and her tone of voice told him she was worried about how he was handling the stress.

He'd manage a hell of a lot better if she'd let him hold her. But he wasn't going to beg. Even so, he looked forward to the rehearsal because she'd be forced to take his arm during the recessional.

He missed touching her more than he'd expected to. His body yearned for hers with a fierceness that kept him from sleeping at night and caused him to seek her out during the day. All morning he'd had a good excuse to hang around her because the whole family had pitched in to decorate the living room for tomorrow's ceremony.

Rafe knew Wyatt and Olivia were thrilled with the results. The ranch hands had carted the heavy living room furniture out to the tractor barn, where it would stay until tomorrow night. In its place all thirty-two dining chairs had been arranged in rows. They would provide plenty of seating because the guest list was small.

Tyler Keller, Alex's wife, had supervised the decorating, which included piling flowers in the empty fireplace and draping vines all over the stones to create a backdrop for the minister and the wedding party. White satin bows adorned each chair, and more flowers in vases gave the room a chapel-like atmosphere.

He glanced toward the driveway again and sighed. "It's not as hard on me as it is on Wyatt. I've accepted what she's like, but I don't think he ever has. He keeps hoping she'll be different."

"I've tried putting myself in her shoes," Meg said. "How would it feel to walk into a place where no one is happy to see you?"

"Nobody, that is, except Wyatt. He'll be glad."

"Okay, one person, then. But a bunch of others who've condemned you for your past actions." She met Rafe's gaze. "If she comes, I give her props for it. She may have done some things that weren't cool, but if she shows up, it proves she has guts."

"I suppose it does. But you're not going to like her, Meg. If you think my father's obnoxious, wait until you've met my mother."

She regarded him quietly for a moment. "Please know that it's not because of your parents that I've decided we don't belong together."

"Oh, so it's just me, then?" He tried to make a joke out of it even though she was slicing him to ribbons. "Gee, I'd rather blame it on them, if you don't mind."

"No, it's not you, either! You're fine. Wonderful. We're just not in sync!"

"Funny, but I remember a few times we were perfectly in sync. I don't know if you realize this, but simultaneous orgasms aren't the most common thing in the world, and yet we—"

"Don't, Rafe." A flush spread over her cheeks. "You'll only make it harder."

"Now who's talking dirty?"

"Make it more *difficult!* Sheesh!"

She was adorable. And he, poor sap, was in love with her. He couldn't convince himself that she was in love with him, though.

Sure, she cared about him or she wouldn't be here helping him sweat out this waiting game. But if she loved him, she'd want to find a way they could be together. Instead she was ripping them apart.

Yet, like a fool, he looked into her green eyes searching for something, anything that would give him hope. As he did, he could swear that her expression relaxed a little, and a soft glow warmed her eyes. Or maybe he was imagining things. Before he could be sure, she turned toward the window.

"Rafe, somebody's coming."

He looked, and sure enough, a little Jeep had turned into the gravel drive. Although it was the kind that could lose its top and side doors for off-roading, it was buttoned up tight.

"Is it her?"

"I can't believe she'd rent a Jeep, but that's my mother getting out." And she was wearing…holy crap. She was wearing jeans. And boots. True, they were red, but they were cowboy boots, not designer heels.

Her sequined red T-shirt was more her style and she had on her trademark Gucci shades. Her hair had recently been colored and styled and hung straight and shining to her shoulders. She looked terrific, but he couldn't get over the jeans and boots. He'd never seen her wear anything remotely Western.

"Are you going out to meet her?" Meg asked. "I think that would be a nice gesture, all things considered, so she doesn't have to walk in cold."

"You're right." Without thinking, he grabbed her hand. "Come with me."

She seemed startled, but she didn't jerk away from him. "I don't know if that's a good idea."

"I do. Besides Wyatt, you may be the only person who's giving her the benefit of the doubt."

"Okay, then." She hurried with him down the hall.

"She's here!" Rafe called as they passed through the living room. "Meg and I will go get her."

"We'll go, too," Wyatt said. "Come on, Olivia."

The four of them piled out of the door and started down the steps as Diana rounded the Jeep clutching several shopping bags in each hand. Now that was a familiar sight. His mother was one hell of a shopper.

She paused uncertainly when she saw them. "Wow, a welcoming party."

"You bet, Mom." Wyatt walked forward with Olivia. "This is Olivia Sedgewick."

"Hello, Olivia. I'm so glad to meet you." Diana's voice trembled slightly. "You're beautiful." She turned to Wyatt. "She's lovely, Wyatt. Just lovely." And then, to everyone's total surprise, tears started running down from under her sunglasses and onto her cheeks. "I'm sorry." Still holding the bags, she reached one hand to wipe her face, knocked off her sunglasses and slammed the bags into Wyatt's chest. "Oh, dear. I'm m-making a mess of this."

Rafe squeezed Meg's hand and let go. "Let me take

those bags, Mom." He was seriously rattled. He'd never seen his mother cry.

"Oh, thanks." She sniffed and handed them over. "It's…it's presents…f-for Wyatt and Olivia. I didn't know what they needed, so I put g-gift receipts…"

Wyatt folded her in his arms. "I'm sure we'll love all of it, Mom."

Rafe grabbed up her sunglasses from the gravel and stood holding the bags, unable to take it all in. His mother was crying. And wearing jeans and boots.

"Let me hold those," Meg said softly. "You go to your mother." She pried the bags and sunglasses out of his hands.

In a daze, he walked over and put his arms around his mother and Wyatt as she continued to cry and apologize in alternating waves. Rafe couldn't decide if she was apologizing for crying, for being late, or for a million and one sins that she'd been accumulating her entire life.

But this wasn't the mother he'd thought he knew. For the first time in his relationship with her, his throat hurt from joy instead of disappointment. She did love her sons, after all. Until this moment, he'd never been really sure.

"Okay, okay," Diana said. "Enough. Back up, you big lugs, and let me get hold of myself." Eyes still streaming, she waved her carefully manicured hands in front of her face. "There goes the Elizabeth Arden makeover."

Rafe laughed with a certain measure of relief. That sounded more like the old Diana. Except as he gazed at her puffy eyes and red nose, he realized something else. "I love you, Mom," he said quietly.

"Me, too." Wyatt squeezed her shoulder. "Thanks for coming to my wedding."

"I wouldn't have missed it for the world. I—" She caught her breath as she glanced at the porch and her hand covered her heart. Silently her lips formed a name. *Jack*.

Rafe turned as Jack came slowly down the steps, his gaze never leaving Diana. Rafe and Wyatt both stepped aside but Rafe was prepared to move in if necessary. He wouldn't abandon his mother now.

She trembled as Jack came nearer, his dark eyes, so like hers, unreadable.

He stopped when he was within arm's length of her. "I wanted to hate you." His voice was strained. "You left a little boy who didn't understand why you'd disappeared."

"I know," she whispered. "Jack, I…" She gulped and blinked very fast.

"I understand a little better now. I'm not excusing you for what you did."

"No." Her voice was thick with emotion. "Nothing could excuse it."

"But I…" He held out both hands. "I don't want to live with anger anymore."

She grabbed hold of his hands and hung on. "I will always live with regret."

"Yeah, me, too." He squeezed her hands. "But it's time to move on." He glanced at Rafe and Wyatt. "Having a couple of bonus brothers isn't so bad, and I hear that one of them is trying to get himself married."

"Right." Diana gave a quick nod, as if willing herself back under control. "I've held things up long enough." She sniffed hard and gazed up at the sky. "Damn, it's blue up there. I'd forgotten how blue the Wyoming sky is."

Then she looked over at Meg. "In all the confusion, I don't think I met you." Walking forward, she held out her hand. "I'm Diana Locke."

"I'm Meg Seymour, the maid of honor." Meg grasped Diana's hand in both of hers. "I'm happy to meet you."

Rafe smiled as he remembered his discussion with Meg that only one person would be happy to meet Diana. After this display of vulnerability on his mother's part, he hoped there would be more. The fact that she'd dressed like a cowgirl and driven up in a Jeep would help.

Diana glanced over at Rafe. "If I'm not mistaken, you came down the steps holding this delightful young woman's hand. Does that mean you're...friends?"

Rafe's heart hammered as he looked at Meg. "Yes, we're friends." But that wasn't all of it, and this didn't seem to be a day for half truths. "No, that's not exactly right. I'm in love with her, Mom."

Meg gasped.

"I see." Diana gazed at Meg. "And how about you? Are you in love with my son?"

Meg gulped. "I... Yes, I'm afraid so."

Rafe's jaw dropped and he stared at her. "You are?"

"But, Rafe," Diana said. "Notice how she phrased it. She said she was 'afraid so,' which means she's in love with you but doesn't think that's wise. Why isn't it wise, my dear?"

Meg took a deep breath. "Because Rafe is focused on the bottom line, and I'm focused on living a happy life, regardless of the bottom line."

"Did he tell you that?"

"Pretty much."

Rafe's mother waved a dismissive hand. "Don't believe a word of it. That's his father talking. Rafe has the most loving heart in the world and he'll never be like his father, no matter how hard he tries."

"And I'll second that opinion," Wyatt said. "Besides, I've seen the way he looks at you, Meg. If you want the guy, you've got him. You just need to tell him how high to jump."

"Hey!" Rafe glared at his brother. "What kind of talk is that?"

Wyatt laughed. "I know what I know, bro. And now I'm going to do you a big favor and get this whole crowd inside so you and Meg can have a little one-on-one. But don't get carried away. We have a rehearsal coming up."

Rafe stood there thinking about what Wyatt had said as Olivia took the shopping bags from Meg and everyone walked inside. He'd been thinking that if Meg loved him, she'd find a way for them to be together. What about the fact that he loved her? Shouldn't he be finding a way?

Well, he had. He'd suggested she move to San Francisco, but city life wouldn't make her happy. He used to think city life made him happy, but how happy would he be without Meg?

Besides, he'd become mighty fond of this ranch and this area. He imagined himself living here, and got excited about the idea. But he couldn't live here and keep his client base in San Francisco…or could he? Why not? So much of his communication was via the phone and the internet. He could always fly back to the city every now and then to have face-to-face meetings.

"You're not saying anything." Meg continued to stand several feet away.

He looked at her with renewed focus, and everything

fell into its logical place. Of course she was the one. And he was the one for her. "That's because I'm waiting for you to tell me how high to jump."

"I doubt you'd be willing to jump that high, no matter what your mother and Wyatt think."

He smiled, because he was so many steps ahead of her. "Try me."

"I personally think you could live in Shoshone and telecommute with your clients, but I doubt that you—"

"I would." He enjoyed the shock that widened her eyes. "In fact, I'd need to try and keep as many of my San Francisco clients as possible because it looks like I'll be earning the lion's share of the family income. You're not going to have an easy time finding a job around here."

"I know, which is why I've come up with a different plan." Her eyes narrowed. "Wait a minute. Did you just refer to a 'family income'? What family are you talking about?"

"Ours." He crossed the distance between them and took her by the shoulders. "Because, Meg Seymour, we're going to marry each other and have kids who will grow up learning to ride, and rope, and ski."

"Is that a proposal?"

"It is, but you're worrying me with this alternate plan of yours. I want us to live here, so I hope you're not about to throw a monkey wrench into that plan."

"You're *proposing*? It doesn't feel like a proposal."

"Why not?"

"For starters, you're not down on one knee."

"You have a proposal scenario on your list, right?"

"Yep."

"Alrighty, then." He dropped to one knee and spread

out his arms. "Done." Then he patted his knee. "Sit here."

"That's not part of the scenario on my list."

"Then it should be. Come here." He smiled at her. "Please."

"Oh, okay." She balanced on his knee and wrapped her arms around his neck. "You were saying?"

He cleared his throat. "Meg Seymour, will you do me the honor of becoming my wife?"

"This is rather sudden."

"I know." He gazed into her eyes. "But tell me honestly, aren't you crazy about me?"

She laughed. "Yes, you egomaniac, I am."

"And I'm crazy about you. And it's not the sort of deluded crazy that gets people into trouble. We fit and we both know we do, once we figure out the whole career/living arrangement thing. So is that figured out or not?"

"It is. I'm going to start a consulting business helping cities experiencing unexpected urban growth and I'll base it here. I'll have to travel, which means you might become the babysitter. Are you okay with that?"

"I'll be happy to babysit our kids if you'll marry me. I know some couples have kids without getting married, but I'm sort of old-fashioned about that, so I'd want the ring, the license, the ceremony, the whole deal."

"Then I guess I'll have to marry you."

"Good. Now that we've settled that, I'm going to kiss you. I didn't want to do it while we were still negotiating, for fear you'd accuse me of taking unfair advantage."

"Oh, please do. That sounds like fun."

"It will be. I promise." He kissed her as thoroughly

as he dared while balancing her on one knee. Falling into the gravel would not be cool.

But, glory and hallelujah, she kissed him back with all of her heart and soul. He'd experienced her kiss when she was holding something back, but that wasn't the situation now. She was giving him everything she had to give.

And he was giving everything he had, too. For the first time in his life, he was laying himself bare because love demanded nothing less. As he reluctantly ended the kiss and they walked hand-in-hand back to the house, he thought about the event that had led to this moment. More than thirty years ago, his mother had made a choice that changed everything. Although some condemned her for that choice, he would be forever grateful.

Epilogue

NASH BLEDSOE WAS LATE to the wedding. No one would notice, because he hadn't planned to be there, despite a personal invitation from his good buddy Jack Chance. Nash's life was a mess, and although he wished the best for Jack's half brother Wyatt and Wyatt's bride, Olivia, he hadn't seen his way clear to attend their nuptials.

Last night, however, he'd thought of all the reasons why he *should* be there. He'd thrown a few things in the car, left his bachelor pad in Sacramento, and headed for the Last Chance Ranch.

As he drove in this afternoon, he took note of the outdoor wedding reception area that had been set up with a platform for dancing, tents in case of rain, and gaily decorated tables and chairs. If it was like most Chance events, it would be a blowout. After parking his truck in an area to the left of the circular drive, he mounted the familiar front porch steps.

Damn, he'd been away too long from a place that he'd cherished from the time he was a little kid. Maybe coming here would help him sort through his options. Ending his marriage to Lindsay had been necessary,

but now he had to figure out what the hell he wanted
to do with his life.

The ceremony was in progress. As he quietly opened
the front door, the minister repeated the words that Nash
remembered hearing three years ago when he'd thought
Lindsay was his forever-after soul mate. He hoped those
words would work out better for Wyatt and Olivia than
they had for him and Lindsay.

Slipping inside, he quickly saw that all the chairs
lined up in the living room were filled. Jack had said
it would be a small wedding, about thirty people, and
Nash had felt honored to be included, even if he'd had to
send his regrets. Fortunately no one noticed him come
in. He would have hated to interrupt the ceremony.

He searched the crowd and found his mother, Lucy,
still a redhead thanks to regular salon visits. Sure
enough, she was sitting next to Ronald Hutchinson, a
widower who ran the local feed store. That was one of
Nash's reasons for coming today. His sister Katrina had
mentioned that Lucy and Ronald had a romance going
on, and Nash felt he should check that out in person.

Katrina hadn't been able to get home for the wedding, though. She trained thoroughbreds back East, and
work had kept her away. Just as well, considering Nash's
other concern, the guy seated on his mother's far side.
Langford "Hutch" Hutchinson, Ronald's son and a talented sports videographer, had been Nash's friend since
they were kids.

In fact, Hutch, Jack and Nash had been close all
through school and into their twenties before life had
gotten in the way. But Hutch was severely testing that
friendship. Nash was still trying to sort out the particulars, but he gathered from what Katrina was *not* saying

that Hutch had seduced her this past spring when they both happened to be in town. Furthermore, he hadn't proposed marriage afterward.

Katrina might be fine with that, but Nash wasn't. In his estimation, any guy who messed with his sister had better show up the very next day with a ring and a plan. Katrina had made no mention of a ring, and the plan seemed to be continuing with their careers on opposite sides of the country.

Nash's dad had died seven years ago, which made Nash the man of the family, the one assigned to watch out for the womenfolk. The Hutchinsons, both father and son, had been fooling around with the Bledsoe women. Nash was here to find out their intentions.

Although that had been his primary goal in driving over, he admitted to being curious about Jack's two half brothers, Wyatt and Rafe, who'd turned up out of the blue. Rafe was handling the best man duties, and if Nash squinted slightly, he'd swear it could be Jack standing up there. The striking resemblance confirmed that Rafe and Jack were half brothers. Wyatt's body build was similar to Jack's, but his coloring was much lighter, so he must take after his dad.

Jack had also said there was a slim possibility that Diana, mother to Jack, Wyatt and Rafe, might show up for the wedding. Nash was pretty sure he'd spotted her because she had features that reminded him of Jack. After witnessing firsthand the damage she'd done, Nash wasn't inclined to be friendly.

He decided to take his cue from Jack on that one. If Jack had made peace with the mother who'd abandoned him more than thirty years ago, then Nash would do his best to suspend judgment. But he'd witnessed Jack battling his demons as a result of Diana's actions, and Nash figured Diana had plenty to answer for.

Nash recognized most of the other wedding guests, who were either members of the Chance family or close friends. But he puzzled over the identity of an old codger in the front row. The guy could pass for Albert Einstein—same wild hair and a nutty professor outfit consisting of a tweed sports coat and plaid pants. Because he sat up front, Nash guessed he was related to Olivia.

The minister finished, and Wyatt was invited to kiss Olivia. Cheers erupted from the guests, who gave the couple a standing ovation. Nash stepped aside to let the happy couple fly past him and out the front door, followed by Rafe and a woman he didn't recognize.

Next came the one most likely to be Diana, escorted by a guy in an expensive-looking suit. He was dry-eyed, but she was in tears. Nash didn't have much time to think about her, though, because the next person down the aisle was Sarah. Nash, along with everyone in town, considered Sarah Jack's real mother.

"Nash!" She stepped out of the procession and rushed over to give him a hug. "You made it!"

"Better late than never." He hugged her back and wished he'd accepted the invitation right off the bat. So what if his life was in the dumper? His old friends wouldn't care about that.

"This is Pete Beckett, my fiancé. I can't remember if you've met him."

"I don't think so." Nash shook the guy's hand. "But congratulations. You're getting a gem."

"I know." The light in Pete's eyes when he looked at Sarah convinced Nash he really did know he'd lucked out.

Nash hoped the same could be said for the Hutchinsons, both father and son. After promising Sarah a dance at the reception, he looked around for his mother. She'd spied him. Bypassing the central aisle, she'd come around the chairs from the other direction and was bearing down on him, trailed by the Hutchinson duo.

"Nash Bledsoe, did you drive straight through? You did, didn't you? You know I hate when you do that." Then she gave him a fierce hug. "Glad you got here safely, you big lunk-head."

"Me, too, Mom." He hugged her back, but over the top of her head he found himself eye-to-eye with Ronald Hutchinson, and behind Ronald stood Hutch, looking decidedly uneasy. As well he should.

Nash called up his most intimidating stare, the one he'd used to great effect against opposing linemen back in high school. "So, Mom, what's this I hear about the Hutchinson men making off with the Bledsoe women?"

His mother laughed as she stepped back and smiled up at him. "Crazy, isn't it? First Ronald was courting me, and then your sister came to town, and…the rest is history, as they say."

Nash's gaze flicked to Hutch, who was trying to look innocent. Ha.

Ronald came forward and offered his hand. "For the record, I plan to spoil your mother rotten."

"Glad to hear it." As Nash shook the guy's hand, he relaxed on his mother's account. Ronald seemed as smitten with Lucy as Pete Beckett was with Sarah. But that still left the issue of Katrina and Hutch.

"Well…" Lucy glanced from Nash to Hutch as if feeling the tension between them. "We'll get on out to the reception. You boys haven't seen each other for a while. I'm sure you want some private time to talk."

"Yeah. See you out there later." Nash was finally face-to-face with Hutch, and the years faded away. Suddenly they were teenagers again, and he felt the way he had when he'd caught Hutch ogling his sister in a bikini. Before he could censor himself, he swung.

His fist connected with Hutch's jaw and Hutch landed on his butt. He looked dazed for a moment, and then he rubbed his jaw and grinned. "Feel better?"

"Infinitely." Nash chuckled and shook his head, a little embarrassed at his gut reaction. "Sorry, buddy, but I had to get that out of my system. It's the big brother thing."

"I do understand. Would it help if I said I'd spoil her rotten? That seemed to work for my dad."

"Yeah, but I believe your dad." Nash extended his hand and pulled Hutch to his feet. "You, my friend, are going to have to prove it. So, are you buying her a big old rock or not?"

Hutch's grin widened. "As a matter of fact, I am, but she doesn't know that yet, so I'd appreciate it if you wouldn't go blabbing to her."

"Excellent!" Nash clapped him on the shoulder. "If you're putting a ring on her finger, then my work here is done."

"You're not leaving, are you?"

"No, at least not until I've congratulated the bride and groom. But I have a messy divorce to clean up back home, and—"

"Are you planning on staying in Sacramento, then?"

Nash had debated that for weeks. "I don't know. We're selling the stable, so…"

"Jack would give you a job in a second."

"I know, but I hate to trade on friendship for a job."

"Bullshit. You're a good hand and he knows it. You've always loved this place. Why not move back for a while, see how it goes?"

"I might. You know, I just might." The idea sounded better the more he considered it. "Right now, though, we have a wedding reception going on outside. And if I remember right, the Chances know how to party."

"They certainly do," Hutch said. "Good booze, good music, pretty women. What more could you want?"

"At the moment, not a damned thing. Let's go." But as Nash headed out to the wedding reception with his friend, he knew that in the long run he wanted more, much more. Maybe, just maybe, he could find it at the Last Chance Ranch.

* * * * *